A note on the author

Douglas Skelton was born in Glasgow. He has been a bank clerk, tax officer, taxi driver (for two days), wine waiter (for two hours), journalist and investigator. He has written several true crime and Scottish criminal history books but now concentrates on fiction. *Thunder Bay* (longlisted for the McIlvanney Prize), *The Blood Is Still*, *A Rattle of Bones* and *Where Demons Hide* are the first four novels in the bestselling Rebecca Connolly thriller series.

Also by Douglas Skelton

Non-fiction
Blood on the Thistle
Frightener (with Lisa Brownlie)
No Final Solution
A Time to Kill
Devil's Gallop
Deadlier than the Male
Bloody Valentine
Indian Peter
Scotland's Most Wanted
Dark Heart
Glasgow's Black Heart
Amazing and Extraordinary Scotland

Fiction
Blood City
Crow Bait
Devil's Knock
Open Wounds
The Dead Don't Boogie
Tag – You're Dead
The Janus Run
Thunder Bay
The Blood Is Still
Death Insurance
(e-novella with Morgan Cry)
A Rattle of Bones

WHERE DEMONS HIDE

A REBECCA CONNOLLY THRILLER

Douglas Skelton

First published in Great Britain in 2022 by Polygon,
an imprint of Birlinn Ltd

Birlinn Ltd
West Newington House
10 Newington Road
Edinburgh
EH9 1QS

www.polygonbooks.co.uk

1

ISBN 978 1 84697 598 1
eBook ISBN 978 1 78885 383 5

British Library Cataloguing-in-Publication Data
A catalogue record for this book is available
on request from the British Library.

Typeset by Biblichor Ltd, Edinburgh

1

SUNDAY

The Island of Stoirm

She ran.

Sharp heather stabbed at the soles of her bare feet but still she ran.

She had to get away.

Far away from the cottage. As far as she could. Far from *it*.

It was back there, somewhere. She did not know if it was following her, she did not know if it could follow her, or if it was somehow tied to that small sitting room, but she wanted distance. She needed time. Distance and time. The blade in her hand, the *athamé*, was short and blunt and would be of little use as defence. Not that any metal of this world could protect her against that which lay behind.

So she ran across the moorland. Blindly. Not knowing where she was going. Just knowing she had to get away.

The moon was full but only fitfully revealed by the clouds that flew overhead, as if even She could not bear to watch the scene below. The land would silver suddenly then darken, and that was where the fear would hide. It

1

would use the darkness, for that was where it lived. Earthly creatures sought out the light, but it pursued the shadows.

The woman did not think it had found her again. Not yet.

It was bitterly cold and a frost hung in the night air, coating the heather and turning the gorse bushes into spectres. She had fled the cottage without thinking and her thin white robe did little to protect the flesh beneath. She felt the chill gnaw at her now, prickling her skin, as she stopped to catch her breath and peer over her shoulder through the flecks of frost floating in the moonbeams, her ears alert for any sound that was not natural.

But then that from which she had fled *was* natural. It was as natural as the elements and the moonlight. It lived both in this world and in the Ethereal Plane.

And it was hunting her, she was sure. It was now free of the confines of the cottage and out here somewhere, moving from shadow to shadow, slowly, methodically, seeking to catch her scent in the air, to hear the blood throbbing through her veins, to taste her fear. She could not outrun it, for she was but flesh and bone and it was not. It did not feel the cold and it did not tire. No matter where she ran, where she hid, it would find her and it would take her.

Unless she protected herself.

Here was as good a place as any.

She fell to her knees and began to dig. She did not have time to work out the exact specifications of the shape she was creating; it would be rough, uneven, and that may mean its efficacy would be reduced, but she had to do something. Further flight was not an option. She had rushed from the cottage in panic but her mind had settled now, though her breathing remained rapid and her heart rattled against her ribs. She could still taste the bitter tea she had drunk earlier and she licked her lips to try to scrape it away.

She dug.

This was her one chance to survive this night. If she could make it to daylight, she could get off the island. If she could get off the island, she could reach the Sisters. If she could reach the Sisters, she would be safe.

So she hacked and hewed with the dull blade of the ceremonial dagger, hauled out clumps of heather with her fingers, scraped at the peaty soil beneath. Fragments dotted the pristine white of her robe, but she didn't care. All she wanted to do was complete the protection before it found her again. Her breath fogged from her lips, hanging in the air for a moment before it evaporated as she grunted and strained at her labours.

And she wept.

She wept because she was afraid. She wept because she was alone. She wept because she had not heeded the warnings. She had been told they were dangerous, these men, but she had believed she could handle them. She had powers, too. She had knowledge. She could protect herself. And yet, they had come for her. They had sent it after her. And she could not control it.

She paused, glanced at the flanks of the mountain, sheened with frost and raked by the moonbeams breaking through the cloud cover. They said it was home to three witches, and she wished they were here now to aid her. They would know what to do: how to combat that which lay behind. And they would know what lay ahead. The witches were but myth, however. The blade in her hand and the creature lurking in the darkness and the terror that escaped from her chest in huge, wracking sobs – they were real.

She dug.

Edging around the damp earth on her knees, estimating the sharp angles needed, wishing she had more time to do the job properly but knew she did not.

For it was close now. She couldn't see it and she couldn't hear it but she could feel it, could sense its consciousness reaching out through the cold, dark night, searching for her, calling her name in a low, seductive voice, as if it were a lover wooing her to bed. She heard it snuffling, faintly, as it sifted the air for traces of her blood and her terror.

It had appeared while she was performing a simple cleansing ritual. It had been more a sensation than a manifestation. The candles guttered, as if being breathed upon. A golden glow spread its warmth from the wood burner in the hearth, but the temperature dropped with unnerving suddenness.

And she knew something had joined her.

She had sensed it prowling in the shadows between the flames and hanging in the dark corners. She had felt its eyes upon her, and her flesh tingled, as if its breath had reached out from the blackness to caress her.

And then she heard the voice.

Deep. Silken. Slithering from the shady spaces, oozing from another dimension, the words unintelligible to her but attempting to burrow deep into her thoughts. Tonguing phrases from an arcane language. Coating her consciousness with slime. And she'd known what it was and why it was there. This creature was not of flesh and sinew, but it meant her harm. It pried and probed at her mind, trying to nestle within, to take root – and if she allowed that, it would shred her consciousness, her soul, as easily as tearing paper.

She could still feel it in her brain when she burst from the cottage, the sensual voice worming after her from the shadows. But as she'd hurtled through the darkness, onto the moors, she felt its grasp of her consciousness weaken, lessen, diminish until she knew she was free. Temporarily.

And now she dug.

Frantically. Urgently. Crafting a symbol that would protect her.

But she could feel it had found her once more. A murmur somewhere deep in her mind, caressing her thoughts and dreams, piercing her psyche like a stiletto.

She dug.

Gulping air as she worked at the earth, a straight line here, a sharp angle there and, finally, as perfect a circle around the five points as she could craft.

Louder now. The voice. The ancient words still obscure, meaningless, but their intent becoming even clearer now that it had found her again.

She lay down in the centre of the symbol she had carved, stretched out her arms and legs, positioning her body into a semblance of the shape she had fashioned out of the cold ground.

The voice died abruptly, like a phone being cut off.

It would hold.

The circle would hold. It had been hurried and frenzied, but it would hold. She was safe.

She felt its presence though, moving in the frost and the night, looking for a way to reach her. She lay there, sensing but not seeing the creature as it circled her, feeling its rage build both at her and the protective circle holding it at bay. But it couldn't get at her, not in here, so it moved round and round and round, each lunge at her defences rebuffed.

And then it howled. A howl of fury. A howl of impotency.

The frost settled around her as she waited for morning to come.

2

MONDAY

Inverness, the Scottish Highlands

'You're looking a lot better these days,' Elspeth McTaggart said as she sipped coffee from a mug so large she'd need a lifejacket if she fell in.

Rebecca Connolly looked automatically at her face on the Skype thumbnail. She hated doing that but just couldn't help it. She wasn't overly vain – just averagely so – but she didn't relish seeing herself at the moment. The fact was, she really didn't like what she saw looking back at her. Not that she was about to take to swinging from the bells of Notre Dame, but she preferred her own version of herself to the reality, thank you very much.

She knew she was looking a lot better, though. There had been a time, a year or two back, when the dark circles under her eyes had resolutely resisted any attempt at concealment by the finest the cosmetic industry could create. Even so, as she sat at the counter that separated her small kitchen from the living room of her Inverness flat, she avoided looking at herself. Video calling had become the new routine and Rebecca regretted the day her boss discovered it. Until then, Elspeth had been content with a phone call to bring her up to date with the jobs in hand for the Highland News Agency. Now she insisted that they Skype two or three times a week, Zoom's need for pre-arranging the calls being beyond her mercurial approach, although she had not completely forsaken the old-fashioned voice call. She was perfectly within her rights as she did own the agency, but Rebecca sometimes longed for the old days.

Elspeth was in the kitchen of her cottage in Drumnadrochit, around fourteen miles south from where Rebecca now sat. It was clear that she shared none of Rebecca's concerns about morning appearance. She had taken to dying her hair outlandish colours and it had been bright red a few months before, but now it had faded to a rusty pink. She had said she was a suicide redhead – dyed by her own hand – but had never bothered to touch it up. This morning it was a tangled mess, as if she had been dragged through a hedge backwards. She wore a shapeless blue dressing gown and sipped tea from the huge mug that bore the legend WORLD'S GREATEST LOVER, which Rebecca presumed was a gift from her partner, Julie. The mug was chipped. Whether there was some kind of deeper meaning to that, Rebecca was unsure. She did know that the relationship was secure if often fractious, Julie being environmentally and socially conscious, a non-smoking vegan who drank little and swore little, while Elspeth was none of the above. They enjoyed bickering, if not actually fighting, but despite it all were devoted to each other. Her boss had acknowledged her true sexuality relatively late in life – she had been married to a man for many years, with whom she was still friendly – and Julie became her life partner. That was how Elspeth put it: 'life partner'. Partner for life. Like a punishment, she often said, but Rebecca knew she didn't mean it. Friction creates heat, she once told Rebecca, and there was plenty of that. Frankly, Rebecca didn't want to know. Other people's love lives were their business, though Elspeth was inordinately interested in hers, and Rebecca knew that her comment on her improved demeanour was merely the precursor to turning to that very subject. Nevertheless, she would do her best to head her off at that particular pass.

'There are some court cases that should bring revenue from the nationals,' Rebecca said, in the vain hope that sticking to a business agenda would do the trick.

'Okay,' said Elspeth, the two syllables carrying liberal amounts of disinterest. There were always court cases bringing revenue, although not as much as they used to.

'There's some research for the telly company – a couple of people to find and interview for their victims show.'

An independent producer had indicated an interest in making a documentary based on Elspeth's book about the Culloden case on which they had both worked. There had been such nibbles before, but at least this London-based company had steered some work to the agency on other commissions they had. It wasn't megabucks, but it – and the other items Rebecca mentioned – kept the sheriff officers from the door.

'There are a couple of human-interest pieces that might generate some heat with the weekly magazines.'

Elspeth's face crinkled in distaste. She hated human-interest stories, insisting they were soap opera and not news, but she also knew that they brought in a little cash, but again less than before. 'Okay,' she said again.

'And this morning, once this news bulletin is over, I'm heading out to Bishop's Park to talk to an alleged psychic.'

'The hairdresser who found that wee boy?'

'Yes, it's a magazine piece for the *Sunday Tribune*. She knows I'm coming.'

'Of course she does. She probably sensed it in the ether, or saw it in the chicken innards or whatever.'

Rebecca smiled – she shared Elspeth's scepticism regarding the esoteric. Tabitha Haley had apparently had a psychic vision which led police to where the boy was trapped. 'More like, I told her on the phone where to meet,' Rebecca said. 'And once that's all done, it's all clear for Stoirm at the weekend.'

Elspeth's lips flattened. 'Hmmm,' she said, causing Rebecca's grin to widen. She was not keen on returning to the island because it held nothing but bad memories for her, but it was nothing compared to Elspeth's reluctance. Her aversion to both weddings and funerals were well known. *It's the end of some poor sod's life*, she often said before pointing out that the song 'Here Comes the Bride' was only an up-tempo version of Chopin's 'Funeral March'. Rebecca had checked out both on the internet and could not hear the similarity, but her boss told her she must be tone deaf. If Elspeth could have body-swerved the proceedings on the island, she would have; but Chaz and Alan were friends, and sometimes you just have to suck it up.

'Are you going to be crabbit the whole weekend?' Rebecca asked.

'Very likely.'

'That will be fun.'

'Contrary to popular belief, weddings aren't supposed to be fun. Marriage isn't a word . . .'

'. . . it's a sentence,' completed Rebecca. 'Yeah, yeah, you've said that before. And I didn't think it was original then!'

'Doesn't matter. People aren't meant to be married. Committed, yes, but not tied together by some outmoded concept that was all about property in the first place.'

Elspeth sat back in her chair, sipping her tea. She looked around her kitchen in a conspiratorial manner, perhaps checking if the fridge was listening or watching, then leaned to one side slightly as she reached into the pocket of her dressing

9

gown. Rebecca didn't need to see what she was looking for to know she was going to light up.

'Don't,' warned Elspeth as she held the cigarette between her fingers. She always said that when she was about to smoke.

'Didn't say a word,' said Rebecca. She always said that, too.

Elspeth grimaced as she rooted around in her pockets, then stood up and stepped out of the frame. Rebecca heard the click of a gas hob and a moment later Elspeth was back in her chair, the cigarette sending smoke signals from between her lips.

'Don't try that at home, kiddies, I'm a professional,' said Elspeth.

'Has Julie given up getting you to stop?'

'Julie never gives up anything. A dog with a bone shows less determination than her. When she catches me, she doesn't say anything now, though, just gives me a look. And her looks can speak volumes.' She plucked the cigarette from her lips and blew some smoke in the air. 'While we're on the subject of friends and lovers . . .'

Here we go, Rebecca thought.

'How are things with Stephen Jordan?'

Stephen Jordan was a solicitor Rebecca had met on a Culloden story. It had taken him a few months to ask her out, and when he did, she surprised herself by saying yes. She had always told herself she wasn't looking for a relationship – not that this was a relationship, of course. She liked him but they were just friends. Anyway, it was all part of the new her.

Rebecca asked, 'Is that the business portion of the conversation over?'

'Aye.'

'And we're on to the prying portion of the conversation?'

'Aye. So, how's it going?'

'We've been out once or twice, no big deal.'

'Seeing someone more than once is a big deal for you, my girl, but you know that's not what I mean.'

Rebecca did know what she meant, but she wasn't going to make it easy for her. 'What do you mean, then?'

Elspeth rolled her eyes. 'Have you seen the lawyer without his briefs?'

Rebecca felt a laugh building and struggled to keep her face straight. 'You expect me to answer that?'

'I'll take that as a no.'

'How do you work that out from me not answering?'

'Because I know you, Rebecca Connolly, and I know you don't just play hard to get; you have taken up professional status.'

'Give me a break, Elspeth, I've only been out with him a couple of times. You want me to jump into bed with him right away?'

'I think it's more than a couple of times. And he's an attractive man. If I was that way inclined, I'd do him.'

'You'd *do* him? When did that phrase enter your vocabulary?'

'Since Julie has me watching these American TV shows. But don't change the subject – it's time you cast off your wimple, Sister Rebecca. You've been celibate long enough. Get out there and enjoy yourself, for God's sake.'

What Rebecca didn't tell Elspeth was that her self-imposed celibacy had ended a few weeks before.

The Island of Stoirm

Chaz Wymark's camera was in the Land Rover but he didn't think his father would be pleased if he hauled out the bag and slotted in a long lens to capture this scene. Having a nosey was one thing but snapping away at a police incident at which he should not, officially, be present was another.

Especially as his father was the attending GP. He did, though, grab a few surreptitious shots with his phone. He justified it to himself by reasoning it was what he did; he was a photographer and he saw the world through a lens. Or, in this case, on a screen. He was too far away and the zoom on his phone wasn't good enough to grab any decent shots, but it made him feel better.

His father had told him to keep his distance, but his curiosity was proving stronger than his desire to obey, so he edged forward. All he had been told earlier that morning was that a woman's body had been found on the moor but, judging by the expressions on the faces of the two police officers, not to mention Dr Charles Wymark, there seemed to be something about the circumstances that was puzzling.

The weather was typical of Scotland's Jekyll and Hyde persona – the sky was a bright blue, although some fragments of mist hung around the tip of Ben Shee like the caress of a lover reluctant to leave. The mercury was off looking for an overcoat: the cold air bit at his nose and cheeks, but he had dressed to combat it in a thick padded jacket over a body-warmer and woollen shirt, heavy trousers and thermal socks in solid walking boots. Even the island's climate was daunted by his layers, but he still thought about Alan, probably still snoring in a warm, cosy bed. His partner consistently denied that he snored but, as Chaz had often pointed out, he didn't stay awake long enough to find out. Alan responded with a flat-out assertion that no one in the history of the Shields family had ever snored – a claim, Chaz would argue, that was impossible to attack or uphold. Chaz had thought about recording the nocturnal nasal symphony but he knew Alan would simply accuse him of fakery. After all, if technology could make people believe the impossible was real, then a counterfeit recording would be a simple task. Sometimes Chaz wondered why he was marrying Alan.

His father knelt at the side of the body, favouring his good arm, while the two other men seemed to be engaged in heated debate. Although their uniforms were encased head-to-toe in forensic suits, Chaz knew the lankier of the two was PC Rory Gibson, and the older, squatter, heavier one was a sergeant whose name he did not know. The young officer was gesturing at something at their feet, and the sergeant, who pulled at the disposable Tyvek suit as if it irritated him, was crinkling his face and dismissing whatever was being said.

Elizabeth Walker stood a good fifty yards away from them, her black Labrador, Bess, on the lead but sitting patiently at her side and watching the activity with great interest. The dog rose as Chaz drew nearer, her tail whipping back and forth, and he was obligated to squat to give her a double-handed pat. He loved dogs but had never had one, not even as a child. He planned to discuss getting a dog with Alan, who would surely not baulk at the idea. After all, his family were part of the hunting and shooting set down south and he had been brought up around them. The fact that they both worked might be an issue, but Chaz would probably be able to take the dog with him when he was on a job. It could be trained to wait in the car, unless hot weather became a problem. There would be a way round it, he was certain.

He knew the woman had found the body, but she showed no sign of being in the least traumatised, which failed to surprise him. She had been his English teacher in the island's secondary school and was the person for whom the word 'unflappable' was invented. She would take the whole thing in her stride, short though that might physically be. She had always been sturdy – that was the only way to describe her – and she had not softened in retirement. Her short hair remained fair, Chaz imagined thanks to the haircare shelf in the village general store, and she was also dressed for the weather: a good quality tweed jacket over a thick jumper, cord trousers tucked

13

into woollen socks and a strong pair of walking boots. Her age had been a matter of conjecture among the pupils but she had to be in her late sixties at the very least, although the years were not reflected on her face, which was still relatively wrinkle-free. She carried what looked like a shepherd's crook, though she was unlikely to hook any lambs from crevasses. He wouldn't put it past her to do it, though, should she come upon one. Not that there were any lambs on the moors at this time of year.

'I heard you were back on the island, young Charles Wymark,' said Miss Walker, humour dancing in her eyes, as ever. She had called him by his full name since the first day he had entered her class. As a youth it had irritated him, but now if she didn't do it he would worry there was something wrong.

'I'm sure you did, Miss Walker,' he said, feeling a smile tease his lips. She was not herself a gossip, but she would certainly listen, if only to snort in derision at the more fanciful rumours that circulate in any community.

'Causing a stir, as usual,' she said, which he knew meant the impending wedding to Alan. There were some on the island who were not yet ready to accept same-sex marriage. 'You always were a bit of an attention-seeker.'

Her smile told him she was having some fun. 'Not as much a stir as this will, I think.' He jerked his head towards the group of men clad in protective cover-alls. Miss Walker nodded, knowing this to be true. A controversial wedding was one thing, but a death in the shadow of Ben Shee was another. Chaz gestured to the mound of tarpaulin lying a few feet away from where the men clustered. 'You think they're going to use that to cover everything?'

'Yes, I told them to bring as much as they could. They'll need it.'

That struck him as strange. 'Why?'

She gave him a mysterious little smile. 'That would be saying, wouldn't it, young Charles Wymark.'

He had forgotten how she could be. 'How did you know to suggest it?'

'I've read a lot of crime fiction,' she said. 'And I watch true crime documentaries.' She caught his surprised look. 'Does that shock you, young Charles Wymark?'

'Well, I . . .' She could still fluster him with one arched eyebrow.

'You thought I'd spend my time reading literature, is that it? Committing Shakespeare and Wordsworth to memory? Booker Prize winners clogging up my bedside table?'

He decided he was on a hiding to nothing, so he asked, 'Do you know who she is?'

'Of course I know who she is. She rents – rented – Rose Cottage from me.' She waved in the general direction of the cottage further down the trail. Miss Walker's own cottage was half a mile further away.

'So what's her name?'

Miss Walker gave him a long look. 'You're some sort of reporter now, aren't you?'

'Photographer.'

'But you are part of the dreaded mainstream media of phrase, fable and sneery initialism?'

Trust Miss Walker to know that 'MSM' was not an acronym. Chaz only knew because Alan had told him. 'Yes, freelance.'

'And are you asking these questions as a concerned islander, or former islander, or as a reporter?'

He laughed. 'I take pictures, Miss Walker, I don't do the words. I don't even have my camera.'

'Don't try the piss-take, my lad. I saw you with your phone just now.'

He felt heat burn at his cheeks. Miss Walker had been the most straight-speaking teacher he had ever had, which was one of the reasons she was his favourite. Now, feeling her eyes burn into him, he felt like he was sixteen again and had been caught lying about his homework.

She smiled. 'You always were a clever lad, young Charles Wymark, but don't think for one minute that I'm not aware what you're up to. Your father would have a fit if he caught you using his position as a doctor in order to peddle some kind of story.'

Chaz hadn't intended to use his presence at the scene to peddle any sort of story. He was only here as his father's driver, and he had taken the shots out of habit. At least, that's what he thought he had been doing, but now that he had been pulled up by Miss Walker, he wasn't so sure. Rebecca's nose for a story would be twitching in an obvious way right about now, and he had worked with her for long enough, so was he deluding himself? Somewhere in the back of his mind did he really think he could turn this tragedy to his advantage?

He looked over at his father, who had recently broken his arm in what his mother dubbed The Great Fall – a tumble from a ladder followed by a bad landing during the pre-wedding redecoration of their home. Terry Wymark loved her husband deeply, and her nursing skills had proved useful for his immediate care, but there was no way she was going to miss the opportunity to mock his lack of physical articulacy – hence the moniker assigned to the accident. Chaz saw his father glance in his direction briefly, then turn to say something to the sergeant before he waved at him to come closer. Miss Walker nodded to them and said, 'I think they want you.'

She still hadn't parted with the dead woman's name. She may have been his favourite teacher, but she was always a difficult customer. Smiling to himself, he gave Bess a final pat. 'Always a pleasure, Miss Walker.'

'I assume you mean meeting Bess and not me, young Charles Wymark.'

'Never assume, Miss Walker. Isn't that what you always said? It makes an ass of you and me.'

'Yes, also unoriginal even then but sadly apposite on too regular an occasion.' He moved away from her but stopped when she spoke again: 'Nuala Flaherty.' He gave her a smile that showed he was both grateful and surprised she had told him. 'You'd find out anyway,' she said. 'You were always a smart-arse but you were curious and tenacious. In other words, downright nosey.'

'And is there something to be curious and tenacious about here? Or even downright nosey?'

She gave him that strange little smile again. 'I think you are about to find out.'

He heard his father calling his name, so Chaz gave Miss Walker a nod of thanks and walked away.

'You've got your camera gear in the car, right?' said Dr Wymark, meeting him halfway.

He nodded. He had left his bag in the back of the Land Rover after a trip he and Alan took to Thunder Bay to see the sea eagle nest. When he had lived here, he had been part of a group of locals who had assumed the responsibility of watching over those rare and magnificent creatures, for humankind was known to be lethal to their health.

'Then go get it. We need photographs of the locus.'

Chaz did not need to be told twice. He started back for the Land Rover.

'And put on some protective gear. You'll find some coveralls in a bag in the boot.'

Chaz waved his acknowledgement as he loped to their Land Rover, parked beside the police vehicle beyond Rose Cottage.

'And mind your step when you come back!' His father called after him. 'Use what stepping plates we have.'

17

Chaz had watched as the young police officer had carefully laid the plates on the heather in order to preserve the locus, which was large. There would only be a certain amount on the island and not nearly enough to cover this particular scene. Chaz found the papery white garments in the rear of the Discovery, took off his thick padded jacket and struggled to haul them over his remaining clothes. His father was the GP called out to any death on Stoirm and he had learned many years before it was best to keep a supply of the Tyvek suits at hand. Chaz pulled the white foot coverings over his boots, draped the hood over his head then grabbed the handle of his bag and sprinted back, catching Miss Walker's knowing smile as he passed. As he neared the three men, being careful to use the stepping plates, he heard the sergeant griping.

'. . . telling you, this is a waste of time. Rory here can take shots with his phone, that'll do. The MIT will have all the gear when they get here.'

'Better to be safe than sorry, Pete,' said Chaz's father, a sigh very evident in his voice as he stared down at the woman on the ground, who to Chaz was still little more than a white shape.

The sergeant grunted and folded his arms. He gave Chaz a sour look as he approached then stepped in front of him, as if shielding the dead woman from the sight of the gutter press. 'He's with the media, is he no'? Your laddie know the score? If I see any of these snaps in the papers, I'll have his baws for marbles.'

The sergeant was not Highland, his accent betraying his Dundee birth. Above his mask and below the rim of the hood, his eyes were hard and suspicious.

'He understands,' said Charles Wymark, even though he hadn't actually laid out the rules for his son. Chaz guessed some kind of promise had been made on his behalf, though, and he would not break it. Curious and tenacious he may

18

be – or downright nosey – but he would never undermine his father's trust.

The sergeant grudgingly stepped aside, still muttering his opposition to the whole thing under his breath. Chaz lowered his bag to the ground, flipped it open and fished out his Nikon.

'We're going to have to cover all this up to protect the scene,' explained the young police constable, jerking his thumb to the tarpaulin. 'Chaz, right?'

'That's right.'

'We'll tent the body but we can't cover the entire scene, so we'll tarp the rest.'

Chaz studied the ground beneath them and the design carved around the woman's body. It was a large area and it was unlikely the local police had a tent large enough.

'But we need a photographic record before we do that,' the young police officer continued. 'You got video on that camera, too?'

Chaz nodded.

'Okay, good. Take the whole area, with particular attention to the design on the ground. Then close-ups of the deceased, her position, her face, the weapon in her hand. Just snap as much as you can; we can't have too many. And when you're done we'll have to seize the memory card, okay?'

The sergeant made a hissing sound with his teeth. 'Waste of bloody time. The woman came out here to look at the stars or something and died of exposure, simple as.'

'Very likely, gaffer, but a suspicious death needs to be properly investigated, right? The team will be over from the mainland on the first ferry, but that's hours away yet.' PC Gibson squinted into the clear sky. 'It's fine now but you know what the island is like, and God knows what could hit before they get here, right?' His next words seemed to be for Chaz's benefit. 'So it's maybe an idea to grab some pictures before we

19

cover everything up, and we'd be stupid not to use a professional when we have one right under our noses.' He glanced
back at the ground before them. 'And you've got to admit, this
is all bloody strange.'

The sergeant did not look as if he was in the mood to admit
anything. 'She was probably as high as a kite. Out her head on
something.' He gave Chaz a sharp look. 'What you waiting
for, son? Get on with it.'

'Quick, as you can, Chaz,' said his father. 'We need to get
this poor woman and the scene under cover as soon as possible
to preserve the locus until the pathologist arrives.'

Chaz nodded, slipped the lens cover off and took a deep
breath. He had never seen a dead person in this way before.
He had watched as a man died after being shot, but that had
been on a dark towpath with sweeping rain blurring details.
He had seen life leave him, just a sigh and then the muscles
on his face visibly relaxed. This was different. It was broad
daylight and he was standing directly over the body and about
to focus through a lens. He wasn't sure if he was fully ready
for it. There was a coldness, a clinical detachment, that felt
alien to him. He covered his hesitation by ensuring his feet
were firmly positioned on one of the few stepping plates and
making a show of adjusting his aperture and ISO setting.

'You're no' out to win any prizes, laddie,' said the sergeant,
smiling as if he'd said something worthy of a comedy award.
'Just point and click. And for God's sake make sure they're in
focus.'

Chaz stepped forward and leaned over the body. It's just
another photograph, he told himself as he looked on Nuala
Flaherty for the first time, just another shot. Focus on the job.
This is what you do.

He estimated she was in her late thirties but death might
have smoothed some lines from her face. She was – had been –
a beautiful woman. Her black hair was long and curled away

20

from her head in damp tendrils. Her eyes were open, staring at a sky she would never see again, the brown pigment taking on a milky-blue tinge. She lay on her back, arms outstretched, the fingers of her right hand wrapped around the handle of an ornate knife with a thin blade, the weapon to which Rory had referred. Her legs were wide apart, the position of the body mimicking the lines that had been hastily scratched from the heather and earth around her. The thin gown etched with curious symbols was thin, and the frost that had settled overnight made it cling to the contours of her body.

He snapped, preserving what had once been a living, breathing human being in thousands of pixels and bytes of memory that would last longer than the flesh. He moved around her, being careful not to tread on the design underfoot as the limited supply of stepping plates petered out. His shutter clicked again and again. His initial shock had worn off and he now noted the details through the prism of his camera lens.

This was strange, unusual. This was a story, but as his shutter clicked, he thought about the promise his father had made for him. Even so, he felt excitement grow inside him, his instincts telling him that something like this would not remain a secret, not on the island.

Especially as there was a hint of hocus-pocus.

Inverness

'Hocus-pocus,' said the woman, smiling.

'I'm sorry?' Rebecca said, slightly taken aback.

'You were expecting hocus-pocus, right?' The skin around the woman's blue eyes crinkled and her mouth puckered, as if she was holding back a tiny smile. 'You thought I'd be sitting in a flowing black gown waving a wand and stroking a black cat.'

21

She was not in a black gown. She wore a baggy, brown woollen sweater over brown jeans and she had slippers on her feet. Old woman's slippers, Rebecca thought. The type with woolly borders. There was no hint of a cat in the vicinity.

Rebecca smiled. 'No, I didn't expect that at all.'

The woman laughed. 'Liar,' she said, but her tone was good-natured.

Before visiting Tabitha Haley, Rebecca hadn't known what to expect, truth be told. The woman was a clairvoyant who had, apparently, provided information that had helped trace a missing child. She was in her fifties, Rebecca estimated, slim and leggy with long, straight, blonde hair tied back in a ponytail. The sitting room of her small flat was comfortable and bright and bore no traces whatsoever of the woman's interests, apart from a single bookcase with a few occult titles but mostly taken up by DVDs. Romcoms, as far as Rebecca could tell from where she sat.

'Well, maybe I expected a crystal ball,' admitted Rebecca.

'Oh, I have one of them. Don't get me wrong – Rebecca, right?'

Rebecca nodded.

'Don't get me wrong, I can do the full bhuna when I need to. But, honestly, it's such a faff. All that ritual and all those incantations don't half take it out of a girl.'

Rebecca laughed, relaxing. When she had been hired by the Sunday tabloid to interview Tabitha, she had felt her heart sink because she thought the woman would be some weirdo who would prattle on about crystals and ley lines and vibrations. But she seemed pretty normal for someone who had apparently plucked the location of eight-year-old Brian Docherty out of the ether.

'I do use crystals,' Tabitha said, once again startling Rebecca and making her wonder if she had somehow spoken aloud.

Tabitha smiled again. 'You were just thinking about that, weren't you?'

'How did you know?'

'Hocus-pocus.' Tabitha burst out laughing. 'Honestly, it was a shot in the dark. We'd talked about crystal balls, so it was the logical next step in any train of thought. And if you hadn't been thinking about them, it wouldn't have made any difference, would it? You'd just put it down as a non sequitur from a dotty cow.'

'So it was a trick?'

'No, just a bit of fun.' Tabitha's expression became more serious as she studied Rebecca's face. 'You don't believe in what I do, right?'

'Another shot in the dark?'

'No, you may not know it but your demeanour since you came in, not to mention your expression, speak volumes.'

That was how many so-called clairvoyants operated. They studied their mark and used their intuition to draw conclusions. Body language could be both a whisper and a scream.

'Let's just say I remain unconvinced by . . .'

Another smile. 'Hocus-pocus.'

'Yes, hocus-pocus. And yet, you helped them find little Brian.'

'I did.'

'How?'

Tabitha sat back on her soft settee and considered her answer. 'You want the truth?'

'When I can get it.'

The woman breathed in and out slowly, the smile gone. 'I don't know, and that's the size of it. That's the way it works with me. I'm not a professional – I don't make money by telling fortunes, I don't read Tarot cards, although I can talk the hind legs off a hanged man about them – history, designs, ways of reading them – if that's what floats your boat. I have a deep and abiding interest in the occult, have had it since I was a girl. My mother did, too. She was from Sutherland, and

23

they said she had the sight. So do I, I think.' She reconsidered. 'No, that's not right – I know I have it.'

'So how does it work, then?'

'I get "snatches", I suppose you would call it.'

'Visions?'

'No, not as such, although yes, that has happened in the past. Sometimes just an image, like a slide projected very quickly on a wall. It's almost subliminal, really; it comes, it goes. Mostly it's just something that comes into my head. A thought, a word, a name, an impression.'

'And is that what happened in relation to the missing boy?'

'Yes. I was at work – I'm a hairdresser, have my own salon on Stephen's Brae, you should come see me.'

Rebecca's hand automatically moved to finger her auburn hair, wondering if she had somehow just been insulted.

'Anyway, I was doing this customer's highlights – she wanted bright orange tips. I tried to talk her out of it, she was not a bright orange tips kind of person, let me tell you, but she was determined. Anyway, that doesn't matter, does it?' The smile flickered again. 'The radio was on, the news, and they mentioned his name, and right away I had this feeling of something damp and dark. And I heard this wee voice, a little boy's voice, calling for help.'

'When was this?'

'The day after the news first reported he was missing. Well, I ignored it. It didn't mean anything, not really. The wee lad was on people's minds, you know? Why should I be any different, right? But all day I kept getting the same things popping into my head – just snatches, like I said. His wee voice. The cloying smell of damp. The feeling of an enclosed space.'

'So how did you pinpoint that particular cellar?'

'I couldn't get it out of my mind, so I read all the news reports. I even phoned the police, but the guy I spoke to more or less laughed me off the phone, which is understandable, I suppose. The thing is, I knew I had something. This has happened before. Nothing as big and as important as that wee lost lad, though. Wee things. Lost things. There's a whole world of lost things out there. Everything's got to be somewhere, you know what I mean? And sometimes I can sense where that somewhere is.' She stopped, a slight smile appearing. 'So I went to my special place.'

'And where's that?'

'You'll laugh.'

'I won't.'

Tabitha was controlling her own amusement. 'Oh, I think you will.'

'I promise I won't.' Rebecca held three fingers above her head. 'Scout's honour.'

'That's the salute from *The Hunger Games*, but never mind.' Tabitha paused. 'My special place is in the bathroom.'

Rebecca laughed. So did Tabitha. 'Please tell me you didn't sit on the toilet!'

'No! I took a bath. There's something about the heat and the steam that helps me focus.'

'And that's what you did?'

'Yes. I don't know about you, but I often find myself drifting in a hot bath and my mind frees itself from my body. I heard Brian's little voice, fainter than before, but he'd been missing for almost two days by that time. And I could smell the damp walls again, and in my mind's eye I saw the basement and the little thin window just at ground level.'

'That was the one he'd climbed through?'

'Yes. And then found himself trapped when it slammed shut behind him. His mum told me later that he was an adventurous child, curious to the point of being foolhardy. That's what got him into trouble.'

'But you still didn't know exactly where it was?'

'No, I needed to get myself out of the basement.'

'But you weren't actually there, so this was all' – Rebecca struggled for a more polite way to say absolute bollocks –'psychic stuff, right?'

Tabitha smiled and for a second Rebecca feared she had plucked the phrase 'absolute bollocks' from her mind. Then she dismissed the thought. Telepathy and mind-reading were also absolute bollocks. And yet, Tabitha really did find the missing boy. She wondered if Brian's mother would let her speak to him about it.

'Yes,' said Tabitha, 'psychic stuff. That is exactly what I used and well done you for coming up with the correct scientific term. As you say, I wasn't actually there, but part of my consciousness was.'

'So you moved your, em, consciousness out of the basement?'

'Yes, I took myself through the walls, out and up. Remember, this comes to me in snatches, like grabbing little handfuls of time and space, do you understand?'

Rebecca didn't but she nodded all the same. She had warmed to Tabitha but she couldn't help but feel she was as nutty as a fruitcake. And yet, and this really was the nub of it all, she had found Brian. Rebecca was having a hard time reconciling her innate scepticism with that simple fact. Despite a search by police and family and friends and strangers who had turned up simply to help, Brian had remained missing until Tabitha came up with her clues.

'What did you see?' Rebecca asked.

'Just more snapshots, but I thought enough to narrow the search. I couldn't see it, but I had the feeling of quite a large house set within a big garden. There was an old tree with the remains of a treehouse. A high wall. And just beyond it, a red car.'

'And when you approached the police again, did they react differently?'

26

'I was luckier this time. I spoke to the officer in charge, a detective chief inspector at Inshes. She seemed more receptive.'

Inshes was the headquarters of the Inverness police. 'Was it DCI Val Roach?'

Tabitha's eyebrows raised. 'Yes, she a friend of yours?'

Good question. Was Val a friend? At one time Rebecca would have said decidedly not but relations between them had thawed, thanks to some under-the-counter collaboration on a miscarriage of justice case. Roach could have been handed her jotters for steering some information Rebecca's way. But friends? Difficult to answer. Rebecca had gone a long way to declutter both her life and her own mental state, but that part remained a question mark.

'We've met professionally,' she replied, deciding that was the best way to put it.

'Anyway, she was really nice, really receptive.'

Val Roach, nice? Perhaps she had taken to drinking at work.

'She listened to what I had to say and said she would check it out herself,' said Tabitha. 'I think, by that stage, I was holding out a straw and she was clutching at it. She drove around herself, looking for a red car beside a house surrounded by a wall. It was two streets over from where little Brian had last been seen. A large, empty villa awaiting renovation, I think. Boarded windows, chains on the gate and doors.'

'And searchers had been around it, but found nothing, right? Everything locked tight, so they assumed he couldn't have got in.'

'That's right. At least, that's what I understand. I suppose they didn't hear Brian call out, or perhaps he'd fallen asleep when they were there – who knows?'

'Or it wasn't searched properly,' Rebecca suggested.

Tabitha jerked her head a little, as if she didn't want to get into that.

Rebecca, taking notes, scribbled *Speak to Val.* 'So how did you feel when you learned Brian had been found?'

Tabitha stared at her, that puckering smile returning. 'How did I feel? Isn't that question a sort of cliché for reporters?'

Rebecca was slightly ashamed. 'Yes, but there's a reason why it's a cliché – it's an important question.'

'I felt elated, obviously. Relieved. Glad I was able to help.'

'And have you spoken to Brian's family?'

'Yes, we met, thanks to Val Roach. They seemed very pleasant.'

'Well off, too. I understand they offered a reward, which you refused.'

'I don't do this for money, Rebecca. I told you, I'm not a professional clairvoyant. I'm a hairdresser.' That little smile again. 'I did think about taking it up professionally – you know, fortune telling and all that jazz – but I didn't see any future in it.'

Rebecca smiled. She liked this woman. She was funny and self-deprecating, and the fact she refused to profit from what she had done spoke volumes, although Rebecca still harboured doubts regarding the whole psychic business. 'But will you help the police again if you can?'

'If I can, but I can't turn it on and off like a tap.'

'Even though a bath helps.'

That smile. 'Aye, even though a bath helps. If anything like this happens again then I will pass it along, naturally.'

'Has anything like this happened before?'

'No, not something as major as this. I haven't tapped into any murderer's spirit, if that's what you mean. Just flashes about people, here and there, now and then.'

'Comes and goes, right?'

'Right.' Tabitha's eyes narrowed and she gave Rebecca a look that was different from before. Previously there had been good humour but now she seemed serious. 'Right,' she repeated, her voice trailing. She moved her head in a circular fashion, as if she was studying the air surrounding Rebecca. 'You've known death, haven't you?' Her eyes narrowed as she tried to focus on something just above Rebecca's head. 'A relative, no, a parent. Your father, is it?'

Rebecca felt her muscles spasm and something tickled the back of her throat. She didn't reply. She sat very still. She wanted to look up, wanted to see what Tabitha could see, but she fought the impulse. She knew she wouldn't see anything.

Tabitha said, 'He's gone now but he's always with you – you know that, don't you?'

She had once thought that, but not now. When she had needed him, he had been there, a shadow of her mind made real. She hadn't needed him for some time, although she felt, as Tabitha had said, he was always with her. But only as a memory. She didn't believe in ghosts.

Tabitha frowned again. 'But there's been more, hasn't there? More sadness . . .'

Rebecca remained silent, for some reason not wishing to halt the woman's flow. Mention of her father could have been a shot in the dark which had hit a mark, nothing more. Tabitha had admitted as much regarding mention of crystals. Rebecca wanted to see what else she came up with, if anything.

'I feel rain. It's not heavy, soft, but it's drifting.'

Rebecca remembered rain, flecking the beams of light on the towpath beside the canal. But, again, that could be little more than a guess. They were in Scotland, after all, and it often felt like rain was either falling or on its way.

Tabitha nodded. It was an absent movement, as if she was half-listening to other voices. Rebecca was unimpressed. So far, the woman had made only vague statements that could apply to almost anyone. A dead father. Rain falling. So far, so what.

Then Tabitha winced and said, 'It hurt, didn't it?'

'What?'

Tabitha closed her eyes, her lips compressing and brow furrowing, as if she was concentrating on something playing on her eyelids. Rebecca watched, resisting the urge to smile. Maybe she needed to go take a bath.

'I don't know . . . It's kind of shadowy. I see shapes. A man, in the darkness.' She rubbed the palm of her right hand. 'The pain, it's here.'

Despite herself, Rebecca once again felt the jarring impact on her own right hand.

'You hit him, hard. Again and again.'

Rebecca saw him reel away, blood erupting from his nose, surprise on his face. He hadn't expected her to fight back.

Tabitha sniffed the air. 'Aftershave. Strong, cheap.' Her eyes opened. 'It was a turning point, wasn't it, Rebecca? You piled all the darkness, all the rage that had been building inside you for years, into hitting that man, didn't you?'

Rebecca could only nod, the chill shivering her shoulders and the back of her neck. He had jumped her in her flat, and she knew he had to be put down quickly if she could, so had put everything she had into one titanic blow. She was grateful for the self-defence classes she had been taking and, indeed, continued to take. A woman has to be able to take care of herself in this life and, after the events on the towpath, she had vowed she would never again allow anyone – man or woman – to put their hands on her.

Tabitha breathed in sharply. 'I feel hate. Strong, abiding.' Her eyes opened and fixed on Rebecca once more. 'Someone hates you.'

Rebecca forced a wry laugh. 'I'm in the media, Tabitha. Whoever it is will have to take a number.'

Tabitha didn't smile. 'No, this is real. This kind of hate is toxic, all consuming. You have to be careful, Rebecca.'

*

The grave was neat and tidy. Someone else had laid flowers, she didn't know who, and not for the first time. White roses every time. She set her own flowers beside them, inspected the wilting bouquet for a card, some clue, but there was nothing. She came here every week, rain or shine, and every now and then she found the white roses left by someone who cared for him, obviously, someone who missed him. An old girl-friend maybe – there had been a few of them. Someone from Inchferry perhaps, a local he had somehow met and helped, because he was like that. He had been respected by many, her Nolan, feared by a few, aye, because he was a Burke, but there was love too, because he was the best of them – she'd seen that at the funeral – but they would not, could not, miss him as much as she.

'Who is it, Nolan?' Mo Burke said aloud. 'Who leaves these?'
I don't know, Ma.

She saw him at her side, as she always did. Not quite there, his flesh transparent. His dark hair shining, his handsome face, so like his father, smooth and clear, his smile broad. That was how she remembered him. That was how she would always remember him. She would grow older, her eyesight would fade, but she would always see him this way. He would never age, and his body would never fail him.

She straightened and stared at the headstone. She had insisted it be plain, just his name and the years of his life, which were too short. He would have hated anything ostentatious.

Too gangstery, Ma, she heard him say.

She smiled as his voice carried on the wind easing around the cemetery, as if it was inspecting the various graves. Too gangstery, even though that was what they were. Crooks. Felons. Neds. Drug dealers. The Burke Clan, they were called. Her man still in the jail, one son also doing time, the other son lying in a grave where the wind moaned.

She felt the chill of the winter ahead seep into her bones, so she took out her gold lighter and fired up a cigarette. Smoke drifted from the corner of her mouth like ectoplasm, the warmth of the tobacco going some way to fend off the nip in the air. She had smoked since she was a teenager and Nolan was forever trying to get her to give it up. Even now she heard him, that windswept voice, and saw him, standing beside her, giving her the earnest look he used to have when he was trying to get her to do something she didn't want.

You should give that shit up, Ma, he said. *It's killing you but you just don't see it. I don't want to see you waste away and die.*

And yet, here she stood while there her son lay.

Parents should not outlive their children. It was a phrase she had heard often but had never thought much about it until she experienced its basic truth for herself. There was a particular pain caused by the loss of a child, no matter how old that child was. It was not the natural order of things. Partners die, but children – at least in the minds of their mothers and fathers – should be immortal.

And yet, here she stood while there her son lay.

She blew out another lungful of smoke and breathed his name along with it. She had often been too hard on him, for he was the eldest. She had not been hard enough on his brother, Scott. Nolan had grown to be a level-headed young man, Scott not so much, but she had hoped some of his older brother would rub off on him one day. Nolan, the dark one, never moved without thinking; Scott, the fair one, never thought before moving. It was all instinct and reaction with Scott, all fire and flash, while Nolan examined and considered an issue before acting. She had hoped that, one day, Scott would learn.

One day.

That day never came, though. In the end Scott went completely off the rails and Nolan ended up dead because of it.

No, not just because of Scott's mental deterioration. There had been another factor involved. A girl. A lassie. A reporter who had turned Nolan's head, led him away from family, where he belonged. Scott had warned Mo about the dangers Rebecca Connolly posed, but she had ignored them.

And here she stood while there her son lay.

The nicotine suddenly tasted acrid in her mouth and she threw the remnants of the cigarette away. It spiralled into the grass, the tip trailing a wisp of smoke in the grey air. She knew she should have ground it under her shoe but the likelihood of it setting light to the grass was slim. The ground cover was too short and too damp and whatever heat remained in the ash would die as soon as it hit ground. Even if it did, she did not care. Part of her would like to see this land burn, even though Nolan lay beneath it. She hated this place because of that. She hated the neat grass and the stately trees and the windsong. Her son had been dead for almost two years, yet time had not cooled the heat of her anger, nor diverted its focus.

Rebecca Connolly.

Mo had wanted her hurt before, had found two men who each promised to do it, but one had failed miserably and the other declined to honour the agreement. The bitch still walked around, free as a bird, while Nolan lay in the ground and Scott rotted in prison. Scott may have pulled the trigger but Connolly had loaded the gun. Mo wanted her to pay for what she had done to her family.

Rebecca Connolly.

Unfinished business.

It was time to do something about that. It was time to call in professional help.

Beside her, she felt Nolan waver and vanish, as if he needed to hide from her hatred.

Loch Ness, the Scottish Highlands

The man stood by the picture window and took in the cinema-scope view over the loch. The water was blue in the sunshine but there was a darkness at its heart that spoke to him on a personal level. There were secrets in its depths, mysteries concealed for centuries far below the surface, and he understood that, for he also had secrets and he guarded them just as jealously. Like the creature said to lurk somewhere in that freshwater lake, his secrets only occasionally slipped into view, but he ensured that they sank again quickly. He could not eradicate his past completely, but he could strive to keep it hidden.

He sipped his espresso, the small cup looking even daintier in his massive hand. He did not drink or smoke but he was addicted to caffeine. It was a weakness, and he recognised it as such, but he gave into it, as he had given into so many things over the years, his own nature being his primary flaw. He did not think of himself as a bad man or a good man. He did not know what a good person was, for he had learned since childhood that goodness was an intangible concept. Even the best of men – the best of anyone – can be overcome when the evil that lies in all souls rises. He had understood that from the day he stole for the first time, from a toy store in the ultra-modern town centre of the ultra-modern town in which he had been raised. If he had asked his parents to actually buy the tiny toy soldiers, they would have done so without a thought, for they doted on their only son, but something deep within him whispered that it would be very much more thrilling to simply take them. So he had lingered beside the rack, surreptitiously looking around him to see who was watching, and then he did as that soft, seductive voice commanded. It had been surprisingly easy in the end. A quick movement, and the box was hidden under the folds of his duffle coat in a display of legerdemain he had never thought himself capable. Figuratively speaking, it was an ability he made great use of in the intervening years. 'Now you see it, now you don't' was at the very heart of his transformation from the boy he was to the man he became as he moved from one venture, one persona, to the next.

He still recalled the thrill of heading to the exit, his swag feeling remarkably heavy under his coat, as some memory kicked in about staff waiting for shoplifters to leave before accosting them. Nervous anticipation gnawed at his stomach as he waited for a hand to descend on his young shoulder to drag him from the doorway into a room somewhere to await the displeasure of his parents and the attentions of the law. But there was no heavy hand, no parental ire and no legal backlash. Instead, he walked out of the shop into the grey concrete concourse of the brutalist town centre, the stolen item now as light as a feather, and then to his home, where he concealed it among his other toys and books. He could not recall if he ever took those little figures out of that box, to prise them from the plastic that held them in place to play with them. That had never been the object of the exercise. Possession – and the power to possess – was the motivation, even then. By any means necessary.

Given that side of his character he might have succeeded in politics, but he chose what they now called the financial services industry, for that was where the organ grinders lived. The politicians were merely the dancing monkeys. Lack of morality was not a pre-requisite for success, but he found it gave him an advantage. He still dabbled in the money markets but he had other interests now. His roots lay in that new town, which now was a sprawling behemoth that had eaten up many of the small villages that once surrounded it. Those roots, though, were partially concealed by the web of lies and distortions he had weaved. At the moment, he was known as

Thomas Smith. Simple. Bland. It was not his real name, which was a matter of public record, but he preferred to keep it in the past where it belonged. In the shadows. There had been a journalist a few years back who may have uncovered some of his secrets, but he met with tragedy. There had been Gerald, of course, but his inclination to snort and squirt substances meant nobody took him seriously. His appetites had proved too much for him in the end. Such is life. Such is death.

He turned from the view of Loch Ness he prized so much – it was the reason he bought the house – when he heard a sharp knock at the door. It opened and Vivian entered. Behind her, the full-length portrait of a Knight Templar gazed down, as if awaiting to hear what she had to say.

'I've had a call from the island,' she said, tension in her voice.

He knew the island of which his secretary had spoken. Stoirm, often mispronounced 'Storm', even though he knew the true pronunciation was closer to 'Stirrum'. Not that he was a Gaelic speaker but he was a man who prized knowledge, for that, too, was a possession of sorts. The island had been very much in his thoughts of late and she knew that.

'What news then, fair Vivian?' he asked, his voice light even though he could tell the news was not joyous. And the woman herself was far from fair of face, although she might be passable if she smiled, but that was something she seldom did. In fact, he could not think of any occasion when she did not look as if she was weighed down by some terrible portent of approaching calamity. She was one of the few women with whom he had never engineered some form of sexual intimacy, but not because she was unattractive. He had bedded many women who were unfortunately featured for the same reason he had taken that box of toy soldiers. Because he wanted to. Because he could. They went willingly not because they found him physically attractive – he was self-aware enough to know

36

that – but because they wanted what he could give them, whether it be money or gifts or to use him as a conduit to power. He did not mind that they did not find him attractive physically, because that mattered nothing to him. No, he had never made any sexual overtures towards Vivian because he needed her on his side, not under him. If there had been any such coupling then their working relationship would have been over, and she knew too much for that to happen. Not everything, of course. She would never know everything.

'The Sister,' was all Vivian said. There was no need for a name, The Sister was all that was required. She had been on the island for some time, poking her nose where it was not wanted.

'What about her?' he asked, his voice as light as the sunbeams teasing the ripples of the water behind him. 'Has she finally found someone who will listen to her?'

'No,' said Vivian. 'She's dead.'

He forced his face to remain impassive.

'I see,' was all he said. 'What happened? Some kind of accident?'

'Details are sketchy, but it seems she was found out on the moors, alone and almost naked.'

He felt his lips twitch at the thought. The Sister had been a fine-looking woman and he would have longed to see her almost naked. Too late now, though. 'That is curious. What was she doing out there?'

'Nobody knows. There may be an investigation.'

'I would imagine so.'

'And if so, it may lead to you.'

He kept his face impassive. 'That depends on how thorough the investigation is.'

'Do we instigate damage limitation?'

He swivelled once more to gaze at his view, but it was merely a way of giving him time to think. He sipped the dregs of his coffee. Cold now. Bitter. But still potent. A pleasure craft edged up the centre of the water, and he imagined the people on board eyeing the surface of the loch for a glimpse of something dark and humped and alien. Monsters, he thought to himself, they seek monsters. Perhaps they should look at each other.

'No,' he said eventually, 'any action now might make it appear that we had something to hide or were somehow complicit in poor Nuala's death.'

'And of course, we weren't,' said Vivian. 'Were we.'

She was not posing a question. The flatness of her tone told him that she was convincing herself that they did not have anything to do with the woman's death. She knew more about him than any other, but she did not know it all and she needed reassurance.

He turned to face her and smiled. 'Of course not.'

Inverness

Rebecca heard the wary tone in Val Roach's voice when she took the call. Their relationship had proved mutually beneficial, even though the DCI had lied once about Rebecca in an attempt to extract information from a witness. She had even threatened to have Rebecca herself charged if she did not reveal a source. Those two linked incidents had frosted relations between them for a while, but thanks to the miscarriage of justice case they had a nodding acquaintance with friendship.

'What can I do for you, Ms Connolly?' Rebecca noted the very crisp and formal 'Ms Connolly'.

'Just a quick call, really, and you may not wish to comment officially. It's about Tabitha Haley.'

'You're doing a story?'

'Magazine piece for a Sunday tabloid.'

Roach cleared her throat, as if the very idea of a Sunday tabloid irritated her adenoids. 'She proved very helpful in the investigation.'

'More than helpful, wouldn't you say? She led you right to the boy, more or less, right?'

'More or less.'

'Red car. Big tree. House with a wall.'

'Yes.'

'You found it.'

'I did.'

'And little Brian.'

'Yes, in the basement. He'd crawled through an open window, very small, which had then slammed shut and he was unable to open it again. All a matter of public record, Ms Connolly.'

The tone was so dry that a carelessly eaten pepper could set it alight. Val Roach could be unresponsive when she wanted, but in this case something told Rebecca that the police officer was not alone. She persevered anyway, because that was what she did. And besides, she enjoyed putting the police officer on the spot.

'What's your impression of Tabitha, Val?'

There was a silence. 'As I said, she was very helpful.'

'I know that, but what do you think of her?'

Another silence. 'I think perhaps you should relay your queries through the Communications Office, Ms Connolly.'

The line died and Rebecca laid the mobile on the desk. If Roach did have someone with her then she would have to be brisk because she couldn't afford her superiors knowing she was getting chatty with the media. On the other hand, she could just as easily have been in a mood.

She made herself a coffee, sat back at her desk and picked up her personal mobile. She'd had three missed calls from Chaz, so she hit redial and he answered on the third ring.

'No, I haven't forgotten I'm coming over on Friday, and yes I have a nice suit to wear,' she said before he could say anything.

'That's not why I'm calling, but good to know anyway,' he said, but her words had obviously sparked something in his mind. 'Are you still coming over with Elspeth?'

Chaz had volunteered Rebecca to bring her boss to the island for the ceremony. It would mean Rebecca would have to drive south to Drumnadrochit, pick up Elspeth and Julie then double back to Inverness to head north-west to Ullapool to catch the ferry to the island. It was, as Rebecca's mum would say, a long road for a short cut.

'Yes,' she replied. 'And thank you very much for offering my services as a taxi.'

'You're welcome.'

'I'll be like a kipper by the time we reach Ullapool.'

'Tell Elspeth not to smoke in the car, then.'

Rebecca barked a laugh. 'Yeah, and then she'll go into a huff and be like a bear with a burnt arse all the way there. And the two of them will bicker, with me caught between them.'

Chaz laughed, too. 'You would have driven them anyway – don't give us any of your old moonshine.'

'My old moonshine?' Her laugh rippled her voice. 'I have never indulged in moonshine of any vintage.'

'You know what I mean – you would have offered to do it.'

Rebecca knew she would have if Chaz hadn't beaten her to it but would never admit that. It was not their way. 'So all set for the big day?'

'More or less. Mum has it all in hand.'

If Terry Wymark was in charge, everything would go smoothly, of that Rebecca had no doubt. Chaz's mother had been her father's nurse, receptionist and general minder for years and she was as efficient as she was beautiful. She was blonde and slim and fit as the proverbial stringed instrument. Charles Wymark's hair was darker but he had a bookish charm, too; and, like his wife, kept himself trim. In fact, the couple would not look out of place in a Cotton Traders catalogue. Chaz had inherited his mother's blonde hair and the gorgeous genes from both parents. Before she first met him, Rebecca had spoken with Chaz many times on the phone when she worked for the *Highland Chronicle*. He had been the weekly paper's contact on Stoirm, and they finally met face-to-face when she visited the island on a story. Initially, she thought he was flirting with her, and she was not ashamed to admit that she had felt the first thrill of attraction, despite the fact that she had been in what passed for a relationship at the time – albeit one that was on the endangered list. Then she found out that Chaz's interests lay in another direction – namely Alan Shields, the man he was going to marry on Saturday.

In the background, she could hear Alan ask, 'Has she got her Best Man's speech ready?'

'I can hear you, Alan, and yes, I have made some notes. And it's Best Woman, by the way,' she corrected.

She imagined Alan pursing his lips. 'Pot-ay-to, pot-ah-to.'

'Penis, no penis,' she said.

'Best Person?' suggested Chaz.

'No, that would be confusing,' said Alan, 'when you have my radiance in the room.'

'Such a diva,' Chaz said, not quite under his breath, and Rebecca heard a blow being struck.

'Did he just hit you?'

'He hits like a girl,' said Chaz. 'No harm done.'

'I need to work out,' said Alan. 'So, Becks, is it funny?'

'Is what funny?'

'Your Best Man, woman's, person's – whatever – speech.'

'No, I didn't think I could compete with your face,' she said.

She heard him laugh with an added *whoo-hoo*.

41

'Have you got a date to bring?' Chaz asked.

'No,' she said.

'What about Stephen?'

What was the interest everyone had in her friendship with Stephen? It was nothing, really. They had only been out a few times and, yes, it had turned physical, but they didn't know that – and nor would they know it, because such things were her business. They could be as open as they like about that sort of thing, but she kept it to herself. She had actually considered asking Stephen Jordan to the nuptials, but she wasn't sure how that would be received. Taking someone to a wedding was a big step, she felt. Or maybe it wasn't. She had no real frame of reference here, but she feared that he might feel the need to say no, and such a refusal could prove counter-productive to their relationship. Not that they had a relationship as such, of course. It was a mutually beneficial companionship – yes, as of a few weeks before, with benefits – but it was by no means, no sir, a lasting relationship. She was not about to take herself down any kind of road by inviting him away for a weekend.

'No,' was all she said aloud.

'Oh, going stag, are we?' Alan said.

'Going hind,' she corrected, knowing he was winding her up, which was Alan's way.

'Tom-ay-to, tom-ah-to.'

'Y chromosome, no Y chromosome.'

'Dates are over-rated anyway,' said Chaz, perhaps sensing Rebecca's reluctance to talk about Stephen.

'Yes, all sorts of dried fruits are available,' observed Alan.

Rebecca sighed. 'Anyway, I'm sure you didn't call to check on my dating plans for your wedding, boys. What's up? Busy woman here. Places to be, things to do.'

'I might have a story,' Chaz said.

'On the island?'

'Yes.'

Rebecca felt something flap around in her gut. The last story – the only story – she had covered on Stoirm had ended with two men dead and a discovery about her own distant family that did not sit well with her. Her father had been born there but had left in his late teens. She had only been months beyond losing a baby due to a miscarriage, and what she had learned about the Connolly clan had hit her hard, even though the events were in the past. It had obviously both shamed and sickened her father, for he made a new life, first at sea then in the police force in Glasgow, and he never spoke about his family there or why he had left. Like Elspeth, but for different reasons, she was not looking forward to returning to Stoirm at all, but Chaz and Alan were her friends and she had to be there.

'Dad was called out this morning to a sudden death, out on the moors near the mountain,' said Chaz. 'A woman.'

'So what was it? An accident?'

'No, she had gone out there deliberately, it seems. And just sort of lay down and died.'

'What from, exposure?'

'That won't be known until the post-mortem.'

'Okay, it'll be worth a few lines, I suppose.'

'There's more to it, though.'

'Okay.'

She waited while Chaz hesitated. 'Look,' he said, 'I'm going to tell you, but you have to promise not to use it till it's officially released.'

Rebecca hated knowing something she couldn't use, but her curiosity had been piqued. She said, 'Fine. What is it?'

Another slight pause. 'Here's the thing – before she died, she carved this design around her. A pentagon.'

'Pentagram,' Alan chimed in. 'A Pentagon is a big building in Washington with lots of people in uniform.'

43

'A pentagram,' Chaz corrected.

Rebecca asked, 'Okay, so what's a pentagram?'

'It's a five-pointed star designed to protect witches from harm.'

'Hocus-pocus,' said Rebecca, her interest really stirring, despite the location.

'Pure Dennis Wheatley,' said Alan.

'Who's Dennis Wheatley?' Rebecca asked, and she heard Alan groan down the line.

'Oh, God, don't start him,' said Chaz, but she could hear the smile in his voice. He had obviously already had this discussion.

'I don't know why I associate myself with such cultural illiterates,' said Alan. 'If it's not on Twitty or Fartbook, it just doesn't exist for you two.'

'Relax, Angry from Surrey, I know who Dennis Wheatley is.' Rebecca's mother was an English teacher in Glasgow and their house in Milngavie was filled with books of all kinds, including a couple by Wheatley. She had tried to read one as a teenager but found it ludicrously dated so had set it aside and started on the *Twilight* series. She had to admit that the image of a woman lying in the middle of a pentagram carved from the earth was decidedly Wheatley-esque. 'I'm familiar with his oeuvre.'

'Did you just use the word "oeuvre"?' Alan seemed surprised.

'Yes, and I'm not ashamed of it,' she said. 'Did you get pictures of this pentagram thing?'

'Yes,' Chaz replied, 'but I don't have them and even if I did, I couldn't use them.'

'Why not?'

Chaz explained about the promise his father had made to the police and of Rory Gibson taking the memory card. Rebecca understood but was still disappointed. 'But the design will still be there, right?'

44

'Yes, for now. The police tented the body and covered the pentagram with a tarpaulin, but they won't last long, especially if the weather turns, so who knows what could happen. You know what the island can be like.' She did. The climate on Stoirm was what the word 'tempestuous' was created for. 'The Major Investigation Team is on its way from the mainland.'

'Do they think this is a suspicious death?'

'It's unexplained, I was told, so that's suspicious. They have to go through the motions, I suppose.'

There was a story here, Rebecca could feel it. 'Who was the woman, do you know?'

'A visitor. Had been on the island since the summer,' said Chaz. 'Name of Nuala Flaherty.'

'And what do you know about her?'

'She rented a cottage which is remote even by island standards. The road leading to it is a dirt track with delusions of grandeur,' Chaz said. 'And that's all I know, really. Apart from the fact she's dead.'

'And she drew a bloody great pentagon around her,' Alan said. 'According to you.'

'That's all you know *so far*,' Rebecca said.

'You want me to dig around?' Chaz asked.

'You got something better to do?'

'Eh, I'm getting married in a few days' time.'

'Your mum's all over that, you said.'

'I'll say she is,' said Alan. 'I made a comment about the flowers and I was more or less told that I know bugger-all about flowers.'

'What do you know about flowers?'

'Bugger-all, actually, but that's not the point. Terry has everything under control. All young Chaz and I need to do is turn up on Saturday, hit our marks and say our lines, which means we are, in fact, free for a bit of detective work.'

Even down the line Rebecca could hear the anticipation in Alan's voice. He lived for this sort of thing, despite the fact their involvement had once almost killed them. That story had been different though, for it had been very close to the island's dark heart: it was about people who had lived there all their lives, who could trace their lineage back generations. But this one concerned an outsider. There was little likelihood that Chaz and Alan poking around would ignite anything.

Tabitha's warning that someone meant her harm sprang into Rebecca's head, but she instantly dismissed it. What she had said was accurate – as part of the media, she was open to all sorts of hatred. Fanned by the use of social media, political discourse had become increasingly nasty, and that toxicity had extended to any kind of difference of opinion. The incident with the man in her flat stemmed from his son's name being printed as part of a court report. Those not in the business find it unlikely, but threats of physical harm are relatively commonplace, especially against female reporters. Most are groundless – just angry, bitter, stupid people letting off steam – but others have to be taken seriously, and her mistake back then was not to take him seriously enough. She was lucky, as she could have paid a heavy price for her lack of care, but in the end it was he who came off worse. Being under-estimated sometimes has its advantages. However, she couldn't take on board a dire warning based on studying her aura, or whatever the hell Tabitha had done.

After all, what kind of danger could she really be in? And from whom?

Pittencairn, the Scottish East Coast

Pat and Mike were always together; at least, that's how it seemed. In Glasgow, their home city, no one who knew them could ever recall an instance when they saw one without the other. Neither could they come up with their surnames. They were known only as 'Pat and Mike', never 'Mike and Pat', and they were a team, a duo, a double act. There was a theory mooted in certain East End pubs, in the most discreet of whispers, of course, that one could not function without the other. On occasion, men had tried to put that theory to the test by forcibly removing one or other from the face of the Earth. Some of those men themselves never troubled the face of the Earth again. Those who survived did not do so in one piece.

Pat and Mike.

You take one, you get the other.

That was the way it was. And always would be.

Mike, however, felt out of his depth in this small fishing village. He was a city boy. He liked the feel of concrete underfoot and the claustrophobic sensation of buildings and humanity crowding around him. He liked the roar of the traffic and the aroma of diesel fumes and light pollution and the knowledge that if he woke up in the middle of the night and wanted – really wanted – something hot and greasy in his stomach then he wouldn't have to drive too far to find it. He didn't like the dark and he didn't like the silence. They unsettled him. They were unnatural.

There was a lot of silence in the village. Sure, during the day, there were cars and tractors and buses, while boats coughed in and out every morning and afternoon – maybe not as many as there would have been when this was a bustling fishing port, but there was still traffic. But there was also a lot of darkness. When the sun sank, it was as if someone had thrown a big black blanket over everything. True, there was street lighting but it seemed weak compared to the onslaught of the night. The conical hill that loomed over the place vanished into the blackness, as if it had uprooted itself and headed off to the sun, and what few streets there were seemed to fall into an apocalyptic torpor where nothing moved and

47

no sound was permitted, except the whisper of the waves scraping at the shale on the shoreline and the clinking of metal cables against the masts of the yachts in the small marina.

They had not come to this land that the twenty-first century forgot for the peace and quiet, though. They had been here for two nights, and Mike was ready to go home – an opinion he ventured often – but Pat said they had come for a job and they would see it through even if a sock had to be shoved into Mike's mouth to achieve it.

So he tried to relax. They enjoyed breakfast in the village inn where they were lodged. They walked the cliffside paths and climbed the hill that gave the village its name – Pittencairn, Pat had explained, means 'place of the hill' in Gaelic. Mike was remarkably unimpressed. It might as well mean 'place of the yawn', he thought. He didn't say that, though, for Pat would just give him one of those looks that told him these were not leisure pursuits. Even when they took those strolls, they were watching a guy. They were often watching a guy. Until the time came not to watch but to act. That time had not yet presented itself, and Mike wished to fuck it would get a move on.

They sat on a bench set against the wall of what was once the harbour-master's small office – but was now locked and boarded – looking down on the marina, which was filled with yachts and small boats moored there by the Pringle knitwear and designer gin crowd. It was an L-shaped harbour, crooked into the North Sea. The guy was in the marina, doing something around a mast. Mike had no idea what he was doing: something seafarerly, probably. Splicing the mainbrace or heave-topping the halyards. He had no clue what a halyard was or how you heave-topped it but that lack of knowledge bothered him not one bit. He had picked the phrase up from an Errol Flynn picture on the telly and it had stuck in his mind.

The weather was fine but cold, and for that he was thankful as he would not have enjoyed sitting there in the pissing rain. Actually, he didn't particularly enjoy it even when it wasn't. But they sat there like two old codgers, Pat reading a small book on local history and places of interest taken from the inn. Mike gave up watching the guy splicing or heave-topping or whatever to stare out beyond the stone harbour to the expanse of matching blue water and sky beyond, both stretching off to meet at a barely perceptible horizon.

'What's another word for "blue"?' he asked.

Pat didn't look up from the book. 'Navy.'

'Aye, I know that, but what else?'

Pat's eyes rose from the printed pages. 'Why you asking?'

'Just want to know.'

Pat's mouth twisted. 'Azure, cyan, turquoise, teal, cobalt, aquamarine . . .'

'That's the one, aquamarine. That's what's out there, aquamarine blue.' He stopped, thought for a minute. '*Aqua* means "water", doesn't it?'

'Aye. So does "marine", in a way.'

This hadn't occurred to Mike until it was pointed out. 'That's right.'

Pat looked back at the book, waited for a moment before throwing in, 'There's ultramarine, too.'

'What's the difference?'

'One's blue, the other's helluva blue.'

Mike narrowed his eyes, trying to figure out if Pat was winding him up, just as a movement in the smooth water between two small boats moored just below them drew his attention and the sleek black head of a seal bobbed into view.

'You see that?' His voice was heady with excitement.

Pat looked up again, followed Mike's pointing finger to where the seal was staring back at them. 'It's a creature. So what?'

'I know it's a seal, Pat, I'm no' a complete dildo.'

'So why you so excited?

Mike said, 'I never expected to see one just come up like that, you know, just a few feet away from me, out of the blue. Or the aquamarine or ultramarine or fuckin' Royal Marine.'

Pat said, 'We're at the seaside, ya bawbag, there's a helluva lot more than that out there.'

Mike frowned. 'I know, but still.'

'Still what?'

'Never thought I'd see one, is all.'

Pat gave Mike a look reserved for when he was being especially dense. 'You going to jump for joy if you see a dolphin?'

Mike's voice grew eager. 'You think we might?'

Pat sighed, looked back down at the book again. 'Simple things, I suppose. Just keep an eye on that bloke, is all.'

'Aye, aye, he can't leave without me seeing him, don't you worry.'

Mike kept his eyes on the seal, fascinated by the way it seemed to watch them with its calm eyes, as if it was waiting for something. He felt a sudden kinship with the creature, for he was waiting for the word to go home. He was done with the quiet life. 'We got any bread?'

'Aye, sure,' Pat's voice was heavy with sarcasm. Pat was good with sarcasm. Sometimes too good, Mike thought. 'I've got a pan loaf here in my pocket.'

'Just thought we could throw it a wee something.'

Pat looked up again from the book. 'What, the seal?'

'Aye.'

'You want to feed the seal?'

'Aye,' said Mike. 'It's no' as if it would follow us home, is it?'

Pat's head shook then dropped back to reading.

Mike watched as the seal slipped silently under the surface again. It was probably bored. He understood that. He was bored, too. He sighed, glanced sidelong at Pat, who ignored him. He sighed again, more theatrically. This time Pat noticed. 'Jeezo, it's like being out with a wean.'

'I'm bored,' said Mike.

'We're working, for God's sake.'

'I'm working. You're sitting there reading.'

Pat's head jerked towards the man on the boat. 'I know where he is, and he isn't going anywhere yet. Have you no' got nothing to read?'

'I don't like reading, hurts my head.'

Pat grimaced. 'You hurt my head.'

Mike fell silent. Pat continued to read. The seal did not make a fresh appearance. The sea stretched off to the horizon. Mike's boredom grew.

If they didn't finish this bloke off soon, he'd have the screaming habdabs. He sat back and tried to get comfortable on the bench.

The Island of Stoirm

The bench had been made completely from wood. There was no metal, not one single nail or screw, no unnatural substance in its frame. It had been hewn from raw timber by Sanctuary's carpenter and locked in place through tongue, groove and wooden pegs. It had not been treated with chemicals and being left open to the elemental fury that was life on the island meant that it would eventually become unstable, be broken up and left to rot naturally. It had been born of the land, and to the land it would return. When that day came, the carpenter would construct a new one to take its place atop the small hill. Birth, death, rebirth. That was the way. That was life. And in between there was love, peace and harmony.

Delia Forbes had watched the bench as it was constructed the summer she arrived in Sanctuary. She had witnessed how the carpenter's hands gently caressed the wood as he would a lover, had wondered at the skill with which he eased each section into place, a gentle touch here, a stronger blow there, until the many became one. She had been the first person to rest upon it and look from the small rise over Sanctuary nestling in the hollow and, beyond it, to the sharp peak of the mountain that erupted from the forestry plantation, as if trying to escape the contamination of the non-native species.

She loved to sit on the bench and feel the breeze as it caressed the island from the sea and listen as it stirred the myriad voices in the earth. She knew there were islanders that believed there were beings who lived in the wind and in the grasses and heathers and that the sounds humans heard were but their songs. Songs of love and companionship, songs of welcome and greeting. When the winds grew strong, as they were prone to do on the island, the songs of summer became a shriek of winter as the rage of the banshee was unleashed and the natural world – the world beyond this world – struck back at what was alien. In that same breath of fury, it smote that which was of itself; the land, the trees that grew from it and upon it, the creatures that fed off it, as if punishing them for collaborating with the enemy. She did not necessarily hold with the belief that elemental beings existed, although she had come to believe during her time in Sanctuary that there were forces in nature that mortals were not meant to understand but merely accept. For a time, she did come to believe that the human condition was the pursuit of peace and harmony amid the turmoil of existence. Sanctuary taught that to find true enlightenment one must see the ructions of life as but storms of emotion that spring up and die. Hatred, envy, lust – for money and dominion over others, as well as the desire for flesh – and jockeying for position were not the way. Love – the ability to offer and receive – along with content-ment through hard work and fellowship, is what Sanctuary offered. It was a haven from the increasingly toxic world of scrabbling for profit and power. It was the way.

Delia, though, was troubled. She did not like being troubled, for it reminded her too much of her old life, the one before Sanctuary, the life far away in the city, the life that had almost been the death of her. It was a brush with mortality that had brought her to the Children of the Dell and then to Sanctuary. A nurse in the private hospital where she was treated had introduced her to their teachings, giving her a pamphlet, which she had read. It had questioned what life meant and made her reflect on whether hers had turned out the way she had expected. Was she caught in a spiral of work and worry and petty jealousy and suspicion and yet more work? Had she bought into the fantasy created by the money-spinners and promoted by the power-hungry that life was all about what you could buy or eat or even throw away?

The issues resonated with her, for such had been her life. Her marriage was flat and empty, her family joyless, her work as the chief executive of a media company rewarding in the financial sense but spiritually void. Her life was based on lies; that she loved her husband, that her family cared for her, that her work had any meaning beyond the new car, the new kitchen, the new dress. Her old life had caused her breakdown of mind and body. A new life would repair the damage.

When she had reached out to the Children, it felt as if they had merely been waiting for her all along. She was invited to Sanctuary on the island and she never left. Something about the place, overlooked by Ben Shee, felt immediately like home. If someone had told her ten years before that she was a spiritual person, she would have spat her Prosecco all over them in derision. Religion was for suckers, she believed then, but after two weeks in Sanctuary she realised that what the Children offered was not a religion, as such, but access to the spirit. She resigned from her job, divorced her husband, liquidated her assets and left her family – the one which believed that the only yardstick to happiness was how much money you had in the bank – and moved permanently north. She gave the Children almost everything she had, because that was a prerequisite. You must cast off all you were before. Come with only the clothes on your back and a small bag with a few other items. Sanctuary will provide, but you will work for it. You will become part of something greater than yourself. You will become one with the world and its wonders. And you will find fellowship and you will find family.

That had been two years before. Two years of bliss and peace. Two years in which she had not needed to think of money or profit or loss. Two years in which she had seldom thought of her old life and what she had left behind.

But that old life was only tucked away like an old photograph in a purse, forgotten until you find it hidden in a fold and look at it. And you remember the day it was taken and where it was taken and how you felt when it was taken. It was words, whispers repeated over and over again, that had found their way into the recesses of her mind, found the snapshot of remembrance and held it up to the light.

She had resisted. She had denied. She had refused to believe. But . . .

The old Delia began to question, softly at first, but those doubts grew louder. She knew that by giving her money to the Children she was effectively buying her place in Sanctuary; not that it was described that way, but there was enough of the hard-headed Delia left, even after the breakdown, to recognise that it was a transaction. Sanctuary was like a timeshare, in a way, and she was buying her little piece of paradise. At the time, that didn't matter, even though she had kept a little back. Some shares. Some investments. The old Delia again, telling her that spirituality was one thing but being prudent was another. She had never told anyone about her insurance policies, and by the time she had fully committed to the Children she had felt so ashamed of herself that she could not bear to mention them. She did not divest herself of them, although the mental snapshot of the old Delia faded away, deep into the recesses, and the new Delia embraced all that Sanctuary offered.

But . . .

Then came the whispers – incessant, convincing – and that old, faded snapshot began to sharpen. The old Delia, the one who scrutinised, argued with the new Delia, the one who wanted peace. And the old Delia was winning.

That was why she was troubled.

As she sat on the bench she loved so much, the sun on her face not carrying any warmth but still welcome, the faint boom of the waves in the caves of Thunder Bay a few miles away, her feelings turned to sadness. She knew she may have to allow the old Delia to fully rise to the surface, and she feared it would be the death of her new persona. She did not want to think about such things; that was what had made her ill, that was what had made her cast off that life of darkness and embrace this new one of light. All she had wanted was to live happily without questioning, without doubting, without having to strive to outdo her neighbour, but now she was becoming more certain that she would have to do all of those things if she was to find any real peace. What was worse, she would have to do it surreptitiously. In business she had often been forced to be underhand, to be ruthless. It had never sat well with her, but she had swallowed any hesitation like a bitter pill and got on with the job because, she had been taught to believe, had come to believe, that getting on meant getting on with it.

The whispers had been bad enough, but the final straw had come earlier that morning when Sebastian returned from

55

Portnaseil. She had been walking across the farmyard, or the Compound as many of the Children called it, though she shrank from that term because to her it smacked of the military or – perhaps worse – prison. Yes, they gathered there, if the weather was fine, for announcements and group exercise, but those assemblies were far from mandatory and there was certainly nothing regimented about them. The believers could drift in and out of the group as they saw fit, for freedom was what Sanctuary offered. Freedom of will, freedom of choice.

She had heard the Land Rover before she saw it. It was old, its blue bodywork battered by the years and speckled with rust like liver spots, while its engine was a testament to the tenacity and skill of Sebastian, who had once been a mechanic on the Formula One circuit. That, at least, was how he described himself, but Delia often suspected he had been more than that, for Sanctuary was reserved for what she had once termed high-flyers. No matter, he worked magic with the Land Rover's tired old engine, but of late it had developed something of a roar, plus other issues, including problems with the brakes which he had not yet fully tackled. It was also due its MOT soon and he was not certain it would pass.

He climbed out of the driver's seat, and she heard the clatter of his keys as they fell from his hand. He kept them all on an old keyring, and the clasp was broken. She moved to help him retrieve them from the cobbled ground. He thanked her but, as they straightened, she could tell by his grim features that something had happened. Seb had been the first person to welcome her to the island, had mentored her during the early weeks, so she knew when something was wrong. They hugged, the customary greeting here in Sanctuary, but when he pulled away, his hands lingered on her shoulders. They had been intimate, on occasion – the Children were encouraged to be free with their affections – so she was used to his touch, but, again, something here was different.

She rested her hands on his forearms. 'What's wrong, Seb?'

He was a handsome, powerful man, his thick black hair only now showing signs of grey. She could feel the muscles tense under her fingers. He looked around, as if searching for unwanted ears, which itself was unusual, for there were no secrets here.

'You haven't heard?'

'Heard what?'

'So nobody has connected it to Sanctuary yet,' he said, relief easing his facial muscles. 'That's good.'

'Seb, what are you talking about?' She forced a smile. 'You're worrying me here. Don't tell me our credit has been cut off at the village store!'

He swallowed, looked around again, then edged closer. She frowned, even though she was happy to have him nearer. Although they had once been lovers, he was now with Serena, another believer. Sexual matters were fluid in Sanctuary, but Delia still adhered to some of her old ways. Seb was aligned – therefore he was off limits. She had not aligned herself with anyone since him.

'It's the Sister,' he said.

She felt nervousness flutter but she kept her voice light. 'What is she saying about us now? Do we sacrifice virgins on the altar?'

'No, nothing like that,' he said. 'Delia, she's dead. And word in the village is that she was found in a circle of protection. She may have believed she was under attack, and you know what that means.'

She did. Contrary to rumour, such rituals were not practised in Sanctuary; they were not occultists in the accepted sense of the word, but they did learn the ways of such believers, call them what you will. Wiccans. Pagans. Black Magicians. White Magicians. Part of the ethos of Sanctuary was that the Children study the esoteric in the hope that understanding

57

might assist them in comprehending the natural world and then themselves. Father had stated in his writings that humans are creatures of the spirit, and the more we delve into the spiritual nature of existence, the more we can explore our own core being. Even so, if it was true that the Sister had been found within a pentagram then sooner or later eyes would turn to the Children.

'Someone should alert Father,' she said.

Seb laid a hand on her forearm and she felt a customary tingle. 'Already done. I called him from the village.'

There was only one mobile phone allowed in Sanctuary. It was used for emergencies and was locked away in a small safe in the compound's office.

Delia's nerves, though, were irritated for a reason other than the erotic charge she still felt when Seb touched her. The Children called the woman the Sister in a dismissive way, but Delia knew her as Nuala. And Nuala was the source of the whispers that had troubled her so, that had disturbed her own inner peace and harmony, that had made her doubt. There was something rotten at the heart of Sanctuary, Nuala had said. Something to do with Father, she had said. Delia had tried to ignore it, but Nuala was very persuasive. She said she had evidence but admitted it was really only notes and questions that led to more questions. The file had not been gathered by Nuala – someone else had done that – but the old Delia had known the man who had originally made them and knew he was capable of uncovering that which others wanted to remain hidden. That knowledge, and the fervency with which Nuala had spoken, had resurrected those old doubts.

And now Nuala was dead. She had always said that there was a danger she would become inconvenient, but Delia had dismissed that as high drama from a highly dramatic woman.

58

The people of Sanctuary would never do such a thing, she had said.

The Sister had merely given her a look and said, uncharacteristically quietly, *There are people behind people.*

Now, as she sat on the bench atop the rise, with the breeze whispering around her and carrying the echoes of Thunder Bay, Delia knew what she had to do.

And she wondered why she had heard the Land Rover cough into life the night before.

Inverness

Rebecca stared at the diagram on her computer screen. The five-pointed star, a pentagram, enclosed in a circle. She read the text with a mixture of fascination and amusement.

Mars is a potent power source in magic and its numerological equivalent is five, so the pentagram with its five radiating points is a very powerful symbol. When the single point is uppermost, it is a force for good; but downward it is a symbol of evil, the twin points at the top representing Satan in the guise of a goat. It is also stated that the five points represent the five wounds inflicted on Christ's body and, as such, it is a powerful defence against demons.

Good grief, Rebecca thought, surely people can't believe all this in the twenty-first century? And yet, this woman had cut the symbol in the earth and laid down in it. What was that all about? She began to read again.

There was another theory, that the pentagram is really a depiction of God – or even the magician – adding himself, or at least his spirt, to the power of the four elements. The image itself could even be viewed as a man with his head, hands and feet forming the five points.

Why was it always men, Rebecca wondered. Why were magicians more or less accepted, while witches were the ones who were mostly hanged, burned or drowned? Setting aside the inherent sexism, she thought about the woman on Stoirm. Was that what she was doing? Was she joining with nature somehow? And if so, why do it in the middle of the night?

She began to read again:

What is agreed is that the symbol is ancient and is important not only to pagans but also Christians, and it can often be seen carved in church architecture. It is even referred to in the old folk song 'Green Grow The Rushes Oh', which mixes Christian thought with more ancient beliefs. The line 'five for the symbol at your door' refers to the medieval practice of having a pentagram etched in the doorway to ward off evil. When drawn within a magic circle, the pentagram is seen as a potent defence against psychic attack.

Rebecca sat back. That has to be what forced her out of the cottage into the cold. The poor woman was convinced she was under attack and she carved the pentagram as a form of defence. That Nuala Flaherty was some sort of pagan or Wiccan was pretty obvious now.

Rebecca had already put a basic story together regarding the discovery of the woman's body and sent it out on the wires, with no mention at this stage of the strange circumstances. Mindful that she was not supposed to know about it, she had skirted around the matter of the pentagram with her contact in the communications department at Inshes – basically, an almost off-hand query if there was anything unusual about the scene – but he had still been very reticent. No one wanted the pentagram angle out there yet, least of all Rebecca, but it would not remain quiet for long, certainly not on Stoirm. Someone always talked, whether it be a loose-lipped local cop or even the joiner from Portnaseil who doubled as an undertaker and who would have been called out to remove the body. The word would be passed on to someone who would drop it into another conversation, and soon it would be common knowledge. It probably already was. Life did not move swiftly on Stoirm, but rumour was supersonic.

The island's remoteness was an advantage, but when the news did finally cross the water it would spark interest among her colleagues and rivals. So she kept her line very brief: tragic death of a young woman, as yet unnamed officially, on the moors of a remote Hebridean island; a Major Investigation Team sent to investigate as a matter of routine, but no suggestion at this stage of foul play. She bolstered the spare report with a comment from a Mountain Rescue spokesperson about the dangers of failing to treat Scotland's wild places with respect. She didn't hint to news editors that there may be anything more to it because she didn't want to get any other noses twitching. She was reasonably confident that nobody else would have the inside track to the circumstances yet, but if it did hit soon, staffing levels even in the dailies were pared to the bone and they were unlikely to send someone to the island. She had the edge, for Chaz was already there.

There was a time when Bill Sawyer would not have touched fast food with someone else's bargepole, but that was long ago when the world was young. Since the injury to his leg – tip: don't travel on the outside of a speeding vehicle – he had been forced to give up his fitness regime and had discovered the delights of burgers in greaseproof paper. He hadn't himself gone supersize – he liked to think he was still reasonably trim – but he did enjoy high street fast food. Thanks to the injury, he now sported a very slight limp and had not walked a proper hill for three years. He should get back to it, he supposed, and eat properly. He had a friend who nagged him constantly about his eating habits, telling him what he should stay away from. Cooking in vegetable oil was his current no-no and he should be using extra virgin olive oil instead. Bill listened politely but justified his surface dismissal of much of what he was told by telling himself that in a year's time the science will change and olive oil will be bad for you. Or, rather, the vegetable oil industry will find their own experts to say it.

Still, he had bought a bottle of extra virgin olive oil. Just in case.

He had no idea how the burger he had in his hand was fried, but he was enjoying it. The world went on its merry way beyond the big windows of the fast-food outlet on Inverness High Street, and he let it. There was a time, when he was a serving police officer, that he found himself involved in other people's lives, but that was then and this was now and, apart from some freelance investigation work for solicitors and Elspeth McTaggart, he was his own man and was happy to allow events to unravel without his interference. He had a large coffee, some fries, that week's edition of *Private Eye*, and he was content.

That contentment evaporated when Cokey Irvine sat down opposite him, his body jerking like someone had wired the plastic seat to the National Grid and thrown a switch. Cokey was a hangover from Sawyer's days on the Job, a fringe dweller who was not quite bent but if he had been a snooker cue he would be used for trick shots. He had proved useful in the old days because he was a listener, the type of guy you paid little attention to, once you got used to the way his body seemed to ripple whenever he was nervous. When he was relaxed, he had the ability to melt into the wallpaper like dampness, so people had a habit of saying things within his earshot, and those things were duly passed on to the law – for a consideration, of course, as Cokey was not public spirited. His first name was really Andrew, but everyone called him

Cokey, thanks to his predilection for snorting the white stuff like a hog in truffle heaven. Although Cokey had once told him the bodily tremors ran in the family and he had an uncle in Glasgow with the same condition, Sawyer suspected they were more to do with the illicit substance, but he could be wrong. He had never cared enough to find out.

Sawyer didn't trouble himself by looking at the little man. 'I'm having my dinner, Cokey. Off you fuck.'

Cokey looked at his watch. 'Bit early for dinner, is it no', Mr Sawyer?'

'What are you? The dinner police?'

Cokey decided not to answer that. 'Saw you through the window, Mr Sawyer.'

'Good, now go look at me from the same vantage point.'

Sawyer turned a page in dismissal.

'Got something for you, Mr Sawyer,' Cokey said, his voice dropping to a whisper, even though there was no one anywhere near them. For Cokey, it was always best to be circumspect, for he knew more than anyone else that walls have ears. And sometimes they have mouths, tongues, fists, boots and, on occasion, knives and guns. It was always best to have any conversations *sotto voce*. In fact, as *sotto* as it was humanly possible for a *voce* to be without resorting to semaphore.

'I'm not on the Job any more, Cokey,' Sawyer said, still not looking up.

'I know that, Mr Sawyer, but you'll still want to hear what I've got.'

'Why is that, Cokey?'

'Because it's about a pal of yours.'

This time Sawyer raised his eyes. 'Oh, aye? Who?'

Cokey sat back, a confident smile appearing. He had even stopped jerking slightly. His movements were now little more than a shudder, as if someone was walking over his grave, which was all very possible given the fine line he tended to walk as a tout between this world and the next.

'I'm a businessman, Mr Sawyer, you know the score. You want the *pro quo*, you've got to come up with the *quid*, you know?'

Sawyer laid his burger down, wiped his lips on the paper napkin and leaned across the table. 'How about I just pick you up and *pro quo* you through that window, Cokey?'

Cokey glanced at the window to his left. 'That's strengthened glass, Mr Sawyer, you'd never get me through it.'

'Maybe not, but it would be fun trying.'

The little man knew Sawyer would do nothing of the sort, but his body did begin to tremble like jelly touched with a vibrator. 'Come on, Mr Sawyer, have I ever given you a bum steer in the past?'

Sawyer had to admit, even if only to himself, that Cokey's information had always been of the stand-up variety. He sighed and sat back again, to appear less threatening. Almost immediately the little man's shaking stilled to an almost imperceptible quiver. 'All right, if I think it's worth it, I'll give you a drink, but if I think you're at the madam, son, I'll no' be best pleased.'

'Och, Mr Sawyer . . .'

Sawyer made a point of looking back at his magazine and picking up his burger. 'Take it or leave it, Cokey.' He didn't look up, merely let the man weigh the pros and cons of parting with his information without any real promise of financial gain. Cokey was sharp – he had to be to survive in his twilight world – and he knew that this was the way it worked, even though Sawyer was no longer a detective sergeant. No money was agreed up front; the usefulness of the information was weighed, graded and rewarded accordingly.

'Awright, Mr Sawyer,' he said eventually, 'I trust you.'

Sawyer faced him once more. 'Okay, so what you got?'

Cokey looked around, leaned in. 'You're pals with that reporter lassie, aren't you?'

Sawyer didn't need to ask which reporter lassie Cokey referred to as he was only ever in contact with two on anything like a regular basis. There was no way on God's little green Earth that Cokey would refer to Elspeth McTaggart as a lassie, so that meant it was Rebecca Connolly. 'Wouldn't say pals, but what about her?'

Cokey had another furtive cast around before he lowered his voice even further. 'Mo Burke.'

Sawyer waited, expecting Cokey to amplify, but the little man simply stared at him, as if he should know what he was talking about. Mo Burke was the matriarch of a criminal family based in Inchferry, which Sawyer viewed as a hell-hole of a housing scheme that sat on the edge of the Beauly Firth like an ulcer. 'What about Mo Burke?'

'She blames your lassie for her boy's death.'

Sawyer knew Rebecca had been present when the family dispute turned to bloodletting. Rebecca herself had been under the gun, but Nolan Burke died instead. 'That's bollocks. She knows it was her drugged-up son Scott who was responsible.'

'That's no' the way she sees it, Mr Sawyer. She wants payback.'

'Where you hearing this, Cokey?'

'Ah, Mr Sawyer, you know I can't reveal my sources. But you know whatever I tell you is gen up. What I hear, she's obsessed with her now. Seems Mo asked a couple of blokes a while ago to do her over. One of them, some bloke up from Glasgow, gave it a knockback but the other one had a go and ended up with a burst nose.'

'Martin Bailey?'

'That's the one. Your lassie gave him a right doing, so she did.'

Sawyer knew the man by repute and knew him to be a card-carrying scumbag, so, like everyone else, he thought Bailey had zeroed in on Rebecca because of a story she had written. Not the case, it now seemed. Interesting.

'Mo's been spitting blood about that, and it's made her even more determined to do your lassie a damage,' Cokey went on. 'You know Mo, she's not the type to let bygones be bygones. I've heard she's obsessed with the Rebecca lassie now. So much so, there's boys in her crew who think she's letting business slip, know what I'm saying?'

Sawyer did know what he was saying. He bit on his burger as he considered what Cokey had told him. Mo Burke was as dangerous and as vicious as any ned he had ever known. Her husband, Tony, had been jailed a few years before for assault to severe injury, and she had held her own against encroachment by heavy mobs from Glasgow and Edinburgh, even though Sawyer had heard she'd reached an accommodation with the former. Now, she ran the family business single-handedly, and she did so with a ruthless efficiency that shocked many a hardened cop. If she wanted Rebecca hurt – or worse – she would not stop until it was done. Mo Burke was like the Terminator in that way. Sawyer realised he could no longer taste his burger, so he set it aside.

'So what do you think, Mr Sawyer?' Cokey said. 'Worth a bob or two, or what?'

'I'll see you right, Cokey, don't worry.'

'Mr Sawyer, I was kinda hoping for cash on delivery, if you know what I mean?'

Sawyer sighed, reached into the pocket of his jacket for his wallet. 'I've got twenty here. I'll give you another just like it after I get to the bank.'

'Forty? Is that all I get?'

Sawyer held out the twenty-pound note. 'This is like my mother's tea-time menu, Cokey. Take it or leave it.'

Cokey didn't hesitate – he snatched the money and salted it away in his coat pocket with a speed that impressed Sawyer. 'It's a liberty though, Mr Sawyer.'

Sawyer smiled. 'You shouldn't have told me what you knew first then, should you?'

The Island of Stoirm

The phone was not new, and a series of cracks ran across the black screen as if in a race to reach the far edge. She kept it concealed under her mattress, confident nobody would find it. Although doors were not locked – apart from the office downstairs – she knew nobody would come into her room without being invited. The charger was a bit more difficult to hide, but she wrapped it up in some underwear and placed it in the bottom of her laundry basket. Nuala had given the device to her – it had no SIM card, but she had placed photographs of the research she had on the Children, Sanctuary and Father in a file. For a time, Delia had resisted even looking at it. Now, she lay on her bed listening to the usual night-time activity in Sanctuary beyond her door with the phone in her hand, its screen dark. Voices, laughter, even someone singing. Life here was happy, peaceful, even fulfilling. Did she really want to jeopardise all that for the delusions of a woman filled with grief and bitterness?

Delia knew the answer. Or, at least, the old Delia did.

She flicked the screen with her thumb to bring it to life and opened the file labelled *SANCTUARY*. She clicked on the first image and looked at the handwriting. It was little more than a scribble that would have shamed a drunken doctor. Nuala had told her she was able to decipher it, and Delia did not doubt her, for she had known the man who had first scratched them onto paper intimately. To Delia, however, the words were little more than fluctuating lines with the only things clear being *Sanctuary* and initials and names with arrows linking one to another.

TS.

COD.

There was another word linked to both. It looked like 'Gorgons', or 'Gordons'. Or a name, perhaps. It definitely had a capital G. It could even be 'Gorgeous'. Delia knew that the notes which had set Nuala off on her quest were vague, but no matter how often she looked at them she still could not make any sense of them.

Another scribble could be made out: *Templesword*. She had no access to the internet, so did not know what it meant. The fact was, she didn't know what any of it meant.

Also in the file were two jpegs: one of a birth certificate in the name Wesley Fairbanks, born forty-eight years before; and the other a theatrical notice from a local newspaper in the south of England in April 1976, which contained a photograph of a young actor called Bennet Lomax, who was appearing in a production of Joe Orton's *Loot*. She stared at the face. She had never seen this man perform, but she knew those features, although he was considerably younger in this image. That, more than anything else, raised her curiosity level.

No, she told herself – Delia, recognise it for what it is. It's not curiosity, it's suspicion.

She laid the phone face down on her chest as voices passed her room. Sounded like Seb with Serena, probably going down to dinner. She waited until the voices faded and vanished before she picked up the phone again and stared at the hieroglyphics on the screen. She could make a guess at one of the initialisations, but not the others. And what did gorgons have to do with it? Or Gordon, whoever he might be? And who the hell were Wesley Fairbank and Bennet Lomax?

She knew she was being drawn into this mystery, but the old Delia was in charge now. She had liked Nuala; the woman had suffered a lot, so the least she could do was nose around. But what could her next step be, she wondered.

And then she thought of Seb and his keys.

Inverness

Stephen Jordan did not trust reporters. Rebecca was a reporter. And yet, he had asked her out. Yes, it had taken him a while but he did it and she said yes and, as she had told Elspeth, they had gone out a couple of times since. Well, more than a couple. His lack of trust, as she saw it, was something she couldn't quite get her head around, even though when they went out – okay, they had gone out a lot – they did not talk shop. Or rather, he didn't talk shop. She told him what stories she was working on, what the problems were, how difficult people could be, how open people could be, how damned contrary the human race could be when you came right down to it. He listened, he threw in an opinion or two, but he never – ever – spoke to her about his work. Sure, maybe a comment here or there about this sheriff or that judge or such and such a depute procurator fiscal, but never – again, ever – did he talk about anyone he represented.

Not even some pillow talk, as she now knew.

Naturally, there was the little matter of client confidentiality; Rebecca got that because she had her own rules regarding sources. But she couldn't shake off the nagging feeling that he didn't fully trust her. And that, well, hurt a little.

The thing was, she wasn't sure why she went out with him anyway. For starters, he was older, by ten years. For another, he was a lawyer and she had bought apples from that cart before. Simon had been pleasant enough, handsome enough, attentive enough. Actually, perhaps too attentive. Clingy, was closer to the truth, and that rankled. He wasn't exactly a stalker, more stalker adjacent. She needed her own space, and he hadn't understood that. Even so, had she not suffered the miscarriage, they might have been together still. Or perhaps not.

She used to hear a baby crying in the dark. She knew, though, it was her own subconscious crying out, her own guilt, misplaced though it was. She lost the child – their child, hers and Simon's, she reminded herself – through no fault of hers. She had not done anything to cause it; it was simply a complication of chromosomes, nothing more, she had been told. Whatever she felt, or thought she had felt, or convinced herself she may – possibly – have felt for Simon died then.

She didn't hear the baby now. Its voice stilled as the storms of her mind eased.

She still saw Simon now and again – at court, at functions – and the atmosphere between them was frosty enough for a penguin to turn up the heating. She had even run into him one night when out with Stephen. Simon was with another woman, of course, a leggy blonde who hung on his arm like she needed the support. Rebecca had known he wouldn't be single for long – he was a catch, after all – but that had been an awkward affair. The men knew each other, the legal profession being a relatively small club in the Highlands, but they weren't friends. Rebecca felt bad about the encounter and she didn't know why, for Stephen seemed completely unfazed by it. More guilt, she supposed, because she had not treated Simon very well towards the end. Actually, if she was being completely honest with herself, she had not treated him at all well. She had ignored his calls, made excuses to avoid seeing him and eventually ended it all in a brief but chilly conversation in a hotel lounge overlooking the river. He didn't deserve to be treated in such a way, even with his annoying, clingy ways.

Stephen was different. He often gave the impression he didn't care if he saw her or not. There were no recriminations if she backed out of plans because of work. There were no questions, no accusations, no real commitment. It was exactly what she wanted, but she still somehow felt insulted.

Over dinner that night she told him about Tabitha Haley. He was attentive, he always was, and he asked pertinent questions. Feeling she had monopolised the conversation, Rebecca queried how his day had been, but he merely shrugged and said, 'The usual.'

The usual.

That was as much as she got out of him. What was it? Was he concerned she would use anything he told her in a story? She would never do that. She had rules, and one was she would not breach a confidence, as Val Roach had learned when she tried to force her to reveal a source. She had thought about addressing the issue of Stephen's perceived lack of trust but decided against it. He might get the wrong idea. He might feel she wanted something more serious between them, more permanent. And she really didn't. At all. Nope, no way, José.

They went to the cinema after eating, some superhero film that she thought she wanted to see, given it had a female protagonist, but it turned out to be as dull, predictable and downright pretentious as the ones with guys in leading roles. Stephen seemed to be enjoying it, so she settled back and allowed her mind to wander during scenes where characters were throwing each other through CGI walls like in cartoons. She thought about work, about Chaz and Alan on Stoirm.

Stoirm.

She didn't want to go back. She wanted to go back. She didn't know what she wanted. Would she return if she didn't have to for the wedding? She knew the island was part of her family's past, but when she had found out about the dark

71

events that occurred more than two generations before, it had shocked her. Her great-grandmother had been a child murderer, disposing of illegitimate babies at birth, drowning them like unwanted puppies or kittens. She had no idea how many she had killed in her lifetime but even one life lost in such a heartless fashion was too much. Rebecca, still reeling from the miscarriage that only she and Simon knew about, was sickened by it, just as her father had been years before. It made her realise why he was always hit so hard by any crime involving children. As a police officer, he had to deal with such horrors efficiently, but she knew it ate him up. Once, she would have been about five or six years old, she heard him talking to her mother downstairs, so she crept from her room and peered through the living room door to see him in his armchair, her mother perched on the armrest, cradling his head against her shoulder as he sobbed – great, whooping sobs – and his hands held her close, fingers digging into her arms as his body jerked and spasmed with the tears. His knuckles were scraped, Rebecca saw, and blood smeared his fingers like a guilty secret. Back then, Rebecca didn't know what had happened but over the years, as she became aware of her father's hatred of anyone who harmed a child, she suspected he had stepped over a line. He had lashed out at one such person, and the grief and rage she had witnessed as he buried his face into his wife's body was not only because of the crime itself but also because of what he had perhaps done. As far as she knew, there had never been any comeback – he became a detective chief inspector eventually – so if he had beaten a suspect, it had not been discovered or covered up somehow.

The last time she had seen him it wasn't really him but another manifestation of her mind. She had been in a dark place then, she knew that now, and the sight of her father sitting on her bed, smiling at her from the corners of her imagination, always comforted her. The sight never terrified her, for she knew he would never harm her – and, anyway, he wasn't really there.

Was he?

The final visitation came soon after she had returned from a Spanish holiday, her first real break in years and much needed. It was there she'd enjoyed her first decent sleep for years, as if the torment had been burned away by the sun or had not travelled the thousand miles to follow her. She woke to see her father standing by her bed, staring down at her, that little smile of his so vivid, even in the dark of her room. In the dreams he was the John Connolly she remembered: the handsome, tall, vibrant man who used to lift her up and swing her around the room as if he was a human merry-go-round and she a brightly painted horse. She never saw the wasted, desolate man he became towards the end, his frail body barely noticeable beneath the hospice bedclothes, his face hollow, his eyes empty and staring into a void only he could see.

'Dad?' she had said, either aloud or in sleep, she was never certain which.

She felt his hand on her forehead, his thumb pushing back a lock of her hair, just as he used to do when she was a child. He had done that before, in her dreams, but this time it felt different. She sensed sadness as his hand lingered on her head.

'Daddy?' she said, once again that little girl with the rebellious bangs.

He did not speak. The touch of his hand was gone and was replaced by a kiss on her forehead. She did not see him stoop or straighten but she felt it, right where his thumb had been: light, airy, there and yet not there. Then he was smiling down at her again and she saw the pride shining in his eyes and she knew that something had changed. She had changed.

Time to live, Becks, she heard him say, the words only in her head. *Time to cast off the past.* He began to back away, the shadows of eternity taking hold.

'Don't go,' she heard herself say. 'I need you.'

No, Becks, you don't need me. Not any more.

He was now almost completely dark. His auburn hair, his face, his bright smile, all gone. He was just a dim outline now.

'What will I do without you, Daddy?'

Live, little one. Live.

She wanted to get up and run after him, to wrap her arms around his neck the way she used to, to feel the scrape of his beard against her cheek the way she used to, to feel warm and safe the way she used to. But she didn't. She couldn't. All she could do was watch as his outline melded with the deeper black until she could no longer distinguish him from it.

'I don't want you to go,' she said.

His voice came to her from the darkness, fainter than before, but still in her head. *I was never really here, Becks*, he said. *But I'm never far away.*

A breath of wind that came from nowhere, went nowhere and did not brush her face or ruffle the bedclothes, carried his voice away. She knew there would be no more visitations in the night. No more cries from a child who never breathed. No more returns to a rain-swept towpath. The memories would remain, but they would never again fill her dreams.

Tabitha had said that he was always with her, and whether or not it was his spirit didn't matter. There was an essential truth in her words. Nobody is really gone, as long as they live in memory.

And as she sat in the shadowed cinema, the screen flickering with lights and exploding with sound, she was aware of Stephen's hand reaching and his fingers meshing with hers as they rested on the armrest between them.

Okay, she thought, this is new.

The Island of Stoirm

The young man was blond and tall and would have been handsome if it weren't for the look in his eye that revealed an inner ugliness. Chaz knew who he was, of course, and he watched him weave out of the hotel bar, threading between the tables of the restaurant towards them. He hadn't reached full drunkenness but he was definitely on the inebriation express. He had a way of looking around him that suggested he was seeking out trouble and, when he spotted Chaz sitting with Alan at their table, decided he had found it. He didn't stop in front of them right away but carried on past, presumably to the Gents to make room for further liquid, satisfying himself with a smirk in their direction. Chaz felt tension begin to tighten around his jaw. He suspected things would not end with that disdainful look.

They had decided to go out for dinner, to get some time alone and also to give Chaz's parents space to themselves. Even older people need alone time, Alan had said, as if Terry and Charles were in their dotage. On the island, eating out came down to one of two choices: the restaurant in Portnaseil's only hotel or a fish eatery on the southern tip of the island. Neither Chaz nor Alan were overly fond of seafood, although their tastes were more sophisticated than Rebecca's, who was only interested in fish if it was served on a polystyrene plate, wrapped in paper and lathered with salt and vinegar. But that night they both had a yen for turf rather than surf, and so the village hotel it was.

It formed one edge of what islanders called the Square, bound on three sides by modern structures mixed with solid Victorian buildings of grey granite imported from the mainland – the Stoirm Hotel, an arts centre formed out of the old police station, the grocery store and post office, and what had once been a bank but was now empty, its safe long since cleaned out, its accounts digitised and only accessible online. The more recent constructions included the hub, made up of a small police station, a health centre, library and community hall, as well as two shop units housing a butcher and a hair salon. The fourth side of the Square was the road leading from the harbour, where the ferry docked, to weave up the hill between houses towards the Spine.

The interior of the hotel fitted its exterior, and if Queen Victoria herself had been somehow transported from the nineteenth century she might not be amused but she would feel right at home. The carpet was in dark green tartan, the woodwork around the reception desk, the walls and on the stairway burnished near black. The walls were adorned with paintings of a life in the Highlands and Islands that Chaz was convinced never really existed – all impressively moustached men with guns, dogs carrying dead animals and subservient locals glad to be of service to their betters. The décor extended into the small restaurant where, thankfully, the artwork was more scenic than bloodthirsty, but there was a large stag's head on the wall above the buffet table that looked disconcertingly real, if somewhat threadbare, after many years of gazing down at people tucking into their full Scottish breakfast.

Alan had nodded to the stag and commented, 'He must have been moving at a hell of a speed to get his head stuck through that wall.'

Chaz knew he was going to say it. He always said it when they came here. It had become a tradition. He showed his appreciation with a slight shake of the head and a heavy sigh.

The restaurant was nearly empty, not surprising given the main tourist season was a rainy, windswept, and occasionally sun-kissed, memory. The bar, through a door at the far end, sounded livelier and they could make out voices, laughter and a TV screening some football match or other. In a far corner of the restaurant, PC Rory Gibson was in civvies – a blue cotton shirt, blue sweater and blue jeans. Even in his off-duty moments he was a boy in blue. He shared a table with two women, one small and fair with the look of a weightlifter, the other taller, older and sharper of face, with brown hair cascading round her shoulders in a tangle of curls. They were both more formally dressed – a blue pinstripe suit and a white shirt for the weightlifter, a more expensive grey number for the other woman – and they all seemed deep in conversation, so much so that Rory didn't notice Chaz was there. As they sat down, he had pointed out the tall, fair-haired police officer to Alan, who scrutinised him as they ate without appearing too obvious.

'He's working,' Alan observed.

'How do you work that out?'

Alan sliced the fat from the steak on the plate before him. He had a horror of eating fat and could often spend more time trimming it away than eating the actual meat. Chaz had once suggested he become vegetarian and, to his credit, Alan did make an attempt but failed in the end, his carnivorous instincts proving too powerful. He shoved the offending tissue to the side of his plate. 'He has his notebook on the table. Also, only the woman in the designer suit – Hugo Boss, if I'm not mistaken – has eaten anything.'

Chaz spotted the black book lying open and the single soiled plate. 'I didn't catch that.'

'Of course not, my dear friend. You see but you do not observe.'

Chaz pulled a face. 'Yeah, okay, Sherlock. And how do you know it's Hugo Boss?'

'Not a clue, I just threw that in for effect.' Alan thrust a slice of rare beef into his mouth and chewed. 'But that's not all . . .'

Alan seemed in no hurry to expand, and Chaz grew impatient. 'So, you going to tell me what else?'

Alan swallowed. 'I was masticating.'

'You'll go blind and we're in public. What else did you spot, master detective?'

'The smaller woman is with the police. While we've been here, she's been asking a lot of questions and PC Rory has been making notes.'

'Amazing, Holmes.'

Alan shrugged, modestly. 'Elementary, my dear Wymark.'

That was when the young blond man came through the bar door and walked past. Alan also caught his look and smirk as he passed. 'Friend of yours?' he asked.

'You don't know him?'

'Should I?'

'That's Andy Yates's younger brother.'

They fell silent, the mention of Andy Yates sobering Alan's usual waspishness. He had been one of a group of youths they called the Moron Squad, casual workers for the then game-keeper on the island's estate. They were an unpleasant bunch who were also homophobic in the extreme and one night had tried to run them both off the road. Chaz had been injured in the car crash, a shard of metal from their vehicle piercing his leg and side; the truth was, he could have died, and even think-ing about it caused a dull ache to spread through his body.

'If there's one law of the West, bastards have brothers,' said Alan, perhaps sensing Chaz's tension and seeking to lighten the mood.

Chaz managed a smile. 'I never should have bought you that Blu-Ray of *Romancing the Stone*.'

'I always see our Rebecca as Joan Wilder.'

'She looks nothing like Katherine Turner.'

'I know she doesn't – she's more that Scottish actor, the one who was in *Dr Who* . . .'

They became aware of the young man heading their way again but kept talking.

'Karen Gillan,' said Chaz.

'Yes, Karen Gillan.' Alan paused. 'I get the feeling she's quite tall, though, and our Rebecca is not. And it's Kathleen Turner, not Katherine.'

'If she was here, I'd apologise.'

The young man stopped at their table this time but didn't say anything, so they made an effort to studiously ignore him.

Alan carried on, 'Yes, I can just see our Rebecca out there in the wilds with a machete, sliding in the mud, being chased by gun-toting treasure hunters.'

'Falling in love with Michael Douglas . . .'

'You two should never have come back here,' said the young man towering over them, his words carried on a zephyr of beer breath that was far from pleasing.

They continued to ignore him. 'Of course, I think Michael in his day would have turned my head, too,' said Alan.

The blond youth tutted. 'Fuckin' gay boys. No place on the island for you.'

Chaz lowered his knife and fork and raised his eyes to stare at him. 'Just keep moving, Darren.'

A slightly skewed smile. 'You remember my name, then?'

'Yes, I remember your name. And I remember your brother's name, too – and the way he grinned from that Land Rover as he forced us onto the Sisters.'

The Seven Sisters was a rock formation; according to legend, they were the wives of men fighting for the clan chief on the mainland who had vowed never to leave the shoreline until they returned. The three witches of the mountain turned them to stone to make their wait easier. Chaz's own Land Rover had careered from the road and slammed into one of them that night.

'Aye, well,' said Darren, 'it's a pity they didn't finish the job. Best thing for the world, getting rid of your kind.'

79

Alan said, 'No, the best thing for the world was getting your brother and his kind behind bars, where they belong.'

Darren's eyes slide from Chaz to Alan and studied him. 'Your fault,' he said.

'No, their own fault,' Alan replied. 'The Moron Squad was always destined to fall foul of the law, one way or another. They were just lucky it wasn't more serious. Chaz almost died.'

Darren returned his attention to Chaz. 'Almost isn't enough. I remember you from school. You were a wee poofter then, too.'

'Yeah,' said Chaz, staring down at the table, trying to control his rising anger, 'and I remember you, showing us all your dick behind the dinner hall.'

'That was for the lassies.'

'There were no lassies there. Just boys.' Chaz looked up again, his teeth gritted. 'What was that about, Darren? You advertising your wares? Hoping one of us would want to touch it?'

Darren's own jaw was clamped, and his words came out in a strangled way. 'I'll bet you liked what you saw.'

Chaz managed a small smile. 'I might have, if I'd brought a magnifying glass.'

'Oh, dear,' said Alan, the corners of his mouth twitching, 'was it a very tiny winkle?'

'Like a worm with depression.'

Darren's rage was building, but Chaz wasn't finished with him. 'I'm sure you and Billy Wyatt enjoyed it, though. You were always going off together, weren't you? And in class, heads together, sniggering. Was he your first crush, Darren? When you were alone, did you both whip it out, compare girth? Such as it was.'

Darren's eyes were hard and bright, and his breathing seemed to sharpen. 'I'm no' like that. Billy neither.'

'You sure about that?' Chaz turned to Alan. 'You remember that guy we met last year? Wee fella, shaved head? He was with that French boy, what was his name, Pierre?'

'Really?' Alan said, with emphasis.

Chaz nodded.

'Well,' said Alan, giving Darren a look, 'I'll go to the foot of our stairs.'

'You're a lying bastard, Wymark,' spat Darren. 'You and your sort just want everyone to be like you.'

'And you don't? You want everyone to be straight and stupid.'

'Straight-ish, it seems,' Alan said.

Darren stepped back. 'Step outside, we'll see who's stupid.'

Alan muttered, 'Stupid people say what?'

Darren frowned. 'What?'

'I rest my case,' Alan smiled.

The young man looked from one to the other, not sure how he had suddenly become the object of ridicule, but he was determined to gain the upper hand the only way he knew how. He moved closer to the table and leaned over Chaz. 'You're so fuckin' smart, aren't you? So clever, so fuckin' witty . . .'

'So kind of you to notice,' said Alan.

'Just shut the fuck up, gay boy. I'm talking now, right?'

'You're also breathing air that is quite toxic,' said Alan, waving a hand in front of him. 'Two words for you, old chum – Tic-Tacs. Lots of them.'

Darren's face rippled with rage and he reached out across the table but stopped when a voice interrupted from behind him.

'We have some problem here, lads?'

Darren turned to face Rory. Darren was tall, but Rory was taller and his body carried considerably more power. Alongside him stood the muscled female officer, ready to weigh in if necessary. The taller woman they had been speaking to had left.

Darren sneered. 'Doesn't concern you or the law.'

'Not the way I'm hearing it, Darren,' said Rory, his tone light but his eyes hard and watchful. 'I'm hearing a breach of the peace, at the very least, maybe even some hate speech.'

'We're just talking, that's all.'

'Talking loudly, Darren.'

'And his breath is probably damaging the ozone layer,' Alan pitched in but was waved away by the police officer. Under the table, Chaz kicked his partner and gave him a look that told him to keep quiet.

Rory's tone was still conversational when he told Darren, 'I suggest you walk away.'

Darren was not about to back down. 'You're no' even in uniform.'

'I don't need to be.'

'I'm not doing nothing.'

'Then do nothing elsewhere. Or would you rather do nothing in the cell across the Square?' Darren seemed to consider arguing the point, but Rory's face was firmly set. 'Don't make me tell you again, son.'

Son. Rory was only a few years older but a certain maturity seemed to have been handed to him along with his blue serge and warrant card.

The young man seethed, his shoulders tight, his fingers bunched, but he knew when he was beaten. He gave Chaz and Alan one final glare that seemed to promise more to come, then brushed past Rory, giving the female plainclothes officer an appraising glance. She glared at him in a way which suggested that if he didn't keep his eyes to himself, she would swing him like a dumbbell. Rory watched him go, shaking his head.

'He's a big man when he's on the bevvy, that one,' he said, turning back to their table.

'So was his brother,' said Chaz, feeling his leg and side burning. 'Rory, this is Alan, my partner.'

Rory smiled as he reached across the table to shake Alan's hand. 'Aye, I know who you are. You guys are the talk of the steamie, as my grannie used to say.' He gave them both a concerned glance. 'Sorry about Darren – he's not indicative of the island in general, you know that, right?'

Alan flicked his eyebrows, as if to say he didn't quite buy that. 'We've experienced that sort of thing before on the island, so perhaps it's more indicative than you think. We used to ignore it but not now.'

'Aye, well . . .' Rory said, giving the bar door another glance. 'Anyway, enjoy what's left of your meal, lads. And, Chaz, thanks for that wee job today. It's a great help.'

'No problem, Rory,' said Chaz. 'Any idea what caused her death?'

Rory shot a brief glance at the female officer and dropped his voice slightly. 'No, it will take time for post-mortem and toxicology results to come through. The woman's body is being stored in the community hospital overnight before it goes back to the mainland tomorrow.' He raised his voice once more. 'We need a wee word with young Darren, so we'll take a wander through the bar.'

The police officer retrieved his thick jacket from the back of the chair at his table. He picked up his notebook and pen and thrust them in an inside pocket. Then, with a quick hand movement to the plainclothes detective, he stepped back to their table. 'Darren is mostly talk,' he said, reaching into the pocket of his jacket and producing a card, 'but if you have any more trouble with him, here's my phone number.'

They thanked him and, with a final nod, he and the plain-clothes officer headed towards the bar.

They resumed eating without saying anything further until Alan said, 'Pierre? Was that the best French name you could come up with?'

Chaz concealed his smile.

'I mean, a rich supply of Gallic Christian names and you go for Pierre?'

'It did the job.'

Alan ignored him. 'What about Yves, Etienne, Antoine, Clément?'

'I was under pressure.'

'And I wonder how this fellow Billy Wyatt will feel when he discovers you outed him – and made him lose his hair!'

'Him and Darren had a falling out, a big one, in fifth year. Billy's family moved away from the island the year I met you. I'm fairly certain they won't be in contact.'

'And if they are?'

'I didn't say Billy was gay. I just said we met a guy. I didn't say it was Billy.'

Alan gave Chaz an admiring smile. 'You can be a devious bastard when you feel like it, Chaz Wymark.' He turned his attention back to his food. 'I like it.'

Loch Ness

The full-length portrait of the Knight Templar stared down from above the ornate fireplace, his face grim, his eyes intense and hinting at secrets only he knew, his long hair hanging freely, his beard neat and trim, his helmet under one arm. The red cross on his white tunic was like a bloody wound, and one hand rested on the hilt of his sword. Behind the figure was a scene of devastation, a city in the Holy Land left in ruins by men such as he. To his right was a pile of treasure: gold, jewels, artefacts. It was not a portrait from life, for there was no way of knowing how the man looked in the flesh, but an imagining, as described to an artist-for-hire, who transferred it to canvas.

Nonetheless, those dark, penetrating eyes seemed to scrutinise Thomas Smith as he spoke into the mobile phone, as if taking in both sides of the conversation. This was one of many numbers Smith used, and this was his personal device. No one else made or answered calls on it, not even Vivian, and it was not used very often, only at times like this.

'Are we exposed?'

The voice on the other end bore only the faintest trace of its origin in Russia. This man had been in the West long enough to have developed the American twang so common among émigrés.

'I don't think so,' said Smith and instantly knew he had made an error.

'You don't think so?'

'No, we are secure.'

A grunt on the other end signified the man was not convinced. 'We had better be, my friend. This business of yours has been useful in a limited manner only. I would hate for my brother and I to be implicated in any way.'

'You are insulated, don't worry.'

A small chuckle but there was little humour in it. 'I do not worry. I let others do that.'

The implication was clear, and Smith did begin to worry. These men were not likely to allow themselves to be drawn into anything that might leave them open to scrutiny. At the first hint of an official investigation, the brothers would shut everything down and sever ties. As he had said, the Children of the Dell set-up was useful, but it was nothing compared to their other enterprises. The Sanctuaries may be seen as assets, but assets could be liquidated.

'You did not have anything to do with this woman's death?'

'I did not,' Smith replied, hoping he sounded convincing. If this man thought otherwise then it may not go well for him.

'How much did she know about us?'

'I don't know. I spoke to her once and she dropped hints, but I had the impression they were nothing more than shots

85

in the dark. As we know, what little information she had was not her work.'

Another grunt. Damn the woman, he thought, his mind already working out how he could salvage the operation if the brothers pulled out. The scheme could continue without them but opening further Sanctuaries without their initial investment would be tricky. That was if they didn't take things to any unpleasant extremes. Perhaps it was time for him to think about moving on.

'We feel we have been on this road before, my friend.'

Smith knew they had. His eyes roamed around his office, drawn first to the painting then to the window overlooking the loch. He saw nothing, for night had fallen, but he could imagine the deep, dark water below, perhaps the surface disrupted slightly by something large and ancient. He would miss this place if he had to move on. He knew he could sell the property easily, perhaps not at a huge profit but a tidy sum nonetheless. He always had an escape route.

'We feel history is repeating itself,' said the Russian.

Smith sharpened his focus, wondering if they knew about Gerald. 'It is coincidence only,' he assured him. 'I had nothing to do with either unfortunate incident.'

There was a silence on the line and he waited. He was a decent judge of character and could read people easily, a gift that had served him well in businesses both legitimate and illicit, but he could not read this man, even when face-to-face. That made him uncomfortable. The silence on the line made him even more uncomfortable, and he did not like that. He preferred to make other people feel uncomfortable. He felt as if his life was the surface of the loch, now being swirled by something unseen.

Eventually, the man spoke again. 'Keep me posted, my friend. Let us hope that this really is nothing but a coincidence, an unfortunate one for the woman.'

'She was an irritation, nothing more. A fleabite.'

'Fleabites can become infected. And infections can spread if left unattended.' There was a slight pause. 'And they can kill.'

The line went dead, leaving him to stare into the blackness of the night. He believed he had a flair for the dramatic, but the Nikoladze brothers made it seem so effortless.

3

TUESDAY

The Island of Stoirm

The Reverend Fiona McRae had already heard of the discovery on the moors. Stoirm was an island that held onto its secrets like a miser with an out-of-date ten-shilling note, but gossip was gossip.

As a log spat in the grate, and the minister rested her head on her knuckles, her elbow propped on the arm of the chair, which was obviously a favourite, for the upholstery was worn and the legs showed signs of abuse from a previous pet. The marks were too deep for cat scratches, so Chaz assumed it had been a dog which had gnawed at the polished wood, probably a pup. He had never seen Fiona with a dog, so he deduced it was long gone. Alan wasn't the only one who could pull a Sherlock now and then.

He and Alan had arranged the meeting to discuss the wedding on Saturday, but Terry really did have it all under control, so the conversation had turned to Nuala Flaherty's death.

'And they think it was exposure?' Fiona asked after Chaz had outlined what he'd seen the previous morning.

'Well, they don't know yet for sure, not until the post-mortem, but it certainly looks that way.'

Fiona's head shook. 'Whatever possessed the poor woman to lie out in the open like that?'

'"Possessed" may be the right word,' said Alan. 'There's a black magic slant here, given the pentagram.'

Chaz shifted in his chair, mention of the design making him feel uncomfortable. Fiona, meanwhile, gave Alan a sceptical look. 'I don't think that's likely, Alan.'

Alan seemed surprised. 'You don't believe in the occult, demons and all that jazz?'

'No,' said the minister, 'I don't. Wearing my collar back to front doesn't automatically make me buy into everything that the church has peddled over centuries. Whatever this poor woman believed was her choice, but it was not a demon that killed her.'

Alan seemed to be disappointed by the response. He may not be religious, but Chaz knew the thought of things that go bump in the night appealed to him.

Chaz asked, 'Did you know her at all?'

'I spoke to her once, that's all. She came here to see me about two months ago.'

'What did she want?'

'She was asking about the Children of the Dell.'

Alan said, 'The Children of the what now?'

Chaz sighed. Alan had developed this way of speaking lately and it was becoming increasingly annoying.

'The Dell,' Fiona repeated. 'They've bought that old farm, the one up near the plantation that leads to the mountain. They call it Sanctuary.'

Chaz searched his memory. 'The old McKenzie farm?'

'Yes. We were all surprised when the estate sold it and some of the land to them, but then His Lordship had to get rid of some things when his plan to turn the estate into an upmarket playground went belly-up.'

The island had been owned by the various Lords and Lady Stuarts of Stoirm for centuries, but over the years they had sold off much of it. They still owned the estate and a few of the businesses, including the small distillery which was now running again after a few years of hibernation, but their influence had waned, particularly under the stewardship of the current incumbent who now spent less time in the ancestral home than ever. He had planned to turn the castle and the estate lands into a resort for the wealthy. Alan had called it Butlin's for the rich and shameful.

Alan said, 'He lost his backers, that right?'

'Yes, that's the rumour, at least. After that, Lord Henry lost interest in the island and now spends his time abroad or in London. The McKenzie place hadn't been a working farm for a few years and the buildings and outbuildings were in a dreadful condition, so I hear the Children of the Dell got it for a song. Even so, there are many of us who wonder about the transaction. His Lordship was never keen on losing what little his family had here, but for some reason he gave this up. Having said that, they've done wonders with the place, apparently.'

'So who are they?' Alan asked. 'Some sort of cult?'

Fiona thought about it. 'A cult? Well, yes, I suppose. They are New Agers. Hippies, is what we used to call them.'

'Satanists?'

Fiona smiled. 'There you go again. No, not Satanism. Perhaps paganism – I suppose you might call it, although they dispute that, too. They study all forms of spirituality, I gather.'

Chaz asked, 'Have you had any dealings with them?'

'No, they're not in the habit of popping into the local kirk for a psalm or two.'

Something like delight crept into Alan's voice. 'Pagans, eh. That's a short leap to black magic, right?'

Fiona compressed her lips in mock severity. 'As I say, I think they would take issue with that. They simply have an interest

90

in the old ways, that's all, ways that predate Christianity, but they also claim to show an interest in all faiths. It's all spirituality, a belief in something other than ourselves. Not everyone follows mainstream religion, Alan.'

'There was a time when your lot burned their lot at the stake.'

Fiona waved that away, as if she were dispersing smoke. 'Yes, but that's frowned upon now by the General Assembly of the Church of Scotland. In fact, we are actively discouraged from it.' She smiled. 'It takes all sorts, Alan. If people want to follow God then they can come to me. If they want to follow older faiths, then fine. If they don't want to follow any faith then they are damned and will burn in the fires of Hell for eternity.' She paused. 'Really, it's no biggie.'

Chaz asked, 'So what did Nuala want to know?'

Nuala. He realised he had never met the woman, but he was already on first-name terms, such was the informality of sudden death.

'She wanted to know if I'd had any dealings with them,' Fiona replied. 'Had there been any rumours, complaints, that sort of thing.'

'And have there?'

'Well, apart from the usual suspicions from the diehards on the island about any incomer, no.'

Chaz asked, 'Did Nuala say why she was asking?'

'She said she thought they were dangerous.'

'In what way?'

'She didn't expand. I didn't ask. Frankly, I thought she was a little, em, weird.'

'In what way?'

Fiona's face crinkled. 'It's difficult to say.'

'Did she wear strange clothes?'

'No, not at all. It was just that there was something, em, dreamy about her, you know what I mean? A feyness.'

On the island, people with the ability to sense thoughts, who showed strong empathy, were called 'the fey'. But Chaz knew Fiona was not saying that Nuala had any kind of second sight.

'She asked me if I'd ever met their founder. They call him Father.'

'And have you?'

'No, I don't think anyone has, apart from selected Children. He's something of a recluse, it seems.'

'Does he live on the farm?'

'No. This Sanctuary is one of a few dotted around the country and abroad, I think. This is one of the newer ones, set up after you left the island, Chaz.'

'Have you been up there since they took over?'

'No, I have had no reason.'

'You wouldn't be welcome anyway, I suppose.'

'Oh, I think I would be. They have a reputation for being very welcoming to strangers. They run residential courses, some as long as a week or a fortnight. All New Age, touchy-feely stuff, getting in touch with your inner angel, that sort of thing. They also offer spiritual retreats to those who need such a thing.'

'So they can brainwash them,' said Alan. 'Lure them into their cult.'

Fiona gave him a sideways look. 'You have a knack for melodrama, Alan.'

'Tell me about it,' said Chaz, rolling his eyes. 'You should see him when he finds a spider in the bath.'

Fiona laughed, but then something appeared to occur to her. 'Chaz, this isn't just idle interest in this tragedy, is it? Are you on the clock here?'

'Not exactly,' he said. 'I'm really just nosing around as a kind of favour.'

'A favour?' Fiona asked, but there was a smile in her eyes

that told Chaz she knew the answer to her next question before she had even posed it. 'Who for?'

He gave her a broad grin. 'You'll never guess.'

Inverness

Rebecca tapped her pencil on the notepad resting on the desk-top, keeping time with the beat of the song on the CD player: Robbie Williams swinging and winning with 'Mack the Knife'. Her dad had been a fan of Bobby Darin's version, not to mention Frank Sinatra's, but even he had appreciated this particular album.

She had already battered out a draft of the interview with Tabitha Haley and had turned her mind to the death of Nuala Flaherty. Her nose told her there was more here than just a curious death, so she had written the woman's name at the top of the page, then set to considering the rule of six which, even in the digital age, was important. A framed image of Rudyard Kipling sat on her desk and the quote:

> *I keep six honest serving-men*
> *(they taught me all I knew);*
> *Their names are What and Why and When*
> *And How and Where and Who.*

She scribbled down her first query.

Who is Nuala?

She already knew the When and Where. The How – the actual cause of death – was yet to be determined. She jotted another line on the notepad.

Why did she carve the pentagram?

Her earlier research had told her the symbol was used as protection, but from what?

Who, or what, was she afraid of?

Chaz had told her about the conversation he and Alan had with Fiona McRae and that Nuala had been asking about the Children of the Dell. Rebecca wrote down another two questions.

Who are CotD?
What made Nuala investigate them?

There was something here, she could feel it. Elspeth – and her own father – had always urged her to heed her instincts, and they were screaming so loudly they almost drowned out Robbie, now duetting 'Something Stupid' with Nicole Kidman.

Her personal mobile rang, and she recognised Val Roach's number.

She barely got out a hello before Roach said, 'What do you need to know about Tabitha?'

Rebecca smiled. Straight to the point, as usual. 'You hung up on me yesterday,' she said accusingly.

'I had a roomful of detectives with me, and it wouldn't do for me to be seen being chummy with the press. Then I had a slew of meetings.' Rebecca heard Roach sigh heavily. 'I thought my job was to catch the bad guy, not to sit in a conference room listening to pencil pushers drone on about human resources, budgets and how much toilet paper is being used.'

'Was that really discussed? The toilet paper?'

'No, but it's only a matter of time before they start counting the sheets and asking why so much is literally being flushed away.'

'And will they ask you to get to the bottom of it?'

A smile crept into Roach's voice. 'Don't give up the day job, Rebecca. So, what do you want to know about Tabitha Haley?'

'What do you think of her?'

'In what way?'

'Well, this business with the wee boy. Her visions. You think it's all genuine?'

She heard Roach take a deep breath and exhale as she considered. 'Is that Robbie Williams you're listening to?'

'Yes.'

'I took you more as a hip-hop type of girl. Maybe garage or grime.'

'I'm impressed you know about these things, Val.'

'Hey, I'm down with the kids. Is Robbie not a wee bit before your time?'

'You like classical music – is Mozart not before your time?' Roach had no answer for that, so Rebecca prodded, 'Tabitha Haley? Visions? Genuine, yes or no?'

'Yeah.' Roach came back on point. 'If you had asked me before we found the boy, I'd've said no. But now? I don't know. If this had been an abduction, I would have been looking at her as a prime suspect, but there's nothing to suggest any kind of criminality here, and even the boy himself refutes it. He climbed in and found himself trapped, simple as.'

Rebecca saw the sense in this. 'So how do you account for Tabitha leading you to that house?'

'I can't. That's the maddening thing about this – and it's causing some snickering in the canteen at my expense.'

'Snickering?'

'Snickering,' confirmed Roach. 'Something wrong with the word?'

'Not at all.' Rebecca paused. 'Is it like a chocolate-covered snigger?'

Roach tutted. 'Seriously, Rebecca, whoever told you to try stand-up was not doing you any favours.'

Rebecca smiled. 'But I'll bet you checked Tabitha out, right?'

'No, I simply accepted what she said because I've not been doing this job for twenty years and haven't dealt with more crazies than you've had hot scoops.'

'We don't say "scoops" any more.'

'Well, pardon me for being so out of touch.'

'You're cranky today.'

'Don't ask bloody stupid questions, then. Of course I checked her out.'

'And?'

'And what?'

'What did you find?'

'You want me to do your job for you, is that it?'

'Frankly, yes.'

Roach laughed suddenly, as if she was letting off steam. 'Sorry, been a bastard of a day again. She seems completely legit.'

'Hocus-pocus aside.'

'Yes.'

'She's a hairdresser, right?'

'Right. But she wasn't always.'

'What was she before?'

'An academic. Philosophy. Anthropology. She chucked it all in.'

'To become a hairdresser?' She couldn't keep the disbelieving tone from her voice.

'Are you being hairdresserist, Rebecca?'

Rebecca laughed this time. 'No, but why did she walk away from the halls of academe to tint and curl?'

'You'd need to ask her that. But she was highly respected in her field and was – probably still is – quite an expert on the occult.'

Tabitha Haley was growing increasingly interesting to Rebecca. She still had a few days before the deadline for the magazine piece to get more out of her. Despite her attempts to shrug it off, she thought about her mentioning her dead father – and that he would never be far away. Then there was the suggestion that someone hated her enough to wish her harm. What was that about?

'So, she genuinely has a gift?'

'There are more things in Heaven and Earth, Horatio,' said Roach. 'That all you wanted?'

Rebecca looked down at the notes on Nuala, decided to take a flyer. 'You heard about this suspicious death on Stoirm?'

'No, what's the story, morning glory?'

'Oasis now, you really are a groovy chick.'

Rebecca swiftly told her what she knew, even the pentagram. She knew if Roach took it into her head to ask around about the incident she would find out that Chaz was there, and she was canny enough to know he would tell her about the strange circumstances. She also trusted Roach now. Up to a point, anyway.

When Rebecca was finished, Roach said, 'Sounds like someone forgot to put her woolly vest on before they went sunbathing in the middle of the night.'

'Yes, but this pentagram thing . . .'

'Stuff and nonsense.'

'More things in Heaven and Earth, Horatio,' Rebecca reminded her.

She heard a chuckle creep into Roach's voice. 'Aye, point taken. Okay, I'll have a look at it, will get back to you. But you owe me.'

'I'll buy you a coffee.'

'Yes, you will.'

The pub stank of the previous night's beer. Barney's always stank of the previous night's beer, it seemed to Sawyer. And the beer from the night before that and the night before that. How hard was it to spray a bit of Febreze around now and again? As a uniform, he'd had occasion to visit this dingy bar situated up an alley in Inverness Old Town, but only ever for professional reasons, as it was like a Wild West saloon back then. All it needed was a piano player. That malarkey stopped when the Burkes took over the place, although the licence was still in the name of the former owner. Being a feared criminal family had its advantages, and one of them was that very few people stepped out of line on the premises.

The last time he had walked across the sticky floor he was with Rebecca to speak to one of the regulars about the death of a doctor. That had been a bad business and it led to them both staring down the barrels of a shotgun in a wee house in the Ferry. He didn't think there was anything like that in his immediate future, but he had his extendable baton tucked up his sleeve when he entered. You never knew with Mo Burke.

Overnight he had thought about what Cokey had told him. The wee tout had seldom steered him wrong in the past but that didn't mean he wasn't wrong this time. Eventually, Sawyer had decided that he needed to look into Mo Burke's eyes. He would know then if there was anything to this.

When he pushed through the door, all eyes turned in his direction. If that piano player had been there, he would have stopped tinkling the ivories right about then. The place was as busy as it got for just after lunchtime on a weekday, which was not very busy at all, and those among the cluster of men at the bar who knew what he used to be either looked away or sneered, while those who didn't know somehow sensed it. Sawyer had long understood there was something about him that screamed police, which was why he would never have been any good undercover. Neds took one look at him and could smell the law.

Mo Burke was at a corner table, a cup of coffee in front of her, a cigarette smouldering in an ashtray, the law regarding smoking in a public space obviously not applicable here in the Republic of Burke. Nobody in this bar was likely to report the contravention, however, for that would be harmful to their health. She saw him coming, of course. From her vantage point Mo would see everyone who entered or left. She sat back, reached out with her hand and plucked the cigarette from the ashtray, gave it a tap to dislodge the ash then raised it to her lips. She let it rest there as she watched him.

'Detective Sergeant Sawyer,' she said, the cigarette bobbing. 'Sorry, former Detective Sergeant Sawyer. What brings you here?'

He sat down without being asked, eyeing the white West Highland terrier in a basket. He had nothing against dogs, but he had learned on the Job to be wary. There was something about the uniform that some dogs did not take to, and even though he was wearing a woollen, mid-length, black jacket and jeans, the wee dog looked like an anklebiter to him. The dog did not even stir, obviously used to people coming to speak to its mistress.

'Need a wee word, Mo,' he said, deliberately using her first name. Old cop trick to keep people on the back foot: be familiar with them but they can't be familiar with you.

'That right, Bill?' said Mo. So much for old cop tricks. 'What could you and me have to talk about?'

Sawyer fought the urge to hunch forward and keep his voice low. The telly was muted but there was no one in their vicinity to overhear, even if they hadn't all been suddenly stricken with three wise monkeys fever. 'Rebecca Connolly.'

Mo's eyes flared as bright as the end of her cigarette as she sucked on it. 'What about her?'

'A wee bird tells me you mean her harm.'

She tapped the dead ash away. 'And what wee bird would that be?'

Sawyer chuckled. 'Aye right, Mo, like I would give you a name.'

He saw something shift behind her eyes as she tried to fathom who might have been carrying tales. 'What's she to you, then?'

'She's a pal.'

'She doesn't have pals. She has people she uses.'

'Stay away from her, Mo.'

'I'm not going to go anywhere near her.'

Sawyer's voice hardened further. 'Leave her alone.'

Mo studied him, perhaps wondering if he was wired somehow. 'I don't know what you're talking about.'

'I think you do. And I'm here to tell you that if anything happens to her, I'll take it badly.'

Her smile was nasty as it gripped the fag between her teeth. 'And what? You're not police any more. What will you do?'

He let that hang for a moment. 'Believe me, Mo, you don't want to know.'

She thought about it, her eyes squinting against the trail of smoke drifting upwards. 'This wee bird has been singing off-key, I think.'

'So you bear no ill will towards her?'

'You know I do, but if she comes to any harm, it won't be my doing. She's a pushy wee bitch and she's put a lot of people's noses out of joint. Only a matter of time before someone gives her a slap.'

'Fella tried it before. Didn't do him a whole lot of good, did it? She broke his nose and now he's banged up.'

'I heard about that. Tosspot deserved what he got for being such a useless tool.'

Sawyer stood, the dog lifting its head at the scrape of the chair on the floor. He kept an eye on it as he said, 'Aye, he did. But just so you know, I'm on the case here. If any other tosspot tries it on with her, they'll have me to deal with.'

Mo seemed to find that amusing. 'Still think you're a hard man, eh?'

He leaned over the table. The dog tensed, so he kept his voice reasonable, even smiled. 'I *am* a hard man, Mo. Some of your lads learned that the hard way. As for me not being police any more, don't let that worry you. I was always able to find evidence back in the day when I needed to, and I can easily do the same now and steer it to some people. Do you catch my drift, Mo?'

Mo didn't reply, but he saw in her eyes that she understood he'd never been one to let lack of evidence get in the way of making a case. He had been mentored by an old-fashioned cop who told him that justice was blind and sometimes needed a wee hand in the right direction.

'Everything all right over there, Mo?' The barman was looking in their direction while two young guys had stepped away from the bar, waiting for any kind of sign that Mo needed them to step in, ex-cop or no ex-cop. Sawyer let the baton slip down his sleeve into the palm of his hand. If any one of them even twitched in his direction, he would start swinging.

'It's all right, lads,' said Mo. 'Bill here was just leaving.'

Sawyer gave all three a look designed to show them he was not in the mood for dancing, and the barman shrugged then turned away while the two neds sat back down on their stools. You've still got it, Bill, he thought, before he faced Mo once more. The dog's head was resting on its paws again but still watched him under its brows. Looked like a cute wee thing, but you just never knew. 'Good to see you, Mo. You're looking well.'

'You're looking old,' she said.

'Happens to us all,' he said. 'And I intend to make sure it happens to Rebecca. Keep that in mind, eh?'

He didn't give her the chance to reply. He turned and left the bar, knowing her eyes were on him all the way. He had stared into those eyes and now he knew that Cokey's info had been correct. Mo Burke really did mean Rebecca harm. The question was, would she give the job to some local lads or bring someone in from outside?

They took him on the third day. They had watched him closely, sometimes together, sometimes singly to let the other have a rest, but the opportunity to move did not present itself. He was either in full view of others or had someone with him. He had rented a small cottage overlooking the sea, and they might have done him there, but so far he'd had a woman in there with him and also on his walks. Good-looking blonde chick, Mike noted – older, sure, but still in good nick. Bloody Don Juan, so he was. Mike didn't know what she saw in this bloke, because he was no George Clooney. They couldn't do him with her around as it needed to look like an accident. There could be no suggestion otherwise. It was a common instruction, the need for it to look accidental, even natural, and it made the job more difficult – much easier to shoot a bloke in the head – but that was why they got the big bucks.

But, just after breakfast, they saw their chance.

They were beginning to think he was on to them, that he knew they were there, which made things more difficult but not impossible. But that morning he left the blonde in the cottage and followed his usual routine. He popped into the village shop where he bought his paper and a coffee from the machine. He walked to the harbour and stepped onto his boat. So far, so routine and Mike had resigned himself to another day of bum-numbing tedium on that bench, or watching from the window of the bar in the village inn or his room upstairs, both having good views of the harbour. He felt his heart quicken when he saw the guy come up through the hatch again and step onto the jetty.

'This is different,' said Pat, and Mike felt like saying *D'you not think I know that?* But he didn't, for he knew it was best not to try sarcasm with Pat. He always lost.

The bloke walked up through the village, heading for the coastal track.

'You think he's going for a walk?' Mike asked.

'If he is, it'll be the last one he takes,' said Pat.

Mike crossed his fingers. From Pat's lips to God's ears, he hoped, because then they could get out of this godforsaken shithole and go home, get some diesel fumes into his lungs. All this fresh air can't be good for them.

The coastal path climbed up some grassy slopes and headed north from the village, following the edge of the land, where it fell away sharply down a cliff face to jagged rocks below. There was nobody else up there at that time of the morning, apart from a woman jogging in their direction with the tell-tale double white lines running from her ears giving away the fact she had music being piped from an iPod. Mike never understood jogging, but he supposed having her favourite tracks playing helped the boredom. She didn't even look at them as she passed.

'I should've got one of they things for this job,' he said, never taking his eyes from the back of the man ahead.

'One of what things?' Pat asked.

'They iPod things, like that woman that just passed us.'

Pat craned round to look at the jogger.

'Listening to my tunes might have made it easier to sit on my arse waiting for this bloke to give us a break,' said Mike.

'She could be listening to a book.'

He took his attention away from the man in front briefly to give Pat a quizzical look. 'On her earphones?'

'Aye,' said Pat, 'lots of people do it.'

'Listen to books? Being read by someone?'

'Aye, big business now, they say.'

'How do you know that?'

'I read it.'

'So, you didn't hear it on your iPod?' Mike smiled, as if he was the successor to Robin Williams.

The path had levelled off now and they were passing by some incredible rock formations, where the sea and the wind had eaten away at the land, reminding Mike there were forces in the world that were more powerful than humanity. Patient, too. The elements had created these towering, jagged shapes over thousands of years. Mike respected that, for he and Pat had to have patience to achieve their goals, too. He had shown that in the past three days, although he did wonder if he could wait much longer. But hopefully they were in the endgame now.

His earlier worries that the target had sussed their presence had now been proved baseless, for he was wandering along the clifftop like he didn't have a care in the world. Neither Pat nor Mike knew why this guy had become a target, and frankly, my dear, they didn't give a damn. They didn't even know who it was that wanted him done, or why. All they were given was a photograph and a few clues as to where he would be. This guy, it turned out, was not where they had expected him to be, and it had taken a bit of digging to track him to Pittencairn. It was Pat who found out; it usually was, for Pat was the brains and Mike was the muscle. A wee chat to a neighbour – *I'm looking for my pal, any idea where he might have gone?* – and they learned about the boat and the mooring in the harbour. So up they popped and waited for their chance.

And here it was, handed to them on a platter. Finally.

Pat looked around them, making sure there was nobody about, nobody to see, nobody to talk. That could prove awkward. The sight-line was clear both ways. Even the jogger had vanished.

'Now or never,' said Pat. Mike didn't need to be told twice. He picked up his pace, leaving Pat to lag behind and keep watch, ready to whistle a warning if someone appeared. It was all down to him now and he felt his heart begin to hammer. It always got him like this, just before the kill. The excitement. The anticipation. The fucking thrill of it all. Pat was all business. Pat felt nothing. To Pat, this was just a job. Mike knew that the bottom line was that it was just a job, but that didn't mean he couldn't get a bit of pleasure from it.

The target didn't hear him. Mike was a big guy but he could be stealthy when he needed to. He could also dance with the grace of Fred Astaire, because big doesn't necessarily mean clumsy. But it did mean power, and that was what he used.

It was all done in a moment. The target was enjoying the fresh air and the sea breeze one second. The next, he was gone. He might have been aware of Mike as he drew level. He would have felt the force of his hands as they propelled him over the edge. There would probably have been a flash of searing agony as his head bounced off a lump of rock protruding from the cliff face, but more than likely nothing after that as he spun slightly in the air before his body crashed into the sharp rocks and churning water. He might have screamed as he went but it might have been the seabirds that darted between the rocks and skimmed the water like they were doing it for a dare.

Mike stood on the edge and watched as the tide tossed the body against the rocks, the arms and legs flopping in the water, as if it was a rag doll. Pat reached his side and looked down.

Mike asked, 'Time to go home now?'

Pat watched the body being thrashed about for a second, as if to confirm that the target was dead. Mike had no idea how high up they were, but he was confident there was no way the guy would survive.

Finally, Pat's head bobbed. 'Aye, we can go home now.'

Ya dancer, Mike thought. He could already smell the fumes.

Rebecca was pinging the text of one of the human-interest stories to the commissioning editor at the tabloid magazine when she heard footsteps on the stairs outside and a shadow loomed on the frosted glass of the news agency door. It opened and Bill Sawyer walked in as he always did, like he owned the place. She gave him a mock glare. 'You don't knock? I could have been entertaining a gentleman caller.'

'You'll never be entertaining, Becks, though it would be just like you to bring a bloke back to the office for some slap and tickle. You'd probably get some sort of story out of him, too.'

That hadn't worked with Stephen, she thought. Sawyer glanced at the CD player on top of the filing cabinet to his right, grimaced at the music and switched it off.

'Hey, I was listening to that!' she objected.

'Did you a favour, Becks. If I want to hear someone mangle a Sinatra song, I'll do it myself.' He fixed her with narrowed eyes, as if seeing her for the first time. 'Never took you for a Robbie Williams fan.'

Everyone's a critic. 'Takes all sorts, Bill. We can't all like accordion music, like you.'

He pulled a face as he limped across the small office and dropped himself into the chair in front of her desk. He took off his tweed cap and ran a hand across his bald scalp, then sighed. 'When you going to get a lift put in? Those stairs will kill me one of these days.'

'Take it up with the landlord. I just work here.'

She watched as he rubbed his leg. He had once been in good trim, but a bad leg break saw him off his feet for some time and he had never fully regained his previous level of fitness. He wasn't fat, by any means, but he had certainly filled out since she had first met him a few years before.

She asked, 'To what do I owe the pleasure, Bill? And I use that word in its broadest possible sense.'

'Was passing, saw the light was on, thought I'd come up and let you make me a cup of coffee.'

'You did, did you? So I'm just a branch of Starbucks to you, right?'

'Aye, if Starbucks hooked their coffee out of a jar and used a kettle. Come on, Becks, it's cold out there. Do an old pal a favour.'

'There's the kettle, there's the jar, help yourself,' she said, before adding, 'old pal.'

Old pal. Whatever she and Bill Sawyer were, she wasn't sure they were pals. Their relationship was similar to that between Rebecca and Roach: a lot of banter and sometimes mutually beneficial, but they weren't exchanging LOLs on social media.

Sawyer sighed again before he hauled himself out of the chair and moved to the kettle, his limp very pronounced. 'You're a hard woman, Rebecca Connolly.'

'It's a hard world, Bill Sawyer. And stop exaggerating the limp, you're not Douglas Bader.'

He turned, his expression one of surprise. 'How does a young girl like you know about Douglas Bader?'

'I saw the film,' she said. 'And I'm a young woman, thank you very much.'

He pursed his lips and shook his head as he turned away to pick up the kettle and carry it to the small toilet beside the office door, the hitch in his step still over-the-top. She smiled. She didn't really care that he called her a young girl. This was the way it was between them. Maybe they were pals, after all. Maybe she and Roach were pals. Sometimes it was difficult to tell without an instruction manual.

She heard him fill the kettle. 'So what really brings you here, Bill?'

He reappeared in the doorway. 'Can't I just come up and say hello?'

'You can but you're not in the habit of it.'

He hit the switch then turned and wagged his finger at her. 'You know, you've become very suspicious of people. It's unbecoming in one so young.'

'Occupational hazard. And I'm not so young.'

'You are from where I stand.' He held up two mugs. 'Can I get madam anything? Coffee, tea? Whetstone for her tongue?'

She laughed. 'Coffee, my good man. Milk, two sugars and a right good stir.'

'Of course, madam.' He bowed. 'Coming right up, madam.'

She watched as he made the coffee. Their relationship was a strange one. They had begun as adversaries – he a former police officer with a cloud over his head, and she a young reporter trying to find out if said cloud was warranted. Then they had become colleagues, of a sort, first working together in a way on that story, then back in Inverness when he occasionally performed investigative jobs for the agency. She knew he also did some work for solicitors who needed defence witnesses interviewed, which was ironic considering his tendency to disparage 'clever' lawyers who get obviously guilty people off. 'Clever' being a synonym for 'corrupt', in his world view. Over the years, though, something had grown between them. Respect, she supposed. Sawyer had been a cop with some very dodgy methods in the past, but she knew that whatever he had done, it was done with the best of intentions. She was also aware of what they said about good intentions and the road to hell. If Sawyer agonised over anything he had done, he didn't show it. The fact was, he had helped her in the past and, with him, the knowledge that her father had been a respected ranking officer in Glasgow went a long way. He also had a grudging respect for Elspeth and, given his man's man views, was surprisingly unfazed by her sexuality.

He set one of the mugs of coffee in front of her, then lowered himself into the chair with a groan. She thanked him, and there was a silence as they sipped their drinks. She waited, sensing there was a reason for his visit.

'So,' she said, eventually, feeling the silence should be breached, 'what will we talk about? Politics? Religion? Don't say football because I support Partick Thistle, so you know I don't know anything about the game.'

He sipped his coffee, didn't smile. 'Bit harsh on the old Jags there. They're a grand old team.'

She didn't reply. It was a Glasgow thing, the automatic slagging off of Partick Thistle. The thing was, she didn't know if it was a good team or not, football really not being something she cared about.

Sawyer set his mug down on the desktop and looked straight at her. 'I hear you're going back to the island.'

Had to have come from Elspeth, she thought. 'End of the week,' she replied.

His head drooped slightly, then came back up again. 'Are you crazy, or what?'

'The boys are getting married, Bill,' she said. 'I can't miss it.'

'And what about His Lordship? He won't be happy with you being back on his island.'

Sawyer's reservations were not for her family secrets, of which he knew nothing. No one did, not even Chaz. Fiona McRae knew it, for she had revealed it to her, but she would never tell. 'His Lordship' was Lord Henry Stuart, the island's laird, who had secrets of his own, which Rebecca and Bill knew about but could not prove.

'He's left the island,' she said, 'seldom goes back. In fact, seldom in the country now, I'm told.'

He did not look convinced. 'His Russian mates might think you're back for a second go.'

Lord Henry Stuart had been involved years before in illicit deals involving the Nikoladze brothers. They did not know how much Rebecca knew, or even how much she could actually prove, but she had the feeling that doubt was the only thing that had kept them from moving against her. On the other hand, perhaps they knew she was no threat at all, which she knew to be closer to the truth.

'I'm going over for a wedding, nothing more.' Her eyes fell on her notebook. 'Well, there might be something else.'

He followed her gaze, even though he couldn't see what she had written. 'On the island?'

'Yes.'

'What is it?'

She told him what she knew about the dead woman in the pentagram. She trusted him, knew he would not talk to anyone else. If there was one thing about Bill Sawyer, it was that he didn't talk to the press. Hell, sometimes he barely spoke to her, and they were supposed to be pals, according to him.

'Lassie must've been a couple of raisins short of a fruit scone,' Sawyer decided. 'And what's this pentagram thing, anyway? Some sort of black magic hoodoo bollocks?'

'Yes, something like that.'

'Aye, well – didn't protect her from the island's weather, did it? Stupid bugger probably died from the cold, this time of year.'

'Very likely, but I'll dig around anyway. You heard of the Children of the Dell?'

He shook his head. 'What are they? Some kind of boy band?'

'A cult, or something. I've not had the chance to dig into them yet. But it seems this woman Nuala was sniffing around them.'

'Cults, aye. The island attracts nutjobs like a shite does flies. Been a few settled over the years – harmless but still nutjobs.'

Rebecca knew of one other cult that had settled on the island, many years before: fundamental Christians. Her own family had stemmed from there.

'So you're bound and determined to go back, Becks?'

'Can't let the boys down, Bill. They're pals, too.'

His lips thinned, not in anger but as if they were trying to prevent him from saying what he was about to say. They didn't manage. 'Then I suppose I'd better come, too.'

'You don't need to do that.'

'I think I do.'

'Then you better tell your face, because it doesn't look convinced.'

'I don't want to go back, I really don't. My bloody leg aches just thinking about it. And I don't want to fall foul of they Russian bastards, if they're still around.'

'They won't be.' Her tone was confident. 'What happened over fifteen years ago is ancient history and there is no proof. If we know that, then they know that.'

He considered that for a second, then shook his head. 'I can't let you go there without back-up.'

'Oh, you're back-up now?'

'Best hope you've got.'

'I'll have Elspeth with me.'

He laughed. 'They'd knock her sticks out from under her, and where would you be then?'

'She could still lacerate them with some invective. And what about you? You've been limping around here like Chester out of *Gunsmoke* since you walked in.'

He was surprised again. 'First Douglas Bader, now Chester? You sure you're only a slip of a lassie?'

'Satellite telly, Bill, it's an education.' Her father used to talk about the old TV show, and when she saw it was being rerun on a satellite channel, she tuned in. It was dated and badly acted, but she now knew who Chester, the limping deputy, was.

'I'm coming and that's it,' Sawyer said. 'I'll bet you don't have a date for the wedding, right?'

She didn't know whether to be insulted by that. Her mind shifted again to Stephen before she said, 'You asking me out on a date, Bill?'

He gave her a stern look. 'Get over yourself. You're no' a bad-looking lassie, but I'm way out of your league.'

'Bill Sawyer, I never knew you cared!'

'Shut it,' he said, but he smiled. 'If you're going, I'm going with you, Becks, simple as. I'll book my room at the hotel – they won't be too busy this time of year. When we for the off?'

'Friday.'

'Right,' he said as he stood up. 'Settled. You can pick me up at the house.'

Great, she thought. Elspeth and Bill Sawyer in the same car for a journey that would take hours. What fun.

'Do you honestly think there's the possibility of danger, Bill?'

He was at the door and he turned back, one fist wrapped around the handle. 'I do, love,' he said, his tone sombre. 'I really do. And better to be safe than sorry, eh?'

Mo Burke was angry as she lit up another cigarette. She was angry when she sucked in a lungful of nicotine. She was angry as she tilted her head back to send the exhaled smoke floating into the beer-soaked air of the bar towards the peeling paint of the ceiling. A young man on her crew approached her, one of the lads who had been ready to step up – but when he saw the smoke signals, he thought better of it and pivoted again. That bastard Sawyer had been gone for half an hour, but she fixed her eyes on the space he had last occupied. Hypocritical bastard, she thought, lecturing me like he was still important, still had some kind of juice. Judge fucking Dredd. I am the law. Like he was pure as the driven. Well, she knew he wasn't. She knew former Detective Sergeant William Sawyer was so bent they'd have to twist him into his grave. She didn't know if he'd taken backhanders, though she wouldn't put it past him, but he'd certainly done stuff when he was supposed to be the guardian of society that really didn't bear much scrutiny. There were just as many crooks in the blue as out of it.

You should listen to him, Ma.

Nolan was sitting in the chair opposite, the one Sawyer had been in. She shook her head at her son; no way was she going to listen to that bent bastard cop.

Her eyes slid to the boy on her crew who had planked his backside at the bar again, watching some shite on TV. A quiz show with some comedian. All colours and flashing lights and questions only a completely brainless idiot would fail to answer. The boy answered one of the questions out loud. Got it wrong.

People were talking about her behind her back. Was it him? Wee fucker was always hanging around here.

He's one of Scott's pals.

Nolan was right. The boy had palled around with his brother so, if anything, he would applaud payback on the reporter. Someone's gums had been flapping, though. Someone had carried tales.

You have been talking, Ma.

Nolan was always the only one who would tell her the truth. Not even Tony faced her down as often.

You maybe don't realise it, but you have been.

She knew she was far from blameless. Too much rage, too much booze. Too much grief. She had no idea what she had said but she had obviously said something out of turn.

You need to watch your tongue.

113

Nolan was right, she would need to watch that. Even so, her temper smouldered. She didn't like being told what to do by any man, let alone that bastard Sawyer. She picked up her bag, told Midge to stay in his basket, and walked through a doorway to her right, past the toilets and then downstairs to the cellar. It was a big space, but crates filled with bottles and cans, as well as boxes of crisps and other savoury snacks, were piled around the walls like insulation. She took a final drag of her cigarette and dropped it on the cement floor, killing what was left of its heat with her shoe, her rage making her press harder than was required, then fished inside her handbag for the mobile phone she had placed there earlier. It was a cheap pay-as-you-go, one of many she had stashed away, and she checked it had a decent enough signal before she hit send on a number her man had given her on the fly during a visit. He had outlined the procedure for her, all sorts of cloak and dagger, but she supposed it was necessary. After all, she wasn't phoning to order a pizza.

Don't.

Nolan emerged from the shadows, but she ignored him as the phone at her ear rang three times.

This is a mistake.

She turned away from him. Another three rings. Had she dialled it wrong? Had Tony given her a snide number?

Hang up, Ma.

He appeared right in front of her. Just appeared, like those guys on *Star Trek*. Another three rings.

You don't want to do this, Ma. Not really.

'I really do,' she said but was growing tired of the ringing. Then, just as she was about to cut the connection, she heard a recorded voice.

'Leave a number.'

'Inverness calling,' she said, feeling ludicrous at using the words her man had told her to use – cloak and fucking

114

dagger – and then rattled off the second number, another burner. Mo dropped the first phone in her pocket and took the second from her bag. Ten minutes, Tony had said, before they would call back. She wandered around the cellar. Looked at her watch. Lit up a fag. Looked at her watch. Wandered some more, cigarette smoke twisting and trailing behind her before it dissolved into the gloom. She looked at her watch.

When it rings, don't answer, Ma.

'I've got to, son,' she said aloud.

Why?

She didn't answer.

Bang on ten minutes, the phone rang. She was impressed.

'How'd you get that number, darling?' The man's voice was straight out of *EastEnders* and was neither friendly nor curt. 'Darling', he'd called her. Nobody called her that, but there wasn't much she could do about it.

'My man,' she replied, knowing that would be answer enough. There was a silence. 'He still away?'

'Aye. You know why I'm calling?'

'There's only one reason folk call that number, darling. So here's the deal. There's a rubbish bin down near the docks, next to that old tower.'

'The Cromwell Tower, right.'

'Yeah, the clock tower. Print the name and a photo of the person in question on a bit of paper – don't write it by hand, and use paper you can buy in any supermarket, nothing fancy – and wrap it up in newspaper. Don't use a local rag or nothing. Use a national, and an old one. Put the fee in, all small notes. We see anything higher than a tenner and the deal's off.'

'What is the fee?'

The man named a figure. It made her eyebrows raise. 'That's a lot of cash.'

Too much, Ma.

'That's the price, take it or leave it.'

Hang up.

When she didn't say anything, the voice said, 'How fast can you put it together?'

She made a quick calculation. 'Couple of hours, maybe.'

'Wrap them all up in the newspaper, bind them with packing tape. I don't need to tell you to use gloves when you're doing all this. You don't do any of that, the deal's off. You got that, darling?'

End it now.

Mo ignored her son's voice. 'Aye, but . . .'

The man on the phone carried on as if she had said nothing. 'Then you walk away. You don't hang around to see who picks it up. You don't have anyone else hang around to see who picks it up.'

'They shy, like?'

There was a slight pause but then the voice continued, 'If you do, if they do, the deal's off. You do all this at six tonight, okay, darling? If you're five minutes early or five minutes late, guess what?'

'The deal's off?'

'Right first time.'

'Hang on, what if someone else comes along and lifts the package?'

'Chance you take.'

'But how will I know you've got it?'

'You won't. The job will either be done, or it won't. You won't hear from me after this, and if you call that number again at any time, for any reason, the deal's off. Understood?'

'Look, I'm not sure I . . .'

She realised she was talking to dead air. She dropped the phone back in her bag – she would destroy them both later – and stood in the centre of the cellar, hearing a faint ripple of applause coupled with some bouncy music from the TV from

116

upstairs and the footsteps of the barman as he paced in front of the gantry. She was uncomfortable leaving that amount of money, which was no small potatoes, in a rubbish bin and then walking away, but she assumed that was why it had to be done at six on the dot. Someone would be there to pick it up as soon as she was out of sight, but she had been warned that if she lingered then the ball was up on the slates. Tony must have used these people before, whoever they were, so they were professionals. She had to trust them.

Still.

Cloak and fucking dagger.

This is wrong, Ma. You know it.

'No,' she said. 'It's the right thing to do.'

Why?

'Because.'

'Because' isn't an answer.

That's what she used to say to them both, when they were boys, when she wanted them to explain why they had done something. They did it 'because', was their reasoning and she didn't accept that, always forced them to explain. And now, here was her son – her dead son – doing the same to her in a dingy cellar that smelled of damp, under a dingy pub that smelled of beer.

She turned to the door, turned her back on him, only to be presented with him standing in front of her.

Tell me why this needs to be done, Ma.

She felt the tears spring to her eyes as she realised he would not give her peace until she answered him. She knew why it needed to be done, knew it was more than revenge, more than payback, more than punishment, but for some reason she didn't want to put it into words. Not to him.

Tell me.

'No,' she said.

Tell me.

117

'I can't.'

Tell me.

Finally, she snapped. 'Because . . .' she began, too loudly. They would hear upstairs. She dropped to little more than a whisper. He would hear her words, even if she only thought them. 'Because it's the only way.'

The only way for what?

She lowered her head. 'Can't you see, son? You're in my head, in my heart. You're a part of me, so you must know. Do I need to spell it out?'

She saw his outline flicker, like a TV picture slightly out of tune, and he floated just a few inches from the concrete floor. He knew why she had to do this now.

It's the only way you can lay me to rest.

Coffee, 12.30

The text was spare, to the point, with no location, but Rebecca knew it would be the coffee house below her office. Roach was very particular about the quality of her brew, but she was satisfied with what they served there. Rebecca would drink any old muck.

Roach's dark hair was as close-cropped as ever, and there were strands of grey showing through, but her features still reminded Rebecca of Audrey Hepburn, her mother's favourite actress.

'So why the face to face?' Rebecca asked. 'Something important?'

'No, I decided all the skulking around was useless. The boss has his mind on other things and I think he's forgotten about the Gregory Stewart business. Anyway, bugger all that for a game of soldiers, I'm sick of pandering to them. They are aware we know each other and, as far as they know, we're just two pals having coffee.'

118

Pals, Rebecca noted. There was that word again. Sawyer had used it. Rebecca herself had used it in relation to Stephen Jordan. It was a short word for a big concept. As for the 'them' Roach referred to, Rebecca knew it was her bosses. After Roach steered some information to Rebecca about a suspect in a miscarriage of justice story, her divisional commander suspected that the info could only have come from one place – and Roach had been threatened with suspension, the rack and imprisonment in the Tower of London.

'I asked about your woman on Stoirm,' Roach said as she stirred her coffee. She pronounced the island as 'Storm'.

'It's pronounced "Stirrum",' said Rebecca.

'Yeah, yeah,' said Roach, 'you want to hear this or not?'

'I'm all ears.'

'It's a suspicious death, so has to be investigated properly. We have an MIT on the island now and they'll follow any line of inquiry, but there doesn't seem anything sinister here.'

'Apart from the pentagram and the fact Nuala is dead.'

'Yes, but initial reports say there's no bruises or lacerations, no wounds, not even scratches or nibbles from local wildlife. There was an old appendix scar, but they can't see that as being cause of death. A search of the cottage she was staying in revealed no signs of a struggle, no overturned furniture, that sort of thing. All seems pretty straightforward, really.'

'So what killed her?'

'Cause unknown as yet. She's being transported to Aberdeen for the post-mortem examination and the toxicology gubbins, but God knows when that will take place. If there were obvious signs of foul play, it would be different, of course, but there's nothing reaching out and slapping our people in the face.'

'So what do you think? Heart attack? Exposure?'

Roach raised the cup to her lips as she looked beyond

Rebecca to the street. 'Or a mixture of both, maybe. Poison obviously can't be ruled out till the PM and tox reports.'

'But why was she out there on that moor? And what was the pentagram all about?'

Roach's eyes narrowed slightly, as if she had seen something, but when Rebecca twisted to see what it was, all she saw was shoppers moving up and down Union Street. 'What are you looking at?'

'Nothing,' said Roach, 'just thought I saw someone. As for the whys and whats regarding your Nuala Flaherty: not my circus, not my monkeys.'

That made Rebecca smile again. 'What?'

'Old Polish saying,' explained Roach.

'You're not Polish.'

'No, but in my teens I went with a boy who was. He used to always say that.'

'I'll bet you can't say it in Polish.'

'*Nie mój cyrk, nie moje małpy,*' said Roach.

'Impressive,' Rebecca said.

Roach raised her coffee. 'I could be saying anything, something obscene, but he assured me that's what it means.'

'So Police Scotland don't think this is anything more serious?'

'Oh, we'll continue to make inquiries, of course, but unless there is some indication of malice aforethought, it's as open and shut as it gets.'

'The whole occult thing is interesting, though.'

'Not from a Police Scotland point of view. Witch hunters were before our time.' She laid her cup down again, her face thoughtful. 'If only there was someone you could speak to who might know more about all this stuff.'

Rebecca had already decided to raise the matter with Tabitha Haley. 'Way ahead of you. And I can't believe you just said "malice aforethought".'

'What's wrong with that?'

Rebecca sipped her coffee. 'Nothing, it's just the nineteenth century called and they want their vocabulary back.'

'Bugger off,' said Roach.

The Island of Stoirm

They had added some outbuildings to the old farm now known as Sanctuary. Chaz brought the family Discovery to a halt on the crest of a small hill, to look down on the place. He had been out here a few times when he was growing up, during his trips around the island on his bike, looking for things to photograph. He had an old shot from the very spot on which they now sat, looking over the farm towards Ben Shee, its pointed summit sharp against the blue sky. The two-storey farmhouse had once been grey stone, reminding him of photographs he'd seen of similar buildings in the Borders, but it had now been painted a white that shone in the winter sunlight. It was clean and bright but, for some reason, he missed the stark Scottishness of the original. It had looked as if it was part of the land back then. Now it was a feature. The courtyard of old stables and other structures were still there but the broken-down tractor that he remembered was gone. He could see the green of what looked to him like an old Land Rover in the corner, and the figure of someone bent over the open bonnet. Like the house, the farm buildings had also been renovated. The new-build structures on what had once been a narrow field to the rear of the stable block were of wood, one a log cabin that he assumed was used by the weekend visitors Fiona had mentioned. Tall fences surrounded the entire complex and, at the end of the drive – which used to be bumpy dirt but was now tarmac – a tall metal gate had been erected.

Alan leaned forward, his arms folded on the dashboard. 'Why am I getting a Waco feel about this place?'

'Yeah, there is a siege-about-to-happen look about it.'

Alan studied the view. 'I don't see any wicker men, though.'

'Disappointed?'

'A bit, but let's go down and see how they go about brain-washing people.'

'What makes you think they do that?'

'There has to be brainwashing. That's how they operate.'

'Generalising much?'

'No,' said Alan, his voice serious, 'people like this are dangerous, darling. We have to be on our guard.' He sat back again. 'Although I think you're safe enough.'

'Why me?'

'You need a brain before it can be washed.'

Chaz started the engine again. 'Well, I certainly need to have what there is examined, given I'm marrying you.'

'Baby, I'm the best thing that ever happened to you.'

Chaz suppressed his smile and pointed the Discovery's bonnet down the incline towards the double metal gates, which lay open.

'No guards,' observed Alan.

'It's not Stalag 13.'

'We'll see about that.' Alan paused to consider the buildings as they neared. 'And there are more subtle ways to imprison people, I suppose.'

They drove into the courtyard and Chaz could see the changes more clearly. In his memory it was covered in mud and manure mixed with straw. There were even chickens back then. All gone now. The yard had been concreted over and scrubbed clean. The buildings had solid doors and double-glazed windows. The old slate roof had been replaced by modern tiles. Fiona had told them that the estate had allowed the farm to run down, and so the Children of the Dell had got the place for a song. They had certainly raised its resale value in the couple of years they had been there.

The man who had been working on the engine of what Chaz now recognised as a late-eighties Defender walked towards them, wiping his hands on an oily rag before thrusting it into the rear pocket of his jeans. He was tall and rangy, broad-shouldered, his long dark hair threaded with grey and tied back in a ponytail, his skin bronzed from working outdoors. His beard, a meld of black and white giving his chin a badgery look, was not quite long enough to be termed hipsterish but it was getting there. Despite the chill in the air, his muscular upper half was clad only in an old T-shirt bearing the logo of a US beer company, and his biceps erupted from the sleeves as if they were showing off. He was, Chaz thought, quite the most handsome man he had seen outside of an ad for men's skin-care products.

'Down, boy,' he muttered to Alan. They were devoted to one another but that didn't mean they didn't notice other men. They were committed, not dead.

Alan's face was a picture of innocence. 'What? I'm almost a married man.'

'Yeah, yeah,' said Chaz as he opened the door, 'just roll your tongue back in.'

'Hi,' said the man, 'welcome to Sanctuary. My name's Sebastian. Seb.'

His voice came from a land somewhere down under. Australia, New Zealand maybe. Chaz was never any good with accents. Seb held out a hand to Alan big enough to float Polynesians across the Pacific, and he seemed puzzled when Alan was reluctant to shake it. Then he saw that he hadn't successfully removed all the oil from his fingers.

'Sorry,' he said, fishing the rag out to scrub his hand again. 'Trying to breathe new life into the old girl. It's a dirty job.' He was unsuccessful in removing all the stains, so he did not offer the hand again.

'Hi, Seb,' said Chaz. 'My name's Chaz and this is my partner, Alan.'

'Welcome, Chaz and Alan.' Seb smiled, revealing more white teeth than any man had a right to have. 'What can I do for you guys?'

'We're staying in Portnaseil for a time and we heard about Sanctuary,' said Chaz. 'It sounded interesting, so we thought we'd take a drive out and have a look. I hope that's okay.'

'Fantastic,' said Seb, 'always happy to meet new people. Sanctuary is open to all.' His voice turned apologetic. 'We don't have any courses running at the moment, though.'

'What kind of courses do you run?' Alan asked.

'All sorts, weekends, some longer. Self-discovery. Self-help. Spiritual awareness.'

'Ah, we could all do with some of that,' said Alan, sounding so wistful that Chaz gave him a quick sideways glance.

Seb caught the tone and gave Alan a fresh look. 'You need some spiritual fulfilment, Alan, was it?'

'Yes,' said Alan. 'Don't we all? Modern life is so empty, so' – he seemed to search for the correct word, which was quite unlike Alan – 'so demeaning.'

Okay, Chaz thought, what the hell is this?

Alan was warming up. 'That's why, when we heard about Sanctuary we had to come and check it out. I'm in banking, my partner is a photographer, and we live on the mainland but life there has become complicated.'

Banking? What parallel universe had Chaz walked into here? Alan worked in administration at the University of the West Highlands' Inverness campus. The closest he came to the bank was checking his statement online. Seb seemed to buy it, for he nodded in a solemn fashion and his smile disappeared like the sun in an eclipse.

'I hear what you say, Alan,' he said. 'It's society, right? It's totally screwed up beyond all help. The need to own and to use and to ultimately throw away. It drags the spirit down.'

'Possessions are anchors,' agreed Alan. 'That can be a good thing because it can ground you, but an anchor also draws you to the bottom. Consumer society is an ocean of need, and we can all drown in it.'

Alan had not warned him that this was the tack he was going to take, and if Chaz didn't know him better he would have thought he had been replaced by a pod person.

'And what about you, Chaz?' Seb faced him. 'You feel the same as Alan here?'

Chaz was about to answer when Alan spoke again. 'Chaz hasn't reached my stage of disenchantment, I'm afraid. He still buys into the whole possession thing. I've tried to make him see sense, but he does love his gadgets. Sure, we can afford them – I make a decent living – but that's not the point, is it?'

'There's more to life than possessions, Chaz,' Seb said, a hint of reproach in his voice. 'Your soul needs more than a flat-screen TV and a brand new car.'

'Yeah,' said Chaz, really not sure how to respond and slightly pissed that Alan made him sound like a kept man. He shot him a quick look designed to let him know that. 'Alan has tried to make me see life that way but, as he says, I enjoy spending his money.'

'You don't make much out of photography, then?'

'He does okay,' Alan interjected, 'but to be honest – and I think Chaz will agree – I'm the breadwinner of the household. My family have money, certainly, but I am very good at what I do.'

'Banking, right?'

'Investment banking,' Alan expanded, and Seb looked even more interested than he had been before. 'Don't get me wrong, Seb, I also enjoy the fruits of my labours. I like good food and wine – I love a Beaujolais that is so nouveau that you have to slap it on the bottom to make it breathe. But when I heard about this place, I thought perhaps this was somewhere that might be of interest. Your courses sound fascinating and might provide what I think my life lacks. Or even just some sort of retreat, perhaps? Breathing space. Somewhere to recharge the spiritual batteries, so to speak.'

'Fantastic! Look, why don't you give me a moment to clean up a bit,' said Seb, 'and then I'll show you around the place, if you want. Maybe tell you a little more about what we do here. How does that sound?'

Alan gave him his best smile. 'That would be fabulous, Seb.'

Seb returned the grin. 'Fantastic! Wait here – it's a nice day, take the air. I won't be a minute.'

He turned and walked quickly into the main house through a door behind the Defender, leaving them alone in the court-yard. Chaz checked to ensure there was no one around but he kept his voice to barely a whisper. 'What the actual hell, Alan?'

Alan kept his smile in place. 'Just play along, okay? You want to know more about this place, then this is the way to do it.'

'Yeah, but what the hell do you know about investment banking?'

'I've picked up a thing or two from my father and my brothers. Enough to get us through a tour, anyway, if he asks any questions. Did you see the way he lost complete interest in you when I said you barely made enough to wash your face? As soon as I suggested I was rolling in it, he was mine.'

'How did you know that was the way of things?'

'Because that's always the way of these things. As the song goes, money makes the world go round, and these places – cults, religions, alternative lifestyles, call them what you will – are all about the bucks.'

126

'But why am I the poor relation?'

'Because you do it so well, dear heart,' said Alan. 'Just play along.'

'Okay,' said Chaz, 'but I hope you know what you're doing. If he even suspects we're at it, he'll bounce us out of here like rubber balls.'

'Oooh,' said Alan with mock licentiousness, 'that might be fun.'

Chaz pursed his lips. 'I told you. Tongue. Back in.'

'Come on, you have to admit he's a bit of a hunk.'

'He's probably old enough to be my father.'

'Oooh, he can be my daddy . . .'

Chaz laughed. 'You really are an anchor, aren't you?'

Alan began to chuckle but forced it back when he saw Seb heading their way again. Behind him, in the doorway, a woman with unruly grey hair watched them. The man's toothy grin seemed to reach them before the rest of him. 'Okay, guys, all set?'

'As we'll ever be, Seb,' said Alan.

'Fantastic! Right, let me take you into the communal hall first, eh? See where we get together as a group, how does that sound?'

'Sounds fantastic, Seb,' said Alan, and Chaz had to look away and feign a cough to hide the laugh that puffed out his cheeks.

Seb led them into what had once been the stable block. It had been hollowed out to form one large room with windows running down one side, facing across the heather to the mountain. It looked like a university common room, except the people reclining in the armchairs and couches reading or talking, or those working in the kitchen area, were all older. They were all in casual clothing, most of the men bearded, and a few studied them as they entered.

Alan asked, 'How many people live in Sanctuary, Seb?'

'It fluctuates but we can accommodate around twenty full-time residents.'

'Do people come and go, then?'

Seb said, 'Not in the way you mean, Alan. Once you become part of the Children of the Dell you don't want to leave, believe me. By taking the first step to joining us, you find yourself on the pathway to enlightenment and true, everlasting peace.'

'Sounds heavenly,' said Alan. At least he didn't say fantastic, Chaz thought.

'Well, not sure about heaven. We don't buy into the concept of paradise packaged by mainstream religion. We believe that it is our duty to make a paradise here on Earth, not in some airy-fairy land in the sky.'

'So why do people come and go?'

'They may move on to another Sanctuary, or help set up a new one.'

'There are others?'

'Oh, yeah. There's one in Cornwall, one in County Mayo, one in France and we're in the process of setting one up in Wyoming, USA.'

'None where you come from?'

'I'd love to set one up in New Zealand and maybe one day I will, but to be honest I don't think I ever want to leave the island. I love it here.'

New Zealand, Chaz thought. The land of the long white cloud. He'll feel right at home with the clouds on the island, although not today.

Alan asked, his face straight, 'So how did you come to take your first step on the path to enlightenment and true peace?'

'I'm a mechanic, by trade. Give me an engine and I can make it sing, although that old darling outside is a challenge, let me tell you.'

'What's wrong with it?' Chaz asked.

'Engine roars like a lion and the brakes are on the dodgy side. I can handle it, but I wouldn't let anyone else take her out.'

Alan asked, 'So what made you give up the roar of the engine and the smell of the oil?'

'I ended up project leader for a Formula One racing team. Do you know anything about Formula One?'

'Lots of cars going round and round, right?'

Seb laughed and clapped Alan on the shoulder. 'Fantastic! That's about the size of it. I made big money – I mean, big money – but all that going round and round came to mean nothing to me. Sound and fury, right? Signifying nothing? Isn't that what the Bard said? So, one day I chucked it all in, took a space in the French Sanctuary and then a couple of years later came here to set up this one. It's been an honour, let me tell you. This is a beautiful island.' He led them through the common area to the well-appointed kitchen. 'This is where we cook all our meals – all organic ingredients and locally sourced produce as much as we can, although being on an island means some concessions have to be made.'

'Are you vegetarians?'

'Some are, some vegan. Some eat meat. It's up to the individual. It's all about freedom, no rules, no judgement.' Seb gestured at the far end of the block. 'And that's the dining area. It can get crowded when we have courses running, but we manage. Come this way and I'll show you the visitors' accommodation.'

As they followed him through double doors towards the log cabin, Alan asked, 'Is that why you chose the island for this Sanctuary? Its beauty?'

'I didn't choose it.'

'Sorry, I thought you formed this Sanctuary.'

'No, I helped. It was chosen by our leader. The Sanctuaries are his brainchild.'

'And who is that?'

'He is a visionary. Oh, I know that's an overused word these days. You know what I mean, right? Someone makes a science fiction movie and he's a visionary or a genius, but believe me, this guy really is.'

'So what's his name?'

Seb's face took on an almost dreamy aspect. 'We call him Father.'

'But that's not the name he was born with, was it?'

'Of course not!'

Alan smiled. 'That's a relief. You can get some strange names these days. I know a Leaf, a River and an Aspen. All I need is a Hawk and I'm ready for a walk in Colorado.'

Seb's laugh was loud and explosive. 'Fantastic!' He clapped Alan on the shoulder again with enough force to send him forward a couple of steps. 'No, the truth is, Father has transcended the need to label himself with a name. He is Father, that's all that's needed.'

Delia had been wondering how she could get her hands on the key to the office safe without Seb knowing, so the two visitors arriving was a stroke of luck. When Seb came into the house to wash up, she casually bumped into him and followed him to the bathroom on the ground floor, where he stripped off his shirt and began to lather off the oil on his hands and forearms. He was in his fifties but he kept himself trim and, as usual, she admired the lean contours of his body, for a fleeting moment recalling the feel of his skin on her fingers and the pressure of his weight on and under her as they moved in tandem.

To distract her from the ghost of carnal pleasures past, she asked, 'How are you getting on with Beatrice?'

He had dubbed the ancient machine Beatrice after an aunt of his, who he had once told her was a woman who never said die. 'I can keep her going a while yet,' he said. 'She's a game old thing. Just needs some love and attention.'

'If you say so,' she said, absently thinking to herself, Don't we all? But she forced that thought from her mind. Admiring Seb's body generated not only a moment of longing, but also a stab of jealousy. She understood that things change, and she told herself that remembering their passion was a memory of something pleasant, no more, but there was that dagger of remorse that he was now aligned with Serena. A sign, she knew, that she was further distancing herself from the basic tenet of Sanctuary. Harmony. Goodwill. A place where there was no room for envy, for bitterness.

But she did feel envy. She was bitter. She was now, thanks to Nuala, suspicious.

'Can you give me the key to the office?' she said, keeping her voice casual. 'I need to have a look at the accounts.'

Sanctuary's office was the only room that was kept locked, and Seb had the only key. Delia's previous dexterity with figures made her the ideal candidate to keep track of their incomings and outgoings. The question that had been on her mind, thanks to Nuala, was exactly where the outgoings ended up.

'Sure,' he said and shook soap and water from his hands before he hauled his old keyring from his pocket. As she had hoped, the keys fell loose and clattered on the floor tiles. 'Damn it,' he said, reaching for a towel.

As he dried his hands, she moved quickly to gather the keys up, palming the one she wanted. 'You need a new keyring, Seb.'

'I know, I know,' he said. She knew why he was reluctant. The fob, a black cat made of some kind of hard-to-recognise fabric worn smooth in places and reeking of oily fingers, had been given to him by his wife many years before. It was her death from cancer that had precipitated his desire to pull away

131

from the world and, in turn, had led him to the Children of the Dell and Sanctuary. She recalled him telling her this after a night of passion in his room, while the winds for which Stoirm was famous raged and howled at the windows, making the frame shake in time to the thrusting and writhing on the bed. Yeah, she was envious all right.

She handed him the bundle of keys, some of them to doors he no longer opened, perhaps to places he had long forgotten, hoping he would not notice the one she had cupped in her hand was missing. He didn't even look at them as he thrust them back into his pocket.

'Won't be too long,' he said as he walked into the corridor. 'I'll show these two visitors around and then meet you in the office.'

She walked with him towards the rear door leading to the courtyard. 'Who are they?'

'Possibles,' he said, which meant they might be thinking about joining, or at the very least attending a course or two.

Delia waited until he took the visitors into the common room before she darted towards the Sanctuary office. She glanced through the window to ensure Seb had not returned for any reason, but the courtyard was clear. She paused as she knelt in front of the small safe on the floor, the key she had purloined not yet inserted in the lock, guilt settling on her now as she stared at the safe door. What she was about to do was a betrayal, not just of him but also Sanctuary, the Children and everything she had come to believe. Or thought she had believed, for she knew now there was that little part of her that had never fully bought into the whole thing. Nuala had sensed that in her.

I saw it in you, even if you didn't know it, Nuala had said during one of their clandestine meetings when Delia asked her why she had focused on her. *I saw it in your eyes, the very first day I spoke to you in the village.*

132

The comment had worried her, for if Nuala could see it, could everyone else? But, despite her concerns, she detected none of the other residents of Sanctuary giving her strange looks, not even Seb, so she relaxed.

She stared at the key in her hand. This was the biggest step she had taken. Up until now her covert actions had consisted of digging around on the computer when dealing with Sanctuary's business accounts. Looking at figures and records on a PC seemed somehow innocent, as if the screen was somehow a barrier to any guilt over the breach of trust. She had Seb's full permission to access the data, and, anyway, she had not told Nuala anything. She would never tell Nuala anything now. What she was about to do was different. This, effectively, was theft. She had stolen the key and was about to access a part of Sanctuary that only Seb had the authority to access.

If she did this, there was no going back. Having rushed conversations with Nuala whenever she was in Portnaseil, and a couple of times in the cottage she rented, was one thing but digging around in the safe was another. She had uncovered a few things in the computer but nothing concrete. Questions, really. The twenty residents currently in Sanctuary had contributed between them over ten million to the funds. Previous residents had added to that figure, but Delia had no way of knowing exactly how much. When one left, another arrived eventually, adding more cash to the coffers. The summer courses and residential retreats brought in more cash over the three years Sanctuary had been active on Stoirm. Some of that was used to keep the place running – power, taxes, food. The question was, where did the rest go? It left the Stoirm Sanctuary account into the main Children of the Dell account, which funded outreach and charitable work, but that was as far as her access reached. She had asked Seb, couched as an idle question, but he denied all knowledge, giving her that smile of his and telling her that was why he left the day-to-day accounts to her. Give him a machine and he was happy, but present him with numbers and he seemed to go blind. He told her not to worry too much about it, that Father dealt with the finances at a higher level. After all, wasn't that why they were all there? To escape such worldly matters? Yes, a certain amount of attention had to be paid to it – they did exist in the twenty-first century, after all – but as long as bills were paid and there was food to eat, there was no reason to be concerned.

Let it go, Delia, he had told her, *don't let the outside world get into your head.*

But it was in her head, and she could not get it out again. Her own reservations, never acknowledged, had risen with Nuala's words.

So she knelt in front of the safe, the key poised before the lock, battling her conflicting emotions. Seb was her friend. He had been her lover but that was over. He had moved on easily enough and now he was her friend. Wasn't he? Was he? Can you really be only friends with someone you had once been intimate with? Wouldn't there still be latent desires, thoughts, needs? He didn't seem to have them. She did, though.

And the other Children, they were more than friends: they were her brothers and sisters. They were family. They shared a home. They shared a future. They shared a belief.

Weren't they? Didn't they?

Nuala was an outsider. Yes, Delia had known her slightly before – her husband was the one she knew better – but, by her own admission, she was out to cause trouble for the Children and Sanctuary. Why did Delia listen to her? Why did that little doubting portion of her mind buy into what she said?

The part of her that lay with the Children and Sanctuary wanted to drop the key somewhere in the office for Seb to find, then leave, go back to her room, go to the common room, do something other than this. It told her it didn't matter where the money went, that it was held somewhere, that it was not her business. She was happy here.

Wasn't she?

Yes, she was settled. She had never felt such peace before but if she put the key in that lock and turned it, if she opened that door, if she found what she thought she would find then she was taking yet another step back to the life that had almost killed her.

Did she want that?

Did she?

She didn't, but the simple truth was she had to know. There was too much of the old Delia still alive within, too many doubts to go back to normal life in Sanctuary. Nuala had told her something was wrong with the whole set-up of the Children of the Dell movement, and the old Delia agreed. Anyway, she had gone too far to stop now. The betrayal of Seb and the Sanctuary was already a fact. It had taken place in her mind and then, in physical form, when she stole the key. The old Delia knew it was a done deal.

She slid the key in the lock, turned it, opened the door.

The safe contained a few folders and documents which she quickly scanned but found nothing of use. She didn't think she would. The object of her search today sat in the centre of the safe. A mobile pay-as-you-go phone. It was old, squat, quite ugly really, but it made and received calls and texts. The internet had not been outlawed in Sanctuary but, as the outside world no longer held much interest, most of the Children had little use for it. Social media was a bridge under which trolls lived, a land made barren and bleak by too many blinkered opinions, too much hate and an excess of narcissistic behaviour. As such, this was the only phone in the compound, the way with which Seb contacted Father, and, with her poking around on the PC proving something of a dead end, it was her only hope of finding answers.

She took out the device and fiddled with the slot on the side to release the SIM card. At the desk, she scraped the mouse a little to bring the PC to life, glancing to her right through the window again. She may have wasted precious time struggling with her conscience and had no idea how quickly Seb might complete his tour with those two young men and be on his way back. She didn't see him outside but that didn't mean he wasn't heading to the office from another direction. The visitors' Land Rover was still parked outside, but she still had to move quickly.

She fished the card reader from her pocket and inserted the flimsy SIM card, then fitted that into the USB socket of the PC. This would have been easier with Bluetooth, but both the phone and the PC were too old for such luxuries. Her acquaintance with technology was more nodding than intimate and she tutted when the ageing computer didn't recognise the card, so she removed the reader again, extracted the SIM and then re-inserted it the other way round. The old Delia had people to perform these basic functions. The new Delia struggled a little. This time the icon flashed up as the PC recognised the card, and she clicked it open, glancing again to the courtyard. Still no Seb. The phone's contents appeared in a new box, and she selected the file containing the contacts stored on the card. She opened a new file and dragged the list into it. There weren't that many. She also found a call list, again not lengthy.

A noise outside drew her attention and she saw Seb with the two visitors again. They were shaking hands.

Shit.

She scribbled the most frequently called number on a Post-it note then snatched the card reader from the PC's single working USB slot, inserted a thumb drive, and dragged the new folder there.

136

Another glance outside. Seb was smiling and talking.

Delia ripped the yellow note from the small pad then, as an afterthought, pulled away the next few blank sheets. With fingers trembling, she struggled to replace the SIM card, finding it difficult to slot it in properly.

Seb shook hands again and turned away from the men, who climbed into their Land Rover.

Keeping the phone below the level of the windowsill, she managed to slide the card in, hoping she had inserted it in the correct way. If Seb was unable to make a call, he would know that someone else had touched it.

He smiled through the window to her as he passed the Sanctuary Land Rover, then glanced under the still-open bonnet at the engine. He reached in to touch something.

The visitors backed up a little, then steered to the gates.

Delia ejected the thumb drive and thrust it into the pocket of her jeans. She clicked on the folder she had created and dragged it into the trash then emptied it.

Seb straightened again then seemed to shrug at something in the engine. He noticed fresh stains on his hands then turned to the rear door to the farmhouse. When he was out of sight, she darted from behind the desk to the safe and replaced the phone.

She heard the back door opening and closing. She had intended to root through what documents there were in the safe, but there was not enough time. The bathroom door across the hall opened. Closed. Maybe she had some breathing space as he washed his hands clean of the oil again. She flicked through the handful of folders, pulled one out, scanned the few sheets of paper, then dropped it back. There was a series of small drawers at the bottom of the safe and she pulled them out swiftly, one by one. All empty but one. She could feel her breath growing ragged, her ears pricked for the sound of the bathroom door opening again, as she unfolded a thin sheaf of papers from the drawer, scanned them. They were the title deeds to the property, or at least copies, signing the farm over from The Stoirm Estate to a company called DKMH Holdings, based in the Channel Islands.

The bathroom door opened.

She couldn't risk taking the document away, so she committed the company name to memory, thrust the papers back in the drawer, slid it shut, then quietly closed the safe, locked it and stood up.

The key. What could she do with the key? Her original plan had been to drop it in the bathroom where he had washed his hands, but that wasn't possible now. She heard Seb's footsteps approaching the door and it opened. Shit!

She clenched her fist, feeling the sharp edges of the metal bite into her flesh, and faked a smile as he entered. Her heart hammered. He seemed surprised to see her standing in the middle of the floor.

'How did it go?' she asked, wondering at how her voice came out evenly, despite the sudden dryness of her mouth.

'Fantastic,' he said. 'They're partners, but like I said, one seems keener than the other. At the very least, we might get a couple of fresh faces at the next course, though. More than that, we have to wait and see. I gave them a couple of brochures.'

More than that. He meant that they might be potential recruits.

He looked from her to the computer. 'Get your work done?'

'Yes,' she said, the key seemingly burning itself into her palm. 'It wasn't a big job, just a bit of housekeeping, cleaning out the hard drive, defragmenting it, that sort of thing.'

He nodded and walked around the desk. He would not have known what she was talking about and, to be honest, she was not too clear either, but it sounded believable. 'I hate these bloody things,' he said, staring at the computer. 'I'm glad you know your way around them.'

'Believe me, I just muddle through,' she said, injecting a little laugh into her voice, which came out more as a nervous giggle. Get it together, Delia. 'Sometimes I have no idea what I'm doing.'

'Well, you do the job, that's the important thing.' Seb fiddled with the mouse and frowned at the screen. Oh God, she thought, has he spotted something? 'I wouldn't know where to begin,' he added as he looked up and smiled. She felt relief ease a fraction of the tension in her muscles. 'This place would be in a hell of a state if you didn't look after all this.' He waved a hand at the PC.

'There are plenty of people in Sanctuary who can do it,' she said, aware her smile was tremulous. What if he wants to open the safe, she thought. He'll realise the key was gone. What then?

Seb moved back around the desk and stood directly in front of her, so close she could smell the lingering scent of engine oil. It should have repelled her, but for some reason she appreciated it on him. Or perhaps it was just him she appreciated.

'Are you happy here in Sanctuary, Delia?'

The question both caught her by surprise and deepened her nervousness. The guilty secret that was the key seared her skin. Why was he asking?

'You've been kind of absent these past few days,' he said, as if he sensed her thoughts.

'I've been here,' she said, knowing that was not what he meant but feeling she needed to say something even though her nerves were climbing to fever pitch.

He studied her face. 'No, not really. It's as if something's been troubling you.' He reached out and grasped her shoulders with both hands. She loved the feel of his hands on her but she still flinched, and he noticed it. 'You're tense. What's wrong, Delia?'

139

She forced another smile, even a slight laugh. 'Nothing, Seb, I'm very happy.'

He wasn't buying it. 'Happy, yeah, but I feel there's something on your mind. You know what we say, a settled mind is a free mind. Is there something you want to talk about?'

Does he know? The single thought screamed in her mind. Had he seen something on that screen when he flicked it on? Had he noticed the key to the safe was missing?

'Honestly, Seb, I'm fine.' She tried to inject as much confidence into her voice as she could, even though her trembling knees threatened to jerk the legs from under her. She tried to think what she had done to make him think there was something wrong but came up with nothing.

He tilted his head. 'No, I don't think so. There's something wrong, and I want you to know that whatever it is, no matter what, you can come to me and talk. You do know that, right?'

'Of course,' she said.

'Anything at all. We have a connection, you and me, a bond. If there's something on your mind, I hope you would come to me, let me help you find peace.'

Okay, was he hitting on her? Was that what this was all about? No, she decided, he's happy with Serena – she could tell that when they were together. This wasn't about sex, as much as she might want it to be. He had picked something up from her and that worried her. She needed to get out of that room, get to the small bathroom and leave the key there before he noticed it was missing.

'Seriously, Seb, thanks for the concern but I really am fine. A bit tired, but this thing with the Sister has got to a number of us.' She almost called her Nuala but used the Sanctuary name for her just in time. The art of a good lie is sticking as close to the truth as possible. It was something she had learned in her corporate days and, now that she was back to being the old Delia, she slipped easily into the routine.

His hands dropped away again and he turned. 'Yeah,' he said, 'that's got us all shaken.'

As he moved back to the desk, Delia said, 'Listen, Seb, if you don't mind' – she dropped her voice – 'but I've really got to pee.'

He laughed but she thought she heard something brittle there, as if it was merely a means of breaking some tension. 'Sure, when you got to go, you got to go.'

She gave him a final grin, which she hoped was airy, and hurriedly left the room. As she crossed the hallway to the bathroom, where she would deposit the key in a corner near to where Seb had been standing when he dropped them, she wondered what that exchange had been all about. He said he had detected something in her, but she sensed something in him in the final moments when she had mentioned the Sister. Prior to that he had been relaxed, solicitous, everything she knew him to be. But in those few moments his body had stiffened, his face grim. He hadn't known the dead woman all that well, so it wasn't grief or even sorrow. It was something else.

She thought about hearing the Land Rover leave that night and again wondered if Seb knew more about her death than he claimed.

Inverness

Sawyer had misjudged the temperature, for the cold crept up his legs from his feet and nipped at the tips of his fingers and his ears, though his cap kept his head warmer. It was like old times, more's the pity. He had been glad to cast off the uniform and get into plainclothes back then. He had thought there would be no more standing in the freezing weather at crime scenes or demonstrations or football matches. He had been wrong. Yes, in CID he was often in the office manning a phone or in a warm car, but there were also times when he would be hanging about waiting for the order to converge on some scrote or other. That's what this reminded him of, and he wished he'd had the foresight to bring a flask of coffee, but then how would that look, a man standing on a busy street corner with a tartan thermos at his feet? He was outside a restaurant and wondered if they did takeaway, but then he might miss Rebecca leaving.

Damn it, Bill, you should have worn that sheepskin flight jacket of yours. That's thick enough to keep out everything short of a nuclear blast, and even then it would do its best.

From where he was on the corner of Church Street, he could see across Union Street to the coffee house where Rebecca was meeting with DCI Val Roach. Rebecca was safe as long as she was with Roach, and he was desperate to get something hot inside him – the Egg McMuffin he'd downed earlier seemed like ancient history – but he didn't want to leave his post. Rebecca had her back to him as they talked, but she suddenly twisted round to scan the street and he had to duck back to avoid being spotted. He waited a full minute before he peered round the corner of the building to see she had turned back again and resumed talking. Narrow escape there, Bill, he told himself. Sure, he would have been able to bluff his way out of it, but he would rather not have to.

He had considered telling Rebecca about the threat over her head but decided against it. There was no point in worrying her about something that still may be the result of Cokey trying to put two and two together and losing count at three. There had been that look in Mo's eyes, though. As a police officer, Sawyer had always relied very much on his instinct: if something looked wrong, smelled wrong and tasted wrong then it was far from right, and all three senses had told him the twitchy wee bastard was bang on the money.

He wondered why he was putting himself out in this way, but he could not provide an answer. Yes, he liked the lassie, even though she was a bloody liberal-minded trendy who would rather see guilty people go free than give justice that helping hand. She was gutsy and she liked the truth, and he respected that. After they had first encountered one another on the island, he had looked into her dad and discovered he was a good copper in Glasgow. She idolised him and that was okay, even though DCI John Connolly was not as lily-white and noble as she liked to think. He had been a big city detective and he had known corners had to be cut sometimes, it was as simple as that.

Rebecca was leaving the table now. Roach was already standing. He edged slightly round the brickwork to watch them as they lingered briefly in the coffee place's doorway to exchange a few more words. He knew he must look as dodgy as hell, but he had to see where Rebecca went. When they parted, she walked up Union Street a few yards to disappear through the street entrance to the office upstairs, while Roach headed in the direction of Station Square, where he assumed she had parked.

He stepped back and leaned against the stonework beside the restaurant sign. Okay, Bill, what now? Drop in on her again? Not a good idea. They were friendly enough but not BFFs, and he was not in the habit of making social calls. He couldn't stand around here all day because it was only a matter of time before someone thought he was up to something and reported him. He could . . .

'DS Sawyer, you taking up busking?'

He found himself facing Val Roach. Shit. He forced a smile. 'DCI Roach, how are you doing?'

She must have seen him through the window, then walked up the street a bit, crossed over and headed back to surprise him. She was tricky.

She didn't reply to his polite query, instead saying, 'So? Are you?'

He was puzzled. 'Am I what?' He bit back the ingrained desire to say 'ma'am'. He didn't have to acknowledge her rank.

'Taking up busking?' she repeated. 'Subsidising your pension, maybe, with a bit of song and dance?' She made a show of looking around him. 'I don't see any instruments, or even a prancing haggis.'

She was funny. She must be a riot at office parties.

'Just standing here enjoying the crisp weather,' he said.

Her eyes narrowed slightly. 'You got Inuit blood in you, have you?'

'On my mother's side. I'd show you my whale harpooning skills but I'm an animal lover.'

'Uh-huh.' She glanced over her shoulder at the coffee house, as if she was confirming what she already knew. 'So what are you really up to?'

He looked as innocent as he could. 'Up to?'

'Don't give me that, detective sergeant.'

'Retired. Which means you have no authority over me.'

'A good cop never retires, and I do have the authority to lift you.'

He laughed. He couldn't believe she was trying to intimidate him. That was his job. 'For what? Lurking without a licence?'

Her eyes softened with a smile. 'Bill, isn't it?'

'Aye.'

'What's the story here, Bill? One cop to another. Why are you so interested in Rebecca Connolly?'

'What makes you think that?'

'I'm a detective and I detected. I saw you standing over here and you hardly took your eyes off her. So what is it? Mid-life crisis? Got a crush on a younger woman? A *much* younger woman, I've got to add. No offence.'

He wasn't offended. He was experienced enough to know how this looked. 'How do you know it's not you I've got a crush on?'

She made a dismissive noise with her tongue against her teeth. 'You'd be punching above your weight there.'

He couldn't argue with that.

'So, what's going on, Bill?'

He could lie, but Roach was sharp and would see through it, even though he was fluent in lies. He decided the truth was the best way forward. He looked back at the coffee house and saw a table in the corner was free, and it had a view of the street door leading to Rebecca's office.

'Can we go inside and get a coffee? I think my frostbite's got frostbite.'

'So much for Inuit blood,' she said but turned and headed across the road.

Rebecca's phone rang as she climbed the stairs to the office. She saw Elspeth's name on the screen, hit the button, saying, 'Rebecca Connolly's the name, exclusives are my game.'

A slight snort greeted her. 'I like the enthusiasm,' said Elspeth. 'You sound out of breath, where are you?'

'Heading back to the office. Just had a coffee with Val Roach.'

'Oh, I thought maybe you were shagging.'

Rebecca made a dismissive noise with her lips. 'You have a one-track mind these days, and it happens to be a dirt track.' Her mind flashed to the night before. Stephen had held her hand for the rest of the film, and the kiss as he dropped her back at the flat was particularly long and, frankly, exciting.

Rebecca had kissed many a boy and man – well, maybe not many, but her fair share – and she could testify that he was good at it. With most of the others it was like kissing a faulty tumble dryer, all rotation but very little heat, but Stephen knew how to make the lip thing work. Push, as they say, came to them shoving each other around in her bedroom. She was not about to tell Elspeth that, however.

'Chance would be a fine thing,' she lied.

'You've had plenty of chances, Becks. You're just too choosy.'

'Nothing wrong with standards.'

'No, but if you don't lower them, you will die a born-again virgin. What is it, five years before that kicks in?'

'Something like that.' Rebecca was at the door to the office and fishing in her pocket for the key. 'So, did you phone me to talk about my love life?'

'Pretty short conversation, that.' Rebecca was glad this was not a video call, for her smile would have given the game away. Elspeth continued, 'No, I was bored so was just calling for a gab. What's happening?'

Rebecca opened the door, kicked it shut with the heel of her foot, set her bag on the desk and settled herself behind the desk. 'Chaz and Alan may have stumbled on something,' she said.

'I thought they were on Stoirm.'

'They are, that's where they stumbled on it.' Rebecca quickly told her about Nuala Flaherty, Sanctuary and the Children of the Dell.

'Children of the Dell, Children of the Dell.' Elspeth's voice was thoughtful.

'You've heard of them?'

'Rings a bell, is all. I've read something about them.'

'I had a quick google . . .'

'Oooh, matron!'

Rebecca smiled. 'What is it with you today? Are you horny or something?'

Elspeth laughed. 'No, I am beyond such temptations of the flesh.'

'What does Julie say about that?'

'She loves me for my mind, not my body. So, you gave yourself a Google, you naughty girl.'

'Yes, and it seems to be quite an operation. There's a handful of these Sanctuaries offering a place to drop out of the rat race and find respite and solace. Their words, not mine.'

'At a price, no doubt.'

'There was nothing mentioned. It was formed by someone they call Father.'

'Ah, the patriarchy at work again.'

'There's a picture of him online looking like someone who would always have a boiled sweet in the pocket of his cardigan. Very few have met him, even among the Children of the Dell.'

'Stupid name.'

'I'm sure it makes some sort of sense to someone.'

'Enid bloody Blyton maybe.' Elspeth paused. 'Still, I know I've heard of them before.'

'Well, maybe you'll remember by the weekend. I've got the boys doing some digging on the island, and I'll do the same here.'

'You've got them working?'

'What's the point of having lackeys if you don't use them?'

'I hope they're doing this for nothing.'

'Of course. It will look good on their CV.'

Elspeth erupted in laughter. This was a phrase trotted out by the owners of the newspaper they had both worked for to justify using people's work without paying.

'They're glad of the distraction,' said Rebecca. 'Chaz's mum has the wedding in hand, anyway. And Alan, I think, is delighted. You know how much he likes to exercise his little grey cells.'

'Bless him.' She paused again. 'But I wish I could remember where I've heard of the Children of the Dell.'

'It'll come back to you. Just don't think about it.'

'It's bloody annoying, though.'

Rebecca knew that there would be something tucked away in the recesses of Elspeth's memory and she would find it eventually. Knowing her, it would occur to her out of the blue, perhaps even in the middle of the night. It wouldn't be the first time Rebecca's own sleep had been disturbed by a call from her to pass on something she had just thought of.

Something else occurred to Rebecca. 'Guess who's tagging along this weekend, by the way? Bill Sawyer.'

There was a short silence as Elspeth took this in. 'Has he been invited to the wedding?'

'No, he invited himself. He's decided he's my plus-one.' For now, she thought. She had decided to risk asking Stephen away for the weekend. Sometimes you just have to take chances.

'What brought this on?'

'He's worried about me, because of Lord Henry Stuart and the Russians.'

'If they've not done anything before now, they're not going to. And it's not as if you've said anything about all that.'

'No, but he thinks he needs to come as a bodyguard.'

Elspeth snorted. It was not a pleasant sound. 'Maybe in his day, but the sun has well set on that as far as Bill Sawyer is concerned.'

Rebecca saw him in a cramped sitting room of an Inchferry house, an extendable baton appearing as if from nowhere as he tackled a man with a shotgun. 'Oh, I think he's still got some moves.'

'Well, maybe, but I'll tell you this, he's up to something. Sawyer was a devious bastard when he was a cop and he's not changed much.'

*

148

When they managed to snag the table, Sawyer saw Roach noting how he took the chair with the best view of the street, but she said nothing. A little smile did play on her lips, though.

'Have you not just had a coffee?' he asked.

'That's fine, you can never have too much coffee.'

'Aye, gives me the skitters, though, too much of it.'

'Thank you for sharing,' Roach said, then added, 'Old age is a terrible thing, though.'

Cheeky bugger: she wasn't that far behind him, though she didn't look it, he had to admit. A mate still serving on the force described her as elfin and he couldn't have put it better himself. He knew her temperament was far from elfin-like, though.

'So, now we're all warm and cosy,' she said, 'what gives? Why the Popeye Doyle routine?'

He didn't catch the reference and she sighed.

'*The French Connection*? Gene Hackman standing in the cold watching for suspects?'

'Never seen it,' he said.

She was surprised. 'You've never seen *The French Connection*?'

He shrugged. 'Don't like cop movies, TV shows or books. All pish, if you ask me.'

'I have to agree with you, but that film's a classic. Anyway – let's have it. What's the interest in Rebecca?'

He stirred five sachets of sugar into his coffee. 'I think she might be in danger.'

She took that calmly, the professional police officer kicking in. 'From whom, where or what?'

'You know Mo Burke, right?'

'Yes, by repute. I've never had the actual pleasure.'

'Believe me, it's no pleasure. You know what happened with her sons?'

'Yes.'

'She blames Rebecca. She thinks she lured Nolan Burke away from the fold and that's what tipped Scott over the edge.'

Roach compressed her lips. 'Scott was a coked-up nutjob who had launched himself off that edge a long time ago, from what I hear.'

'Aye, but she loved them both. She's many things but she loves her family.'

'And she's coming after Rebecca?'

'So I'm told.'

'By whom?'

'An old tout of mine.'

'Name?'

'Doesn't matter.'

'Reliable?'

'Can be. Not always.'

'But you think so this time?'

'I spoke to Mo Burke.'

'She confirmed it?'

'Her lips said no but her eyes said yes.'

Roach's gaze drifted to the street as the thought about this. 'Rebecca was attacked a while ago in her home.'

'Aye.'

'Connected?'

'My tout says yes.'

Roach looked back at him, her mouth puckering slightly as she took this in. 'Why are you doing this?'

'I like Rebecca. I don't like Mo Burke.' He knew Roach understood. Like all decent cops, she would despise the likes of Mo Burke. They leeched from the world, corrupting everything they touched. Sawyer had been neither surprised nor sorry to hear her boy had died at his brother's hand because Scott Burke had been heading towards murder from the day he was born. When he was a cop, he had tried to make some charges stick on the family, but Mo Burke was always

150

too slippery for him, always too careful. Her man, Tony, had proved an easier target and, when he took a steak knife to a rival, he was not as careful as he should have been. The attack, which fell short of murder only by the narrowest of margins, was motivated by rage and hatred, and Scott had inherited his father's temper while Nolan had taken after his mother. Tony Burke was due out in a year or two, but Sawyer doubted if he had mellowed while inside, and God help anyone who got in his way.

So now, the coffee thawing the chill in his bones as he spoke to Roach, Bill Sawyer finally understood at least part of why he had turned bodyguard. It wasn't just that he liked Rebecca: it was because he wanted to get Mo Burke. She had avoided him years before, but if he could somehow nab whoever she may send to take Rebecca out, then hopefully it would lead back to her. He had no doubt that the woman would have insulated herself, but maybe, just maybe, there would be a tiny chink in her precautions. Like her husband, this time she was motivated by hate, and that could make her careless.

'You should have reported this,' said Roach.

'Aye, and where's my evidence? The word of a tout?'

Roach accepted that. 'You should have told me.'

'I'm telling you now. And I didn't know that you and Rebecca were coffee pals.'

She brushed that aside. 'You can't watch her twenty-four hours a day.'

He had already thought of that. 'I know. I wasn't too happy with her going back to the island at the end of the week, but, as it turns out, that might be a good thing.'

'Island?'

'She's going to Stoirm for a wedding. I'm going with her and so is her boss.'

'Elspeth McTaggart, right?'

151

'Right.'

'And you're going as what? Her date?'

He pulled a face. 'No, I've blagged my way in as protection detail.'

'But I thought you hadn't told her about this Mo Burke thing?'

'I haven't.' Sawyer paused. He had opened another door here and he wasn't sure if he should walk through. 'There are other, em, variables on the island.'

'What other variables?'

He hesitated and Roach leaned forward. 'Bill, what other variables? What else does she need to be protected from?'

The sound he could hear was that door slamming behind him. 'I met her for the first time on Stoirm, a few years ago now. She was following up a story . . .'

He told her about the man who years before had been cleared of a murder charge on a Not Proven verdict, a man Sawyer had charged and who he firmly believed was responsible. His return to his island home provoked all sorts of reaction. Rebecca and Sawyer learned of other illegal activities involving Lord Henry Stuart, who owned much of the island, and the Nikoladze brothers.

Roach's face and tone was severe. 'And you didn't report any of this, either?'

'What we learned had happened over fifteen years before,' he said. 'We had no proof, just the word of a former junkie who was, at the time of the offence, strung out to buggery. We had no corroboration at all.'

'And you think Rebecca going back will place her in danger there, too?'

'Aye.' He changed his mind. 'No.' He thought about it again. 'The truth is, probably not. The parties involved know there is nothing to connect them to what happened back then. They are as insulated as they possibly can be.'

'But you used it as a ploy to tag along, right?'

'Right.'

'And she accepted it?'

'I didn't give her the option.'

Roach stared out of the window again. 'You think a warning from me will call Burke off?'

'No. I've tried.'

'You're retired. I have the weight of Police Scotland behind me.'

'She doesn't give a toss about that. You don't know her, DCI Roach . . .'

'For God's sake, call me Val.'

'You don't know her, Val. She has held the business together since her man was jailed. She's come through a feud with a Glasgow crew and she's lost both her boys, in one way or another. And she's still standing. I don't like her but I have to respect the sheer force of will that keeps the woman going. She's got Rebecca in her sights and she's not going to be happy until she sees it through.'

The clock tower was a finger of reddish stone flanked by a self-storage facility and large oil tanks. Cars slid past on Cromwell Road, a fitting name given the origin of the building standing in a neat patch of paving stones and gravel. On the other side of the road was a line of railings and beyond it a patch of wasteground and then the River Ness snaking out to the firth. Mo had pulled the car into a space in front of the oil company's offices, the small car park empty as it was after hours, then walked the few yards to the tower, where she found the litter bin. It was dark – with only light from the streetlamps – so she couldn't read the legend on the plaque. Not that she needed to. Years before, Nolan had told her about the tower, and why it was built – he'd had an interest in history and had read up on Inverness's past. And as Mo stood there in the shadows, she saw him again, but this time as that little boy, dark hair needing combed, eyes eager and excited. A little boy for whom the past was a source of fascination. A little boy who did not know he had no future. Even though her mind was once again spanning the years, past to present, she still heard her son's voice, not yet broken, echoing from the red stone and filtering through the thin branches of the bushes behind her and the slim trees beyond the tower.

It's one of four strongholds built by Cromwell, Mum.

The words replayed in her mind, just as they were uttered then. A recording locked in a databank she didn't know she had.

'What,' she'd said with a smile, 'did he come up here with a brickie's hod and slap the mortar in himself?'

Nolan gave her that look he reserved for when she had said something really dumb. He could be a serious lad, often missing her tone. *No, he didn't build it himself, Mum!*

It was always 'Mum' back then, she recalled. When did it change to 'Ma', she wondered. And why?

It was after the civil war, after he'd beaten the king. The Scots had sided with Charles, and Cromwell needed to subdue the Highlands, so he built citadels here and in Perth and Leith and another one, can't remember where . . .

'Ayr,' she'd said, and she recalled the stunned look on his little face. She didn't tell him she'd read it on the plaque. She had squinted up at the tower with its clock. 'It's no' much of a fort, is it?'

That look again. *It was bigger than this, Mum! Much bigger, stretched all around here, covered four acres. Must have been huge.*

She would have laid good money that Nolan had no idea then how big an acre was. She had only a vague idea, but she agreed it must have been huge.

There's earthworks somewhere here, but the tower is all that's left of the actual building . . .

He had gone on to outline the history, and she remembered it all. His face. His voice. Her son. Her boy. Despite what he might have thought, her favourite. She knew she shouldn't have had favourites, but she did. She was harder on him because he was the oldest and because he had the most promise. She was soft on Scott because she thought that was what he needed. He needed a mother's love, her guidance, where Nolan did not. He would always do what was right in any given situation, and for a while she had forgotten that.

Until Connolly came along and got her claws into him.

She slid the package from under her arm and looked at it. It was neatly wrapped in the pages of *The Guardian*, the newspaper Nolan favoured. She had found a few copies under his bed when she finally tidied his room, although she did not clear it out. She never would. He was her son. He was her boy. He would always be a part of her, and she could not bring herself to dispose of anything connected to him. She had stood in that room and tried to imagine him in there, reading, watching some documentary on the small TV. She had opened his wardrobe and touched his clothes, raising the fabric to her nose, as if the scent of him would make him miraculously appear. But he didn't. He was gone. Only the idea of him and the sound of his voice remained, but they were mere echoes, memories bouncing in the walls of her mind. Not real. Not present. Not any more.

She checked the time then stepped to the little bin, solid on all four sides with openings at the top for the refuse to be deposited. The package would not be seen by anyone walking past, not that there were any pedestrians. Motorists were unlikely to give her so much as a glance as they zipped by, for at this time of night all they wanted was to get home. Even if they did catch sight of her, all they'd see was a woman dropping some rubbish in the bin. Nothing suspicious there. All the same, she hesitated, the package held in both hands. It was a lot of money. It was a big step. Once she put it in this bin, there was no going back. The man she spoke to said that she should not, could not, contact them again. As soon as she left the package here and walked away, the contract was sealed.

Mo Burke had ordered men hurt before; in her line of business it was not a daily occurrence, but it happened. This, though, was different. She was going to have a woman killed. All it would take was to put the package in the bin and walk away. Simple as that.

Tony had argued against it. She had been warned off by that bastard Sawyer. Even Nolan – the one in her head – was against it.

It's a big step, Ma. She could hear him again, his voice older, the little boy gone, the man in his place. *It's no' like doing a damage. This is permanent.*

But she has to pay, son.

Maybe, but you have to know that there's no going back from this, Ma. You drop that in there, you're changing things. You're changing. She's not some ned from Glasgow. She's not someone muscling into the family business. She's a straight arrow.

She caused your death!

No, Scott did that. You know it. Scott, my brother, out of his head on coke.

No! She is responsible. She did it!

She stared at the bin, the package in her hand, Nolan in her head, aware that it was already six. Time was running out.

M90, Perth

They were on the way back to the city when Pat received the phone call. They had waited a few hours, just to ensure there were no last-minute issues, such as the target actually surviving the fall and swimming to safety like Aquaman. Pat had argued that it was best not to leave in any haste, for haste can draw attention, and the last thing they wanted was to draw attention. They liked to simply merge with the crowd, just two faces among many, nothing particularly memorable. They had lunch in the bar downstairs, ears and eyes alert for any sign that the target's body had been spotted, but there were no sirens, no boats or helicopters. Life went on as it had done for the few days they had been in the village – in other words, as slow as a week in the jail. Mike had done time only once and he'd hated it, vowed never to go back, and he vowed he would never come back here either. He was done with rural Scotland, thanks all the same.

Finally, Pat relented, so they packed their bags, checked out and began the drive home down the A90. They were about a mile from the Broxden Junction outside Perth, at which point they would nose south-west on the A9 for Glasgow, when the call came on Pat's personal number. They had one for work, and each had their own. They were all small, lightweight units because they couldn't have their pockets weighed down. The weapons they often carried were bad enough. Pat knew which pocket this one was in and fished it out as Mike kept his eyes on the road ahead, taking in the illuminated sign that pointed to Glasgow.

Pat checked the number on the tiny screen and frowned before answering. 'Aye,' Pat said into the phone, eyes flicking towards Mike, 'it's been a long time.'

'Who is it?' Mike asked, his voice low enough not to be picked up by the caller.

Pat's head shook. 'We're a wee bit busy, right now.' A sigh. 'Aye, I know, I know.' Pat listened and sighed again, lips stretched into a tight line. Whatever was being said was not welcome. 'Okay, fine. We'll be there.' Listened again. 'Soon as we can. Email the necessary to this address.' Pat rhymed off a

157

secure email address. They used to use EncroChat for this sort of thing before the law got wise and broke it all up in 2020. Still, the web was a big place and there were lots of dark corners for businesspeople to hide. Mike was always impressed how easily Pat reeled off the address, for they had a host of such accounts and most of them were used only once. Mobile phones, too. You can never be too careful. But Pat was able to dredge them up at will, something he could never do.

The phone was abruptly hung up and thrust back into a coat pocket.

Mike said, 'So you going to tell me who that was or just keep me in the dark?'

Pat's voice was flat. 'Aye, there's a job for us.'

'Tell me it's in a city, any city.'

A cheeky smile played on Pat's lips. 'It's a city.'

'Where?'

'Up north.'

Mike felt the rug being pulled from beneath his feet. He could see the big roundabout up ahead that would take them back to Glasgow. 'Up north? Teuchterland?'

He made it sound like a wilderness.

Pat said, 'Inverness.'

Mike thought about this. Okay, it wasn't Glasgow or Edinburgh or London, but it wasn't the back of beyond. It had streetlights and it had properly paved streets. It would do. He changed lanes and followed the road that would lead them north, giving a final wistful look to the arrow pointing south and home.

Inverness

Val Roach didn't get along too well with the man on the other end of the phone, but professional courtesy went a long way. Detective Chief Superintendent Joseph Lonsdale was with the specialist crime unit that dealt with serious organised crime and counter-terrorism, two strands of criminality linked because often one washed the blood from the hands of the other. His voice had been cool and detached when she was put through, but something like warmth crept in when she mentioned the Nikoladze brothers.

'We've been after those bastards for years,' he said, his Yorkshire accent sounding nasal. 'What's your interest?'

'Officially, I have none.'

'Unofficially?'

'Their name cropped up in a conversation regarding a friend.'

Lonsdale's voice was business-like. 'Is your friend mixed up with them?'

'No.'

'Just as well, because they are as dangerous a pair as you can get.'

'What can you tell me about them?'

'Ichkit is the eldest and he bases himself in London. Keeps himself to himself, lives in a multimillion-pound penthouse flat in Belgravia. Jarji is the youngest and he likes to move around: London, New York, Paris, Munich . . .'

The words of an old song came into Roach's head, but she kept them to herself. She didn't want to interrupt Lonsdale's flow. He seemed to be enjoying himself. But now she had the damned tune in her head.

'He likes to mix with showbiz and sporting types. A few government ministers and advisers all over the globe. It helps create a sheen for them and their reputable businesses, of which they have many.'

'And disreputable ones?'

'Oh yes. If there's a criminal pie to stick a finger in, they have more digits than Little Jack Horner. All the old hits – drugs, prostitution, extortion, fraud, people trafficking . . .'

159

She knew about the people trafficking but, again, said nothing.

'. . . plus a few newish wrinkles. Cybercrime, that sort of thing. They are well insulated, of course, that's why neither we nor the National Crime Agency have ever been able to lay a glove on them. They are clever, those two, and they mix with clever people, and ensure their less-than-legal incomes are well hidden and well washed.' He paused, coughed a little. The first time she had met him he was stricken with a cold, and it sounded like he was developing another. Some people should overdose on echinacea.

'The single-line pitch is that they are bad bastards, and if your friend has fallen foul of them then he or she should tread warily,' Lonsdale said, pausing again for a sniff. 'There's a list of unsolved murders across the UK and on the continent that have their fingerprints all over them, figuratively speaking. They don't forgive and they don't forget, and if someone crosses them, lets them down or just generally pisses them off, that someone more often than not ends up dead or disappeared.'

The Island of Stoirm

Alan fingered the blue-and-white tape stretched across the doorway of Rose Cottage, tutting loudly. Chaz watched from a few paces away, the island's darkness stretching off across the moors, a faint breeze disturbing the voices in the grasses and heather. He imagined it probing the tarpaulin covering the pentagram hacked from the earth, as if curious to see what had disturbed the land.

They should have known the cottage would be sealed by the police. This was where Nuala had been living, and it was from here she fled. As far as Chaz was aware, there was no evidence of a crime, but he knew the Major Investigation

Team would treat it as one until certain there was nothing sinister.

Alan reached through the criss-crossed tape and tried the door handle. Locked, which was unusual for a cottage this far away from Portnaseil, but then the police had probably instructed Miss Walker to secure it. Alan stepped back and studied the windows on either side.

Chaz guessed what was going through his head. 'We're not committing burglary.'

'Of course we're not,' said Alan, sharply, then added, 'It's called housebreaking in Scotland.'

'Whatever it's called, we're not doing it.'

Alan faced him. 'Where's your sense of adventure?'

'Hiding behind my fear of ending up in a cell with a tattooed hairy guy called Bubba.'

Alan tutted his dismissal. 'We're in the Highlands and Islands, not Arkansas.'

'No matter, we're not doing it, Alan. I mean it.'

Alan sighed. 'I really wanted a look inside.'

'And see what exactly?'

A shrug. 'I don't know. Maybe . . .'

A strong beam of light swept over them, and Alan jumped back as if he had been stung. Chaz shielded his eyes against the glare but couldn't see who was holding the powerful torch as he or she approached from the moorland, although that mystery was solved when a black figure bounded towards him, tail wagging, and he heard Miss Walker's voice booming.

'And what would you two be up to, then? You wouldn't be planning a spot of housebreaking?'

Chaz caught Alan's superior smile but ignored it. 'Sorry, Miss Walker, but we're . . .'

'Snooping.'

Chaz, kneeling to rub Bess's ears, considered lying but decided it would do no good. She had a way of seeing through

161

such things. 'Yes, we did want a look. We called at your cottage, but you weren't in.'

'Obviously,' she said dryly, now beside them and flicking the light more fully on Alan. 'You will be Alan Shields, I presume?'

Alan gave her his most appealing smile. 'My fame has spread.'

Miss Walker cleared her throat. Only she could make it sound like a reprimand. 'I recall seeing you about the island when you lived here. As for your fame – notoriety, I think is the proper term.' From the light cast back towards her, Chaz saw the humour sparkling in her eyes. 'So, young Charles Wymark, can I take it as read that you two are playing at being the Hardy Boys?'

Chaz had no clue as to who the Hardy Boys were, but he assumed they were detectives of some kind. He stood up, and Bess, deciding he had lost interest in her, turned her attention to Alan, who smiled and stooped to rub her head. It reminded Chaz that he still hadn't talked to him about getting a dog. Now was not the time, though.

'I also take it you are now on the trail of some sort of story?' Miss Walker asked.

'Yes. Ms Flaherty's death is intriguing.'

'Intriguing. Yes, that is most decidedly what it is.' Miss Walker studied Chaz closely, then looked around again. She swung the beam over the door and windows, as if checking they were undisturbed. 'So what did you expect to find, had you been able to gain access?'

'We don't know,' said Alan. 'Something. Anything, really.'

'The police have already searched the cottage, you do know that?'

Alan asked, 'And do you know if they found anything?'

The torch beam was back blinding them again and, in the pause, Chaz suspected his former teacher was considering whether or not to answer the question.

162

'They took a few things away,' she said. 'A used mug they found on the floor of the sitting room, candles that had been placed in the fireplace and on the table, as well as various ephemera of an esoteric nature. I let them get on with it, on the understanding that if anything was broken it would be replaced at Police Scotland's expense. I don't think they knew what they were looking for, either.'

'And did they ask you about her?'

'Of course they did.' Her voice suggested that he had asked whether the sun rose in the east.

'And may we ask what you told them?'

'Yes, you may,' she said and waited. Chaz smiled. She really hadn't changed and Alan had met his match.

Alan realised he was expected to actually ask. 'So what did you tell them?'

'I'm not sure I can really discuss that.'

'But you said . . .'

'I said you may ask; I didn't say I would answer.'

Alan stared at her, his mouth slightly open before it transformed into a smile and he wagged a finger at her. 'You're a tricky one, you know that? I can see why you were Chaz's favourite teacher.'

It was true, but he had never told Alan that, to the best of his memory. Miss Walker seemed to appreciate it, though. 'Well, young Wymark is perhaps a better judge of character than the evidence suggests.'

'Current company excepted?'

'Not necessarily,' she said, but the good humour was plain now, and Alan picked up on that.

'Well, I'll try to change your opinion on that score,' he said.

'Uphill battle, I fear.'

'I like a challenge.'

Bess had tired of being obedient and had wandered back to Alan, who this time got down to her level to give her a rough, two-handed stroke. 'You're a lovely girl, aren't you?' He looked over the dog's head to Miss Walker. 'Your dog likes me.'

'She also likes eating sheep shit, so what does that prove?'

Alan chuckled and stared into the dog's eyes. 'I'll win your human over, wait and see, girl.'

Chaz decided it was time he tried appealing to his old teacher. 'Come on, Miss Walker, what can you tell us about Nuala Flaherty?'

She exhaled. 'Not much, to be honest. She rented the cottage from me, as you know. She paid her rent on time. She kept the place clean and tidy. I'm just down the track, so we met now and again, but that's all.'

'Do you know where she was from?'

'Despite her name, she was English. I think she mentioned Chigwell originally.'

Alan kept patting Bess. 'So what brought her here?'

'Research, is all she told me. I believe she may have been writing a book.'

'But she didn't actually say that?'

'No.'

Chaz said, 'And what did you think of her?'

'In what way?'

'Well, did you think she was in any way strange?'

'I think most people are in their own way strange, young Charles Wymark.'

'Does that include you, Miss Walker?' Alan asked.

'Most decidedly. Ask anyone on the island, especially my former pupils, and that's what they'll tell you. Old Miss Walker: strange.'

'I never thought you were strange, Miss Walker,' said Chaz, honestly.

'Well, I find that strange,' she said. 'I did my best to be different. But Nuala' – she considered her words – 'Nuala had a touch of the fey about her, most certainly. She was an attractive woman; I know some of the young men in Portnaseil had noticed her, though she never had any time for them. I saw that Yates lad trying it on with her, even though she was far too old for him.'

Chaz frowned as he felt that twinge in his leg and side once more. 'Darren Yates?'

She nodded. 'Dar, as he likes to be called.' She paused to give Chaz a pointed look. 'I do so hate it when people contract their Christian names, don't you, Chaz?'

She had a knack of making him feel guilty even when there was nothing to feel guilty about. 'Well, Charles is my dad, so "Chaz" makes it easier at home. It's just stuck, I suppose.'

Alan said, 'He had never fancied being Charlie, and Chuck was completely out of the question, thankfully. His mother tells me he thought Chaz infinitely cooler.'

Miss Walker cleared her throat again, as if the idea of Chaz being cool was something horrible that needed to be dislodged and expectorated.

Chaz asked, 'So Darren was chatting her up?'

'Yes, while she was in the hotel bar. I was having some lunch when I saw them.'

'Did she go in there often?'

'I really couldn't say. I saw her that one time only, just on Friday there. Darren Yates, though, is something of a permanent fixture in the bar, I understand.'

Alan said to Chaz, 'I wonder if she ate lunch there regularly.'

'I'm not sure.' Miss Walker paused. 'But I can tell you she was not alone.'

Alan waited, then realised she again expected him to ask the question. 'Who was she with?'

'I really don't know who the person was.'

'Man or a woman?'

'Woman.'

'Not local?'

'Not as far as I knew. I don't know everyone on the island, though.'

'Did you tell the police this?'

'Of course.'

Chaz asked, 'Can you describe her?'

Miss Walker rhymed off the description without thinking. 'Tall, slim, long dark hair, not terribly attractive, but, frankly, Nuala put most women in the shade. Pale skin. Maybe about forty. Had the look of a businesswoman. She was wearing a smart, grey, three-piece suit that was not off the peg, let me tell you.'

Alan gave Chaz a meaningful look. 'Now,' he said, 'where did we see someone answering that description recently?'

Chaz recalled the woman they had seen Rory Gibson talking to in the restaurant the night before, then asked Miss Walker, 'But you didn't catch her name?'

'Nobody mentioned it. But they were deep in conversation until the boy Yates interrupted. Nuala deflected him, though. I'm sure, looking as she did, she had great experience of discouraging unwanted attention from men.'

4

WEDNESDAY

Inverness

Tabitha Haley's salon was on Stephen's Brae, a steep incline leading from the pedestrianised Eastgate up the hill to the Crown area. The room in the basement, where Tabitha and her two staff members had their breaks, was larger than Rebecca had expected, but it was made smaller by the piles of haircare product boxes along one wall. There was a sink, kettle, filter coffee machine, toaster and microwave. A door to the left led to what Rebecca assumed was a toilet. Upstairs, the narrow space was all chrome, mirrors and stone floor tiles and smelled of hairspray, but down here it was drab, functional, with the heady aroma of brewed coffee. That coffee was good, even Rebecca recognised that, and Tabitha had laid a plate of biscuits between them before she sat down opposite Rebecca at the small table. Rebecca selected a Club Fruit, for which she had an inordinate fondness. Tabitha picked up a Penguin.

'You didn't tell me you weren't always a hairdresser,' said Rebecca as she unwrapped the foil.

'We've all been something else at one time, haven't we?' Tabitha said as she peeled the paper from her own biscuit. 'Anyway, you didn't ask and I didn't think it important.'

Good point, Rebecca thought. 'I looked you up.' Rebecca bit off some of the chocolate and chewed as she glanced at her notepad. 'Professor of Anthropological Studies at the University of Southern Scotland. A particular interest in ancient religions and beliefs. You've written three books on the occult and contributed to various magazines.'

'I also cut hair,' said Tabitha.

'All this was done under your married name, Tabitha Houseman, but you reverted to your maiden name when you divorced five years ago. Then, the year after that, you resigned your position at the university and came to Inverness.'

'Where I opened this salon.'

'Yes – why?'

'I told you, I also cut hair.'

'Tabitha . . .'

She sighed. 'Is this important?'

'Yes. You agreed to this magazine piece and that means this is important. A news story just reports the facts . . .'

She saw the beginnings of a mocking smile form on Tabitha's lips.

'Okay, it's *supposed* to report the facts,' Rebecca amended, 'but a magazine piece goes further, digs under those facts to the people behind them.'

'Even in a Sunday tabloid mag?'

'Yes, even there.'

Tabitha was not convinced. Rebecca could see it in her face, in the way she fiddled with the biscuit wrapper, so she decided to be more honest.

'Look, I'm interested, okay?' Rebecca said. 'I like to know who I'm working with. Yes, I can write the magazine piece with what I know, but I need to mention your background. If I didn't then someone will pipe up, especially if there's something to pipe up about.'

'You mean a skeleton in my closet, in there beside my broomstick, my cauldron and my pointy black hat?'

Rebecca waited, hoping her expression revealed she would not give up. 'Tabitha, it is uncommon for someone with your academic background to end up owning a hair salon, even if you do also cut hair. If there is a skeleton then you can put money on someone coming forward when they read the story to give those bones a right good rattle.'

Tabitha exhaled deeply and dropped the remains of the biscuit on the tabletop. 'There's no deep, dark secret. I had a breakdown after the divorce – not because I mourned the loss of my husband, who was a shit of marked distinction, but because the pressure of my married life and the pressure of my work life grew too much for me. I told you I had an interest in the occult, and that was fine with the faculty as long as it was purely academic, but when I began to take more of a practical interest they became concerned.'

'So you are a Wiccan?'

'I don't believe in labels. I have my beliefs, let's leave it at that.'

Rebecca sensed the honesty in the woman's words. 'Okay, good. Sorry to press the issue, but I have to be careful. What you did in finding that little boy was impressive, even though I don't fully understand it . . .'

'Or believe it,' Tabitha added.

Rebecca inclined her head to acknowledge that. 'I am sceptical but, as it has been pointed out to me, there are more things in Heaven and Earth. But yes, I am having a hard time believing in a psychic link.'

Tabitha smiled. 'How you make the words "psychic link" sound like absolute bollocks is quite something, Rebecca.'

'I'm sorry, I didn't mean to . . .'

Tabitha waved her apology away. 'Don't worry about it. You don't believe, I get that. Many people don't.'

'It's just that I have to remain objective. There are many things here that I cannot explain, though.'

'Do they need to be explained? Can you not simply put them down to things being what they are, without having to rationalise?'

Rebecca let that go and nibbled on her biscuit. She had a limited amount of words for the magazine piece and the newspaper wanted a by-the-numbers account of finding the boy, not a serious probe into second sight. What she was doing now was, essentially, extra-curricular in regard to the article, although she did need to have some sort of assurance that the woman had not been caught with her fingers in the till. Or, indeed, anything else.

Tabitha was not about to let it go. 'The modern world is trained to view mysticism with mistrust, to dismiss, to mock,' she said. 'But we all have that part of us that we don't understand, those little moments we cannot explain. Déjà vu. Intuition. A feeling that something is not right. Flashes of insight into what we cannot see, hear, feel or touch or taste.' She sat for a moment, her lips working slightly as she considered what she was going to say next. 'Intuition, insight, instinct. There's a reason why they all begin with "in" – because it's something that comes from deep within, something inside us that we don't fully understand, may never understand.'

'They say we only use ten per cent of our brain, right?'

'They do say that but it's not true, actually. What is true is that while science understands more about what goes on in our heads than people realise, they are still learning all the time. What I'm talking about is something more primal, something that cannot – and perhaps never will – be measured by science. And it's something I believe we all have to some degree or another.'

'But you've never experienced this kind of psychic link before, right?'

'Not personally, but this sort of thing, astral projection, has been documented. St Paul wrote about it, the Egyptians believed in the *Ka*, a manifestation of the soul outwith the body, the Japanese call it the *Ikiryō*. Even Michael Crichton, the *Jurassic Park* author, experimented with it.' Tabitha had plumped for tea rather than coffee and she took a mouthful. 'But you're not here for a lecture. There's something else on your mind, I think.'

Rebecca was about to ask how she knew when Tabitha smiled. 'No psychic bollocks involved, Rebecca. You haven't made any notes, so none of this is of interest to you.'

Rebecca set her coffee mug down and leaned forward. 'Have you heard about the death of a woman on the island of Stoirm?'

'No,' replied Tabitha.

'It's been on the news.'

'No offence, but I tend to avoid newspapers and the news now. Too much death, too much destruction and hatred. Too many politicians being allowed to lie with impunity. It all harshes my mellow.'

Rebecca was secretly horrified, but she let it pass. 'A woman named Nuala Flaherty died on the moors. She was clothed in only a very thin gown and was found in the middle of a pentagram surrounded by a circle, which she had dug out of the heather and peat with a small dagger.'

Tabitha's eyes narrowed. 'A pentagram? Was the dagger an *athamé*?'

Rebecca stammered a little. 'I . . . I have no idea. I don't even know what an *athamé* is.'

'It's a ceremonial dagger used in rituals.'

'So we really are talking Satanic stuff here?'

'Not necessarily, but the presence of the pentagram does suggest something dark. The *athamé* is not a practical blade – you're not going to go all *West Side Story* with it, if you know what I mean – so if she used that to dig out the circle then it must have taken a great deal of effort. This woman must have been highly motivated. She must have felt she needed protection.'

Tabitha's interest in this was clear. Rebecca felt the excitement that ran through the woman reach across the table. 'Yes, but protection from what?'

Tabitha picked up her mug, moved to the sink and filled the kettle again. She clicked it on and turned back to Rebecca, her back against the worktop. 'There was an incident on Iona years ago, back in the 1920s, I think. A woman was found dead, much like this poor soul. She didn't dig a pentagram – it was a cross – but she did use an *athamé* because she believed she was under attack.' Tabitha paused. 'A psychic attack.'

'Okay,' was all Rebecca said, but she knew Tabitha caught her tone.

Tabitha closed her eyes, took a deep breath. 'I don't expect you to believe it, but you've asked so I'll tell you. The story was that she had fallen foul of black magicians.' She grimaced slightly when she saw Rebecca's eager expression. 'Yes' – the word was coming out as a sigh – 'Satanists. The point is, what happened on your island . . .'

'Stoirm.'

'Yes, what happened there has parallels in what occurred on Iona. What do you know about this poor woman?'

'Not much. She rented the cottage from someone who says she was a bit strange . . .'

Tabitha smiled. 'Aren't we all?'

'She had been on the island for two or three months, maybe more.'

The kettle switched itself off and Tabitha turned to drop a teabag into her mug. 'Why was she there? Had she moved? On an extended holiday?'

'No, she was asking about a group who have taken over a farm steading. They call themselves the Children of the Dell. Have you heard of them?'

Tabitha poured the water and stirred the bag. Agitating the tea, as Rebecca's mother would say. 'No, but that doesn't mean anything. There are a number of groups who flock to isolated areas. Most are harmless.'

'Most? Some are not?'

'Well, we don't have the militias in this country that they have across the pond, but we have our share of nutters.' She laid the spoon down and turned back to the table. 'I take it you want me to look into them?'

'Would you mind?'

'So you think there's some sort of occult network that I can tap into for information not normally freely available?'

'I don't know, is there?'

'Of course there is. I just wanted to know if you thought it.' Tabitha smiled. 'It's not so much a network, really, more a few private Facebook groups and a chatroom or two. We like to gossip as much as the next person.'

Rebecca smiled. She really liked this woman. Then she recalled someone else she had liked while on a story – that person had turned out to be a murderer. 'I'd appreciate your take on all this.'

Tabitha raised the mug and sipped. 'My take at this stage is that this poor woman felt under threat, tried to protect herself and died because of it.'

'Under threat like the woman on Iona?'

'Yes.'

'A psychic attack?'

'Yes.'

'So what are we talking about here? Some sort of demon?'

Tabitha stared at her for a moment, then swallowed a mouthful of tea, before she simply replied, 'Yes.'

Despite knowing Tabitha's beliefs, Rebecca had still expected her to dismiss that idea. 'Come on, Tabitha. Demons? Goblins? Things that go bump in the night?'

'You asked me, I've told you. That would be what she was fleeing – you said she ran away from her own cottage. Something occurred in there that sent her out into the cold, something that scared her so much that she believed she had to protect herself. She didn't pick up a heavy object, she didn't reach for a weapon of some kind or even a phone to call the police, so it's a fair guess, given the circumstances, that whatever it was frightening her was not of this dimension.'

Rebecca knew this story had that kind of angle but hearing it put into words seemed so unreal. Demons. Psychic attacks. It was all so unbelievable.

Tabitha recognised her struggle. 'Look, I know this sounds like madness, but my point is that if you believe in these things they can be very real.'

'So you don't believe that she was really threatened by a demon?'

'I don't know. I wasn't there.'

'Do you believe in them?'

Tabitha thought about this for a moment. She laid her mug down carefully then faced Rebecca again, leaning against the worktop and folding her arms. 'I have never – ever – experienced anything malevolent on a personal level. I've had feelings, yes. I've sensed something in the air, just as I did with you the other day. Did anything come of that, by the way?'

Rebecca shook her head and Tabitha remained silent for a moment as she gazed into the space between them, as if looking for an answer. Finally, she nodded but Rebecca could tell she remained concerned about whatever it was she had felt.

'That little boy, I knew, was in no danger from anyone,' Tabitha continued. 'He was lost, he was scared, but there was no malevolence. But that doesn't mean that evil does not exist in the world. We all know it does.'

Yes, it does, Rebecca thought. She had seen it herself.

'There are forces all around us that we don't understand, Rebecca. Deep, primal forces that surround us, occupying and moving within the space between the atoms. Psychic dark matter, if you will. I believe those forces, whatever they may be, can be tapped into and used, yes. But demons? Flesh and blood creatures that prey on us? No. I don't believe they do exist. Evil does exist, though, and those with the will and the knowledge can use the forces to do evil things.'

'So evil is a state of mind?'

Tabitha thought about it, then nodded. 'Yes, put very simplistically, I suppose it is.'

'What you're saying is that Nuala believed in demons, or whatever, and someone has perhaps used that against her?'

'Yes, that's one explanation.'

'Is there another?'

Tabitha picked up her mug once again. 'That I'm wrong . . . and demons do exist.'

Pat and Mike knew what Rebecca looked like, of course. Her photograph, along with all the personal information they needed – including her home and business addresses, the registration number, make and year of her car and even a list of close friends and their addresses – had been provided. In their business, there was no such thing as too much information, and although they didn't know everything they might wish, it was enough. They had left their chain hotel before sunrise to get to her flat and then followed her into the town centre, where she left her car in a car park on a side street near the railway station. Mike, who was driving, let Pat out to trail her to her office while he found a space. They wandered up and down Union Street, sometimes together, sometimes separately, but in contact by text if needed, until she left to walk to a hairdresser's shop on a lane that curved up the hill. They stationed themselves at the entrance to a shopping mall, managing to look inconspicuous with casual ease but still alert to all around them and also for her reappearance.

'Think she's getting her hair done?' Mike asked.

'She could do with it,' said Pat.

'Oooh, bitchy.' Mike smiled and received a sharp look from Pat.

'What? I'm no' supposed to notice when a lassie needs her hair done? And you could do with a trim yourself, by the way. Getting a bit mullety back there.'

Mike ran his fingers through his hair. 'I like it longer.'

Pat glanced towards the salon. 'If she is getting a do, we could be hanging around here for a while.'

Mike pulled his thick woollen coat closer to his body. 'Why is it always so cold in the sticks?'

'It's cold in Glasgow, too.'

'Aye, but it's different here, know what I'm saying? Maybe 'cos we're further north.'

Pat's head turned in his direction again. 'We're no' at the North Pole, Mike.'

'I know, I can tell that by the lack of polar bears. But it's still bloody freezing.'

Pat looked back the way they had come. 'There's a bakery down there. Go get a coffee and a sausage roll or something, that'll give you some central heating.'

Mike followed the direction of Pat's chin jut. 'Good idea, you want anything?'

'Aye, get me a cuppa and a roll and sausage, if they do them.'

'No' a sausage roll?'

'Naw, a roll and a sausage. And brown sauce.'

Mike nodded. 'Right, got it.' He didn't move straightaway, though.

'What's up?' Pat asked. 'You waiting for the money?'

Mike's eyes were fixed on where he had last seen the lassie. 'No. I was just thinking that she's awfy young.'

'So?'

'So, I don't like it that someone wants her dead. What is she? In her late twenties maybe? I mean, what can she have done that's so bad she needs to be taken out?'

Pat's mouth fixed in a straight line. 'It's no' our job to worry about things like that, you know that, Mike. We do what we're asked to do, no questions, no second thoughts.'

Mike knew that was how they had survived in this game for so long. Always delivering, always careful. He remained uneasy, but he would see the job through. 'I'll go get some scran,' he said. 'Cuppa tea and a sausage roll for you, right?'

'A roll and sausage,' Pat amended, the words carrying an irritated edge.

'Aye right, red sauce.'

'Brown sauce.'

Mike squinted, as if trying to remember. 'You said red sauce.'

'I said brown.'

'You sure?'

Pat's head shook. 'How long you known me, Mike?'

'Long time, Pat.'

'And have you ever – I mean, in all that time – have you ever heard me ask for red sauce on a roll and sausage, or a bacon roll, come to that?'

Mike tilted his head as he considered this. 'Naw, can't say I have.'

'Then why in the name of holy fuck would I want it now?'

Mike turned this over in his mind for a moment. 'I dunno. Variety?'

Pat's mouth opened, no doubt with a sharp comment but none came as realisation struck. 'You're winding me up, ya bastard.'

Mike couldn't contain his grin any longer. 'You're too easy, Pat.'

When Rebecca left Tabitha's salon, she passed Stephen Jordan's office and found herself in two minds about popping in to invite him to the wedding. It amused her to think that his place of business was on a street that bore his name, as if he had chosen the site specially. However, he had inherited the practice from his parents, and it had been established before he was born. Perhaps they named their son after Stephen's Brae. She hesitated just out of sight of the office door, little more than a slight hitch in her step, before she decided against it. She had never dropped in unannounced before and wondered if it would be seen as some sort of signal, one she was unsure she wanted to send. She liked him – he was handsome, in the way of one of those rugby players who had been good-looking before taking up the scrum and were now attractive in a somewhat battered way – and found herself wishing to see him, but now was not the time. Anyway, his receptionist had taken an instant dislike to her, and she didn't feel like running that single-woman gauntlet.

That's just an excuse, Becks.

The thought was her own, but it popped into her mind in her boss's voice. *Damn you, Elspeth McTaggart, for getting in my head.*

She was confused, she knew that. Contradictory thoughts and feelings pulled at her as she kept walking. She didn't want a firm relationship but there was something appealing about having one, especially after all this time. She didn't like the difference in their ages, but it was only a few years. She also didn't like the fact that Stephen was a solicitor, given she had been with Simon before – she didn't want to be seen as some kind of Law Society groupie. However, she liked his independence and the way he put no pressure on her at all.

Dear God, Becks, pick a position and stick with it!

It was cold but dry, the kind of day she really enjoyed, so she took a leisurely walk back to Union Street, stopping to look in shop windows as she went. She didn't have that much to do, workwise. The Tabitha piece was all but done, just a few paragraphs to add about her academic background. A couple of court reports, which she could rattle up in no time, so used was she now to the formula. And they were formulaic; most stories were. There was some research work for the TV production company in London, but nothing needed done until the following week, when she returned from the island.

The island.

She had vowed never to return, and perhaps going back was a bad idea, but she had no choice. She did believe that Sawyer was worrying unduly about the dangers she might face, although there was also Tabitha's dire warning that someone meant her harm. Rebecca was still sceptical about the whole hocus-pocus thing, but she was grudgingly coming round to the idea that some things cannot be explained and perhaps are not meant to be. Tabitha seemed pretty level-headed to her, had the least airy-fairy approach to the subject that Rebecca had ever experienced. And she had found that young boy.

Something crawled at the back of her neck and she stopped in her tracks to look back the way she had come. She didn't know why – all this talk of the supernatural getting to her, she supposed – but something was niggling at her. A mental shrug and she continued on her way.

She thought about Nuala. The island was beautiful and strange, a place where you could believe in other worlds. A place where creatures lived and sang in the heather and on the wind. Even she had heard – convinced herself she had heard – voices on the breeze both on Stoirm and elsewhere in the Highlands. She dismissed it as nonsense, naturally; ridiculous stories planted there by her own father, of all people, when she was a child. She had been born and raised in Glasgow. She went to university there. The city woman within was tough-minded and had little time for silly notions of magic and mysticism.

But then there was that other woman, the woman who shared the blood of her father and carried the tang of the sea in her veins and the song of the wind in her ears, the woman who longed to believe in something more.

Something prickled in that blood now and she stopped once again to look around her. She could not fix on what troubled her, she only knew that something did. It was something vague, elemental even, like a faint unsettling scent carried in the air but with no obvious source. Still, she saw nothing out of the ordinary. A woman veered around her, tutting at her standing on the pavement like a human round-about. A man with a dog crossed the street between traffic. A young woman waited outside a bakery, rocking a pram back and forth, its wheels screeching slightly.

Life in Inverness. Modern. Bright. Bustling. Nothing unusual. And yet . . .

Pull yourself together, Becks. All this hocus-pocus is getting to you.

She thrust the sensation from her mind and forced her thoughts onto Tabitha Haley. That she had somehow known the boy was trapped in that cellar could not be denied. She had somehow sensed his presence. And the vision had come while she was in her bath, steam-cleaning reality from her mind to let the psychic waves flow.

She made a mental note to remember that phrase, even though it needed work.

The Glasgow in Rebecca resolutely refused to accept the idea: second sight, what the islanders called the fey. Astral projection. These things cannot be. There had to be a logical explanation, though that did not matter for the story. The newspaper wanted a straightforward interview with Tabitha and that was what she would deliver. That was the job.

She had reached the top end of Union Street when that sense of something being off kilter hit her again. She had felt this before, when she had sensed that creep Martin Bailey was around. She clenched her fist as she scanned the street again but all she saw were shoppers, cars passing. Buses. Taxis. The rumble of a train pulling out of the station opposite. A middle-aged man and woman walking hand in hand. That's sweet, she thought, then realised she was being patronising. A child chasing a pigeon on the concourse between the entrance to the shopping mall and Station Square, his mother calling after him to stop. Two men in dark coats standing on the corner, one looking at a restaurant door, as if contemplating whether to go in for a late breakfast or an early lunch. All commonplace, everyday scenes of life on any city street. All very ordinary.

And yet, there was the feeling that someone was watching her.

One of the men looked in her direction, just briefly and probably wondering why this young woman was standing stock still and staring around her, then turned his attention back to his friend. The pigeon fluttered away, but not too far, and the little boy chased it again.

Rebecca shook her head, told herself she was letting all this talk of the occult get to her. She continued walking but still simply could not shake it off, and one of the few lines of Shakespeare she knew popped into her head.

By the pricking of my thumbs.

Absolute bollocks, said the Glasgow woman within her, you're letting your imagination run away with you.

The island woman inside knew, however. Something was coming.

Something wicked.

The Stoirm Hotel had been managed by a Sikh family, but they had moved back to the mainland and now it was run by an English couple who had yearned to escape the city and breathe the clear, clean air of the islands, much as Chaz's family had done when he was an infant. He had met only the woman, the small, bird-like Mandy Newcombe, who at first sight could have been mistaken for being shy and timid, but his mother told him she was a tough Geordie who could not only handle anything Portnaseil's more rambunctious element chose to throw at her, but could probably throw it back too. Chaz had met her the previous Sunday to discuss the booking of rooms for the wedding, and she'd struck him as being smart and business-like, with a mind like an adding machine. He had never met her husband, Bernie, a burly former oil worker, but had seen him from afar. He tended to look after the bar while Mandy handled reception and managerial duties for the hotel. The chef, a cousin of theirs, was in charge of the kitchen.

Mandy studied them across the reception desk as if they were selling religion door-to-door. They had described the woman they wished to speak to and received a nod in response. Chaz had hoped Mandy would provide a name but all they got was that nod.

'Is she still staying in the hotel?' Alan asked.

Mandy thought about this, perhaps turning over in her mind whether she was breaking any rules of the hotel trade. 'She is still registered with us.'

'Can you give us her room number?'

'No, I don't think so.'

'We just want to talk, Mandy,' said Chaz.

'I can't give you her room number. If she wanted you to have it, she would have given it to you.'

'We've never met,' said Alan.

'Even more reason not to, then.'

They were getting nowhere. 'Do you know if she's in the hotel right now?'

Another pause as she mentally flicked through the good hotelier's rule book. 'No, she went out.'

'I don't suppose you know where?'

Mandy's face was blank. 'No, I'm not in the habit of asking where guests are going.'

'Is it all right if we wait for her to return?' Alan asked, giving her his sweetest smile. Only Chaz knew it had been plastered there like paint over a damp patch of wall.

For a second Chaz thought Mandy was going to refuse permission but she waved across reception to two armchairs on either side of a low table. 'Help yourself, lads,' she said, her own smile unexpected. 'Can I get you some coffee or anything?'

Both Chaz and Alan were caught unawares. Of course, they did not think for a minute that the refreshment would be free but, given the frosty responses so far, even the offer of commercial hospitality was a surprise.

'Yes, thank you,' said Alan as they moved to the armchairs. Mandy gave them another broad smile – wonders never ceased – and vanished through the door behind her.

They settled themselves in the chairs. 'I think your friend Mandy is a complex individual,' said Alan.

'I've only met her once and she was all business then. Although she did give me a free coffee.'

'Any biscuits?'

'Of course! She's not a barbarian.'

Alan smiled as he leaned forward to pick up a tabloid-style magazine from the table and began flicking through the pages. He stopped at one page and said, 'Who are these Kardashians and what exactly have they done to merit all the attention they get?'

'Reality TV.'

'Oh, dear.' He studied the images on the page. 'They certainly do seem very pneumatic.'

'Healthy living,' said Chaz.

Alan squinted at the page. 'Yes, that will be it, I'm sure.'

Chaz glanced at the door, hoping they were not in for a long wait. 'So do you think this woman, whatever her name is, will talk to us?'

'I'm sure we can charm her.'

Chaz laughed. 'We?'

Alan was not noted for his charm. If you wanted acerbic wit, patronising comments and a tendency to pontificate, he was your man. To his credit, Alan recognised that. 'Fine, I'm sure you can charm her with that boyish Robert Redford thing you have going.'

'Who do you think she is?'

Alan continued to flick through the magazine pages. 'I have no idea. Obviously, Nuala knew her, unless she met her in the bar and struck up a conversation, which is always possible. Both outsiders, bonding over a cheeky chardonnay.'

'And Darren chatting them up – what do you think about that?'

'I would imagine he was on to a loser. That gentleman does not strike me as being particularly adept in the art of wooing.'

'Wooing?'

'Yes, wooing. I have a vocabulary and I'm not afraid to use it.'

Don't we know it, Chaz thought but kept it to himself. 'But what if Darren took the knockback badly. If Fiona is correct, he has access to drugs. What if he slipped Nuala something?'

Alan looked at him over the top of the magazine. 'Bit of a stretch, isn't it?'

'Just thinking aloud.'

'And how does it sound now that you've heard it?'

'Bit of a stretch, to be honest.'

Alan laid the magazine down. 'Just keep thinking, Butch, that's what you're good at.'

'So what do you think? Okay, we don't even know what caused the poor woman's death yet.'

'There's something dodgy about it. I mean, who goes out and about in the middle of the night with nothing on but a thin gown, carves a pentagram and then lies down and dies? That's not normal behaviour. Then we have the Children of the Dell, as creepy a place as I have ever been. Did you see them all, with their smiles?'

'They were just friendly, I thought.'

'No, that's more than friendly. That's a "hand me the Kool-Aid" level of creepiness. That's a "I'm off to divest myself of my garments and climb a mountain and await the rapture" level of creepiness. That's a . . .'

'Fine, I get it.' Chaz cut him off before he could develop his analogy even further. 'They're creepy. But if they're behind Nuala's death, how did they do it? You think there's something mystical going on?'

'Honestly? It's doubtful. As much as I get excited at the thought of the strange and esoteric coming into play, I just know that whatever this is about will be down-to-earth, mark my words.'

Alan fell silent as Mandy reappeared from behind the reception desk with a tray carrying two cups with matching sugar and milk bowls and a cafetière. She gave them another smile as she laid the tray down and made a point of resting a finger on the bill. 'There you go, lads. Just pay in the bar before you leave.'

The phone on the desk rang and she left them to answer it. Chaz watched as Alan depressed the plunger on the cafetière and began to pour, his partner's quote from *Butch Cassidy and the Sundance Kid* raising a question in his mind.

'You really think I have a boyish Robert Redford thing going?'

Alan handed him his cup. 'Not my words. Becks's.'

'Becks thinks I have a boyish Robert Redford thing going?'

Alan raised his cup to his lips. 'She toyed with the idea of there being something between you two when she first met you.'

This was news to Chaz. 'She did?'

'Very briefly. Until she discovered that you played for my team.'

Chaz sat back in the chair. 'I didn't know that. She told you?'

'I saw it in her face that first time she and I met, at the public meeting, remember? When you introduced me to her, it was there. You wouldn't notice because you never do, dear heart, and sometimes our darling Becks is not terribly skilled at hiding her thoughts.'

'You're right, I didn't notice it.'

'That's because you only have eyes for me. And who can blame you?'

Chaz grimaced. 'Yeah, keep telling yourself that. You'll do until someone better comes along.'

'There is nobody better. You hit the jackpot with me and you know it.'

Chaz agreed but it was something he would never ever tell Alan, mainly because he already knew it, but also because they did not indulge in overt displays of affection. The feelings they had for each other were deep and abiding and they had no need to put it into words or underpin it with meaningless romantic gestures. Valentine's Day came and went. Even birthdays were treated as just another day, apart from the customary greetings and a card, generally something insulting. Christmas was a time they both loved, and they did tend to splash out then, but never anything stupid. Nothing soppy, as Alan would say.

'I wish Becks could find someone,' said Chaz.

'Maybe she already has.'

'Stephen?'

They had met the solicitor on a number of occasions and they both liked him. He was the only person they had known her to go out with more than a couple of times.

Alan said, 'Have you noticed how she lights up whenever she's with him?'

'She does seem more relaxed, even happier. You think there's something more there?'

Alan nodded. 'Without a doubt. She doesn't know it, though, but as I said, she is not as adept at concealing her innermost desires as she thinks she is. Not from me, anyway.'

'You think he feels the same?'

'I really don't know. He's more difficult to read, to be honest.'

Chaz gave him a double-take. 'Good grief, I never thought I would live to hear you say there was something you don't know!'

'Make the most of it, it does not happen often.'

Inverness

Rebecca didn't know why she was nervous as she listened to the phone ringing. She was phoning a friend, after all. That's what Stephen was. A friend. Okay, maybe a little bit more. But she was phoning him for a chat, and she could feel the tension begin to tighten on the muscles of her shoulder and neck. What's that about?

'Hi.'

She had dialled his personal mobile number, not his office number. He always sounded delighted to hear from her – and why shouldn't he? She was delightful.

'Hi, how's it going?' she said. 'Not disturbing anything?'

She knew she wasn't disturbing anything. She'd spoken to him the night before and he said he was spending the day in the office on paperwork, with only a couple of clients to see. That was the most he had ever said about his work. She was honoured. They spoke every night – that was what friends did, right? Spoke often. Kept in touch. She spoke to Chaz and Alan regularly, Elspeth too. Fine, maybe not every night, but what was wrong if they did? Did it mean anything? No. Just friends being friends and keeping in touch. But she wasn't sleeping with her other friends, was she? That was different.

'No, glad of the break, to be honest,' said Stephen. 'Elaine is cracking the whip.'

She would like that, Rebecca thought. Elaine was his receptionist and office manager, and Rebecca often wondered if she had a secret yearning for her boss. That might explain why she really didn't like Rebecca, although the woman also shared Stephen's mistrust of the media.

Stephen said, 'So, what's the skinny?'

'What's the skinny?' She giggled. It was a release of nerves, but she actually giggled. What the hell was going on with her?

'Yes, as in, what's happening, what's going on, what's the score, or, as you're from Glasgow and you Weegies like a bit of rhyming slang, what's the Hampden roar?'

'Yeah' – her voice drier now as she kept the giggles in check – 'we generally just say, "what's the Hampden?" You teuchters just can't pull it off.'

'Ah well, I'll keep trying. Maybe one day I'll be sophisticated enough to use words that rhyme, rather than just say what I mean.'

'You'll never be that sophisticated.' She took a deep breath. Here we go. 'Listen, there's something I need to ask you.'

'Sounds serious.'

'No, not really.' She swallowed. This is ridiculous, Becks, why are you making this so difficult? She and Stephen had been going out for a while now. She had seen him naked and everything. She had an old friend in Glasgow, Sophia, and she could hear her voice in her head saying, *Pull yourself the hell together, Becks, and get yourself sorted.* She pulled herself the hell together. 'You know Chaz and Alan are getting married this weekend, right?'

'Yes.'

'Well, I was wondering, and feel free to say no, but I was wondering if you'd like to come. With me. As my plus-one.'

He didn't reply immediately.

'I mean, I know it's maybe short notice . . .'

'I can't, Becks.'

The words hit her like a slap. Despite her trepidation, she thought he would simply say yes. Friends said yes. Yet he hadn't. 'Okay,' she said, and even she heard the disappointment in her voice. Get a grip, Becks.

'I've got a family thing. I think I told you it was my sister's anniversary.'

Damn it! He *had* said that, although it had slipped her mind. She closed her eyes and cursed herself for not remembering. All this build-up for nothing. It was like watching a TV thriller show for weeks then feeling let down in the final episode. She wondered why she put herself through it.

'That's okay,' she said. 'I'd forgotten about that – no worries.'

'Sorry, Rebecca,' he said, and he sounded as if he meant it, which went some way to assuaging her self-recrimination, but she still needed to end this call. Something stung behind her eyes. Allergies, she decided, probably some new product the office cleaner used.

'Listen,' she said, her voice just a little cracked, 'I need to go. Places to be, people to see.'

'Sure,' he said. 'But listen, sorry again, I can't miss this. Family, eh?'

'Seriously, it's not a problem. But I really need to go, speak later.'

'Sure.'

She clicked off, feeling she had been a bit abrupt, but that damned stinging was making her eyes water.

The Island of Stoirm

They had waited about half an hour before they saw the woman enter the hotel, unbuttoning her thick sheepskin coat to reveal clothes that were more casual than the suit she had worn in the restaurant on Monday evening. Chaz wondered if perhaps she liked to dress for dinner. Even so, everything about her screamed money. Her black jeans, black knee-length boots and white blouse no doubt carried designer labels that might have been familiar to Chaz but about which he cared very little. Her hair dangled over the collar of the thick coat, framing her narrow face and the brown eyes that studied them with suspicion as they approached. The boxy, black leather bag with a silver chain draped across the front was crooked in one arm. All smart, all carefully casual, and, added together, she was probably wearing the equivalent of a small independent state's national debt.

'Excuse me,' Alan said, 'sorry to disturb you, but I wonder if we might have a chat.'

He had donned his friendliest of smiles and, when the woman looked from him to Chaz, he made sure he sported his best boyish Robert Redford grin. He was a bit self-conscious about that now – he had always visualised himself in the Brad Pitt mould – so he hoped it looked natural.

The woman did not smile back, which was not hopeful, but then why should she when two strange men were accosting her in a hotel reception? She flicked her eyes at Mandy, who was watching from behind the desk. Chaz assumed the owner's presence and lack of alarm allowed her to relax a bit, but there was still a hint of caution in her voice.

'Who are you?' English accent. Not a surprise, really. Nuala was also English, and they seemed to have known each other.

'My name is Alan Shields, and this handsome young man is Chaz Wymark,' said Alan. 'We're not selling anything, don't worry. We'd like to talk to you about poor Nuala.'

There was not even a hint of surprise in her face, as if she had been expecting it. 'You're not police, though.'

'No, we're not police.'

'Then what's your interest?'

'I'm a journalist,' said Chaz, before Alan could lie.

'And there's a story in Nuala, right?'

'Yes, there is.' Chaz recalled Rebecca's view that it is often best to be honest about these things. *We can dress up our interest as much as we like, but people aren't stupid.*

Again, no surprise. Just a slight nod, although Chaz didn't know if it meant she agreed or if it was merely that he had confirmed her suspicion. 'Why?'

'Why do I think it's a story? Being blunt about it, this is unusual – the manner of Nuala's death, I mean.'

Something flickered in the woman's eyes, pain perhaps. 'Nuala had a weak heart.' Chaz saw Alan's eyebrow rise, as if that explained everything. 'I think perhaps it just gave out.'

'But why?' Alan asked. 'Had she not taken her medication? And what made her go out onto the moor on a freezing cold night? What do you think happened, Mrs . . . ?'

Alan had let the question of her name dangle, but she did not pick it up. 'I don't know,' she said. 'I wish I did. She knew it was weak and had to be careful.' She paused, then said, 'I'm not sure I want to talk to the media.'

'We're simply looking into it. You won't be quoted without your permission.' Chaz had no idea if he could make that promise, but he could bend the truth as quickly as Alan. 'We

just want some background. At the moment, she is just a name, a tragedy. By doing a story we can help make her a person.'
Again, he had heard Rebecca use that argument in the past. He wasn't sure if he was able to sell it quite as well as she could, even with his boyish Robert Redford charm. 'You knew her well, didn't you?'

He could tell she debated answering but finally said, 'Yes, we were at school together.'

'Don't you think she deserves to have whatever happened investigated?'

She looked from Alan back to Chaz and then over to Mandy, who was watching the conversation and could obviously hear every word. The woman appeared to reach a decision and looked at her watch. 'I'm hungry,' she said. 'I think we should go into the bar. Let me eat and then we can talk.'

Before they could say anything further, she walked off towards the restaurant and bar. Chaz and Alan followed.

'Don't forget to pay for your coffees, lads,' said Mandy, but when Chaz looked back, her head was bowed over the computer terminal.

The bar was empty, which came as a relief to Chaz because he had felt some concern that Darren might be there with whatever mates he had. He had learned that showing fear was never a good idea, but neither was finding himself in such company unwittingly. Nine out of ten times they were satisfied with looks and sneers. But then there was that one out of ten, the one that can turn nasty.

He felt the pain again in his leg and side.

He saw the windscreen wipers sweeping furiously, back and forward, back and forward. The monolithic shard of rock jutting from the shore as his Land Rover left the road and flew through the air. The engine screaming – or was it him? – as he twisted the wheel, as if that would make a difference.

Laughter. Fading. The youths in the other vehicle speeding away.

The wipers. Still working. Back and forward. Back and forward. Back . . .

He closed his eyes briefly to blot the memories out, but when he opened them again he saw Alan staring at him, his features not revealing the concern that shadowed his eyes. He always sensed when Chaz was transported back to that night. Alan had been uninjured in the smash, which was a miracle, and there was some measure of guilt, even though he had no reason to feel that way. Chaz had been driving, and the way they had skidded from the road at speed in wet weather meant that he had taken the brunt of the impact. He had walked with a stick for over a year afterwards and had been unwilling to get behind the wheel of a car, and certainly not whenever it rained. These moments, the memory of the pain and that night, were less common now, but Alan had previously voiced concerns that something would trigger it again when they returned to the island. However, familial duty superseded that consideration and, anyway, memories can't cause lasting hurt. The pain he felt now was only a phantom, the echo of a sensation from the past.

The TV bracketed to the wall was on and Bernie, Mandy's husband, leaned over the bar as he watched the BBC News channel. He nodded to them as they entered and smiled, waving a hand at the empty tables and chairs. 'Afternoon, folks, we're a bit busy as you can see, so just sit down where you can. I'll come over and take your order.'

They gave him a smile and ignored the seating in the small bar to step down into the lounge area. Should any locals come in for a lunchtime tipple or a bar meal, they were more likely to shun this space. It was for visitors. True islanders crammed into the bar, sometimes standing shoulder-to-shoulder. Through the open door that led to a small entranceway, Chaz saw a woman, her hair grey, her body wrapped in a thick padded jacket and denims, standing at the payphone fixed on the wall. He felt he had seen her before but couldn't quite place where. She had a yellow Post-it in one hand, and the other rested on the phone, but she didn't make any move to pick it up. She became aware of them behind her and glanced over her shoulder, her face reflecting a sudden alarm. Chaz gave her a reassuring smile as he followed Alan and Nuala's friend down the two steps into the lounge.

They settled at a table and the woman shrugged the heavy sheepskin from her shoulders and draped it over the spare chair, but she kept the bag resting on her lap. She plucked the cardboard menu from where it was propped up between the salt and pepper shakers and scanned it. Chaz realised he was also hungry and when she proffered it he took it, even though he had already decided a cheese and ham toastie was in his immediate future. Bernie appeared, a small notebook in his hand, and he took their order – the woman ordered a ploughman's and Alan fell in step with Chaz. The woman also ordered a large gin and tonic, while Chaz and Alan went with bottled water.

As Bernie left them, the woman waited for a moment before she said, 'So what do you want to know?'

'Perhaps we could start with your name?' Alan asked.

'Cynthia Danvers.'

'Mrs Danvers? As in *Rebecca*?'

She nodded as if she had heard that comment before, which she no doubt had, then gave him a quizzical look. 'How did you know I was married?'

'Wedding ring.'

She looked down at her left hand resting on the lip of her handbag, as if she had forgotten about the gold band nestling beside an engagement ring with a diamond large enough to be seen from space.

'May we call you Cynthia?' Chaz asked, and she nodded her permission. 'I'm Chaz Wymark; this is Alan Shields.'

'And you are both journalists?'

'I'm a photographer, but I'm doing some work for a news agency.' He did not add that the work was more than likely unpaid.

Her gaze dropped to his hands. 'You don't have a notebook.'

'Ah, sorry,' he said and rummaged in his jacket pocket for the small black notebook he used to record the names of people in photographs. This was not his trade – he dealt with the visuals, not the words – but he supposed he should play the part.

Cynthia looked at Alan. 'And you work in pairs?'

'I'm his minder,' Alan said.

Her eyes flicked him up and down, and some amusement crept in. 'You don't seem quite burly enough for that.'

'Looks can be deceiving. Underneath this studious, boyish exterior lies a crouching tiger.'

'Alan is my partner,' said Chaz, the words somehow sounding like an apology.

She nodded as if she had already guessed as much. 'What do you want to know?'

'What can you tell us about Nuala? Why was she on the island, for instance?'

Cynthia was silent for a moment, then inhaled sharply and let her words carry on the exhale. 'She needed a break. She needed to get away from home for a time.'

'And home is where?'

'Cheshire.'

Chaz recalled Miss Walker saying that Nuala had mentioned Chigwell, but her memory had seemed hazy. Could it have been Cheadle?

They fell silent as Bernie appeared in the doorway leading from the bar carrying a small tray with their drinks. He set them on the table and said, 'Food won't be long.'

They thanked him and he stepped away, tossing the tray in the air like a baton and catching it with ease, a man obviously happy with his work. Somewhere a phone began to ring and, as he stepped up into the bar room, he veered to the left, heading for the entranceway. Chaz glanced out the window and saw the grey-haired woman he'd spotted at the phone hurrying across the car park then vanishing behind the Police Scotland incident van parked outside.

Alan asked, 'What was your relationship to Nuala?'

'We are' – she stopped to amend the tense – 'were friends. Close friends.'

'And you came here to visit?'

'Yes, I'm due to leave at the end of the week. After what happened – with Nuala – I would have left before now, but I didn't think it right, somehow. You know, just to go home, with her lying dead somewhere.' She raised her gin and tonic to her lips and sipped it. 'I think I may head home soon, though.' She looked out to the small car park, her gaze resting for a moment on the police vehicle then moving beyond it to the road that rose from Portnaseil up to the Spine.

'It's a beautiful place but it's tainted now.' She returned her attention to them. 'Does that make sense?'

'Of course,' said Chaz. 'When did you see her last?'

The woman blinked three times in rapid succession. 'The night she died. I'd rented a car from a man who has a car workshop, a Mr Drummond?' Chaz nodded to acknowledge she had the right name. 'I drove out to her cottage.'

So Cynthia Danvers was perhaps the last person to see her alive. Chaz wondered if she was being economical with the truth when she said she had felt it best to stay. Perhaps Rory Gibson, or the plainclothes officer, had asked her not to leave the island for a few days.

'And how was she?'

She sought the correct word. 'Agitated, I think you would say.'

'Do you know why?'

Bernie appeared with the food on a larger tray. 'Here you go,' he said as he laid the plates before them. 'Enjoy.'

They thanked him again and he left them, but there was no toss of the tray this time. Cynthia stared at the baguette stuffed with cheese, tomato and lettuce as if her eyes had been bigger than her belly. She still had her handbag clutched on her lap like a security blanket.

'Why was Nuala agitated, Cynthia?' Chaz asked again.

Her fingers tightened on the bag. 'Nuala didn't choose this island by accident for her break. She had a reason.'

'She had an interest in the Children of the Dell,' said Chaz, picking up one half of his toastie, then biting into it. He didn't realise how hungry he was until he felt the hot cheese on his tongue.

Cynthia's eyebrows shot up. 'You know about that?'

Chaz chewed and nodded as Alan stepped into the breach. 'Why was she so interested in them, Cynthia?'

'She believed the group and the Sanctuaries are nothing more than a scam to relieve gullible people with wealth of their money. They use spirituality as a front, offering respite and haven from the pressures of life in return for giving up all their assets. They say the money goes towards keeping the Sanctuaries open – and good works in developing nations – and some of it does. But Nuala had come to believe that the bulk of it went into the pockets of the people behind it all.' She reached out for her food at last. 'She wouldn't tell me much – she could be very tight-lipped when she wanted to be. I knew she was looking into the Children, I knew she was obsessed with them, and I knew that she was close to getting something.'

'But you don't know what that something was?'

She cut the baguette in half with the knife provided. 'No, she didn't say. To be honest, I didn't ask. It was Nuala's obsession, not mine, but I took the view that if it kept her mind occupied it could only be a good thing.'

'Why did her mind need to be occupied?'

She laid the half baguette down and sat back, gathering her thoughts, or debating whether to reply. Finally, the words came out as if being forced. 'Nuala can be . . . could be . . . was emotionally naive. I recognised that very early in our friendship. Did you ever see her at all?'

Only in death, Chaz thought, but chose not to express it. He shook his head.

'She was a beautiful girl,' Cynthia Danvers went on. 'I mean, really beautiful, and she drew men like moths to a flame. Even here. There was a young man who had begun to pester her.'

'Darren Yates?'

'I don't know his name, I only saw him once, in the restaurant here, but she said he had gone out to her cottage a couple of times. But he was too young for her and there was something unpleasant about him, I thought.'

You bet there is, Chaz thought, filing this information away.

'But that's the way it was with Nuala. Men just automatically fell for her. I was the less attractive friend and sometimes I'd pick up her cast-offs, but she had a habit of falling in love very easily, too easily, and often not wisely. More than once, when we were teenagers, I had to pick up the pieces. She'd had tragedy in her life – her partner died a few years ago – and she'd had a few disastrous liaisons since. Men just saw the package, you see, and didn't realise what was inside was a mess. She was getting over one such disappointment and she felt she needed to get away.'

'What sort of disappointment?' Alan asked.

Cynthia looked uncomfortable and she shook her head. 'It doesn't matter. The point is, she felt she had to get away. She already had this Children of the Dell bee in her bonnet, so she came up here. The island's mysticism also appealed.'

'She was a . . . what?' Alan asked. 'Wiccan? Pagan?'

'We don't label ourselves, Mr Shields. "The Sisterhood" is as far as we go.'

That surprised Alan. 'You share her beliefs?'

'If I do, would that surprise you?'

'Well,' said Alan, obviously struggling to express himself, which was such an unusual occurrence that Chaz was glad he was there to witness it. 'You don't look . . . em . . .'

A smile began to ghost her eyes and haunt the corners of her mouth. 'I don't look what?'

'New Age-y,' said Alan, somewhat lamely Chaz thought.

'That was Nuala's style, not mine. I prefer stylish clothing, while she was the more obvious of all the Sisters. She enjoyed playing the part. She liked the kaftans and the chanting and the burning of incense. But there is more to being in the Sisterhood than that.'

'For instance?'

'A belief in the natural world; that there are elements of life that are, well, elemental; that it's not all about pounds and pence and what they can buy.' She caught Chaz's eyes dropping to the handbag on her lap and the ring on her finger. 'Yes, I know. I wasn't as into it as Nuala. I like my Givenchy bag and my Gucci watch. I like nice clothes and I like to look good, and I can afford it. I don't see that as a crime or a disgrace.'

'So you don't fully buy into it?'

'No, it was fun, that was all.'

'So apart from being in the Sisterhood,' Chaz asked, 'what drew you to Nuala?'

'Opposites attract, I suppose. I had known her since our teens, we were at school together and we bonded. She was that weird girl in class, beautiful, but the one that nobody wanted to go near, the girls anyway. I found her fascinating. I suppose there was something of a crush there, adolescent hormones being what they are, not that we ever experimented with lesbianism.' She considered her next words. 'The thing was, she didn't try to make anything of her looks. I do what I can with what I've got, but with Nuala it seemed effortless, and I was envious of her ability to be so attractive without seeming to work at it. As I said, I basked in her glow for a time, until I found my own way. Then we left school, adulthood brought its pressures and we drifted apart for a few years. I got married. Then she reappeared in my life, and we reconnected.'

'And she joined the Sisterhood?'

'She *formed* the Sisterhood, drawing women from our village and a couple of others nearby. Even when we were kids she was fascinated by the occult and enticed us into dabbling – you know, séances in candlelight, experimenting with spells and incantations. I grew out of it, but Nuala had obviously bought into it all, and when we reconnected she said she wanted to start a woman's occult group. I went along with it. As I said, it was fun.'

'And the other Sisters? How many are there?'

'Half a dozen, but it fluctuates. We never reached coven proportions, not that we were interested in all that. Apart from Nuala, none of us take it that seriously. Personally, I think much of it is mumbo-jumbo, but being in the Sisterhood was an opportunity to get together with other women, have some fun, drink some wine and let our hair down.'

'So you don't cast spells or do whatever is done at these things?' Alan asked.

'Oh yes, but we never know if they work! Frankly, it's all suggestion, isn't it? Smoke and mirrors. Incantations, chanting, this and that, but in the end when the incense clears, things are the same as they were before. But believers convince themselves that they have made a difference, that they have changed something in their lives, in the world.'

'Nuala believed all of that?'

'Oh yes, she was really into it, and our lack of commitment pissed her off at times. She would often become quite incensed – no pun intended – by our levity. She felt we were betraying the gods, or the craft, or something. She would lecture us all about squandering the powers that nature had given all women.'

'Is that why she focused on the Children of the Dell?' Chaz asked. 'If they are fleecing people, did she see that as some kind of a betrayal?'

'Yes. She didn't like the idea of someone using the one thing she loved to cause harm.'

Alan said, 'But if it's rich people who are stupid enough to part with their cash, where is the harm?'

'Rich people can't be victims – is that what you're saying?'

'No, but it's not as if the food is being snatched from their mouths and their children being thrown on the streets. And we've seen Sanctuary. It's pretty comfortable, and they seem happy. It's creepy, certainly, but if they want to hole up there, surely it's up to them?'

'Well, that's what I said, but Nuala pointed out that these people were expected to sign over everything to the Children. So, perhaps, children could end up on the streets as inheritances vanished overnight. She felt there was evil there and was determined to find out what it was.'

'Evil as in wrongdoing, or evil as in an actual entity?'

'She believed it existed, that the only thing that is pure are the forces of nature that are within us and surround us all.' A small smile then. 'Like the Force in *Star Wars*. I said that once, and she was not pleased. She accused me of belittling the natural world, that these forces were very real and could be dangerous. In Nuala's eyes, humanity was not pure, and those forces could be harnessed for good and for evil, depending on the individual's intent.'

Chaz asked, 'And what do you think of the pentagram she carved?'

'You know about that?' Chaz nodded but didn't amplify, and Cynthia Danvers didn't ask. 'I don't know what to make of it, to be perfectly honest. She was agitated when I was with her, but then Nuala could be like that. Nervy, jumpy, if you know what I mean. Her attention could be flighty, flitting from one thing to another even in mid-sentence. Apart from that, she seemed fine. We chatted, shared a cup of tea – I was driving and she didn't drink. Or smoke. She took care of herself.'

'She didn't talk about the Children of the Dell?'

'Just that she was confident of a breakthrough.'

'What kind of breakthrough?'

'She said someone on the inside was going to find something that would link them with God-knows-what. I assumed that was the cause of her agitation.'

'But she didn't say what that link might be?'

A shake of the head. 'No. To be honest, I didn't much care.' Her brow puckered slightly, as if something had occurred to her. 'You might try her spell book.'

Alan asked, 'Her what now?'

'Her spell book. It's where she kept a record of the rituals and spells she had performed or cast, but she also used it as a diary. Nuala wrote everything down – how she was feeling, who she spoke to, what she did, her medication, even what she ate. I've never read it, but the chances are her writing style will be the same as her mental state – all over the place, jumping from one subject to another. If she wrote the person's name down anywhere, it would be in there.'

*

202

Delia had walked from Portnaseil up the hill towards the parish churchyard and now hesitated at the drystone dyke separating the old graveyard from the road. To anyone passing, she had only paused to catch her breath and perhaps take in the view of the blue waters of the Sound and the mainland rising beyond it, lit by the final rays of the low winter sun. From this elevation, she could see the unmistakable bulk of the last ferry of the day making its way away from the island. She could also feel the bite of the breeze on her nose as it rose from the chilly waters.

She wasn't here to take in the view, though, and there was more to her hesitation than composing herself after the steep climb. Just beyond the kirkyard was the dark stone bulk of the manse. It looked forbidding, a throwback to when the island church was more glare than welcome. It was different now, of course, Delia knew that, even though she had never met Fiona McRae, the minister. The Sister had, however. Nuala, she amended. She had to stop thinking of her as the Sister – that was the Sanctuary way, and by the thoughts she'd harboured and the actions she had already taken, as well as those she was about to take, she had left that way behind her.

Even with that in her mind, she knew what she about to do was a major step. She took a deep breath, her hand slipping into the pocket of her thick jacket to close around the hard plastic of the thumb drive and the phone Nuala had given her. She had no way of knowing whether the numbers she had pulled were important, and perhaps the minister could help, even if only to tell her that she had nothing to be concerned about. But something in her gut told her that was not the case. There was something rotten at the heart of the Children of the Dell.

Time to decide, Delia. Either follow this through or go back to Sanctuary and try to make the best of things. Or pack your bags and leave. They won't try to stop you. Unless they suspect something. And by 'they', she meant Seb. When it came to the Sister – to Nuala – she had seen a different side to him, just flickers of the man below the smile.

No, she was too far down the rabbit hole now. Moving forward was the only way, whether for good or ill. She began to walk to the manse gate, hoping Fiona McRae was at home.

Inverness

Rebecca was having trouble handling Stephen's knockback. Yes, she should have remembered his sister's anniversary – he had told her – and could have saved herself a lot of internal debate over whether to ask him to the wedding. She was still disappointed, though: bitterly disappointed, if truth be told, and that puzzled her. *What's going on with you, Becks?*

Her PC bleeped that she had a Skype call, and Elspeth's name flashed up. Rebecca forced a slight smile as she clicked open the app and saw her boss. Her hair was combed this time and there was no shapeless blue dressing gown.

'Hi,' said Rebecca, trying to keep the dull edge from her voice and not quite making it. She hoped Elspeth wouldn't catch it.

'You okay?' Elspeth had caught it.

'Yes, all fine.' Rebecca forced lightness into her voice. *What the hell, Becks? It's not the end of the world.* Then why did she feel something hollowing out her guts?

Elspeth nodded her acceptance and leaned into the screen. 'Listen, I've remembered where I heard of the Children of the Dell before. I had to make a few calls, but it's all come back to me now.'

'Okay, where?'

'A few years ago, it was. Just a mention, but it's one of those names that sticks in the memory. Well, in mine, at any rate.'

'So what was it?'

'Do you remember the case of Sam Walters?'

'No, should I?'

'Maybe not, you would still have been in uni. He was a free-lance journalist down south, investigative stuff mostly. Wrote a couple of books, was on telly and radio now and again. He was a friend of a friend of a friend of a colleague, that sort of thing. I heard some of the details through an NUJ pal down there.'

'The name doesn't ring any bells. What about him?'

'He was found dead one day, in some woods outside Manchester. It looked like suicide but there was no note, no signs beforehand of any deep depression, although he did have some issues.'

'Don't we all?' Rebecca observed.

'Speak for yourself, dear. The coroner recorded an open verdict. Anyway, he was working on a few things at the time – something to do with the security services being involved in protecting a member of the cabinet from some scandal or other, another about a cover-up regarding widespread abuse in care homes. And, way down the list, he was looking into the Children of the Dell.'

Rebecca felt the thrill of curiosity fill the void in her stomach. 'Really?'

'Yes, indeedy. His partner was never convinced that he killed himself, refused to accept the open verdict.'

'She thought he was murdered, I'll bet.'

'Yes.'

'And do you know what he'd found out?'

'No, that was never released. From what I could glean, he had only been on it for a short while. But listen, this guy was good – I mean, really good. He could find out in a few days what would take others weeks. Even us.'

'But these other stories sound big; surely one of them was more likely to lead to murder?'

205

'You'd think so and you'd probably be right. Except for one thing.'

'What?'

Rebecca felt the familiar tingle grow at the back of her neck. It was the same as the one she felt when she thought someone was watching her. It had told her something was coming. It told her that now.

'His partner was Nuala Flaherty.'

Mo Burke stared across the table at the man juddering before her and marvelled at the changing nature of the world. Mobile phones had been large and unwieldy when they first appeared and grew gradually smaller as the years passed: she used to have one that fitted in the palm of her hand like Little Jenny Wren. Then, as technology grew, so did the phones, to accommodate the various bells and whistles people demanded. They weren't as large as they once were, nor as heavy – she remembered her man braining a guy with his brick-like mobile. Try doing that with the lightweight units they carried now. They were vital, though, for day-to-day life.

Touts weren't so useful, and she supposed they had changed, too, at least the way they were labelled. Way back when, the police would have called the twitching man in front of her an informant, but that was shortened to grass, snake, squealer. Then came CI, for Confidential Informant, and now it had grown even further to Covert Human Intelligence Source, or CHIS.

She called them clypes, a word from her childhood meaning tattle-tale, and she despised them, even though she recognised they had their uses. Cokey himself had been used by first Tony then her, to help them remove people who had proved inconvenient but who were not worth the trouble of damaging in any way. They would have Cokey drop a few words to a copper like Sawyer, provide some evidence to help corroborate and let justice run its course.

As she had walked away from the tower the day before, she had turned her mind to the source of the whispers about her. It had been an easy journey to reach the conclusion that Cokey Irvine was the piece of slime who had carried tales to Bill Sawyer. She had no evidence, but she wasn't a lawyer. She knew it was him, and that was good enough.

She had been surprised when he twitched his way into Barney's, but then she reasoned that it was the smart thing to do. Had he avoided the place altogether he might have raised suspicions. Of course, he didn't know that she had already decided it was his flappy little tongue that had been whispering in the former cop's ear. She had been in her usual corner, watching him as he bought his pint and moved to an empty table. He even gave her a wee nod as he passed, cheeky bugger. She had discussed the possibility that Cokey had outlived his usefulness with some of the boys, and all it would take was a nod from her. Nothing would happen in the bar itself because there were straight arrows present and you could never tell what they would do in such a situation, but three of the boys had positioned themselves in a semi-circle around Cokey's table. They didn't look at him at all, didn't even speak to him. It was all very casual, natural even. He saw them coming, of course, but he was canny enough to know there wasn't much he could do about it. He wasn't stupid, Mo knew that; he would know what was happening but would also know there was no point in heading for the door because her boys would intercept him and politely, but firmly, invite him to stay. She watched him calculate those odds but then resign himself to bluffing it out.

Then one of the boys began to whistle the song 'Whispering Grass' and at that point Cokey would have known his goose was cooked and Mo was sharpening the carving knife. His bones jolted like a string puppet whose operator was having a fit.

Mo slid into the chair opposite him and lit up. She didn't say anything, just sat there, the cigarette in one hand while she twirled her gold lighter between the fingers of the other then tapped it on the tabletop. As his nerves frayed, Cokey's convulsions increased to such a degree that he could barely lift the pint to his lips without spilling it. She was impressed when he managed it, though, and he took a long swallow, perhaps hoping the beer would calm his electric nerves. It didn't.

He raised a trembling hand to his lips and wiped the excess froth away, then forced a smile, but it had no grip and tumbled away. 'How's it going, Mrs Burke?'

She didn't reply. Her gaze didn't waver, her only movement the occasional drag on the tip of her fag and, of course, the tap and twirl of the lighter. His eyes were drawn to the movement and he watched with fascination, as if it was a particularly impressive move, even though to her it was only a flick of the wrist and a twist of the fingers. He reached out for his glass again but seemed to think better of it when he saw the palsied shake had grown worse.

'You've been talking out of school, Cokey, old son,' she said at last, and his eyes swivelled to her face.

'Me? Naw, Mrs Burke, I wouldn't . . .'

'Don't speak, Cokey, just listen. I know you like to run off at the mouth to that bent bastard Bill Sawyer, and while I find it fucking reprehensible – I mean, where's the honour in this world? – I don't really care. Until you start running off at the mouth about me and my business. Then I do care – especially when you're telling lies.'

His head shook, though whether it was his nervous condition or in denial she wasn't sure. He looked like he was going to say something, but she raised the hand holding the cigarette between them. 'Don't talk, Cokey, I told you.' He watched the smoke drift off the tip to the ceiling, his eyes wistful, as if he was wishing he could float away with it. 'Here's the thing. I did consider sending you back to him to tell him that you'd got it all wrong – which you have, by the way. I don't know what you heard, or think you heard, or just made up, but you are as wrong as a wrong person can be. Anyway, I thought about getting you to tell him that, but the damage is done, you see what I'm saying? He wouldn't believe a word of it.'

She drew in a lungful of smoke, held it for a moment, then released it. 'I can't let this go, you know that, don't you?' She waited for a reply, but his body did the talking for him. 'You know physics, Cokey? Newton's Third Law?' She waited again for a response, but Cokey still couldn't speak. His eyes darted to the three boys at her back, all sitting casually, no eyes in his direction, but he would know they were listening. And waiting. Cokey was a rat bastard clype, but he knew the score. 'My boy told me about it years ago,' Mo continued. 'Nolan, you mind him, right, Cokey? My boy, Nolan?'

She couldn't see Nolan. It was as if even her memory of him didn't want to be part of this.

'Newton's Third Law states that for every action there is an equal and opposite reaction. That's what's happening here. This is my reaction to your action. You flap your gums, and I show my extreme displeasure. Now, here's what's going to happen. You're going to go with my lads here, downstairs, where they'll have a wee word with you, make you see the error of your ways. Don't worry, you're not going to meet your maker, but I do want you to repent, Cokey. Your days of telling people anything, even if someone stops you in the street to ask for directions, are over. Got it?'

Cokey nodded, then stammered, 'Mrs . . . Mrs . . . Burke . . .'

She raised her hand again and waved it in front of his face, the smoke zig-zagging behind her fingers. 'Ah-ah! No' a word,

Cokey. Go with the lads and take your medicine. You've had a good run, old son. You've got away with clyping for years. But it's all over now, okay?'

Whether or not it was okay mattered nothing to her. What mattered was that a message be sent out on the street. Mo Burke was not to be messed with. Anyone who did would be dealt with. She sat back and gave her boys the nod. The three rose from their chairs and stepped closer to Cokey, who shrank back, his body jerking with increasing violence.

As she looked over his head into the mirrored wall behind him, she saw Nolan's reflection staring sadly back at her.

The Island of Stoirm

Chaz and Alan thanked Cynthia Danvers for her time and headed to the hotel car park. Although it was unspoken between them, they knew what they had to do next.

Chaz dialled the number PC Rory Gibson had given them in the restaurant and it was picked up on the fourth ring.

'Rory, it's Chaz. How you doing, mate?'

'I'm okay. You having trouble with Darren again?'

'No, nothing like that. It's about Nuala Flaherty . . .'

'You know I can't tell you anything.'

'No, but I can tell you something, or at least ask you. Do you know anything about a' – Chaz hesitated to use the words 'spell book', as it felt somehow alien to him – 'about any sort of diary?'

'Nuala's diary?'

'Yes, sort of.'

'She kept a diary?'

'Yes.'

'How do you know?'

'We spoke to Cynthia Danvers.'

Rory fell silent. 'She didn't mention a diary to me.'

'Well, she told us. You didn't see it when you searched the cottage?'

The line fell silent as the police officer considered the implications of answering Chaz's question. 'No.'

'But if it was lying in plain view, you would have taken it?'

'Yes, we would have seized it.'

Seized it. Police jargon was so manly. 'So that means it must still be in the cottage.'

'Maybe,' said Gibson, his guarded tone resonating in Chaz's mind, which was already itching. Cynthia Danvers had said something, he didn't know what, that had tickled at his memory, but he couldn't reach in and scratch it.

'You think there's more to Nuala's death, don't you?'

'The death is still under investigation.' Rory was being cagey, a skill handed to police officers on their first day. 'We're down at the south end right now. We'll get to the cottage in an hour or so and have a look.'

'Okay.'

The call ended and Alan pursed his lips. 'So we have done our civic duty. What now, Butch?'

'Shouldn't I be Sundance?'

'Don't quibble. What's our next step?'

Chaz was considering that when his mobile rang. He thought it might be Rory calling back, but the read-out told him it was Fiona McRae. He clicked on the hands-free again.

'Fiona, everything okay?' He exchanged a look with Alan, both thinking the same thought, that there was something wrong with the wedding plans.

'It's nothing about Saturday,' Fiona said, hurriedly, as if she had some sort of telepathic link. 'I just wondered if you had a minute to pop by the manse.'

'What's up?'

A slight hesitation on the line, then the minister said, 'There's someone, something, I think you might want to see.

To be honest, I'm not terribly sure what to do with it, or even what it means.'

'You're being very mysterious, Fiona,' said Alan.

They heard a slight laugh in the minister's voice. 'All part of my mystique. Can you come by?'

'Yes, we're just turning onto the Spine now – be with you in a couple of minutes.'

'Okay, good.' Fiona cut the connection, leaving Alan frowning as he looked ahead towards the church and the manse.

'Has to be something to do with Nuala, don't you think?' he ventured.

'Could be anything.'

'Yes, but it has to be that. It's not the wedding, so what else could it be?'

'We'll know soon enough,' said Chaz as he steered the Discovery onto the grass verge beside the low wall that bordered the manse property.

Chaz recognised the woman as the person at the payphone in the bar, the one who had seemed so startled when they passed behind her, yet he still felt he had seen her before somewhere. She seemed no less ill at ease in Fiona's comfortable study, where the fire crackled as usual in the grate, spreading welcome warmth.

'Delia's from Sanctuary,' Fiona explained, prompting a raised eyebrow from Alan. 'But she's having doubts about it, right, Delia?'

Delia nodded as she scrutinised their faces. 'I saw you both there yesterday. You were showing interest in joining.'

'We were undercover,' Alan assured her.

That's where he had seen her before, Chaz realised. He had glimpsed her standing in the doorway when Seb came out to take them on the tour.

Fiona said, 'She has something to show you.'

The woman had a laptop on her knee with a data stick jutting from the USB socket, and she looked down at the screen as if searching for reassurance that she was doing the right thing, before she turned it in their direction. Both Chaz and Alan were still standing and they craned forward to look at the screen. They saw a list of numbers.

'That looks like phone numbers,' said Chaz.

'It's a call log, am I right?' Alan asked Delia, and she nodded. 'Is it yours?' She shook her head. 'Then whose is it?'

Delia glanced once at Fiona, who nodded her encouragement. 'You can trust them, Delia.'

Reassured, Delia took a breath. 'It's from the only mobile phone allowed in Sanctuary.' Her voice wavered with nerves. 'The phone is kept in a safe in the office, and only Seb has access to it.'

'Ah,' Alan said, 'Captain Fantastic.'

A tiny smile tugged at the woman's mouth. 'Yes. He's the closest Sanctuary comes to a leader. He's been with the Children of the Dell for years and he is the only one who talks to Father.' She paused. 'Or whoever.'

Chaz caught the tone. 'Whoever? You don't believe Father exists?'

'Well, that's the thing, isn't it? I've discovered a few things but I can't connect the dots, if you know what I mean.'

Alan asked, 'And you accessed this phone without Captain Fantastic knowing?

Fiona jumped in again to explain. 'That's why we're talking to you and not going straight to the police. I'm not sure of the legalities here, and if this is evidence of anything – although I'm still not sure what – then the fact that this information has effectively been stolen from the safe could make it inadmissible, or whatever.' She smiled. 'You're with the media, Chaz, so you would have no qualms about it.'

Chaz cleared his throat. 'Yes, there's hardly a day goes by that I don't intrude into somebody's privacy or steal their data.' He leaned in for a closer look. 'So what is it you want us to see?'

Delia leaned over the top of the screen and used her finger to highlight a section in which one number was called several times over a period of days. 'That's the most common number on the list, it's a mobile. I felt it logical that it would be the one that Seb used to contact Father.'

'Or whoever,' Chaz said, and she nodded.

'And what about this one?' Alan pointed to the number that seemed to be the next most used.

'A company called Templesword International,' said Delia.

Chaz recalled her standing beside the public phone in the hotel. 'You phoned these numbers?'

'Just the two that appear most.'

'And who answered?'

'A woman, both times.'

'Do you think the same one?'

'Yes.'

'What did she say?'

'Just hello, that's all for the first number, and then the company name for the second.'

'And what did you do?'

'I hung up right away.'

Chaz fell silent. He had the feeling that Delia calling the numbers was a mistake, but he understood why she had done it.

'This woman, did she have an accent?' Alan asked. 'Scottish, English, anything?'

'Scottish but well-spoken. She called me back – at least, I'm guessing it was her. I'd barely put the phone down before it rang.'

'You didn't hide the number?'

Delia shook her head. 'I didn't think to do that.'

That confirmed it. She had made a mistake. Chaz didn't know why, he just knew. He recalled the phone ringing and seeing her hurrying across the car park. 'You didn't answer it, though.'

Delia replied, even though he had not meant it as a question. 'No, of course not. I just got away from there as soon as I could.'

Alan nodded his understanding. 'So whoever that woman was now knows someone from the island called that number.'

'Is there any way you can do a back trace?' Fiona asked. 'Use the number to track the owner?'

'We can try simply putting the number into a search engine or a reverse phone number service. But that's not my area. I'm a photographer, Fiona, the detective work is done by Rebecca, or rather, Elspeth. Anyway, we have this other number, what was it again?'

'Templesword International,' Delia said. 'I've seen the name in the accounts. They perform services for Sanctuary.'

'What kind of services?'

'I'm not sure. I think it's accounting or financial advice or something along those lines. It's not really clear in the books.'

Chaz looked to Alan. 'I'd say that's the place to start, right?'

'Absolutely.' Alan pointed at the laptop still on Delia's lap. 'May I?'

She handed him the device and he seated himself on the settee beside her. He peered at the bottom of the screen. 'Your internet connection is, not to put too fine a point on it, Fiona, absolute crap.'

Fiona shrugged. 'It's an island thing.'

'Should be enough for a Google search.' His fingers began to stab at the keys.

Chaz asked, 'Why are you doing this, Delia?'

She sat in silence for a moment and when she spoke, her voice was low, as if shame was suppressing it. 'The sister – Nuala – recognised me from years ago. I knew her partner,

Sam. He died, committed suicide, but she never accepted it. She believed he was murdered because he had been looking into the Children of the Dell.'

'And was he?'

'No. Sam was troubled, he always was. Intense, I suppose. I wasn't on the newsgathering side of things but I knew him to be a good journalist who, once he was onto something, didn't let go. That kind of tenacity can be wearing, I suppose, especially when the bean counters like me who run the business don't see the merit of long-form investigations.'

There was a note of shame in her voice, whether at her inability to do something about the man's death or her contribution to the overall decline in investigative journalism.

'From what I understand, Sam was ill, mentally ill,' she continued. 'He had burned some bridges, lashing out at editors and commissioners, saying things he probably shouldn't. He was also, by nature, paranoid. It's true to say that he had never met a conspiracy theory he didn't like, and he had begun accusing people in boardrooms of being part of plots to hide the truth from the public. The media business can be very petty and does not forget such transgressions. Also, things weren't going too well between him and Nuala. There were tensions and she had a couple of affairs. I didn't know her too well, but I had the feeling her head was easily turned by men.'

Cynthia Danvers's words came back to Chaz – *she loved too easily and not wisely.*

'I think that's part of the reason she refused to accept the truth of his death,' Delia went on. 'She felt guilt, I suppose. When she saw me one day in the shop in Portnaseil, she approached me. We had known each other slightly back in the day, not well, but I knew her as soon as I saw her. She told me that coming to the island was no accident: she had heard from mutual acquaintances that I had joined Sanctuary and she'd come here to seek me out. She could be very persuasive, could Nuala. I hadn't known that Sam had been looking into the Children of the Dell – as I said, that was not my field, although I had met the man on a number of occasions – but she had his notes, which she showed me.'

She reached into the pocket of her thick jacket and produced a battered mobile phone. She flicked at the screen to activate it and handed it to Chaz.

'This, basically, is what she had.'

Alan asked, 'Why didn't you use that to call the numbers?'

'It has no SIM card. It's just an electronic file now, really.'

Chaz looked at the photograph showing handwritten notes, most of which were indecipherable. 'What are these initials? TS, COD? Children of the Dell, perhaps?'

'I would say most definitely.'

'And the arrow to TS? What is TS?' Chaz expanded the image on the screen. 'And what's that, underlined three times? Starts with a G – gorgeous? Georgia? And here's Templesword again.'

'Yes, I know,' said Delia.

'Templesword International,' said Alan, his attention on the screen. 'Financial services company, based in the Channel Islands. The number you called is a mobile, so they could be anywhere, I suppose.'

'Is there anything with TS?'

Alan's eyes followed the screen as he scrolled, clicked and opened. 'Not that I can see right now.'

'I also found a document in the safe relating to the purchase of the farm,' said Delia. 'That mentioned a company called DKMH Holdings.'

Alan typed the name into the search engine, waited, his impatience evident in the drumming of his fingers on the keyboard. 'At last,' he said, stabbing at the mousepad as if it was responsible for the delay. 'There's a DKMH Holdings with a London address.' He clicked again. 'No other information but it seems to be a property company. Buying and selling perhaps, some property management, that sort of thing. Another name to check with Companies House.'

Fiona asked, 'How long will that take?'

'A quick search can be done in minutes online, a deeper one longer. But your connectivity really sucks, Fiona – this is like dial-up with a really bad hangover. You need to get your router looked at.'

'Will that help?'

Alan shrugged. 'Not a clue, that's just something people say. I know how to use the technology; I don't know how it works.'

Chaz stored this admission of a gap in Alan's knowledge for later use. 'And what about these images,' he said, looking again at the phone's screen. 'Who is Wesley Fairbank? What's his birth certificate got to do with this?'

Delia shook her head. 'I don't know.'

'And this newspaper clipping – what's that? Bennet Lomax is some sort of actor, so what's he got to do with it?' He narrowed his eyes as he gave the grainy black-and-white shot on the cutting a closer look. 'Alan, you still got one of those brochures from Sanctuary on you?'

'Never leave home without it,' Alan said, producing it from his back pocket. Chaz opened it, compared the two, then noticed Delia watching him, as if waiting for him to make the connection.

'You see it, too?' she said. 'That could be Father, although much younger.'

'Let me see,' Alan said, holding out his hand. He scrutinised the two images. 'Yup, definitely the same guy.' He laid them down and keyed words into the laptop.

Chaz asked Delia, 'So all this is enough to convince you that there's something rotten in the state of Sanctuary?'

'Let's just say that they raised doubt,' she replied.

'How much money do you think has been filtered into the place?'

Delia considered her response. 'Between all the Sanctuaries, I'd say we're talking in the millions.' She caught the look of disbelief Chaz exchanged with Alan. 'Those in Sanctuary are all former high-flyers, remember. We're not supposed to talk about our past life but naturally some of us do. We've got former merchant bankers, hedge fund managers, chief executives, even a baroness. Each one handed over their fortune willingly. I was not the most successful but I parted with over a million once I had sold off stocks and property. If everyone in Sanctuary contributed the same, we're looking at a tidy sum from the island alone.'

'You think it's a scam?'

'I have no idea. It could all be above board. I certainly looked into it first and saw nothing to set off warning signals, but I was not in a good place then. I could have missed something. Nuala just made me question the lack of accountability, that's all.'

'But there has to be a trail. Perhaps not a paper trail now, but certainly a digital one.'

'If it was me,' Delia began, 'I'd cover my tracks with a host of shelf and shell companies – I'm betting the offshore one is one or the other.'

Chaz asked, 'What's the difference?'

'A shelf company is one that has been left to lie dormant – on the shelf, as it were – and can be bought from lawyers or accountants without having to go through the bureaucracy, if you want to set up quickly. A shell company is a fictitious entity used to cover fraud or money-laundering. If Sanctuary is a scam, but now that we're talking I think it's more likely it's a way to clean up dirty money, then whoever is behind it will have created a labyrinth of companies to obscure them. By the time forensic accountants have unravelled it, they'll be long gone.'

'And do you think it possible that whoever is behind it is capable of murder? I mean, it seems convenient for them that Nuala's partner took his own life then she died under mysterious circumstances.'

'Sam had barely scratched the surface, according to his notes. But, of course, Nuala dying gave me pause, especially because—'

She stopped talking suddenly. 'Especially because of what?' Chaz asked.

Delia dropped her eyes. 'It may be nothing,' she said, then came to a halt again, her eyes losing focus a little as she battled with herself.

'What may be nothing?'

She looked at Chaz, then at Alan as he clicked links on the laptop, then finally at Fiona. 'You've gone this far, Delia,' Fiona said, her voice gentle.

Delia blinked a few times, then resumed her study of the computer. 'The night Nuala died, I heard the Land Rover start up. I went to my window and saw it pulling away, heading for the gates.'

'And is that unusual?'

'Yes. We're not confined to barracks or anything, it's not a prison, but we seldom leave Sanctuary after dark, even in the vehicle.'

Chaz asked, 'And do you know who was driving?'

Alan was way ahead of her. 'Captain Fantastic, right?'

'Yes. Seb is the only person with the keys. Nobody else drives it.'

'And has he ever done that before?'

Delia had to admit that he had. 'But it stuck in my mind because of what happened to Nuala.'

Alan looked at Chaz over the top of the screen. 'I've found a couple of references to Bennet Lomax. Small-time actor, had a couple of walk-ons in *The Bill*, once swilled some beer in the Rovers Return and chatted up Elsie Tanner. Not been active since the nineties.'

'And where is he now?'

'The big repertory theatre in the sky. He died ten years ago.'

Loch Ness

He kept his voice even as he spoke, but inside he was seething. Nuala Flaherty had been an irritation, but even after death she was pissing him off. A call from the island directly to the mobile that was reserved for that particular Sanctuary was a cause for concern, and he was not one for keeping such concerns to himself. He believed in spreading it around, and at that moment he was pushing it through the ether towards Seb.

'Nobody should have that number,' he said.

'No,' agreed Seb.

'And yet someone does. And they called from a landline on the island. In the local pub.'

The mystery caller hadn't had the sense to block the number before dialling, so as soon as they had hung up without speaking, Vivian had hit Call Back. It rang quite a few times, but Vivian was tenacious and hung on. Eventually a man had answered, a Geordie she said, and told her it was a public phone outside the bar in Portnaseil. No, he didn't know who had used it, he didn't pay attention to these things.

'Do you have any idea who could have the number?'

'No, I . . .' A slight hitch in the man's voice told Smith that something had occurred to him mid-denial.

'Who is it, Seb?'

'I'm not sure.'

'Who, Seb?' Smith placed such heavy emphasis on the two words that they were like separate sentences.

'I dropped the key to the safe earlier.'

Smith's voice remained even as he repeated Seb's words, but the accusation was clear. 'You dropped the key to the safe.'

'Yes. In the bathroom.'

He struggled to keep his temper. The sheer stupidity of this was staggering. 'You *dropped* the key to the *safe* in the bathroom.'

'It was along with all my other keys, and I was certain I had them all, but maybe I didn't. I found it later in the corner of the bathroom.'

'And tell me, Seb, was someone else present when maybe you didn't have them all back in your possession?'

'Yes, Delia Forbes.'

Smith clicked over the Sanctuary membership in his mind. There were some he knew intimately, women mostly but a few men, all of whom had been steered towards him by people such as Seb as being ripe for getting closer to Father. Of course, they didn't get close to Father – that would be difficult – but they did get close to him. He didn't have total recall, and this name didn't mean anything to him.

He asked, 'And does this Delia Forbes have access to the office and the safe?'

'Yes, the office isn't locked, you know that, but she helps us out with the accounts.'

Smith considered this, feeling a faint tingle of tension in his fingers. The accounts. This woman, who may or may not have somehow taken possession of the safe key in order to find the Sanctuary mobile and then the number, dealt with the accounts. Some very clever money men had worked hard to ensure that there were sufficient hurdles for anyone to leap before even the most tenuous of financial links could be made to him or those who backed and profited from his services. Still, it was yet another cause for concern. He began to wonder if the time really was coming to pack up his tent and move on. He could feel tension begin to stiffen his neck.

He would have to have Vivian rub it. She was very business-like when she kneaded the muscles, there was nothing
sexual in her touch, and he needed that now.

'And tell me, Seb, do you know if this Delia Forbes had any
connection with the Sister?'

He knew Seb would have already considered this. He was
canny, despite this latest idiocy – to drop his keys in a bloody
toilet while this woman was present and then not to notice
that one was missing, if indeed that was what had occurred,
was idiocy of the highest level.

'I don't know,' he said, then cleared his throat. 'But there's
something else.'

Smith felt his jaw clamp. 'What?'

'The police were here, asking us about the Sister.'

'And what did you tell them?'

'The truth,' said Seb. 'That we had nothing to hide.'

Smith knew that was not completely true, but he doubted
very much if rural plods looking into a suspicious death would
stumble upon it. 'It would be routine, I imagine.'

'That's what they said.'

'How many officers, and did you get their rank?'

'Constables, one in uniform, the other plainclothes.'

Smith gave himself a satisfied nod. It was merely routine.
Anything more serious would have seen them send at least
one officer of higher rank. 'So tell me, Seb, is Delia Forbes in
Sanctuary at this moment?'

'No. She was seen walking to the road earlier today.'

He had visited the Stoirm Sanctuary only once, so he had
only a vague knowledge of its location. 'And is it likely she
could have gone to the village?'

'There's a bus comes by here twice a day. Just a minibus,
really. She might have caught that.'

The evidence was mounting against this woman; circum-
stantial, it might be argued, but he believed that when

223

circumstance led you to a conclusion, it was more often than not the correct one.

'Find her, Seb,' he said. 'Deal with this.'

Inverness

Sawyer hated hospitals. The only one in which he had personally spent any length of time was the small community hospital on Stoirm, when he had broken his leg, and it had been a pleasant enough stay – apart from the injury – but he had still been restless and uncomfortable. Hospitals were for sick people, and he had never had an extended period of illness. But more than that, hospitals were where people went to die, and he had encountered enough of that in his private and professional life. His mother had died in a hospice, which was just a hospital with a softer name, while his father and two of his uncles had each died in wards like the one he was in now. He had only been a boy then, but he well remembered walking along what seemed like an interminable ward lined on both sides by beds with men in striped pyjamas and skin the colour of parchment – and the smell, a mix of disinfectant and air freshener still hung in his memory. Hospitals had transformed since then, but a ward was a ward, and no amount of refurbishing would change that in his mind.

Cokey was sitting up in the bed, which was something, but his hands were swathed in bandages, as were his lower jaw and head. Both eyes were blackened and the first he knew Sawyer was at his bedside was when he said his name. The swollen eyes opened to little more than slits, and he physically flinched, as if he had been slapped. And he *had* been slapped. He had also been punched and kicked. And worse.

'Take it easy there, Cokey,' said Sawyer, the queasy rolling in his gut he had felt since entering the place deepening. He had been tipped off about Cokey's condition by an old pal on the job, but he was still shocked. Cokey was a tout, not a friend, and Sawyer didn't like him much, but he felt a rash of guilt colour his neck and face.

He wanted to apologise, but he could not find the words. He merely stood by the bedside of a little man he didn't care for very much – whose body was beaten and broken yet still jerked, as if it had a mind of its own – and felt his rage build.

The Island of Stoirm

Chaz offered Delia a ride back to Sanctuary, adding that they would have to drop her off a mile or so away, as she could not risk being spotted with them. The sun had already drowned itself in the sea beyond the mountain, and its death throes had stained the sky a rapidly darkening pink, which cast a glow inside the cab of the Land Rover as they travelled south on the Spine. As they drove, she asked them if anything could be done with the information she had provided, and Chaz was honest enough to tell her he didn't know. He had decided he would not only pass it all on to Rebecca and let her make something out of it but also to the police via Rory Gibson. Delia accepted that calmly, as if she had not expected anything else. His impression was that she had done what she had done in order to do something, however ineffectual it might be. She struck him as being fairly level-headed – not what he would have expected from someone drawn to such a cult.

It was Alan who used that word – cult – as they travelled through the gathering gloom, and she had been very quiet for a second or two afterwards. 'Yes, I suppose that's what they are. But, to be honest, I never really thought of the Children in those terms,' she said. 'I just needed somewhere to be, I suppose. Somewhere I felt welcome and at home, and Sanctuary provided that.'

'At a price,' said Alan.

'Everything comes with a price. Even something that appears free can often have hidden costs.'

'So what will you do? Go back into business?'

She shook her head. 'Not right away. I'll see. But I now know Sanctuary is not for me.' She pondered again. 'Perhaps I'll reconnect with my family. They might not be much, and I still disagree with their values – even though they were once mine, too – but family is family, right? No matter what, you're still a part of it.'

'Right,' said Alan. Chaz had no siblings, but he knew Alan was thinking about his family. He was not a part of their set: his father was the epitome of something big in the city; his mother was unable to fully accept the fact he was gay; and his brothers were men's men, who hunted, fished, played rugby and chased women – and yet he knew that, no matter what, they all shared something. Blood. A common history. Memories. A bond that comes only with family. Not even Alan understood that bond; he merely accepted it. And it sounded as if Delia had reached the same conclusion.

It was pitch black when they dropped her off, and she assured them she would be fine. There was very little traffic on this narrow road during the day and even less after dark. She would hear any oncoming vehicles long before they reached her, she said. The last Chaz saw of her was when she vanished beyond the range of his headlamps. One minute she was there, the next she was swallowed up in the island's darkness.

Inverness

Rebecca was just about to lock up the office when Tabitha's call came through. After the preliminary hellos and how are yous – God, Rebecca hated these conversational conventions – Tabitha said, 'So, the Children of the Dell.'

'You have something?'

'Let me start by stressing that much of this is rumour. There's a reason these sites are called chatrooms.'

'Okay.' Rebecca moved back to her desk, set her bag down and dropped into her chair. 'What have you got?'

'Lots of unrest but nothing concrete.'

'What kind of unrest?'

'That it's not quite kosher. As I said, no real evidence. There was a reporter a few years back who started to nose around, but he died.'

'Yes, Sam Walters. The unofficial version is he committed suicide.'

'So they say,' said Tabitha. 'Naturally, there's a lot of conspiracy nonsense in the chats – I can't wait until news of Nuala Flaherty's death hits. They'll go ballistic.'

'Do they suspect the Children of the Dell had him killed?'

'No, not the Children directly, but the men behind them.'

'And who are they?'

'This is where it all gets even hazier. There was a former member – the guy used to be in the music business, made a bundle then went all fruit loopy. Started investigating comparative religions, dropped out, finally ended up in one of the Sanctuaries. Some sort of leader, I was told. Anyway, he left eventually – thrown out, actually, for enjoying various substances too freely. They don't like that sort of thing, apparently. He started talking about what went on in Sanctuary, the first one.'

'And what does go on?'

'Nothing, that's the thing. It's everything it says it is on the tin – a sanctuary for those who are troubled enough to need an escape. As long as they have the money. I think that's what this is all about.'

'Isn't it always?'

'Follow the money, isn't that what you reporters say?'

227

Rebecca had no memory of ever saying that, but as a rule, it wasn't a bad one.

Tabitha didn't wait for her to reply. 'They don't cater to the hoi polloi in Sanctuary. You need to have a tidy bundle to sink into the coffers. This guy, the music business guy – Gerald Frame was his name – tried to raise a stink about where the money went and there was some interest shown by the tax man, but it didn't go anywhere.'

'Why not?'

'Maybe it's all above board. Maybe the Revenue didn't have the manpower to really have a look. If it is some kind of scam then they will be smart and pay just enough tax to keep HMRC off their back and disguise the rest. Or – and this is what the conspiracy fans favour, big surprise – maybe strings were pulled. I managed to reach someone who knew Gerald Frame – who shall remain nameless, so don't ask – and he told me that Gerald knew the whole Children of the Dell thing was dodgy and was determined to expose it. The problem was, he was out of his skull half the time on those illegal substances. And he also spouted all kinds of nutjob theories about aliens and international masonic conspiracies, so nobody took him seriously.'

'Sam Walters did, but, from what I gather, he was also a bit of a conspiracy nut and viewed by the industry as a liability because of his mental state.' Rebecca paused to consider this, the phrase 'just because you're paranoid doesn't mean they aren't after you' coming to her mind. She asked, 'Where can I find this Gerald Frame, do you think?'

Tabitha paused. 'I'd need to get out my Ouija board.'

'He's dead?'

'Heart attack last year.'

Rebecca frowned, her mind turning over what Tabitha had told her. Three deaths, all linked in some way to Children of the Dell. This had transformed from a simple story of a mysterious death into something infinitely more serious. And Chaz and Alan were on the island, nosing around.

She hurriedly thanked Tabitha for her help and hit Chaz's number. When he answered, she could hear the sound of a car engine.

'Hi, Becks, we're just heading back to the cottage Nuala was staying in. We've got lots to tell you . . .'

'Okay, but Chaz? I need you to leave this alone for now.'

The roar of the engine was the only thing she heard for a moment or two. Then he responded in a puzzled tone, 'Why? What's up?'

She quickly told him what Tabitha had heard. 'I think we need to pull back for a while, think about what we're doing here. Maybe pass it all on to the police. Three deaths can't be ignored.'

'I'll add another death – an old actor called Bennet Lomax,' Alan said. 'It's his image that's been used on Sanctuary literature as being Father. He died in the nineties, natural causes, it seems.'

Rebecca took this in. 'That's before the Children were even set up, so someone must have simply used his image. But the level of death surrounding the group should make somebody's eyebrows go up, right?'

'Unless the Children of the Dell have friends in high places.'

'Don't even think that, Alan. This is already a conspiracy theorist's wet dream.'

Chaz, ever the reasonable voice, piped up again. 'Look, we're going to meet Rory Gibson, the cop I told you about. We've spoken to a friend of Nuala's who was here on a visit, a woman called Cynthia Danvers who's known her since childhood. She said that she was being pestered by a local dickhead who fancies himself as some kind of drug kingpin. We'll pass all this on to Rory, let him take it from here. Okay?'

Rebecca agreed.

'But do us a favour,' Alan said. 'See what you can find on the internet about a couple of companies, DKMH Holdings and Templesword International.' He spelled out the two names. 'We've also just spoken to a woman called Delia Forbes who is part of the Children of the Dell, and Nuala gave her some material.'

'Why?'

'Long story and we can explain later but I need you to have a nose around in the ether. I tried here, but the connection was so slow I was losing the will to live. Look for anything with the initials TS. Also, a Wesley Fairbank.'

She scribbled the names down. 'Who's he?'

'No clue, but Nuala had his birth certificate. We'll text it to you, and a cutting on the actor.'

'This doesn't sound terribly like pulling back to me.'

'It's an internet search, Becks, that's all. We'll tell Rory everything, such as it is.'

She was already typing into Google. 'Okay, but for God's sake be careful.'

The Island of Stoirm

There was no moon to light the way, but Delia had come to know this narrow road well. She walked through the darkness, the cold night attacking her nose and ears. Her hands were thrust into the pockets of her coat, and she wished she had thought to pick up gloves and perhaps her wool hat. She had not intended to be absent from Sanctuary for so long but talking to the minister and those two young men had taken up more time than she realised.

She had done what she'd set out to do, and now she had to make a decision – whether to remain in Sanctuary or leave – although something told her that it was a no-brainer.

She couldn't stay now. Perhaps there was nothing in Nuala's suspicions, but she had lost her faith in the Children of the Dell. She doubted now whether she ever really had it, suspecting that the group and Sanctuary had merely been a diversion at a crucial point in her life, a means of escape for a time. It had been a lovely dream, but now she was awake and the warm fuzzy feeling was but a memory. This had been coming for some time, she knew that now, and there was little point in delaying the inevitable. She would leave in the morning.

There.

Decision made. She felt a smile crack her cold cheeks and she felt better than she had for weeks. All the doubt, all the second-guessing, all the suspicion that had tormented her evaporated now, just as it used to with the old Delia. Once a course of action was decided, she always felt satisfied.

Climbing a fairly steep rise in the narrow road and caught in her own thoughts, she didn't see the vehicle sitting in the darkness, so she was startled when the beam from the headlights exploded around her. Her breath caught in her throat and her heart thundered, sending blood tingling down her arms to her fingers as she shielded her eyes against the glare, trying to see who it was. She heard the door open and a lanky figure moved from the blackness into the dazzle of the lights, becoming little more than a silhouette. The Land Rover completely blocked the road and he'd had to squeeze between the bonnet and a high hedge.

'Seb?' It was a question, but she knew the answer as she squinted against the light. 'What are you doing sitting in the dark like that?'

'I've been looking for you, Delia,' he said. He sounded different. There was no charm in his voice, no fellowship. His Australian accent had flattened, as if he was trying to keep a lid on anger.

231

'I went into Portnaseil,' she said, unable to come up with a convincing lie and deciding that the truth was easier.

He leaned against the bonnet, folded his arms. 'I looked there, didn't see you.'

She felt something intangible reach through the darkness, something she had never felt from him before. She swallowed and struggled to conceal her growing nervousness. 'You must have missed me.'

'It's not a big place, Delia.' His tone was still featureless. 'Not easy to miss someone.'

She forced a smile. 'And yet you did.'

He shifted his position slightly. 'It's late, Delia.'

'Not that late,' she said, her mind working at speed to come up with an explanation for her extended absence. She should have anticipated something like this, but she had been acting very much on impulse and without a great deal of forward planning. She felt her mind hemming in as she sought for an explanation he would believe. Finally, she decided the truth would set her free. 'I met those two young men you showed around Sanctuary the other day and thought I'd see if I could convince them to at least come to one of the courses.'

'And where did you meet them?'

'In the Square.'

'And you stood in the Square all this time? In the cold? I was in the Square and didn't see you.'

'No, we went to the hotel bar.'

'I checked there, too.'

Of course he did. 'They're staying in the hotel and, well, I found being in the bar uncomfortable, so we went to their room to talk.'

'You went to their room? Two men you've never met before, and you went to their room?'

Her laugh was partly genuine. 'I was perfectly safe, Seb. They're nice lads and, anyway, they're gay.'

232

Her explanation was weak, she knew that, but it was the best she could come up with and she could only hope that he would buy it. The silence between them, broken only by the ticking of the still-running engine, was as deep as the darkness that surrounded the pool of light created by the headlamps.

'And were you successful in convincing them?' he asked eventually.

'Who knows? You know how these things go – you've said it yourself. Sometimes we don't know until they book a place. But I'm hopeful.'

'And they're both interested?'

'Yes, very much so.'

'Both of them?'

She realised then she had made a mistake. He must have sensed something when he had shown them around. 'Eventually,' she said. She tried to think which one of them would have been less capable of hiding his scepticism. But she knew nothing about them, not really. She had to take a guess, that was the only way. 'Chaz, the younger of the two, I'm less certain of him, to be honest. But I think there's every chance he'll come around.' She made a show of shrugging deeper into her coat. 'Seb, it's freezing out here. Are you going to give me a lift back to Sanctuary or what?'

She couldn't tell if she had guessed correctly. He didn't reply or make any moves back to the cab. She couldn't see his face clearly but could still feel the intensity of his gaze carrying the sense of menace that had gripped her earlier. Just as the old Delia had made a reappearance, she wondered now if she was seeing the old Seb. The real Seb.

'Did you use the phone in the pub, Delia?'

Shit. 'No,' she said, trying to remain as natural as possible. 'Why do you ask?'

'Someone called Father's number today, and they used the public phone in the bar in Portnaseil.'

'It wasn't me.' The words didn't sound convincing at all, she knew that. She was out of practice with telecommunications, and she should never have phoned either of those numbers, but her curiosity had got the better of her. Now she also knew she should never have headed back to Sanctuary. She should have asked to stay with the minister – she was certain Fiona would have agreed – then left the island on the first ferry in the morning. Leave what few possessions she had and just go.

'Who do you think it could have been, Delia?' Seb's voice seemed reasonable, but that undertone was still present. He knew it was her.

She forced herself to remain calm and decided to go on the offensive. Such tactics had served the old Delia well, but she was unsure if she could still pull it off. She injected some defiance into her words. 'What exactly are you accusing me of, Seb?'

He was silent for a moment, then he unfolded his arms and let them drop to his sides. 'Let's stop playing games, Delia, how about that? I know you took the safe key. I know you've been snooping around in the computer. I know you accessed the call log. I know you phoned Father's number.'

Seb was not stupid. She contemplated carrying on with the charade but the certainty in his voice told her there was no point. 'Okay,' she said.

'That all you have to say?'

'What more do you want me to say?'

'An explanation would be nice.'

She shivered. 'Can we do it somewhere warm?'

'No,' he said. 'We do it here. I don't want to risk anyone hearing.'

'How about in the Land Rover?'

'Not much warmer in there, the heater's busted. So what's the story, Delia? Why the breach of trust?'

She sucked the cold air in through her nose, let it out, willed the hammering in her chest to slow. 'Because there's something not right about Sanctuary, Seb.'

His figure, still backlit by the headlights, shifted slightly. 'She got to you, didn't she? The Sister.'

'She had a name, Seb. Nuala. That was her name. Nuala Flaherty.'

She saw him twitch that away, as if discarding it. 'She was a nutjob, Delia, you know that.'

'She was eccentric in many ways, but it didn't make her wrong. Where does all the money go, Seb? This Sanctuary alone must have brought in a good few million. I can't see it in the accounts.'

'It's there.'

'Only so far, then it seems to vanish in a miasma of figures and accounts, most of which I had no access to.'

'You don't need to access them, Delia. All you needed to do was make sure our day-to-day accounts were okay and the bills were paid. That was all. Beyond that was none of your concern.'

'I made it my concern, Seb.'

'Yes, you did.' His voice seemed sad. 'Yes, you did. Aren't you happy at Sanctuary?'

She thought about this, then answered truthfully. 'I was.' Until I woke up from the fantasy, she thought but didn't say.

'Then why do this, Delia? Why betray us? Betray me?'

Her first impulse was to deny that she was betraying anyone, but she knew that wasn't true. 'I just need to know the truth, Seb.'

'What is truth?'

She felt irritation rise. 'Oh please, let's not get all existential. You know what I mean. Father doesn't exist, Seb: he's just an old photograph of an actor who died years ago. Did you know that?'

He didn't reply. 'Who have you really spoken to, Delia?'

'What makes you think I've spoken to anyone?'

'You didn't spend all day wandering around the village. There's not that much to do there.'

Something told Delia not to tell him. 'I haven't spoken to anyone. I just walked around the beaches, sat on rocks for a while, considered my options.'

'And they are what, exactly?'

'Stay or leave. Right now, given this conversation, I think those options have halved.'

She saw him nod. 'If you leave, you don't get your money back, you know that.'

'Yes, I'm aware of that. I've seen the accounts, Seb, I know Sanctuary has enough to pay the bills but no more. Which is why I want to know where the rest goes.'

'Expenses. Outgoings. Charitable work. You know the drill.'

'I know what we're told, but I don't see it in the record.'

'We've been through that. You don't need to see it. It's all above board, don't worry.'

'That's it, though, I do worry. I didn't before but now I do.'

'Thanks to the Sister.'

'Thanks to Nuala, Seb.' They were talking in circles, and she'd had enough. 'Look, this isn't getting us anywhere. Give me a lift to Sanctuary, Seb, I'll be gone in the morning. I don't expect my money back, I know the way it works. But we both know I'm done with it all.'

He remained still for a moment, then he pushed himself away from the grille. 'I'm wedged in on the passenger side,' he said. 'Move along the road to the gate back there and I can get the door open for you.'

She looked over her shoulder down the steep slope. The thick hedges on both sides tapered the road even further as it vanished in the gloom beyond the beam of the headlights. She couldn't see the gate, but that didn't mean it wasn't there. Seb knew this road well and every point that could be used as a passing place.

'Okay,' she said as he moved to the door on the driver's side. She turned away from the glare and paused to give her eyes time to adjust. The way ahead was still lit by the beams, but some detail began to emerge beyond their limit.

She began to walk, looking for the gate he had mentioned. Behind her, she heard the engine being manhandled into gear.

Inverness

Rebecca looked at the notes on her pad. She had logged into Companies House and typed 'DKMH Holdings' into the search box and saw it had been incorporated in June 2002 and, over the years, had a list of nine directors, five of whom had resigned at various times. This was not unusual, and none of them had the initials TS. Its returns were up to date, the next not due until January the following year. Templesword International was also prompt with its returns and listed seventeen directors, eleven of whom had resigned over the years. There was one with the initials TS, a Thomas Smith, but the correspondence address listed was the same as that of the company. She checked her watch, saw it was almost 7 p.m. and decided against finding a number and calling. She had clicked on the man's name and found that Thomas Smith was a director of three other companies. She scanned the records for each of them, spotted a name she recognised – a Mrs Vivian Ward, who also listed her correspondence address in the Channel Islands. She followed her name and there she was – a director of DKMH Holdings, but this time she had listed an Edinburgh address. Had to be the same person. Rebecca smiled, feeling the warmth of discovery flood through her.

She dialled Directory Enquiries, betting with herself that it would be unlisted. She lost the bet. The recorded voice relayed a number as if it was bored. Rebecca wasn't bored. Despite her admonition to the boys, she could feel the excitement build. She dialled the number. It rang out.

Damn.

She hung up and stared at her notes again, then sat back and let her head rest on the back of her office chair. Okay, Becks, what have we here? The boys had texted her the files Delia had, the ones containing Sam Walters' notes, and they were pretty scant. She assumed that what he had was gleaned from Gerald Frame. The jpegs of the birth certificate and the news cutting didn't really lead anywhere: a search for the name Wesley Fairbank brought nothing, another for Bennet Lomax only a reference to his death in a care home in Devon, noting he had appeared in a few popular TV series in the seventies and eighties, bit parts only, as well as with touring productions around the country. There were some scribbles on the notes that none of them could decipher, and some initials with arrows linking them and the word Templesword. One of the numbers in the call log was to Templesword International, based in the Channel Islands. One of the directors of Templesword was also a director of the company involved in the purchase of the farm from the Stoirm Estate. A further internet search revealed that DKMH also provided property management services. The initials TS could relate to Thomas Smith, who was also a director of Templesword, but not DKMH.

On an impulse she hit redial for the Edinburgh number. It rang out but she let it continue. She was about to hang up when she heard a soft-spoken voice answer. A man, elderly, she guessed.

'Hello, sorry to bother you,' she said. 'My name is Rebecca Connolly and I'm a reporter calling from Inverness.'

'Yes?' said the man, both curious and guarded. She was used to that.

'I'm looking for Vivian Ward. I wonder if she's there?'

'No, she's not.'

'Are you Mr Ward?'

'No, Ward is her married name. I'm her father.'

He didn't offer his name and she didn't press for it. 'Is there any way I can reach her?'

His voice might have been delicate, but he was not. 'What's this about?'

'I'm researching a story up here in the Highlands and she may be able to help me.' She paused for a beat then thought, why the hell not? 'It concerns Templesword International.'

'What newspaper did you say you were from?'

'I work for a news agency. Does Templesword International mean anything to you?'

'That's where she works. What is this story, Miss Connolly?'

'It relates to a group on the island of Stoirm called the Children of the Dell. Have you heard of them?'

'No, I haven't. Should I?'

His words carried the ring of truth. 'Not particularly. But the name of the company came up and I see that your daughter is a director.'

'Really? I didn't know that. I know she works for Mr Smith but . . .'

She couldn't keep the excitement from her voice. 'Thomas Smith? She works for Thomas Smith?'

'Yes, she's his secretary, didn't you know that? That's why she's away. It's one of those live-in positions. He has a large house up there . . .'

Up there. 'Here in the Highlands?'

'Yes, up by Loch Ness. She loves her job, but I didn't know she was a director.' The man's slight laugh that followed was rheumy and carried the memory of a smoker. 'She kept that quiet.'

'Is there a number I could reach her at?'

'I don't think I can pass that on, but I'll tell you what I can do: if you give me your number, I'll get it to her and she can phone you back. How does that sound?'

Rebeca thanked him and gave him her number. 'If you dial 1571, you can check you have it correctly.'

'Yes, I will,' he said. 'Thanks for calling.'

He hung up before she could say goodbye. She didn't think he was being abrupt – there was just nothing more to be said. She sat back again, her eyes still on the phone, as if it would ring immediately.

So much for backing away from the story, she thought.

The Island of Stoirm

The headlights picked out Miss Walker, Rory and the plain-clothes officer at the door to Rose Cottage. As Chaz brought the Land Rover to a halt and climbed out, he saw Rory frown.

'What are you two doing here?' Rory asked, moving towards Chaz and Alan. 'I said we'd look for this diary.'

'We have more information, regarding Sanctuary and the Children of the Dell,' said Chaz.

Miss Walker muttered something about the Hardy Boys again.

'They have nothing to do with this,' the plainclothes officer said. Rory introduced her as DC Bernadette Dwyer from the Major Investigations Team.

'We think they might,' said Alan.

'They could be a scam outfit,' said Chaz. 'And Nuala – Ms Flaherty – was here investigating them.'

DC Dwyer's face hardened. 'Don't you think we know that?'

'Yes, but did you know that the man they call Father was an actor who died before the first Sanctuary was set up?'

Chaz waited for a reaction but received none, although Rory did shoot the detective constable a quick look, but her face was so stony it could adorn Mount Rushmore.

'And the only phone number that connects to this Father is answered by a woman?' Alan added.

'So?' Dwyer said. 'That means nothing.'

'Have you heard of companies called DKMH or Templesword?' Alan didn't wait for them to reply. 'They are connected to Sanctuary and the Children of the Dell.'

Chaz could see that Dwyer had little patience for this, so he addressed Rory directly. 'We'll send you what we have. This Father of theirs is a fiction; there's money coming in and vanishing; they are linked to companies that might be shell companies, or shelf companies, or whatever – something dodgy, anyway – and anyone who looks into them seems to wind up dead. Nuala was the third.'

Rory was interested. 'Where are you getting all this?'

Chaz wasn't sure how to answer that. On the one hand, he felt the police should know about this; on the other, Delia had to be protected. Also, like Fiona, he wasn't sure of the legality of what she had done. 'Let's just say I have a source for now, okay?'

'A source.' Dwyer was unimpressed.

'Yes, don't you have them in the police?' Chaz spoke without thinking, and he saw immediately that Dwyer's mood turned even more belligerent.

Dwyer moved closer to them. 'Listen to me, none of this has anything to do with you, understand? We don't care about this Children of the Dale nonsense. It has nothing to do with our investigation.'

'Dell,' Alan corrected. 'Not Dale.'

Dwyer gave him a look that suggested she wished there were some stairs nearby he could accidentally fall down. 'You think we're just blundering around waiting for two amateur sleuths to crack the case for us? We've been working on this since Monday and we know a hell of a lot more than you think. In fact, we know a hell of a lot more than you. So, thank you for your input, but I suggest you let us take it from here, okay?'

She motioned to Miss Walker to unlock the cottage door and turned away from them. It was a dismissive gesture, and she left the boys with Rory, who said, almost apologetically, 'It's been a long day.'

'You know something, don't you?' Alan asked.

'I think DC Dwyer just told you we did. She's right, though, you two should butt out and let us do our job.'

'Do you think you'll find the spell book?'

'I thought you said it was a diary.'

'Nuala used it as a diary, too, Cynthia Danvers said.'

Rory processed this. 'Cynthia Danvers seemed to open up to you, then.'

'She really didn't tell you about it?'

Rory took a deep breath and stared at the door, from which light now flooded. Through the window they saw DC Dwyer circling the living room. 'No. But I don't think we'll find it here. We would have found it the first time.'

'So why are you looking again?'

'To be thorough,' Rory said, his voice falling hard on the words.

Chaz studied his face. 'You think you know where it is, don't you?'

Rory permitted himself a slight smile and he walked past them to enter the cottage, leaving them in the cold. And in the dark.

Miss Walker still stood at the cottage door, a mocking half-smile turned in their direction. 'Hardy Boys,' she said and then followed Rory inside.

'Who are these Hardy Boys?' Chaz asked Alan.

'Australian lads,' said Alan. 'They make wine but solve crimes in their spare time.'

Chaz knew from the tone of voice that Alan was having fun, but he didn't pursue it. He felt a slow burn of rage at Dwyer's dismissal of them.

Inverness

Rebecca had been stretched out on the couch in her small flat when she heard – thought she heard – the noise.

She had been turning the Nuala Flaherty story over in her mind, Hayley Westenra singing her heart out from the CD player. Her mother had given her the album of songs featuring music by some Italian film composer, telling her she found it ideal to soothe a troubled mind. Rebecca had thought what the hell, she'd try anything. And she was troubled. That there was a story connected to Nuala Flaherty's strange death was indisputable. Whether she should allow Chaz and Alan to continue to dig was not. She needed them to stop, but she also knew they were big boys and would do whatever they wanted.

Three deaths relating to the Children of the Dell. Among the many books she had picked up at home as a teenager was an old paperback copy of the James Bond novel *Goldfinger*. She hadn't thought much of it, but one thing had stuck in her mind, something that the villain said about meeting Bond: that something happening three times is enemy action. Three people in some way connected to the cult all dying has to mean something. But what? She didn't include the death of Bennet Lomax as he was gone before the Children of the Dell was formed. Whoever was really behind it, the real Father, perhaps knew his name or picked him at random, used an image of him in character from somewhere. She was guessing, of course. As to who Wesley Fairbank was, she had no idea. She wished Sam Walters' handwriting had been more legible because the scribbles might have cast some light on the notes that could be read. And what was that G word?

At some point she must have drifted to sleep but she woke with a start, her eyes springing open. The CD had come to an end and the flat was silent. Outside, she heard the noise of a car starting in the car park then driving away. But the noise she'd heard – thought she heard – had come from the rear of her flat. What she didn't know was whether it had emanated from outside – or someone was inside.

A footfall. A stumble. Then nothing.

There were four flats in her block and the soundproofing was adequate, but noises still bled through. She often heard her upstairs neighbour walking around, his TV if it was too loud, even talking when voices were raised. Sometimes she even heard his cat. The flat above was silent, though. No clumping feet, no TV, no conversation.

She lay on the couch, her breath in stasis, her eyes fixed on the doorway to the short hall that led to the bathroom, her bedroom and the rear of the flat. The window blinds were drawn, the only illumination in the living room from a small table lamp in the corner. The hallway was shadowed, but some light slanted through the back door from the street beyond the small communal rear garden. She rose slowly, trying to remember if she had locked the front and back doors. She was certain she had, but had she forgotten? Inverness was far from the murder capital of Scotland, but it still had crime. There had been three break-ins in the area over the past two months and leaving a door unlocked might be too much for the local scallywags to ignore. She thought hard, remembered turning the key in the lock of the front door but not the back. Had she even opened it recently? She couldn't recall.

All day she had been unable to shake off the feeling that someone was watching her. She had experienced that before, when Martin Bailey had been up to his tricks, but he had advertised himself. He had threatened her in person. He had sent her texts. He had tied a dead rat to the agency's door. She had known he was lurking somewhere. But her feeling this time was vague and indistinct, little more than an impression, like a draft that comes from nowhere then vanishes.

She held herself still in a half-upright position and listened again. Nothing. No creaks. No footfalls. No movement.

She swung her legs over the side of the couch, feet probing automatically for the slippers she had kicked off before settling down, the feeling that all was not as it seems niggling at the flesh around her neck and making her scalp itch. She thought about fetching the Louisville Slugger baseball bat, a gift from Chaz and Alan not because she was a baseball fan but after the Martin Bailey attack they wanted her to have something with which to defend herself, domestic ownership of an Uzi 9mm being frowned upon in the UK. When the going gets tough, the tough get swinging, Alan had said as he handed her the bat. But she was in the living room and the Slugger was in her bedroom, so if someone had broken in they could be in there waiting and get to her before she could get to it.

Becks, get a hold of yourself. You were drowsing, the noise could have been anything. She looked at the clock, ten past ten. She had been asleep for around two hours, so more than a drowse. She must have dreamed it, then, it was just a noise that . . .

She heard it again. The scrape of a boot on concrete, indistinct, coming from the back door.

She kicked off her slippers again – they were too loose and would be a hindrance for either fight or flight. She moved into the kitchen, her eye falling on the block holding knives, rejected the idea as she was not convinced she could ever stab or slash someone, then settled on a metal meat pounder. She baulked at cutting flesh, but she could sure as hell tenderise it. She edged towards the rear hallway, each step taken carefully, softly, deliberately. She reached the door and peered into the gloom. A shadow flicked across the glass doorway, confirming someone was out there. The police, she should call the police, but what if it's something innocent?

What could be innocent at the back of ten?

She had to know before she phoned anyone, so she took the final few paces to the door and peeped out. There was someone there, in the corner of the small garden, bending down. A man, but what the hell was he doing? She clicked on the exterior light above the doorway and he whirled round, startled, something cradled in his arms, something that wriggled.

She relaxed instantly, unlocked the door and stepped out, the bite of the night air instantly nipping the flesh of her face.

'Sorry,' said her upstairs neighbour, struggling with the cat in his arms, 'hope I didn't wake you.'

'No, you didn't.' She wasn't about to tell him she had been dozing on the couch. 'I heard a noise.'

'Sorry,' he said again, 'I didn't want this one out all night and I saw her nosing around here.' His eye fell on the meat pounder in her hand, but he didn't comment. Self-conscious now, she hid it from view behind her back.

'No worries,' she said. 'Goodnight.'

His back door was directly beside hers and it lay open. He walked to it. 'Night,' he said, his head down, but not so far that she couldn't see the slight smile on his lips.

She closed her door. Okay, so the guy upstairs thinks you're a complete nutter, coming to the back door with a bloody meat mallet like some cut-price Viking berserker. *Becks, you are imagining things. All this talk of psychic attacks and*

*demons – bloody hocus-pocus, for goodness sake – has you well
spooked. Not to mention dodgy cults and suspicious deaths.*

As Sophia would say, get yourself sorted, girl.

And then someone knocked at her front door and she felt
her guts lurch.

Mike had slumped down in the driver's seat of their rental, his
eyes half closed but still fixed on the block of four flats on the
other side of the small car park. He had wrapped his arms
around his chest to hug what heat he could into his body.
Beside him, Pat seemed impervious to the cold. Extremes of
weather never seemed to bother Pat, whereas Mike didn't like
it too cold or hot. He liked nice, even temperatures, thank you
very much for asking.

Pat's mobile rang and Mike wondered who the hell would
be phoning them. Pat answered it and said with a roll of the
eyes, 'You're up late.'

Mike could make out the buzz of the voice at the other end
but not the words. He could guess, though. They were being
checked up on. He hated that.

A car pulled into a space close to the building and Mike
watched as a tall man climbed out and made straight for the
Connolly girl's door.

'Aye, we're outside her place now,' said Pat, eyes on the man
as he rattled the knocker, then listened for a moment before
saying, a bit testily, Mike thought, 'It'll happen when it'll
happen. These things don't get rushed, no' if they're to be
done right.' Another pause, another buzz of speech, another
roll of Pat's eyes. 'Look, you put us on this 'cos we know our
business, right?' Pat's head bobbed as the man agreed. 'Right,
so let us do what we do, okay? This won't be as simple as a
bullet to the head, you know that. This lassie will take watching and studying, then the move will be made. Believe me,
we've got it covered. We know what we're doing, okay?'

Pat hung up without saying goodbye, thrust the phone back into a pocket, watched as the man waited for the door to open.

'I don't know why you put up with that guy,' said Mike.

'You know why,' Pat said, and that was that portion of the conversation over. This fellow at the door was more interesting to them.

Mike said, 'That the boyfriend we were told about, d'you think?'

'Aye.'

The girl opened the front door.

'Coming for a wee bit of how's your father, I'll bet,' said Mike.

Pat craned forward. 'What's that in her hand?'

Mike couldn't quite see. 'Dunno. Maybe she knew he was coming and it's something for some kinky fuckery.'

They watched as the girl stepped back to let the man enter.

'I felt bad about our last chat,' Stephen said as Rebecca closed the door behind him, then flicked a finger at the meat mallet still in her hand. 'Did I come at a bad time?'

She was grateful the dim light of the entrance hall wouldn't reveal the embarrassment that flushed her face. 'I always carry it about. You never know when you'll come across an emergency meat-flattening situation.' She moved into the kitchen and laid the utensil on the draining board beside the sink. 'Don't worry about the chat, Stephen. I'd forgotten about your sister.'

'I know, but I still wanted to apologise.'

'You already did.'

'I wanted to apologise again.'

She smiled, even though the refusal still stung a little and she didn't really know why. 'Apology accepted.'

'I know I could have phoned but wanted to do it in person. I should have waited till tomorrow, I suppose.'

She also supposed he could have but was glad he hadn't – it was good to see him. Okay, maybe she did see him as more than a friend. With benefits. That realisation made her uncomfortable, though. She wasn't ready for any kind of emotional complication. She had too much to do.

'So why the mallet, then?' he asked.

She told him about hearing the noise and the upstairs neighbour retrieving his cat from the garden. He leaned against the doorframe as he listened, his face serious. 'So what's making you so jumpy?'

'The Nuala Flaherty story has taken a far more serious turn.'

'Okay,' he said.

She almost began to explain when she remembered his lack of openness over his own job. Maybe it was time to open that conversation. 'You know, I tell you everything about my work, yet you don't tell me anything about yours.'

'That's because there's nothing to tell.'

'You're in criminal law, there's always something to tell. Even just gossip.'

'I don't gossip.'

'That I know!'

He shifted his position. 'You know I can't talk about my clients.'

'Yes, I know, but don't try to tell me that solicitors don't do it all the time with people they trust.'

'Not me.'

'Not you? Or just not with me?'

His mouth opened then closed and he glanced into the living room. 'Can we sit down?'

Chaz was thinking about asking Alan for a cuddle to help ward off the creeping chill but decided against it. Neither of them was prone to public displays of affection, and they knew the search would not take very long. It wasn't a large cottage and it had already been gone through once, but when Rory and DC Dwyer emerged from the cottage empty-handed, just as the young police officer had predicted, Chaz was slightly deflated. Although part of him was relieved that it meant they could soon get away from the cold. Miss Walker trailed behind the police officers, making sure the door was firmly closed and locked. She gave Chaz a little smile as she turned, letting him know that she was ensuring he and Alan didn't come back to have a look for themselves.

'Nothing, I take it?' Alan asked.

'No sign of any book or notebook. Not even a collection of Post-it notes,' said Rory.

'Cynthia Danvers was adamant that Nuala kept it with her and was religious in recording her day.'

Chaz noted a look between the officers at the mention of Cynthia Danvers. He had no idea what it meant, but it only confirmed that they knew more than they were saying. It also stimulated that itch in his mind. Something she had said during their chat. He would have discussed it with Alan, even Rory, but whatever it was continued to dance just out of reach.

'Well, it's not there now,' said Dwyer.

'Someone must have taken it,' Alan said, stating what seemed obvious to Chaz. 'Who?'

Another glance between the police officers. Chaz was certain he and Alan had either missed something or didn't have all the information. Rory's mobile rang and he stepped away to answer it.

'Never you mind who,' Dwyer warned. 'You two have interfered enough. It's time to walk away and leave it to us.'

'And what about the Children of the Dell?' Alan insisted.

In the bright light of Miss Walker's torch they saw more irritation flash across the detective's face. 'Let me spell this out for you. If I hear that you, either together or singly, ask anyone else about the death of Nuala Flaherty, or interfere in any way, you will be arrested.'

'You can't . . .'

'I can and I will.'

Alan stood his ground. 'On what charge?'

'Interfering in and impeding a police investigation, tampering with witnesses, attempting to pervert the course of justice, being a pain in the arse without a licence. This is not your business, so keep your nose out.'

'This is my business,' said Chaz, his tone harsh. He had been freezing his nuts off and the woman had now annoyed him. They may have been blundering about but he shared Rebecca's dislike of being threatened. 'I can follow up this story. We haven't interfered or impeded anything; in fact, telling you what Cynthia Danvers told us might be seen as assisting police with their inquiries. We haven't tampered with witnesses – we've spoken to them. And nobody has been charged with anything yet; so they're not even witnesses, they are private citizens. As for attempting to pervert, don't make me laugh, DC Dwyer. The pain-in-the-arse charge may have some merit but when you show me your licence, I'll show you mine.'

She was about to argue back, but Rory stepped back into the light and asked to have a word. Alan had listened to Chaz's speech slightly open-mouthed, and he stepped closer to whisper, 'My God, if Miss Walker wasn't here, I would jump your bones right now.'

'Please resist that temptation, Mr Shields,' Miss Walker said. Chaz should have warned Alan they called her Batwoman for a reason.

Rory moved closer but Dwyer walked past them into the dark without a word, heading back to their vehicle, every step an angry exclamation. 'We're done here, guys,' said Rory. He must have heard Dwyer's threats and seemed slightly embarrassed. 'There's been an RTA and we're needed.'

Chaz frowned. 'A road traffic accident on the island? At this time of year? And at night? What's happened?'

Rory glanced after his colleague, made sure she was out of earshot. 'A woman's been knocked down by a Land Rover, sounds pretty tragic to me. Your dad's on his way now to the locus.'

Chaz asked, 'Who was it, do you know yet?' He caught Rory's hesitation, so he explained, 'I was brought up here, Rory, you know that. I may know her.'

Rory paused, debated with himself. 'This is off the record, right? You don't use this until officially released?'

Chaz nodded, a feeling of unease stirring.

'I need to hear you say it, Chaz,' Rory insisted.

'I won't use any of this until it's officially released.'

Rory glanced at Miss Walker, as if letting her know she was a witness, then said, 'I don't know the name yet, but it's someone from Sanctuary . . .'

Right away, Chaz knew it was Delia.

Inverness

Sawyer stood in the shadow of a doorway on Baron Taylor's Street, his eyes seldom straying from the lane opposite. He could see the sign for Barney's glowing above the door halfway down the narrow passageway. He had been there for an hour, snug this time in his thick sheepskin flight jacket, a birthday present from his wife on his fortieth, back when things had been good between them, or at least he thought they had been. They were no longer together, so he learned he was wrong. He had taken some abuse from mates – cracks about Biggles and Sopwith Camels abounded – which he took in good humour, but he couldn't resist a smug smile when they stood on the terraces of the Inverness Cally Thistle ground, their teeth chattering and skin grey, as the breeze carried the chill of the Moray Firth towards them.

Punters walked by, some heading to or away from pubs, others just passing down the cramped street on their way to somewhere else, more clustering in and around the fast food outlet that was doing a roaring trade. A few spotted him and hastened their step. After all, a big guy standing in a shop doorway was suspicious, but he didn't care. Let them phone the police; he was confident he would have no trouble smoothing that over. He still had pals in uniform.

It would soon be closing time and that's when he would make his move, his reasoning being that there would only be a few diehard boozers remaining inside Barney's. Alcohol could make the bar's average punter more aggressive, but it also made them less co-ordinated and slow to react. Sawyer himself was stone-cold sober. He kept his breathing even, refusing to allow the rage he had felt kindling as he stood over Cokey's bed to take control. Like booze, unbridled anger could be a liability; but, unlike alcohol, if channelled properly it could work to his advantage. He would need that edge. So he let the fury turn cold in order to ice up his resolve.

It was almost midnight when he decided the time had come. Nobody had entered or left the pub for fifteen minutes, so he reasoned whoever remained inside would be well oiled and easy to manage. She wouldn't be, though. Mo Burke was out of control, otherwise this would not have been necessary, but she would never allow herself to lose focus through booze.

He crossed the street and entered the lane, which was barely wide enough for two people to pass. If he had to make a run for it – not that he planned to – this would also work in his favour as whoever might be chasing him could only come at him one at a time. Another edge, should he need it.

He came to a halt at the pub door, took a deep breath, then pushed it open. As before, he felt as if he was breathing the exact same beer-fuelled air and seeing the same small, bedraggled group of men at the bar. Three of them: two in their twenties, one older. He took note of their positions and tried to gauge which of them posed the greater threat. The same barman as last time was collecting empty pint mugs and whisky glasses from the tables.

And there she was. Mo Burke. Sitting at the table, as usual a cigarette wedged between her fingers, a half-filled glass of red wine on the table, her wee dog in the basket at her feet, fast asleep by the looks of it. Mo saw him come in, of course, and he thought he spotted a flicker of a smile as he marched straight towards her. Keep smiling, hen, he told himself, that'll just make me worse.

'Is it no' past your bedtime, former detective sergeant?'

Sawyer noted she placed a lot of emphasis on the 'former', reminding him that he had no power any more, and certainly not in here. He didn't give a toss.

'I saw Cokey today,' he said, in no mood for banter.

A twitch of one eyebrow. 'That right? And how is the twitchy wee bastard?'

'You know how he is, Mo. He was in hospital, and you put him there.' He jerked his head over his shoulder. 'Or rather, you got some of the brains trust there to do it.' He craned round to study the men at the bar. 'Although they don't look tasty enough to open a bag of crisps, let alone damage someone.'

Mo tapped ash into the ashtray. 'Don't know what you're

talking about, *former* detective sergeant.' That emphasis again. He still didn't give a toss.

He faced her. 'He got done over. Two, maybe three people gave him a kicking, broke his fingers.'

'That's a shame,' she said, the words carrying as much sincerity as a politician's hopes and prayers. 'I'll need to send him some grapes.'

'He can't eat them. His jaw is dislocated. And you know what else?'

She gave him a wide-eyed look. 'What?'

He leaned over and placed both hands on the tabletop to stare straight into those innocent but not-so-innocent eyes. 'They pulled out some teeth, Mo. Maybe using pliers.'

She didn't sit back when he loomed over her. She seemed relaxed as she stared up at him. 'Maybe he had cavities and he went to the wrong dentist.'

The slight scuff of a foot on the dirty floor told Sawyer that the boys behind him had shifted position. As he straightened again, he flicked his eye to the mirrored wall above Mo's head, saw the two young ones had left the bar and were stringing out behind him, waiting for the nod from their boss. Even the barman was edging towards him, a pint pot in his hand. The older guy remained where he was, but he watched the proceedings with studied indifference.

'You're the dentist, Mo. Let's cut the crap, eh?'

She stuck the cigarette between her lips again, her other hand doing the tap-and-twirl thing with her gold lighter. 'I told you, I don't know what you're talking about. I do know Cokey had a habit of flapping his gums. Maybe he'll no' do that so much now.'

He shot another look in the mirror. Neither of the young men moved, they simply stood watching them. He noted that they both swayed slightly, so they would be slow, and he knew the barman was no real threat. He might throw that glass, but that's about all. It was the last guy, the older one still standing with one elbow on the bar, who drew his attention. He seemed to regard the whole thing with cool disinterest, his eyes dead but not drowned by booze. If there was anyone in this room he needed to watch, it was him. And Mo, of course.

'You know something, Mo? I think you're losing the place.'

She shrugged. 'You're entitled to your opinion.'

'No' just mine, love. That's the word. Mo Burke's gone off the rails, they say. She's so screwed up by grief and hate that she's lost focus, ripe for the Glasgow boys to really come in and take over. And who's going to stop them? Scott's banged up, so's your man.' He gave it a beat before he said slowly. 'And Nolan? Well, he's dead, isn't he?'

That hit the mark. He saw heat flash in her eyes, but she dampened it down quickly.

'Aye,' he went on, 'you've lost it big time. You'll soon be nothing, sitting here in this shithole with your wee dog, your looks gone – you need to give up the fags, darling, you're taking on a leathery look.'

'I don't need beauty tips from the likes of you,' she said, and by the stretched tone he knew she was beginning to get pissed off. Come on, he thought, don't fight it, let's do it. He could feel the need to inflict damage rising within him.

'You'll just be here, at this table, your looks, your past glories all faded. And all because you let your emotions get the better of you.' He paused, just long enough to add weight to his next words. 'Typical bloody woman. It was always bound to happen.'

He hadn't seen her signal the boys at his back, but one of them moved anyway. It was one of the younger ones, spurred on by either drink or eagerness to please. He lunged, a knife in his hand, but Sawyer was poised for some kind of move. He spun, stepped aside and parried with his left arm, the blade sliding off the thick leather-and-wool lining. That was another reason he loved this jacket – it would take a bullet to get through it. Sawyer lashed out with his foot, his heavy walking boot connecting with the boy's knee. He grunted and tipped to one side just as his pal jumped forward, but he was too unsteady on his feet and he mistimed his attack, giving Sawyer the opportunity to dodge away. The boy's momentum carried him onwards and he slammed into the table, sending the ashtray flying and tipping Mo's red wine over her lap. As he tumbled over to sprawl on the floor, Mo cursed and stood up, her dog awake and on its feet, barking. It might turn out to be an anklebiter, but Sawyer didn't have time to worry about that, for the barman did as predicted: threw the beer glass but didn't follow through. His aim was bad, the missile went wide, smashed against the mirror. The dog's bark grew increasingly shrill, but it didn't make any move to join the fray, for which Sawyer was grateful because he didn't relish having to kick the wee shit back into its basket. He would if he had to, though. A bar fight was no place to be Dr Dolittle.

The boy with the knife came at him again, favouring his right leg, but Sawyer had another edge, literally up his sleeve. He let the slim baton slip into his hand, flicked it expertly to extend it and swung it in a swift sideways arc. As an officer he was not supposed to aim at the head, but, as Mo kept pointing out, he was no longer an officer, and he still didn't give a toss. The baton may have been lightweight, but in the right hands it could do damage, and Sawyer had ensured over the years that he was adept in its use. The aluminium casing cracked against the young man's skull and his eyes rolled as he pitched to the side, the knife clattering on the hard floor. The table-turner was struggling to get to his feet, but Sawyer put him back down with a foot to the face.

That only left the older man.

Sawyer whirled in his direction, ready for his move. He would not be so easy to deal with, he knew that. Those two were the worse for the bevvy, the barman had backed away as if throwing the glass had been an accident, but this guy was sober. He hadn't moved during the brief burst of action and there was a slight smile in his heavily lidded eyes as he turned them to Sawyer, who stood in a half-crouch, the baton held easily in his hand, the tip resting against his shoulder.

Sawyer was panting slightly when he said, 'So we going to do this, mate, or just stand here and look at each other?'

The man looked back at the younger men, both on the floor and bleeding, then smiled, holding up his hands. 'We're cool, man,' he said and backed to the door. 'This isnae my fight.'

And then he was gone. Sawyer couldn't help but feel something of an anti-climax.

Mo decided to fill the void. She snatched up her now empty wine glass from where it had landed and smashed the rim against the top of the table. Sawyer jumped away and swung the baton quickly, but pulled it before it connected, allowing it to rest on her throat. 'Don't think I won't hurt you, Mo. I don't care if you're a woman.'

They glared at each other over the upturned table while her dog continued to bark, the effort making it bounce on its back paws. It didn't seem to have the stomach to do anything more than that, though.

'You've stepped over a line, Sawyer.' Her voice was hoarse with rage, and the lines on her face looked as if they had been etched with a blade. She still held the broken glass at shoulder level, as if she was about to strike.

'No, hen – you stepped over it when you damaged Cokey.'

Her brow furrowed. 'I don't get it, what do you care about a wee bastard like that?'

He ignored the question. He was not going to explain himself to the likes of Mo Burke. 'You're on a road to hell,

Mo. If you don't pull yourself back, you're done, I mean it. Call off the job on Rebecca Connolly. I won't tell you again.'

He sensed the moment of her glassing him had passed, and he lowered the baton but did not put it away. He nodded to the red wine spreading across the legs of her jeans like blood. 'I'd try some soda water on that smartish, if I were you. It's not a good look.'

He backed away, the baton held slightly out from his side as the two felled warriors groaned and began to rouse themselves. Mo's eyes burned after him. The dog barked. Once outside, Sawyer telescoped the weapon down again and thrust it back up his sleeve as he hurried along the lane, feeling the excitement of the action still singing in his veins. It had been a while since he had tangled with scrotes like that, and it felt good.

5

THURSDAY

Inverness

Rebecca and Stephen had talked until after midnight. He hadn't stayed over. She hadn't wanted him to stay over. It wasn't that she was angry with him, and they hadn't argued, but they did have an open and frank conversation which really didn't get them anywhere. Stephen didn't talk about his work because he couldn't, was his position. He didn't talk about his work because he didn't want to, was hers. What it boiled down to, she told him, was that he didn't trust her. He had stared at her for a long time after that, but he didn't deny it. He couldn't. And that was fine because now she really knew where she stood, in that regard at least.

Then he asked the question.

'What are we?'

'What do you mean, what are we?' she had countered, knowing full well what he meant.

'What is this? Us, I mean. What's going on? Between us?'

'Right now, or in general?'

'I know what right now is,' he said. 'This is "the talk", isn't it? This is the one where we establish what we are and where we're going.'

She permitted herself to force a smile. 'You're not going to propose, are you?'

He smiled back. 'No, you're safe there.'

He waited for her to respond, and she struggled to find the words. 'I don't know, Stephen. We're . . . friends?'

His head tilted in agreement. 'But more than that, right?'

'Well, yes,' she said, feeling uncomfortable. She was not one to think too deeply about emotions, not hers anyway. She didn't think Stephen was, either, but obviously she was wrong.

'So what are we then?' he pressed. 'A couple?'

Now she was sorry she had opened the door to him. Simon had often wanted to have 'the talk' but she had always swerved away from it, she thought with the grace of an Olympic skater, but Simon no doubt had a different view. 'Well, em, yes, I suppose we are,' she said, wondering if she could sound any more grudging. Then she added, for no reason she understood, 'Yes.'

Stephen ignored the way the words had come out like pulled teeth. 'So we're in a relationship?'

Oh God, the R-word, she thought, but resisted the temptation to roll her eyes. 'Well, yes, I suppose so.'

He had sat back then. 'Okay.'

'Okay,' she repeated.

'I just needed to know.'

'Okay,' she said again, beginning to fear that someone was going to use the L-word. Nobody did, though. Clearly, the R-word was enough.

He had left shortly after that. There was a goodnight kiss, of course there was, and it was a good one. So good she almost suggested he stay over, but then he was gone.

The following morning, she replayed the conversation in her mind and realised that, limited though it was, stilted though it was, it had gone further than she had ever allowed such an exchange to go with Simon. That meant something,

261

but she didn't know what. Or rather, she chose not to recognise what it meant because she wasn't prepared to consider the fact that – vomit alert – they really were in a relationship. Rebecca didn't do touchy-feely.

Her agency mobile rang as she wolfed down a toasted bagel and banana before setting out. She glanced at the screen, saw the number was withheld and was going to ignore it, then decided she had better answer. If this is someone asking/telling me I've been in an accident recently, she vowed, I'll go all Glasgow on their arse.

'Is this Ms Connolly?' A woman's voice. Crisp as fresh linen straight out of the freezer.

'Yes, who's this?'

'My name is Vivian Ward. I understand you've been trying to contact me?'

Rebecca almost knocked over her orange juice as she reached for her bag on the counter to haul out her notebook and pen. 'Yes, Mrs Ward, thank you so much for calling me back.'

'I only called to say I have nothing to say.'

'You don't even know what I'm going to ask, Mrs Ward.'

'No matter what it is, I have nothing to say.'

Rebecca sensed this was not true. If she really had nothing to say, she wouldn't have called back. 'I'm following up a story about Children of the Dell.' She waited, but the woman said nothing. She didn't hang up, either. 'You know what I'm talking about, don't you? Children of the Dell. Sanctuary.' Rebecca inserted a very brief pause. 'Father.'

'What kind of story?'

Rebecca smiled, the whole awkward feeling over the previous night consigned to the 'think about it later' file. This was where she was on firm ground. 'I assume you are familiar with the name Nuala Flaherty?'

'Why would you assume that, Ms Connolly?'

262

There was a hollow sound to the call and Rebecca wondered if she was on loudspeaker at the other end. That suggested they were not alone in this conversation.

'Okay, what about Sam Walters? Or Gerald Frame?'

There was another silence on the line and Rebecca wondered if the woman had cut the connection. Her personal mobile vibrated and she saw Chaz was calling her. She let it go to voicemail.

There was still no sound on the woman's line so she said, 'Mrs Ward?'

'I'm here.'

'You recognise these names, don't you?'

'I do not propose to discuss this over the phone, Ms Connolly.'

'Then where are you? I'll come to you.'

Silence again. 'Kether House, near Foyers.'

'On Loch Ness?'

'Yes. We'll expect you at 12.30.'

Rebecca looked at the clock, four hours away. 'Fine, I'll be there but . . .'

This time the line had died. Rebecca popped a bit of stray banana in her mouth as she thought about the conversation. Vivian Ward had recognised the names, she was certain, and she had said, 'We'll expect you.' Someone else had been listening, Rebecca was sure, and probably directing the woman's responses. That someone had to be Thomas Smith. She felt the familiar sense of excitement build as she picked up her personal phone to return Chaz's call.

'I think I've tracked down Thomas Smith,' she said as soon as he answered.

'Delia Forbes is dead,' he interrupted.

She took that in then said, 'What? How?'

'She was run over on the road leading to Sanctuary.'

'Dear God,' said Rebecca. She had never met this woman, but this was a shock. 'When?'

'Last night, it must have been just after we left her.' Something clouded Chaz's voice. Guilt, Rebecca assumed. 'She was hit by the Land Rover from Sanctuary. That guy Seb was driving.'

Another death connected to Sanctuary, Rebecca thought. That made four.

'He said it was an accident,' Chaz said, heavy emphasis on the word 'said'. 'She was walking down a hill so he could get to a place where he could get his door open to let her in. The brakes gave out and she was crushed.'

'What do you think?'

'I saw him working on it the other day. It's an old machine.'

'So it could be true?'

'It could be. The guy was pretty devastated by it. Babbling about it, crying.'

'Did you see him?'

'No. Dad did. He was called out. Mum drove him because Alan and I were at Rose Cottage.'

'Has this Seb been arrested?'

'They kept him overnight, don't know if they've let him go.'

'What do you think, Chaz?'

She knew he would understand what she meant. Another death connected to Sanctuary. 'It could have happened just as he said,' Chaz admitted. 'I know that hill, it's near Sanctuary and it's pretty steep, with hedges on both sides so there's room for one vehicle with passing places, but not nearly enough of them. When the hedges aren't cut, they can scrape paintwork. It's possible that Delia couldn't get out of the way.'

'But wouldn't she have heard the engine coming, maybe seen headlights?'

'Seb said he had stopped at the top of the hill and climbed out when he saw her. They talked, he said, and he was going to take her back to Sanctuary.'

'But the brakes failed.'

'Yeah, the brakes failed.'

His voice remained dull, and she knew he blamed himself. 'It wasn't your fault, Chaz.'

'I know.'

'It really wasn't. It may well have been an accident.'

'Yeah,' he said, but she could tell he wasn't buying it.

Sawyer was still in his dressing gown when Val Roach turned up at his front door, making him feel somehow at a disadvantage. She looked him up and down and commented, 'You'll not be at your post anytime soon, I see.'

He knew she meant watching Rebecca. 'As you said, I can't do it 24/7.'

'So you choose your moments?'

'Something like that.'

They stared at each other over the doorstep for a moment before Roach said, 'Are you going to invite me in, or should I ask you if you've found Jesus?'

He stepped back, adjusting the front of his robe, pulling it tighter together. He was wearing pyjamas underneath but there was something disconcerting about having a woman in his home when he wasn't fully dressed. Roach walked past him and into the sitting room. She knew the way because she had been to his house before. He was grateful he had vacuumed a couple of days before and that he had ferried nearly a full tea set of dirty dishes into the kitchen just before she arrived. They hadn't made it to the dishwasher yet. These things take time.

'To what do I owe the pleasure, DCI . . . Val,' he amended.

She didn't take a seat, contenting herself by standing on the worn hearth rug in front of the gas fire. Maybe she was warming herself, he thought.

'I'm catching the 10.46 to Edinburgh.'

'Sightseeing?'

'Seeing something,' she said. 'Someone paid Barney's a visit last night.'

The rage and resulting euphoria had long since worn off and Sawyer knew he had made a mistake the previous night. It didn't matter how much he enjoyed it, or how much those scrotes deserved what he'd given them – he really had crossed a line. He might have got away with it before, but he was a civilian now. and auld lang syne only goes so far. He might be about to find out just how far.

'That right?' He decided it was best to keep playing the game.

Roach gave him a long look. 'Yes. Someone gave a few of the patrons a hiding.'

'Someone?'

'Yes, said patrons couldn't provide a clear description.'

He fought back a small smile. 'It's a ned's watering hole, could've been anyone.'

'Indeed,' she said. 'Anyone with an extendable baton.'

He feigned surprise. 'That what he used?'

'Expertly, it seems.'

They regarded each other for what seemed like a long time. Sawyer wondered if she expected him to confess. That wasn't happening. 'I'm sure they deserved it.'

'So am I. However, if this individual is intent on waging some sort of war then I would recommend that he reconsider.'

'My gut tells me this was a one-off incident.'

Roach continued to study him. 'Glad to hear it, because my gut tells me that if this individual does anything like that again, I will have him enjoying the amenities of the custody suite quicker than he can say, "What the hell happened to my pension?"' She let that sink in before she added, 'Whoever he is.'

She moved towards the front door, and Sawyer opened it for her. 'What are you going to Edinburgh for?'

266

She crossed the threshold, stared across the road at the trees and field beyond, then turned back. 'It's my day to advise people against courses of action that might irk me.'

Drumnadrochit, Loch Ness

Elspeth was leaning against the low wall that surrounded the outdoor eating area of the small tearoom and bookshop she ran with Julie. It enjoyed a good situation for trade, right on the A82 that ran along the western edge of Loch Ness and near to the village hotel and famed monster exhibition. There had been some lean years of late but Elspeth's other business interests, the news agency, the money from the books and some canny investments, meant she and her partner didn't go hungry. She straightened when she saw Rebecca's car approaching, plucking her walking stick from where it was propped beside her. A few years before she had damaged her hip and had declined the offer of surgery to fix it, her mistrust of anyone wielding a blade while wearing a mask overcoming her need to walk unaided. Rebecca had called her when she was five minutes away from the village, to ensure she would be waiting for her, stressing that it would take a little time to drive back to Inverness and then on to Foyers on the loch's east side. She realised this was a dress rehearsal for their journey the following day to the ferry, which would also be time-sensitive.

Elspeth climbed into the car with some difficulty and tucked her stick between her seat and the door, then re-arranged the plaid-like wrap that blanketed her body. 'Do you still think this trip is necessary?' she asked.

They had discussed it at length on the phone. Given the level of sudden death surrounding this story, Elspeth had advised against meeting up with the mysterious Mrs Ward and the even more shadowy Thomas Smith, reminding

267

Rebecca that she had told the boys on the island to back off. Rebecca, however, was curious. That was why she had first become a reporter: her need to know was always strong. It was either that or follow in her father's footsteps and join the police, but she knew, even as a teenager, that she didn't have the discipline to accept someone else having authority over her. That was part of her problem when working in the newspaper industry – Elspeth apart, she resented someone telling her what she could or could not do. She was, as her mother had commented more than once, a thrawn bugger. Thrawn, a Scots word meaning ill-tempered or truculent. In this case, her mum meant stubborn, and Rebecca recognised the truth in it but reasoned that a good reporter has to be stubborn, even truculent.

'Needs to be done, Elspeth,' said Rebecca, checking her wing mirror before she pulled a U-turn. 'Anyway, you're here to protect me.'

Thrawn she may be, but she was not stupid and there was no way she was going to this meeting without back-up. She had considered asking Bill Sawyer to come along, but he was already in Sir Galahad mode and she didn't want to play further into his male fantasy. She was confident Elspeth was more than a match for anyone. Anyway, it was highly unlikely there would be unpleasantness.

That's what she told herself, anyway.

Mike had driven past the lassie's car when she pulled in at the front of the tearoom then stopped where he could and watched in the rear-view mirror. Pat kept an eye on the passenger-side wing mirror. He hoped she was going in for a cuppa because he was gasping for a brew himself, but she was only stopping to pick up a stocky woman with a walking stick.

'Where do you think she's headed?' Mike asked.

'I left my prediction meter in my other coat,' said Pat. Touchy today, Mike thought. But then, when was Pat anything other than touchy?

'She's turned around,' said Pat.

'I can see that,' said Mike, who could be touchy, too.

'Who is that?' Pat wondered.

Mike waited until the car had vanished around a bend before he turned the wheel fully to the right and waited for a car to pass before he pointed the car back in the direction of Inverness. 'I left my cast list beside your prediction meter.'

Pat tutted. 'Nobody likes a smartarse, Mike.'

'That explains how nobody likes you.'

The Island of Stoirm

Chaz had been willing to follow Rebecca's advice to back off, but then Dwyer had issued her ultimatum, and now he wanted to go back to the hotel and have another word with Cynthia Danvers. The missing spell book bothered him, but so did the niggle in his mind for reasons he couldn't explain. Alan was the one who urged caution, which was a role reversal for them.

'I'm not letting this go, Alan,' he said. 'I owe it to Delia.'

They should have stayed with her or got her to remain in the village. They should never have let her walk alone on that road. Chaz knew the guilt would stay with him for some time.

'Chaz, darling, you hardly knew the woman.'

Chaz knew that was true, but he couldn't find the words to explain properly. All he could say was, 'It's something I need to do.'

Alan gave in. 'A man's gotta do what a man's gotta do, is that it?'

'Something like that.'

Mandy Newcombe buzzed Cynthia Danvers's room to tell her that they were in reception to see her. She didn't object this time – perhaps the fact that the three of them had shared a convivial bar lunch fitted the good hotelier's guidelines as to who could be admitted and who couldn't. She offered them coffee, which they declined. She then commented that it was a terrible thing that had happened, that poor woman going under the wheels of the Land Rover, and how the hell did it ever pass its MOT? Chaz knew that MOTs were often more guidelines than rules on the island, but if Seb had known the brakes were in danger of failing, he should never have been driving the damn thing. But he didn't say that aloud. He didn't want to talk about it.

Cynthia Danvers appeared fifteen minutes later, as before perfectly made-up but casually dressed in designer jeans and a baggy woollen sweater. The ring that looked like an asteroid searching for a world to flatten was still perched on her finger, but Chaz noted she didn't carry the designer bag she had clutched when they first met her. She took a seat beside them in front of the dark fireplace and crossed her legs, all the better for them to see her expensive high heels. Chaz had felt the first time they met that she liked to be conspicuous in her ostentation, and he saw nothing now to contradict that view.

'I'm catching the next ferry for the mainland, so we'll have to be quick,' she said.

Chaz acknowledged with a nod. 'We won't be long,' he said. 'We didn't find the spell book.'

Her delicately plucked eyebrows shot up. Chaz felt it was a pose, rather like her display of accoutrement. 'So where has it gone?'

'Well, obviously someone took it,' said Alan.

'Who?'

'Ah,' Alan said, 'that's the question.'

'Is it likely that Nuala would have hidden it somewhere?' Chaz asked. 'The police searched pretty thoroughly, so was there a chance she might have put it in safekeeping outside the cottage?'

She considered this. Or made a show of it. Chaz couldn't help but feel there was more to her posing than just showing off her style.

'I can't see it,' she said. 'She never let that book out of her sight. She put everything in there – her "essence in words", she used to say. She wouldn't be comfortable leaving it somewhere that wasn't within easy reach. No, if it's gone, then someone has taken it.'

'If that's the case, then it was taken for a reason,' Alan said. 'There must be something in there that incriminates them in some way.'

B862, the Scottish Highlands

The narrow road to the east of Loch Ness was less used by tourists and lorries and in many places was a more satisfying drive than the busier A82 on the western side. It veered inland, now and again offering a tantalising glimpse of the loch's blue waters, and rewarded travellers with some fine Highland scenery. Not that Rebecca or Elspeth paid much attention, even though the weather remained clement. They were used to the stunning vistas their small country often afforded, and the splendours of the landscape passed them by relatively unnoticed.

Rebecca brought her boss up to date with what had happened on Stoirm, telling her about Delia's death the night before. Elspeth stared at the countryside as it zipped by, her lips pursed, her hand gripping the handle of her cane.

'We shouldn't be doing this,' Elspeth said eventually. 'Especially given what's happened.'

'I know,' said Rebecca, 'but then again we should. This is what we do, Elspeth. Get the story, right? Above all, get the story.'

'Yeah,' said Elspeth, 'use my own words against me. But I didn't mean put yourself in harm's way. Four deaths, Becks.'

If three times was enemy action, what was four, Rebecca wondered. 'We're not in harm's way,' she argued. 'We don't know if these deaths are anything more than coincidence. What else was it you said once? Be wary of seeing patterns that aren't there? Like seeing faces and figures in wall-paper or floor coverings, the more you look, the more you see, but it doesn't mean they were there in the first place. Nuala and her partner were obviously not the full shilling. Gerald Frame had been an addict. What happened to the woman on Stoirm could simply be what it appears – an accident.'

Elspeth kept her silence, still looking out the window.

'Anyway,' said Rebecca, 'I doubt we'll be hauled off to some dungeon or disappeared somehow. They don't know who we've told about this interview.'

Elspeth looked at her. 'Sure, but that doesn't mean there couldn't be another tragic accident.'

'There could be an accident on this road,' Mike observed, and Pat considered this.

'She's not alone, though.'

'Collateral damage.'

Pat considered this, too. 'Maybe. Possibly.'

'I'd say definitely. If it's going to happen, there might not be a better opportunity, right?'

Pat's eyes narrowed, playing the permutations over. 'I'm no' sure, Mike. Witnesses are tricky, you know that. Accidents happen, sure, but what if one survives? Let's wait and see what presents itself. We just need to be ready to move when the time comes.'

'I was born ready,' said Mike, grinning.

*

272

Tabitha Haley phoned when Rebecca's satnav told her they were two miles from Kether House. She clicked the hands-free. 'Hi, Tabitha, I'm driving. I've got my boss in the car.'

'Elspeth McTaggart, Tabitha.'

'Okay. Hi, Elspeth.' Tabitha's voice sounded somewhat taken aback by the awkward niceties of hands-free calling. 'Just a quick call, Rebecca. You mentioned a group called the Sisters, right? Connected to Nuala Flaherty?'

'Yes. She formed it, apparently, down in Cheadle, right?'

'Right. I managed to speak with a member of the group late last night – well, chat online, but I suppose that's the same as speaking.'

Elspeth made a sucking sound with her teeth, making Rebecca smile. She disapproved of the way social media chats had replaced actual conversations, and Rebecca understood that was why she had reluctantly agreed to come along to meet Mrs Ward. She had raised objections as any good boss or friend would, but, when it came down to it, she knew you learned more by facing the person than speaking on the phone.

'Okay,' said Rebecca, 'so what did they say?'

'Nuala formed the group almost as soon as she settled there.'

'Okay.' Rebecca already knew that, but to say so seemed petty. Perhaps even thrawn.

'There are maybe eight or nine women at any one time.'

She knew that, too. 'So not a full coven, then? That would be thirteen, right?'

'Well, theoretically, yes. Nuala insisted on a women-only membership because she wanted to harness the power of the female, not that the rest of the women were all that interested. The way my contact put it, meetings were an excuse for a piss-up, a laugh and, for some of them, a chance to experiment with drugs. Everyone but Nuala. Did you know she had some kind of heart condition?'

'Yes, I'd heard. What kind of drugs?'

'Started with the usual – grass, mild stuff. But one or two developed a taste for stronger hallucinogens. LSD, psilocybin, even mescaline. That was a trip, apparently.'

'Psilocybin? Mescaline I've kind of heard of.'

'Shrooms,' Elspeth said. 'Magic mushrooms, like the green-flush fibrecap, wavy cap, Laughing Jim. They can all be found here in Britain, if you know where to look and know what to do with them. And mescaline comes from the peyote cactus in the USA. It's not readily available in the UK, but you can get anything if you want it badly enough and are willing to pay. These are all strong medicines.'

Rebecca darted a look at her boss. Elspeth shrugged and said, 'I did a story on hallucinogens once.'

'Uh-huh,' said Rebecca, knowing that Elspeth had a past life that sometimes leaked out through comments such as this. However, now was not the time to snort for that particular truffle. 'So they liked to turn on and tune out?'

'Yes, but all was not rosy,' Tabitha said.

'In what way?'

'According to my contact, Nuala liked men and they liked her.'

'Yes, we'd heard that.'

'But did you hear why she decided to get away from Cheadle for a while and go to your island?'

'She was investigating the Children of the Dell.'

'Yes, she was obsessed with them after her partner died, but that wasn't the catalyst that made her board up the homestead and head north. She'd had an affair with the husband of one of the Sisters. It turned quite nasty, with a screaming match during a session and, well, things were said. A lot of repressed feelings spilled out during the fight.'

'And this was done in front of witnesses?'

'Yes, everyone in the group. It seemed the wronged wife

was out of her head on whatever substance she favoured at that time. Anyway, she could be fiery at the best of times, apparently, and my contact said the two of them had a history. They'd known each other as kids, her and Nuala, and it seems Nuala was always stealing her boyfriends. When she moved in on her husband, that sent her off the deep end.'

'Hang on,' said Rebecca as she steered the car to the right to pull into a passing place on the single-track road. She kept the engine running as she asked, 'In what way did she go off the deep end?'

'Threats.'

'Death threats?'

'Yes, but my contact says she can be a little dramatic. The thing is, it's not that she even loves her husband. He's wealthy, apparently, and she only likes what he can buy her. But she didn't like Nuala once again taking what was hers.'

Rebecca leaned closer to the phone clipped onto the dash. 'Her name wasn't Cynthia Danvers, was it?'

'Yes, how did you know?'

The Island of Stoirm

'Tell us again about the night Nuala died.'

Cynthia Danvers' face crinkled in irritation. 'Why? I've told you everything.'

Chaz forced his best Robert Redford. Whatever had been eating at him since yesterday was still only a shadow, and he had to give it shape if he could. 'There might be something you've forgotten.'

'There's not. I told you and the police everything.'

Alan pitched in. 'You didn't tell the police everything.'

'What didn't I tell them?'

'You didn't mention the spell book to them.'

'I must have forgotten. Or the conversation didn't lead me to it, or something. Anyway, I told you.'

Chaz pressed ahead. 'Neither of you drank, right?'

'No, I was driving. Nuala didn't drink, I told you that.'

'Did you have anything at all? Water? Coffee?'

'Tea, we drank some tea. I think I said that, too.'

That was what had been niggling at him. He recalled Miss Walker's words about the items the police took away after their first search. Among other things, there was one mug, unwashed. One mug. Why would Nuala wash one mug and not the other? He didn't know what it meant, but he knew Cynthia Danvers was lying.

His phone rang – Rebecca calling. He apologised, stood and moved away from Alan and the woman. 'Not a good time, Becks, I'm . . .'

'Cynthia Danvers,' said Rebecca, 'is she still on the island?'

'I'm with her now.'

'Why?'

'Asking her about the night Nuala died again. You once told me that it was a trick you picked up from your dad – go back and ask the same questions, see if the answers vary.'

'Nuala had an affair with her husband.'

Chaz shot a glance back at the woman, who was in conversation with Alan. 'Okay.'

'It wasn't pretty, apparently,' said Rebecca, 'Screaming, shouting, might have developed into something physical if they hadn't been arguing in front of their friends. She threatened Nuala, Chaz. That's why she decided to come to Stoirm.'

Chaz turned away again and kept his voice low. 'And you think Cynthia came here to carry out her threat?'

'We don't know.'

'We?'

Chaz heard Elspeth's voice on the line. 'I'm here, Chaz.'

'We're on our way to see Thomas Smith, we hope,' explained Rebecca.

'I thought we were backing off from this story,' Chaz said accusingly.

'Yes, I'm backing off, just as you have,' said Rebecca, her voice dry. 'Anyway, we think there's a chance that the Danvers woman slipped Nuala some sort of mickey. Something hallucinogenic.'

'Like what?'

Elspeth said, 'Rebecca's contact said they were dabbling in drugs like mescaline.'

'What's that?'

'It's powerful stuff, a strong psychedelic derived from the peyote cactus in southwest USA and Mexico. The Apache and other tribes used it because they thought it was a gateway to reach the gods. It's illegal but there are exceptions, like the Navajo members of the Native American Church, who see it as sacred.'

'How can this be taken? Do you smoke it or what?'

'You can eat it or drink it. It can be packed in a capsule form or turned into a tea, although that can be quite bitter.'

Chaz realised now why the missing cup might be so important. 'You seem to know a lot about it, Elspeth.'

'I did some research a while back.'

'Practical research, I think,' chipped in Rebecca.

He heard Elspeth about to argue, so he decided to keep the conversation on track. 'Where are you getting all this about Nuala and Danvers?'

He listened without interruption as Rebecca relayed the conversation with Tabitha Haley. 'Okay, so what should I do?'

'She's there, right?'

He saw Cynthia Danvers had risen to her feet, so he glanced at his watch. 'Not for long. She's leaving on the next ferry. What should I do?'

'Ask her straight out about the affair,' said Rebecca. 'Watch her reaction. She's not a hardened criminal – well, not as far as we know – so she won't be able to mask completely.'

'Okay,' said Chaz, 'need to go.'

He hung up as Cynthia Danvers headed for the stairs. He could feel the nerves of his legs trembling. This was not what he did. He took photographs. He distanced himself behind a lens, he didn't put himself directly in front of someone to prevent her from leaving. And yet, here he was.

'One question, Mrs Danvers.'

She made a show of looking at her watch. 'I'm sorry, but . . .'

'Nuala and your husband were having an affair, right?' The question came out more bluntly than he had intended, but it was done now.

Her eyes widened slightly and she blinked a few times in quick succession. 'How . . . ?' Then she decided on a flat denial, even though it was too late. 'No! Of course not!'

'So you didn't have a blazing row with her about it? And threaten her?'

'She was my friend. How dare you even suggest it.' She tried to step around him, but he intercepted her. Her eyes flared and her mouth became an ugly, tight line. 'Get out of my way.'

Alan approached them, frowning, and Chaz was aware of Mandy heading his way from behind the desk.

'I don't think so,' Chaz said, swallowing hard, but determined not to give way. 'Hallucinogens, Mrs Danvers. You and your Sisterhood didn't just enjoy a few puffs and a glass of wine. You experimented with drugs like mescaline.'

He saw that hit home and it emboldened him. Mandy was at their side now, her face tight as she glared at him for disturbing her guest. He ploughed ahead. 'You said you both had tea, but the police took only one used mug from the cottage. Why only one? Where did the other one go, Mrs Danvers?'

'I washed my mug. I had finished and I washed it before I left.' That would have been reasonable if she wasn't so flustered and if her eyes didn't scream liar. At least to Chaz.

Mandy decided it was time to bring this to an end. 'Mr Wymark, I think it's time for you to leave.'

Chaz ignored her. He was going to do this. 'Here's the thing, Mrs Danvers. If this is all true then you not only caused Nuala's death, whether intentional or not, you may also have set an innocent woman on her way to death. If Nuala had not died, a woman named Delia Forbes would be alive today.'

Cynthia Danvers waved a hand towards Alan and Mandy. 'That's slander. You've slandered me and there are witnesses.'

Chaz looked beyond her to the hotel entrance. 'We'll see, Mrs Danvers.'

She followed his gaze to where Rory Gibson and DC Dwyer stood with a tall, bald man Chaz had seen at a couple of crime scenes on the mainland. He was a detective chief inspector based out of Burnett Road in Inverness. Chaz returned his attention to the woman in front of him and saw all her rage and bluster leave with a deep sigh.

Kether House, Loch Ness

Rebecca pulled into the drive that led to Kether House. It dipped into a long slope and through a break in the trees she saw blue water, so she guessed the house, which she still could not see, overlooked Loch Ness.

'So what are we thinking?' Elspeth asked. 'This Cynthia Danvers woman killed Nuala because of the affair?'

'Tabitha said Nuala often poached boyfriends from Cynthia, so the affair would have tipped her over the edge,

279

especially if she was in the habit of imbibing too much of the illicit substances. You know what that can be like.'

'Only in a theoretical sense,' Elspeth said, not quite hitting a believable note.

'Uh-huh,' said Rebecca.

Elspeth chuckled. 'You sound as if you don't believe me.'

'I'm sorry, but if that's the way it sounds then it's only because I don't. Anyway, she comes up here intent on having it out, either brings the mescaline or whatever with her, or even buys it on the island – the boys told me there's a young guy there who punts drugs who was paying attention to Nuala Flaherty.'

'It's not so easily available here, but it can be synthesised.'

The house loomed up ahead, a large Scots baronial painted white, gleaming in the winter sunshine. Whoever this Thomas Smith was, he wasn't short of a bob or two. The tyres crunched on the gravel as Rebecca slowed the car to a halt in front of a large stone fountain.

'She slips the drug to Nuala somehow and lets it do its thing,' she said. 'I don't know if she meant to kill her, or just meant to scare her, but from what Tabitha said, Nuala didn't partake of these substances. She wouldn't have been prepared for what she experienced.'

'The visions can be intense,' said Elspeth. 'Mescaline can increase the heart rate. If Nuala had a weakness, coupled with the terror of the hallucination and then the effort of cutting that pentagram . . .'

'Plus exposure.'

They sat in silence for a moment, both studying the massive door ahead, Rebecca trying to imagine what the poor woman had gone through, wondering what terrors she had seen. Thought she had seen. If this was true, and it seemed to fit together, Cynthia Danvers may not have set out to kill, but she did. She didn't pull a gun or a knife, but she murdered Nuala Flaherty.

She looked at the clock on the dashboard. 12.28 p.m. Rebecca liked to be prompt. Good timekeeping can often surprise people.

'There is something that occurs,' said Elspeth.

'What?'

'If Nuala's death had nothing to do with the Children of the Dell, then it is always possible that Sam Walters really did kill himself, Gerald Frame died of natural causes and that poor woman on the island was the victim of a tragic accident. A pattern that isn't really there so this visit may be redundant.'

Rebecca considered this and rejected it. 'There's still something dodgy about the Children of the Dell, I can feel it.' She opened the door. 'Anyway, we're here now and my boss won't let me claim the petrol if I go back empty-handed.'

'Quite right, too,' said Elspeth, as she began to manoeuvre herself from the car.

Edinburgh

The Georgian terrace in Edinburgh's New Town would once have housed the upper middle class and lower upper class, but the handsome buildings were now almost exclusively used as office space. Val Roach emerged from the taxi she had picked up outside Waverley station and studied the windows around her. One or two still looked as if they were residential, but the majority were clearly business premises. She recalled a story she'd heard about a madam running a brothel from a street like this, back in the seventies, she thought. If there was one thing she had learned as a police officer, it was that appearances can be deceptive. On the surface, buildings – and people – can appear to be one thing, but all sorts of things happen in the shadows behind the windows. Or the eyes.

She climbed the flight of steps from the street to the large black door. Below the company name was a security button and a camera lens. She pressed the button and almost immediately a woman's voice answered. Roach identified herself and gave the name of the man she wanted to speak to.

'You do not have an appointment.' The woman's voice was very lightly accented.

'I'm on official police business,' Roach said, knowing this not to be strictly true; if it was, she would have had another officer with her, but she was gambling this unseen woman would not know that. There was a lull in the short conversation, presumably as instructions were sought from someone higher up the pay scale.

'Please hold up identification to the camera,' said the voice.

Roach held her warrant card to the lens. Another wait for a few seconds, then the door swung open with a click. She stepped into a narrow but brightly lit hallway and was met by a tall, blonde woman so unnaturally thin that Roach suspected she would gain weight if she so much as looked at food.

'Can you state the nature of your business?' It was the same voice she had heard on the intercom.

'As I said, it's a police matter.'

'My employer is a very busy man and he is unaware of any police business that might need his attention.'

Roach bit back the temptation to laugh at that. Her employer was well aware of every dirty little bit of police business that needed his attention. 'Tell him that I wish to discuss certain matters on the island of Stoirm.'

The blonde squinted as she struggled with the island's name. 'And where is this Storrim?'

Roach permitted a smile. 'Mr Nikoladze knows.'

Vivian Ward was not as severe in person as she sounded on the phone, despite the look of suspicion she cast upon Rebecca and Elspeth as they faced her across a desk. In fact, she was an attractive woman in her forties with medium-length dark hair, stylish glasses that hung on a chain around her neck, and a mouth that might be capable of a wide grin if it wasn't clamped so tightly it looked as if she was trying to keep her teeth in place. She was wearing a smart grey business suit and a pale blue blouse. At her throat was a simple chain. No rings, not even a wedding ring, so either she had no time for such accessories, or Mr Ward was no longer in the picture.

'Will Mr Smith be joining us?' Rebecca asked.

'Mr Smith is very busy. He will not be joining us.'

That was disappointing, but Rebecca sent a meaningful glance to the door to the woman's right, then to the intercom device on her desk.

Mrs Ward clasped her hands in front of her. 'What can I do for you?'

'DKMH Holdings and Templesword International,' said Rebecca. 'You're a director of both, correct?'

'Yes, and that matters exactly how?'

'As I said, I'm following up a story.'

'What story?'

'As I told you on the phone, I'm looking into the death of Nuala Flaherty.'

Rebecca waited to see if there was a reaction. She knew Elspeth would be studying Mrs Ward closely, too. They had agreed that Rebecca would pose the questions, Elspeth would say nothing. A pressure interview. Someone like Elspeth doing nothing but listening would hopefully unnerve her.

'She was investigating a group called the Children of the Dell and a place called Sanctuary. Have you heard of them?'

The woman gave nothing away. 'Should I?'

'Both companies have links to them.'

'What kind of links?'

'DKMH was the firm that bought the land on which Sanctuary sits and may even have continued to service the property.' That was a guess but Rebecca saw no harm in throwing it in. 'Templesword's phone number is one that appeared on the group's only phone.'

'And how did you obtain that information?'

Whatever she said couldn't hurt Delia Forbes now. 'It was obtained by a woman named Delia Forbes.' Rebecca paused again for any reaction, but still nothing, not a flicker of recognition.

'Well, I'm afraid you've had a long journey for nothing, Ms Connolly.'

'Not that long, really.'

'Either way, I know nothing about this group, the Children of the – what was it?'

The absent-minded act wasn't fooling Rebecca. This was not a woman who forgot something that had been said only a few seconds before. She played along, though. 'Dell.'

'Yes, Children of the Dell. Nor do I know anything about this poor unfortunate woman who died on that island. So, if you'll excuse me . . .'

'It was actually two women, Mrs Ward.'

'I'm sorry?'

'Two women died on the island. Delia Forbes was killed last night. And there have been other deaths, all related to the Children of the Dell.'

It may have looked as if the deaths were only coincidentally linked to the group but Rebecca threw it in anyway. She wanted to see how the woman reacted.

'As I said, Ms Connolly, I know nothing about . . .'

'Gerald Frame,' said Rebecca. 'Sam Walters. Delia Forbes. Nuala Flaherty. All connected in some way to the Children of the Dell and Sanctuary. And all dead.'

Vivian Ward stared at her.

'Does that not strike you as taking coincidence too far, Mrs Ward?'

'I really could not comment. I know nothing of the circumstances . . .'

'Gerald Frame was a former member of the Children of the Dell,' Rebecca continued, 'one of the earliest, I believe. He became disenchanted with it all and began to investigate the group. A great deal of money goes into these Sanctuaries, Mrs Ward, but it's difficult to see where it ends up. He passed what he had on to Sam Walters, who was an investigative journalist who gathered further information. Nuala Flaherty was his partner and, after his death, she inherited all his notes.' She paused before she added, 'And they are quite extensive.'

Rebecca waited to see if the lie had any effect, and she wouldn't have caught it if she hadn't been looking for it. Just a quick flick of the eyes to the intercom on the desk. Rebecca was convinced Smith was listening in.

She switched tack, something her father had told her to do. It keeps the other person on the back foot. 'By the way, I called the numbers I had for those two companies, Mrs Ward,' she went on. 'DKMH just rings out, but Templesword now seems to be unobtainable. Curious, don't you think, for commercial concerns?'

She was firing in all directions, simply to see if anything hit a mark.

'I'm not involved in the running of the companies, Ms Connolly. I'm a director on paper only.'

'Of course.'

The woman began to rise. 'So as there is clearly nothing I can . . .'

'Delia Forbes had access to the computer files on Stoirm and she made a number of copies. They may include various accounts and other correspondence.'

Rebecca was bluffing again, and much of what she had said was little more than stones dropped in the water to see which way the ripples spread. This time she was rewarded by a slight tic in the woman's cheek. Could have been anything, but Rebecca was certain it was a reaction. That was why she liked to see the whites of their eyes. On the phone, a silence was just a silence, but in person nerves and body language can be a soliloquy.

'May include?' Vivian Ward was no fool. She had caught the qualifier. 'You have not seen these files?'

'They are with the police. The death of Delia Forbes, coming so quickly on the heels of that of Nuala Flaherty has generated interest. They will be going through them with a forensic eye.'

Rebecca now knew Nuala's death had nothing to do with Sanctuary or the Children, but she gambled that the woman didn't. Delia had also said the accounts revealed very little, but it wouldn't do any harm to throw a bloody great boulder in that pool.

'I'm sure they will be knocking on your door soon,' Rebecca added.

The woman swallowed, as if she was drinking the ripples. She recovered quickly and pushed her chair back. 'We have nothing to hide here, Ms Connolly, but perhaps we should terminate this conversation. I wouldn't want to pre-empt any official investigation by talking with the press.'

As the woman rose, Rebecca said, 'Bennet Lomax, Mrs Ward,' and was rewarded by a slight freeze. So she tried the final name: 'Wesley Fairbank. Do these names mean anything to you?'

The bewilderment seemed genuine. 'No, should they?'

'Perhaps not,' said Rebecca, feeling this was the first time Vivian Ward had told the truth.

As Elspeth drew the woman's attention by making a meal of struggling to her feet, Rebecca rose, stepped closer to the desk and made a quick study of the intercom. There it was, a little red light. Self-satisfaction was most unbecoming, she knew, but she couldn't help a little smirk. The last two names she had mentioned may not have registered with Vivian Ward, but she would lay odds that they did with whoever was listening in.

Rebecca paused at the door, shot a quick look back to the desk and the intercom, and dropped her voice. 'Are you certain there is nothing you want to say, Mrs Ward?'

'I can't help you, Ms Connolly. I know nothing about the death of this drug addict Frame, the reporter, his partner, or the poor unfortunate woman last night. As for the companies, as I say, I am a director on paper only and know nothing of the day-to-day affairs of the businesses.'

Rebecca gave it a beat, then a smile, then raised her voice again. 'I don't remember mentioning that Gerald Frame was a drug addict, Mrs Ward.'

Thomas Smith sat back in his chair, considering what he had heard on the intercom. The reporter knew both a great deal and very little, but he suspected that situation would change. Vivian's blunder regarding Gerald Frame was both inevitable and unforgivable. Damn the man. He had been with the Sanctuary project from the start – he was Seb before there was a Seb – but his unreliability made him a liability, so he had been let go. Smith had known him for years; had, in fact, been his financial advisor when Smith still used the name Wesley Fairbank. He had thought Gerald to be like Smith himself – venal, realistic, avaricious – but he had that one flaw that prevented him from achieving true commercial freedom. Not his addictive nature, although that was bad enough, as Smith learned. No, his old friend Gerald Frame had a conscience. He should have been silenced permanently, but Smith had baulked at the move, despite it having been promoted by the Georgians. He was many things – a liar, a thief, a seducer – but he was not a murderer. It was, he recognised, a flaw in his own character. So he had simply ensured that nobody took Gerald's claims seriously by poisoning the well regarding his addiction, making his grasp of reality tenuous. And damn Sam Walters, too. That paranoid freak would, of course, have taken Gerald's claims seriously, but again Smith's luck had held, for the reporter's star was waning thanks to his mental deterioration. Then came his partner, followed by that traitor Delia Forbes. He could not say for certain that Seb had not deliberately hit her with the vehicle, but he suspected not. Seb was a greedy man – he would not be in his position if he wasn't – but he enjoyed not only the financial benefits that Sanctuary brought but also the sexual. He would not jeopardise it all by committing murder.

Smith was not a fool: he knew how it all looked. These deaths were merely an unfortunate series of calamities, but they could easily be conflated into a design. Unless the Georgians had somehow engineered each death. He shifted at the thought, his eyes resting on the painting of the Knight Templar. Legend had it that the man was ruthless in his ways, and his modern followers could be equally as single-minded. He certainly would not put it past his partners' capabilities and Smith knew professionals existed who specialised in making such removals look accidental, even natural. He did not relish informing them of the new development.

The reporter had his real name although he suspected she did not know it. Gerald again, he presumed. That was the end of it, he supposed with a deep sigh. Time to move on.

He spun his chair around to stare out of the window at the loch, its waters blue, its banks green and brown. He would miss this view, he thought, as he reached for the phone.

Edinburgh

Jarji Nikoladze was not a man who tended to worry. He was, as he often pointed out, a man who let other people worry. He also sometimes liked to be the cause of that worry. He was not worried by what the female police officer had said to him, but when he also took into account his subsequent conversation with the man Thomas Smith, it did make him contemplate and reassess current business arrangements.

He had agreed to see the detective; it would be stupid not to, for the police here in Scotland were not like those of other countries, where currency being passed, favours granted or even lusts slaked could deflect undue attention. He was curious, too, for he had not had a visit from a police officer for some time, and she was attractive, if a little too slim for his tastes.

So he had allowed her ten minutes of his time, had even offered coffee, which he poured himself from his cezve. He deployed the long-handled pot with ease, the thick, strong cinnamon-based aroma spreading between them like an old friend. But even as they each sipped the brew politely, her appreciation of its wild Russian taste plain, he knew they were not friends. She was there to exercise her authority, although he suspected it was purely in an unofficial capacity. The incorruptibility of the Scottish Police was a generalisation. There were always those whose heads could be turned, so had this visit been in any way official, Jarji would have heard.

Nonetheless, he listened politely as she mentioned she had a particular interest in Stoirm. That interest was both vague and yet curiously specific. She seemed to know a little about past interests he had in the island, but it was not that which caused him concern. After all, he was sufficiently insulated from what had occurred there years ago, although her suggestion that she would seek out the island's nobleman, Lord Henry Stuart, did trouble him. A few years before, there was a worry – no, a concern – that their joint venture into the transportation of human resources had been uncovered, but the evidence was so sketchy that nothing further was said. His brother, Ichkit, had counselled that Henry was a weak link and had urged severing that link with some finality. If this police officer followed through her threat to dig into those events, and reopen the investigation into a young woman's death, then Lord Henry's vulnerability may become an issue. Perhaps it was time to listen to his brother's advice.

He had understood her message. Her eyes were upon both him and his business dealings. He was unconcerned about that. But, although she had not mentioned more recent events, her visit did set him to reconsider his association with the man named Thomas Smith. He always thought of him in such a way, for he knew that was not his name. Jarji had harboured doubts about the Sanctuary project for some time. It had been a useful means of cleaning up the income from interests that were best kept out of sight of the law. They donated money through various fronts and then charged it back by providing services through DKMH, Templesword and other companies. There was a little cream from the money harvested from those misguided and unhappy souls who joined the Children of the Dell but, frankly, most of that went on keeping the Sanctuaries afloat, the genuine charity work and paying legitimate taxes. Jarji and Smith knew well that allowing governments to dip their nose in the trough was the best way to keep them looking the other way. Jarji was wise enough to know that such arrangements had a shelf life and the Sanctuary project, he believed, was about to go stale.

And now the man named Thomas Smith had told him that two journalists had attended his home and interviewed his secretary. Jarji was unsure how much she knew of her employer's dealings – she had always been designed as a shield, a distraction, but it seemed she had fulfilled that function. For the time being. When it was necessary, she would be thrown to the dogs.

The turn of events was, if not worrying, certainly disturbing, and Jarji did not relish being disturbed. Like Lord Henry Stuart, the man named Thomas Smith had perhaps reached the end of his usefulness. Time, he decided, to bring the relationship to a close.

He picked up his personal phone and dialled a number only he knew.

Inverness

It had been a day, Rebecca decided, as she left her car in the car park and trudged along a path she had walked a number of times in the past year or two. It was late afternoon and the light was fading. It wouldn't be too long before it was fully dark at this time, as winter heralded the death of one year and birthed a new one. She studied the pink-stained skies, looking for some hint as to how the weather would shape up for the next three days; not that it mattered, for Stoirm could be as contrary in its climate as humanity is in its nature. It could be clement on the mainland, yet the island's shores would be buffeted by King Lear's cataracts and hurricanoes.

Events across the water had moved with storm force that afternoon, Chaz had told her. Cynthia Danvers was taken in for questioning by the police and her room searched. Tucked away in her fancy handbag, Chaz was informed on the QT by the local police officer, was the spell book and the mug in which she had served the mescaline tea.

291

'The detectives on the MIT pumped air into her and she burst like an over-inflated balloon,' said Chaz.

'Is that what your cop pal said?'

'No, those are Alan's words.'

Rebecca laughed. 'Tell him that needs a little work.'

Chaz didn't share her amusement. 'She insisted she hadn't meant to kill, just to frighten, but hadn't taken account of Nuala's heart.'

'What do you think?' Rebecca asked.

'I don't know,' said Chaz. 'Could be true, could just be a defence. Everything she did after that was on the fly, so maybe there's something in it. If it was premeditated, you'd think she would have covered her tracks, wouldn't you?'

'So she took the book because . . . ?'

'Nuala wrote everything down in it. She had recorded the argument they had in Cheadle and the conversations they'd had on the island. Cynthia pretended to leave after she gave her the tea because Nuala wanted to be alone to perform some sort of cleansing ritual. She knew Nuala would have recorded her visit in her book beforehand, and she knew she would have mentioned the tea. It was what she did. So after she fled the cottage, Cynthia followed to see where she was going. She could tell that Nuala had seen her but not seen her, if you know what I mean. Cynthia had become whatever it was that she believed was stalking her.'

'Your cop told you all this?'

'Well, some. The rest Alan and I have pieced together.'

'Guessed, you mean.'

'Educated extrapolation,' corrected Chaz.

'Alan again, right?'

'Yeah, anyway, she took the mug because she didn't want it to be tested in any way. Her plan was to drop it and the diary off in the Sound on the way home.'

'Why didn't she do it before?'

'She said she was worried they would be found if she dropped them off the coastline, apparently, and her DNA would be traced. She really didn't think it all through, which suggests it was all spur of the moment.'

'So why point you in the direction of the book?'

'The only reason I can think of is that it was a bit of misdirection. She knew it wouldn't be found but telling us about it might help clear her of any suspicion.'

It made some sense. There were many criminal cases in which the guilty party helped the police to divert guilt. Hell, Rebecca thought, Columbo relied on the idea for years.

'What she told us was off-the-top-of-her-head stuff,' Chaz continued. 'One of her mistakes was not thinking about it when she spoke to Rory.'

'It does all seem very haphazard.'

'She was panicking, I'd say. Firing off in all directions, even trying to implicate Darren Yates, the drug dealer I mentioned.'

'Did she buy the drugs from him?'

'No, she brought it with her. And it was mescaline, by the way. When the MIT decided this might be murder, or at least culpable homicide, they managed to get a hurry-up on the post-mortem and toxicology. But when she heard – from Mandy at the hotel, by the way – that Darren was the local drug connection, she thought she'd use that against him. She already knew he was trying to chat Nuala up.'

'What made the MIT think it wasn't accidental or whatever?'

'They did a background check on Cynthia Danvers, and the local law in Cheadle spoke to members of their coven. They told her about the affair, the falling-out and the threats. And the occasional drug use. They had also clocked the curious incident of the missing mug.'

'Alan again?'

'Did you need to ask?' This time he managed some levity in his voice. But it was forced, Rebecca knew that. 'Anyway, when I told Rory about the missing spell book – which she hadn't mentioned to him – that strengthened their suspicions. Of course, finding the book and the mug sealed the deal.'

'So no big conspiracy. No secret society. No secrets. All so simple it's almost a disappointment.'

'But Delia Forbes still died because of it,' said Chaz, and Rebecca could hear the guilt cracking his voice.

She tried to console him, but she knew it would be a process he had to see through himself. He was not responsible for the woman's death, and they could not have foreseen what would happen, whatever it was that actually happened. Rebecca was more or less convinced that the deaths associated with Sanctuary and the Children of the Dell were coincidental, Ian Fleming notwithstanding.

She weaved her way through the gravestones to the one she had visited many times.

Pat and Mike had pulled up in the small car park beside the cemetery and watched the young woman talking on her phone before she climbed out and headed along a path towards the rows of headstones. Dusk closed in around them and they surveyed the area with an expert eye.

'What do you think?' Mike asked, although he already knew the answer.

Pat considered for a moment, neck craning to look through the rear window. Mike understood the thought processes because he had already considered the options. Theirs and the girl's cars were the only vehicles here, but that didn't mean there weren't people on foot in the graveyard, although it was getting darker by the minute. He didn't think there would be any groundkeepers on site.

Pat said, 'If it's going to happen, this is as good a place as any.'

Mike nodded his agreement just as a set of headlights swept up behind them, forcing them both to duck down.

Tabitha Haley's back and legs ached. All she wanted to do was to climb into a hot bath and ease away the hours of standing beside the chair. She also needed some silence because she suffered from a severe case of hairdresser's earache. She loved cutting and styling hair, but the downside was that she had to listen to some customers pontificating on current events. They were all experts in epidemiology, politics, international affairs and the royal family, so any given appointment can become an audible social media without a block function. However, it was part of the job and all she could do was smile, let the often ill-informed deluge of opinion wash over her and resist the temptation to pull a *Reservoir Dogs* with her scissors. If Gerry Rafferty's 'Stuck in the Middle With You' hit the airwaves, she would not be responsible for her actions. Her last appointment had been in the middle of the afternoon, thank God, so after a bit of clearing up, she had left the salon in the hands of her two young staff members, who were more than capable of handling any walk-ins, as well as their own remaining appointments and locking everything up.

She sat on the edge of the bath and watched the water flow from the tap and froth up the bubbles, the steam rising like a fine mist.

Rebecca didn't know why she laid the white roses at the grave every few weeks, she only knew she had to. Nolan Burke had, after all, saved her life at the expense of his own, and it was the least she could do. As she stood over the grave, looking down at the simple headstone, she recalled him bringing her flowers one night. She had been perturbed that he had actually traced her home address, but he had managed to entice her out for a drink with the promise of information on a story she was following. He clearly wanted to take things further, but she resisted, not simply because of the baggage that being a Burke brought – although that was considerable – but also because she didn't want relationships to cloud her life. She wanted to concentrate on her career, and men were, simply, a distraction.

She had dated a few people, mostly once and never more than twice, and it wasn't always her choice not to continue. She knew she had been emotionally distant and, although she knew there were reasons for that, she was certain some of the men she went out with thought she was a cold bitch, but she didn't really care.

Now there was Stephen.

She wasn't sure what that was all about. She didn't understand the wrench of her gut when he declined to go away for the weekend. She knew he was neither being cruel nor disinterested. He genuinely could not come, but why did it still cause a twinge of regret? She was still the same Rebecca, forged out of grief and pain, although she had learned to cope with it all. And yet, when she was with him, she felt different. *What's it all about, Becks?*

She raised her eyes as she asked herself that question and found Mo Burke glaring at her from the opposite side of the grave.

Tabitha sat up suddenly, the image jarring her out of her heat-induced doze. It had merely been a fragment, frayed and bleached of colour like an old photograph, and she didn't know what it meant. She had seen a woman, blonde, her face somehow familiar. A customer? Someone she had seen in the street? She didn't know. But her face had been twisted with rage . . . no, more than that. Hate.

She cleared the sweat from her eyes and focused through the steam on the tiles at the far end of the bath. She didn't know what this was about, but she knew she had to do her best to understand. She blinked a few times, then settled back again and closed her eyes. She blocked all other sound – the cars passing in the street outside, voices carrying from neighbouring flats, the slow, methodical drip of the tap – and concentrated. She could still see the steam against her eyelids, swirling, twisting, and gradually it formed into vague shapes, just briefly, then it unravelled and moved on to something else.

She didn't know how long she lay there – time had no meaning when she was in the zone – but finally the images shattered the steamy veil and broke through. Shards of light merely, piercing the darkness.

The woman again, her mouth tight as she snarled out words that Tabitha could not hear.

Gravestones . . .

Rows of gravestones . . .

And Rebecca, her face splashed with shock . . .

Rebecca had chosen her times to visit Nolan's grave to minimise the risk of bumping into his mother – always around dusk or early in the morning – so she was startled to find Mo Burke scowling at her. That was not the only reason she was surprised. The woman had aged since last she saw her. Her hair was still blonde, but the dye was losing the battle with the grey. Her make-up was still carefully applied, but it was struggling against the dark circles around her eyes, and the lines in her flesh were deeper now, the tell-tale creases of the smoker puckering the upper lip more pronounced. She had lost some weight, too. Her cheeks were hollower, her jaws beginning to sag. But it was her eyes that Rebecca noticed more than all that, even as they threw hate in her direction. There was something clouding them that Rebecca had once seen in herself.

'You have no right to be here,' Mo Burke said as she moved around her son's gravestone, taking in the fresh flowers Rebecca had set down at its foot. 'So you're the one leaving these.'

'Yes.'

'Why?'

Rebecca answered carefully. 'It was something I felt I had to do.'

Mo Burke's mouth narrowed. 'Guilt.'

'No, not guilt,' said Rebecca, still trying to choose her words sensitively. 'Gratitude.'

'Because he died and you didn't?'

'Because he saved me.'

Mo Burke looked back at the grave, stooped to remove a fallen leaf, brown in death. 'It should have been you.'

Rebecca didn't know how to respond to that. She remained silent and wondered if she should walk away, leave this mother to her grief. Yes, that's what she should do. 'I'm sorry if you feel I have intruded. That wasn't my intention.'

'I wanted you dead.'

Mo Burke's words were delivered in a flat monotone, as devoid of heat as the shadows clustering around them, but they made Rebecca turn back. She was still looking down at her son's grave and she twitched a finger in its direction. 'This should have been you, not him.'

'Mrs Burke . . .' Rebecca began but stopped when the woman's head snapped in her direction, her eyes blazing now.

'No, you don't get to speak. You don't get to say anything. You caused this. You turned my boy's head, turned him against his family and his people. And me.'

'That's not true, Mrs Burke, I . . .'

'Don't even try to deny it. I saw it. I've seen it before. You bloody straight arrows who like the thrill of being with a gangster. He was nothing more than that to you, right? A thrill. A bit of rough. And now he's dead, and you caused it.'

It wasn't true, but Rebecca knew she would never convince her of that. She turned to go again. 'I'm sorry, Mrs Burke.'

'I've seen you dead many times, Rebecca Connolly,' said Mo. 'I even contacted professionals. Fair bit of money, too.'

Rebecca felt something crawl up her back and recalled the sensation of being watched. She stopped again, every nerve telling her that she should just go – run – but she couldn't. She had to know. She waited for Mo to expand on her statement, but her attention was fixed on something over Rebecca's shoulder. Rebecca risked a look behind her but saw nothing but the gathering gloom, heard nothing but the wind playing on the branches of the trees at the edge of the cemetery. When she faced Mo Burke again, there was something like humour in her eyes.

'He doesn't show himself to you, does he?'

'Who doesn't?'

Mo gave her head a little shake, as if clearing it. 'Not your business. None of it ever was, yet you stuck your nose in. That's what you do, isn't it? Stick your nose where it's not wanted. And look what happens.' She returned her attention to the gravestone. 'Look what happens.'

Rebecca's phone rang and she moved to take it from her pocket, but Mo said, 'Leave it.'

Rebecca was tempted to ignore her, but then the woman's hand shot into her own pocket and seemed to grip something. 'I said, leave it.'

Rebecca left it.

Tabitha stood in her sitting room naked, water dripping from her body to the rug, listening to the phone ringing out then jumping to voicemail.

'Rebecca, it's Tabitha,' she said, trying to inject some urgency into her voice that fell just short of panic. 'I need you to call me back as soon as you can, okay? Can you do that? Thanks.'

299

She ended the call.

She didn't know who the woman was. She didn't know where they were, if it was happening now or in the future. That was the problem with these visions: they could be both precise and vague. This was the usual jumble of images, but Tabitha was certain of one thing. Once again she had felt real malevolence towards Rebecca.

This was the woman who meant her harm. And she intended to see it through.

Rebecca feared whatever it was that Mo Burke had concealed in that pocket. She had confessed she had arranged to have her killed. She was capable of violence herself. Rebecca may not have ever witnessed it, but she had heard the stories. She was a career criminal and had access to guns. Rebecca scanned the area around her but there was nowhere really to hide, even if the nerves that had frozen her legs allowed it.

Then, in the dimming light, she saw a figure heading their way, a tall woman. Relief thawed some of the ice in her blood. The figure was a distance away and not moving with any resolve, but she was still a witness and Mo wouldn't do anything in front of a witness. Would she?

'Mrs Burke,' she said, playing for time and willing her voice to remain even and not quite making it, 'I understand how you feel . . .'

'You understand how I feel? How the hell can you understand how I feel? I lost my boy, my son, you have no idea how I feel. You've never lost a child.'

'I have,' said Rebecca, bringing the woman up short. Mo stared at her for a moment, no doubt wondering if Rebecca was lying. 'I lost a child, a miscarriage. A few years ago.'

The hatred in Mo's eyes softened but didn't vanish completely. 'Not the same,' she said. 'You didn't watch that child grow to be a man, a decent man.' She straightened as if

Rebecca had sneered. 'Aye, decent. He was smart, clever and funny. And he was taken away from me.'

Her gaze moved again to something behind Rebecca, but this time she did not turn around. She had guessed what Mo saw. Grief is a wound that heals but it leaves a scar, and Mo Burke's was still livid.

'No, that's true,' Rebecca said. 'But I still mourned for that child, and I always will. I've known loss, Mrs Burke, and I've suffered from it. Grief is powerful and it can twist the mind, make us believe things that aren't true and see things that we want to see.' Mo's eyes flicked back to her. 'That's who shows himself to you, isn't it? Nolan?' She didn't wait for confirmation; she saw it in the mother's eyes. 'For a long time, I saw my dead father and let him comfort me, and I heard my child crying for me in the night, a lost soul in search of its mother. But it was me who was crying. It was me who was in search of something. An answer, I think, to the question why.'

'And have you found it?'

'There is no answer. The why of it all remains a mystery. In the end, there's just what is.'

'And what about your father? Why did you see him?'

Rebecca risked a glance towards the woman on the pathway, saw she had moved in another direction, as if looking for a particular grave. She struggled to keep the despair from her voice. 'Because I needed to see him. Because I wasn't ready to let him go.'

'And have you? Let him go?'

'Yes. I don't see him any more. I don't hear the child. I mourn for them, but they're not part of this life now.' And I don't hear the shot in the dark and see Nolan bleeding out on that rain-swept towpath, she thought but didn't add. That was not her grief to bear. 'But they live on. As long as we remember them, the dead live on.'

*

301

Tabitha had pulled on a bathrobe and was pacing the room like a caged animal, her phone still in her hand, willing it to ring. Unusually, she'd had another vision, another flash, and this one was the most disturbing. Before it had been faces, the gravestones and the strong sense of extreme ill-will, but this time it was a brief glimpse of something else. It had sliced into her brain like a sharp blade and left just as quickly, leaving the memory of it to bleed through her mind.

She knew she had to warn Rebecca, knew that she was – would be – in danger. She had nobody else she could call, and she didn't know where Rebecca was, so she couldn't call the police, even if they would accept a vision as evidence of current or future threat.

She hit redial, the image of a hand holding a gun still fresh.

Rebecca's phone rang again, but this time she made no move to answer it, even though she desperately wanted to. Mo had not removed her hand from whatever she gripped in that pocket, and the woman she had seen was still on the other side of the graveyard, although she did seem to be moving gradually closer. Not quick enough, though. Rebecca had considered flight, but if there was a weapon in that pocket then she wouldn't get far. She had considered fight, but Mo had kept herself a good distance away from her and, again, Rebecca doubted she would get close enough to put her self-defence skills to use. So she let the phone ring and allowed her mind to race through what options she had. Which were damn few.

'If that bastard Martin Bailey had done what he promised, this wouldn't be necessary,' Mo said, making Rebecca frown. Had Mo been behind that attack in her home? 'I just wanted to you hurt then. But then he failed . . .'

He didn't fail, I stopped him, Rebecca thought, but again kept it to herself.

'. . . and someone else let me down. So now it's down to me.'

Someone else. Rebecca recalled the man who had appeared in her doorway just after she had put Bailey on the floor. He hadn't seemed threatening, whoever he was, but had he also been part of it? And she had said it was down to her now, but hadn't she hired somebody? Did you really get professional killers? Rebecca's eyes flicked back to the woman heading their way.

'You don't want to do this, Mrs Burke. Nolan wouldn't want you to do this.'

Mo's voice raised. 'I told you no' to talk about him!' She swallowed hard. 'He's no' for you to talk about.' Her voice caught. 'You're no' fit to even say his name.'

The stranger was closer now. Rebecca knew she had to keep Mo talking, hoping that some semblance of sense remained within her and that somehow she could talk her round. Killing Rebecca for what she imagined was a sound reason was one thing, killing an innocent bystander was another. There weren't many rules in Mo Burke's world but not involving witnesses was an important one.

But was this woman innocent? The fear had been growing in Rebecca's mind. What if she was the person Mo had hired?

She had to continue playing for time. She had no other choice. 'But he's what this is all about, so how can I not talk about him? And the thing is, you know he wouldn't want this. You must know he wanted out of the life.'

That surprised Mo. 'He told you that, too?'

'Yes, that's all I was for him, I think. A possible means of getting out.'

The woman wasn't far now. Even in the near complete darkness Rebecca could make her out. Tall, fair-haired, long black coat. Mo remained unaware of her approach, Rebecca realised, and she didn't know if that was good or bad, just as she didn't know if the newcomer was angel or devil.

'You put that into his head,' Mo accused, desperately clinging to the belief that something other than her family's lifestyle, someone other than herself, was to blame.

'No,' Rebecca argued. 'It was his decision. He'd had enough . . .'

The stranger's eyes were fixed on them, and something about her body language suggested that the meander through the gravestones had been an act. Rebecca felt her legs begin to weaken with fear. She may be able to talk Mo round, although she didn't feel as if she was making much headway, but if the stranger was a hired killer then no amount of talking would help.

Mo still had not noticed the newcomer. Her eyes filled, glistened slightly, and the tears erupted. Her hand shifted in her pocket. 'He was my son, and you took him away from me. He was my son, my blood, and now all I'm left with is memories and a fuckin' gravestone, and you caused that.' The tears were flowing now, the words punctuated by sobs. She wiped them away with the back of her free hand and her voice hardened again. 'I've heard enough shite from you.'

Mo's hand began to move.

The approaching woman saw this and picked up her pace.

Rebecca backed away a little, instinctively trying to put a little more distance between them.

Mo became aware of the newcomer and turned slightly, her hand half out of the pocket. She definitely had something gripped there, but Rebecca still couldn't see what.

The woman came to a halt a few feet away and held up a hand in Mo's direction. 'Take it easy, hen,' she said. Glasgow accent. Calm. Confident. Professional.

Mo half-turned to face her. 'You keep out of this, fuck all to do with you,' she snarled, but her hand had stilled. Her other hand hurriedly wiped away what was left of the tears. She seemed more ashamed of being seen in a moment of weakness than anything else.

'Aye, it has. I don't know what you've got there, but I wouldn't pull it, if I was you.'

'And what are you going to do about it?'

The tall woman smiled. 'No' me, hen. My man over there. He's the one who will do something about it. And if he does, you'll no' like it.'

Mo turned. So did Rebecca. A burly man dressed in a similar black coat to the newcomer had emerged from the cover of the trees. He had his right hand down at his side and he raised it slightly to let them see the pistol, then he returned it to the folds of the coat. Rebecca had little doubt it could, and would, be snapped up again if the need arose.

'Who the fuck are you?' Mo asked, defiant to the end.

'Who we are doesn't matter. What matters is we're here, and there's no way we're going to let you harm that lassie.'

Rebecca preferred the term 'woman', but she was definitely prepared to let that pass at this moment in time. Her mind buzzed, though – who were these people?

Mo looked from one to the other. 'So you're here to take me out, is that it?'

'No' unless we have to. But we will, if you make us. So, here's what I suggest you do – let me see that hand, nice and easy like, and if there's anything in it other than your fingers then my man will put you down. Believe me, he's a more-than-decent shot. Practises all the time, so he does.'

Mo looked as if she wasn't going to comply but then relaxed and slowly slid her hand free. The woman stepped closer to her. 'I'm going to check there's nothing nasty there, okay? I'm sure you've got a mean left hook, hen, but don't try it because I'll put you on the ground and it won't be fun, right? So, we okay?'

A reluctant nod from Mo and the woman added, 'Anything in there that might stick me? 'Cos I would not be hyper chuffed about that.'

Mo shook her head, and the woman, satisfied, reached into the coat pocket. Her eyes locked with Mo's for a second and then she withdrew it again, staring at the metal object she had removed. 'Nice lighter.' She held it closer to her face for a better look. 'That a Dupont?'

'Aye, it was a gift from my husband. You going to steal it?'

The woman smiled. 'We don't do that.' She handed the lighter back then patted the other pocket, reached in and withdrew a packet of cigarettes, which she handed to Mo. 'We're done here. But this is over, Mrs Burke, okay? Anything happens to the lassie here, if she even stumbles and falls and there's any doubt about it whatsoever, me and my man will be back. And we will not be so chummy. Understand?'

Mo didn't reply. She glared at the woman then at Rebecca, but something had changed. It was as if everything that had been bottled up inside her had washed out with the tears. Rebecca wondered if she had wept at all since Nolan's death. The stranger sensed that, too, for she nodded once, then gestured to Rebecca to follow.

She stopped beside Mo. 'I really am sorry, Mrs Burke, but you know it wasn't my doing.'

Mo said nothing but she did bob her head once.

'Let him go,' Rebecca said. 'Let him rest.'

Mo's eyes shifted slightly, focused again on something just before her, her eyes glistening again. Rebecca didn't follow her gaze, for she wouldn't see what Mo saw. It was a projection of her own mind. As someone had once told her, we only haunt ourselves.

The woman lingered a few feet away and Rebecca caught up with her. Her partner remained motionless for a few seconds then followed in a sideways walk, his eyes remaining fixed on Mo, the gun still at his side.

'Who are you?' Rebecca asked.

'My name's Pat, that's my man Mike. Bill Sawyer asked us to look after you for a wee while. We've never been far from you for a couple of days now.'

Bill Sawyer. So that's what that concern about her well-being had been about. She made a note to ask him how he had heard about Mo's intentions. And to thank him.

'So, you two are' – she tried to think of a word that didn't make her squirm – 'what exactly?'

Pat smiled. She had a pleasant smile. 'Let's just say we're contractors. We owed Bill a favour or two, from way back. He cashed them in. We followed you here then we saw your woman there arrive. Sawyer had sent us her photie, so we knew her being here wasn't good news.'

Mike cast a glance back at Mo. 'What you think, Pat?'

Pat followed his gaze as they walked. 'Dunno, Mike. Difficult to say.'

'You want me to go back and make sure?'

'No!' Rebecca said, horrified.

'Might be for the best, hen,' Mike said. 'Folk like her don't like unfinished business.'

Rebecca stopped and looked back at Mo, the night gathering around her like a dark pall. Something had changed. Rebecca understood now – Mo hadn't hired anyone in the end; that was why she said it was down to her. Rebecca was convinced she had never seriously wanted her dead. If she had, she wouldn't be breathing now. Even making her think there was something in her pocket was just to make her stay, a means of forcing the confrontation. Now she was alone in the dark, haunting herself with regret.

'It is finished,' Rebecca said. 'It's over.'

Mike was doubtful. He glanced at Pat. 'What you think, Pat?'

Pat studied Mo, then Rebecca, then shrugged. 'It's her funeral.'

307

6

FRIDAY

The weather was still fine, and Rebecca had caught the forecast on the morning news and it looked set to stay that way over the weekend. She was glad of that. There had been stormy emotions enough in the past few days and she didn't need the island's climate to add to them. She threw a few final items into her bag, not bothering to fold them because why break the habits of a lifetime?

The night before, after a glass of gin and tonic – or two – she had spoken to Bill Sawyer on the phone and he agreed there was no need for him to tag along now. There was no immediate threat from Mo – Rebecca remained unsure how much there actually had been, although the mysterious Pat and Mike remained unconvinced – and any danger remaining from what had occurred all those years before on Stoirm was, he admitted, slim. She thanked him for providing her bodyguards and asked him about the history.

He became vague. 'Let's just say that maybe, at one time, there were two folk who did what the law would see as wrong but society might not. And let's just say that there might have been a police officer who had the goods on those two folk and decided it might be in the best interest of the law to arrest them, but not in the interests of justice. But let's also say that

308

the police officer filed that away in the box labelled *Favours, for future use of.*'

Rebecca couldn't help but smile. She could only guess at what Pat and Mike had done that Bill Sawyer had uncovered back in the day, but she was grateful.

She also returned Tabitha's calls and assured her she was fine. She was candid about what had occurred – after all, she had seen the salient details in her visions. When Rebecca told her that it was Mo Burke she had seen, Tabitha knew then why she had been so familiar. Mo's face had often graced the pages of Inverness's press. Rebecca could not rationalise what Tabitha had seen. The visions were pretty specific. Perhaps there was something in this hocus-pocus business, after all.

She left her flat, ensured the door was locked, and walked to her car. It was bright and cold and was the kind of morning that made you feel glad to be alive. She opened the boot to stow her bag then reached up to slam the door shut.

Over the roof of the car, she saw Stephen smiling at her. She couldn't help a smile of her own.

'Come to see me off?' she asked as she moved around the car. That was when she saw the large sports bag at his feet. Something inside her started to leap around like Tigger with ADHD.

'I decided that my sister will have other anniversaries,' he said. 'Chaz and Alan will only get married once.'

Rebecca didn't know what to say. All she could do was stand there and grin like a fool.

Mike had just come out of the shower and found Pat poking the keys on their laptop, looking at a file.

'New job?' he asked.

'Aye.'

'Where?'

'First one's up here, as it happens.' She turned the computer round on the top of the bed to let him see. He leaned forward and read the address of the target.

'Here, isn't that . . . ?'

'Aye, coincidence, eh?'

She clicked on the first of three jpeg images attached.

Mike read the names. 'So who is this Thomas Smith?'

'Does it matter?'

He smiled and straightened. 'No' really.' He rubbed his hair with a towel. 'You said the first one – there's another job?'

'Aye, London.'

Mike groaned. He liked cities but he wasn't too fussed with London.

'Ach, suck it up. It's a job,' said Pat.

'So who is it down there?'

'Some Lord something or other. And before you ask, I don't know why.'

'Ours is not to reason, eh?'

'Aye. Our is just to do – but leave the dying to the targets . . .'

Author's note and acknowledgements

The island of Stoirm does not exist, neither do Inchferry or Pittencairn. I made them up.

As usual, I have people to thank.

I am grateful for the time Professor James Grieve spent with me and also Sophia Noor for allowing me to use her as Rebecca's down-to-earth friend. Get yourself sorted is something Sophia has often said to me. I remain a work in progress. Thanks are due to Karin Stewart for her particular advice on hairdressing.

Author friends who have either read the book or listened to me moaning about my rather haphazard process (you'd think I would get myself sorted) include Caro Ramsay, Neil Broadfoot, Michael J. Malone, Theresa Talbot, Gordon Brown (aka Morgan Cry) and some fella called Denzil Meyrick.

Thanks are ever due to the team at Polygon: Alison Rae, Kathryn Haldane, Ellen Cranston, Jan Rutherford and Fiona Brownlee – Hugh Andrew for spotting that wee plot hole! Also Craig Hillsley for his editing skills.

Finally, a big shout out to my agent Jo Bell for keeping me on the right track and always having my back.